The Summoning

Dr. Stuart Knott

Harriet Everend

Jessica Huntley

with contributions from

Alice Stone

Shantel Brunton

Tom Schnipke

Daria Lavrenteva

First published in 2022 by Amazon

Copyright (c) Dr. Stuart Knott, Harriet Everend, and Jessica Huntley

Cover art by Ivan Semonchuk

Edited by Mallory Wiper

ISBN: 979-8-77-004396-9

Dr. Stuart Knott, Harriet Everend, Jessica Huntley, Alice Stone, Shantel Brunton, Tom Schnipke, and Daria Lavrenteva have asserted their moral right to be identified as both authors and contributors of *The Summoning*.

This is a work of fiction. Unless otherwise indicated, all the names, characters, businesses, places, events, and incidents in this book are either the product of the imagination of the authors or used in a fictitious manner. Any resemblance to actual persons, living or dead, or actual events is purely coincidental.

www.drkwaitingroom.com
www.harrieteverend.wordpress.com
www.jessicahuntleyauthor.com
www.alicestonewrites.mailchimpsites.com
www.shantelbrunton.ca

TRIGGER WARNINGS:

Violence, supernatural horror, depictions of abuse (domestic, physical, and emotional), trauma, swearing, rape, suicide, depression, panic attacks, loss of a child, blood and gore.

These voices change

And remain the same

Placed in a glass frame

Where I have no name.

A shadow's life of make believe

Lost in time we live and breathe,

They take me down to my knees

Choices are made not being free

Another pull and give as if to need

The ones that speak of what is me

- Tom Schnipke

Prologue

A Rainy Horror Three Years Prior

Corey scratched the dried blood from his skin as he drove out into the dark. The storm rapped against the car while the radio dipped in and out of stations and homes turned into open fields. His insides quaked under his thoughts, his breathing shallowed, ticking over with the window wipers. The cold swallowed him so completely that he barely felt his toes wrapped in wet canvas, which was oddly comforting. He stared blankly through the speckled windshield, and he hardly noticed as the car came to a stop. Foot still resting on the accelerator, hands still gripped around the steering wheel, his gaze dropped to the dashboard and watched the red needle slowly fall past zero into true emptiness.

'Fuck.'

The rain grew heavier and the lights dimmed. Corey pulled his phone from his back pocket, the screen shattered but still usable. The lock screen blinded him for a moment before he was greeted by a picture of a younger version of himself with a small girl clinging to his back like a spider monkey. Her toothy smile caused him to gulp and, as he peered at the time, he realised that he'd crossed over into the next day. The road outside was quiet, the tarmac stretched out into the night, the horizon disguised with rain drops, and Corey watched his breath form clouds around his face as the car took its last breath as a fizzing sound leaked from the engine.

The darkness settled and seemed to cause the rain to grow violent. Corey twisted his body around to the back seat, stretched his arms out, and fished a large duffel bag through the narrow gap. The frames of both seats dug into his flesh as he writhed the bag onto his lap. Corey flung the door open and pulled himself from the car and the downpour immediately washed his blond hair a mousy brown. As he stumbled away from the car, his feet skidded in the mud, and the rubber soles of his trainers held no grip on the grassy bank. Rain gushed through the grass like a murky waterfall that followed the line of the roadside, and Corey marched forward as lightning spread across the sky, his eyes glazed over, ignoring the silent mocking from the tangled trees. It wasn't long before he reached a grand steel gate entwined with thick growing weeds that glistened beneath the flashes of lightning.

Corey stopped, pushed his head between the bars, and stared deep past the pulsating overgrowth at the mansion that lay beyond. All the windows were dark…except for one. An orange light glimmered through a small window at the very top of the house, and shadows augmented by the flash of lightning danced about the exterior. The house seemed to taunt him, and an overwhelming sense of urgency swept him all at once as his feet grew numb. His arms shook uncontrollably, rattling the bars like a gorilla trapped in a cage. The metal shifted and tore apart the winding, thick leaves as the gate announced Corey's entrance and he forced his grip to loosen and took his first step into the estate. He felt a light prick in both ears, a sound from which most dogs would turn rabid, and he buried his fingers deep in his ears to block out the noise. The gate creaked gently shut behind him as Corey drew closer to the house, lifting his feet high to avoid tripping on the long, tangled grass. The garden stretched out for what seemed like miles. He hunched his shoulders as he walked and couldn't shake the feeling he was being hunted.

As Corey reached the middle of the grounds, something whipped by his ankle, and he froze. He gulped and glanced at the ground behind him.

Nothing.

Suddenly, something gripped right around his knee. It flung him to the ground, and he yelped as his shoulder met a large rock. Its grip tightened as it pulled him through the grass. The skin on his back was torn open by thorns, and Corey struggled with his duffel bag as he desperately kicked at the invisible force, but it was like kicking thin air. He squirmed as the force dragged him deep into the hedges, where twigs and rotting berries pelted across his face at such speed that they nearly ripped his eyes out. He hid his face beneath the sleeves of his jacket and lost his bag to the garden. The back of his jacket served no protection; his bare skin swept across the wet grass in zigzags.

Finally, it stopped, and he sat up to realise that he'd been left like roadkill on the steps of the house. The grand wooden doors opened, and the world fell silent. Each door was carved with stories of the past, solidified in gold. He looked back over the garden, eyes narrowed, watching for movement, and found none.

Slowly, he scrambled to his feet and edged his way into the house. The warmth took him by surprise…as did the silence.

'Hello?' he wheezed, hardly any sound leaving his lips. He pulled his hand over his mouth and coughed, disturbed to find a small blob of congealed blood and phlegm stuck to his palm. He casually wiped it on his dark tattered jeans and attempted to speak again. 'Hi? Urm...I'm sorry! My...my car broke down, and...' he drifted off, distracted by his new surroundings.

The room was filled with antiques and finery, despite the thick layer of dust dancing in the air. Everything, whilst not disgusting, held a tea-stained hue. In front of him, two large staircases led to the second floor, the old, glazed floorboards lined with thick red carpet. His hands wandered over to a chest of drawers on which sat tiny woodland taxidermy. He stared into the beady eyes of a red squirrel, which glittered in the warm light from the lamp fixed around its tale. He circled around, taking in all the sights at once until his eyes met his own.

A large mirror with an elaborate frame hung on the wall directly opposite him and he strode towards it, running his fingers over the lines of his cheeks. He dropped his coat to the floor and lifted his t-shirt to examine his pale skin. He framed each scar with his hands and twisted to see his back, which looked like he had been lashed with a whip; the wounds tainted with brown and green. He pressed his nose up against the mirror; his breath blurred his reflection as he rubbed dirt from the gashes in his face with the corner of his shirt. A harsh buzz came from his jeans pocket, and he pulled out his phone just in time to see it go dark. He sighed. Any hope of charging his phone lay in his duffel bag, which was lost amongst the thicket outside, slowly filling with rainwater.

Corey flinched. A loud clatter followed by muffled argument came from the top of the staircase. Corey armed himself with a gold-plated candle stick and cautiously crept along. He watched his footing, too aware of the creaking wood beneath him, and ran his fingers along the smooth varnished wood of the banister as it twisted onto the second floor, which was just as grand as the first. His attention was immediately stolen by the rattling of a pair of dusty glass double doors leading out onto a balcony. The glass vibrated as he drew closer, shaking violently within the frame.

'Hello? Is someone there? Are you okay?' Corey raised the candlestick, ready for whatever might come for him.

'Let me in!' a voice whispered from the storm. A tiny pale hand planted itself against the window, and Corey immediately reached out for the handle and tugged at the French doors.

'Hello? Is someone out there with you? Are you alright?!'

The tiny palms turned to fists and battered against the glass. The screaming grew louder and higher as Corey tugged at the handle, but it wouldn't budge. He searched for a lock and tried pushing, but still…nothing. Screaming turned to words that whistled through Corey's ears…a little girl's voice, pleading in the wind.

'Stand back!' Corey swung the candlestick over his head and brought it down, hard on the glass pane. Nothing. Not a crack, a fracture…nothing. He looked up and saw her face staring back at him…she was so pale. Corey's jaw went slack, and his saliva turned to sand in his mouth as she looked up at him with her toothy grin and dark eyes, a face like his but far more beautiful. Corey's heart skipped. Tears filled his vision.

'CeeCee, let me in! I'm cold!'

Without a second thought, Corey charged at the window with his shoulder. The doors burst open, and he found himself alone on a great balcony lined with white marble and gold. He peered out into the endless dark and searched for the little girl…his little girl.

'Rachel!' her name stuck in his throat.

He processed the height. Thick bushes spread out for miles below, spelling out some regimented pattern. A maze. The wind tickled Corey's ribs, his stomach churned, and yesterday's dinner splattered against the side of the house. He sank to the floor and scrambled back to the doors. Shaking, he fumbled with the handle as the rain soaked quickly through his shirt and then his skin. He stood up, knees still shaking, and sank against the wall. The grey storm clouds cast a ghostly hue over the moon, dancing around it like great swarms of moths. Demons moving about the sky to their own song as the clap of thunder joined by veins of light.

Corey's trance was broken as the next window along gave under the pressure and shards sprung out into the night. He slid to the side of the balcony and peered over the edge to see the broken window. Pieces of broken glass still clung to the edges of the frame, and he stared at the gap where he would plummet to his death as rivers of water streamed from his eyes and down into the creases of his face. His shaking feet met the ground and he straightened his back. He clutched the thick marble ledge with his sodden fingers as he raised both knees up onto it. Trembling, the front half of his body teetered over the edge. The ledge seemed further now, but also thick enough to hold him.

He took a deep breath, moved his left knee out from under him, and his foot stammered against the marble. His fingers saved him, and he quickly planted his second foot on the balcony. The rubber soles of his trainers brought him no comfort; his knees shook as the storm played with his balance. Vision blurred, he took his chance, and leapt. His knees hit the window ledge, and, as his arms shot through the window frame, the remaining shards of glass buried deep into his forearms. Hot blood ran down his elbows and curdled with the rain. Corey wheezed and clamped his fingers around the inside ledge, and slowly pulled himself up. Relief came as his knees met the window ledge and he clambered back into the house, his body landing in a bloody heap of glass on the floor of a narrow hallway.

Corey groaned and dragged himself from the broken window, glass fragments chimed as he stumbled to his feet. He looked down at his wrists, which streamed with blood. Slowly, he picked at the shining splinters buried into his flesh. He growled at himself and plunged his skinny fingers deep into his wounds.

'Fuuuck.'

He swore through his teeth, ripped his shirt to rags, and tightly wrapped them around his forearms; the material was still cold from the rain and stung his open tissue. He finally looked around at the rich mahogany walls, which shone like honey beneath the dim lamplight. There were no paintings or trinkets, only the carvings within the wood; flowers and faces and ladies dressed finely draped over antique furniture all interwoven with the walls. Corey ran his shaking fingers over the curves in their faces, releasing dust into the air. That same red carpet which lined the staircase lay over dark floorboards, except the colour was deeper, somehow more authentic.

He walked…and walked.

He must have walked a mile, maybe two, but the hall stayed the same. He picked up his pace, hobbling ever faster. He grasped at the walls on either side, frantically searching for a door, but they were solid. As he ran, each step sent daggers clawing at his calves. Still, he ran, blurry-eyed and staggering, until something solid rammed into his side. It was the corner of a small table, and on it sat a typewriter. Corey held his side and bit his lip; the typewriter seemed to gleam at his misfortune. He gently fingered at the keys. It was clean, no dust fell from its surface.

Corey examined it (antique, no surprise), and a piece of dulled cream paper was still in it; the top corner was marked with:

'H. E. 1820.'

Corey looked to his right, there was another small typewriter some feet away. He strode over to it. The same typewriter; different date, different letters.

'A. S. 1825.'

Again, he looked, there were more and more. The dates went forward as Corey followed the trail.

'S.D.K. 1910, J. H. 1946, S. B. 1956,' he read aloud, running along until he fell to his knees. His breathing became louder, erratic; tears fell over his cheeks, and he could still feel the wind seeping in through the broken window. A chill raced down his spinal cord. He curled up, his forehead pressed into the carpet; dust tickled his nose as he heard feet shuffling towards him.

'CeeCee?' Corey kept his eyes closed tight and trembled at the sound of the little girl's voice.

'CeeCee, why are you ignoring me? Did I do something wrong? Please, *pleaaase* don't be mad at me!' Corey felt a tiny hand gently comb through his damp hair. It was skinny and cold, paralyzingly cold.

'Rachel…' he mouthed.

'What's up, buttercup? I'm just a ray of sunshine, here to brighten your day!' The girl began to sing. Corey smiled, sniffed, and slowly lifted his head…and there she was. In pink pyjamas, her long light brown hair in wispy pigtails. She stared at him with bright eyes that mirrored his own, her grin missing odd teeth.

'Rach, I...I'm sorry, I couldn't stop him...' The words hitched in his throat. He bowed his head and stared hard into the carpet.

'I wasn't there, I should have been, I should have been with you, I couldn't...' Rachel cocked her head, still smiling.

'I'm just a ray of sunshine, here to brighten your day. Rain won't make you sad! You'll be okay!' Corey sobbed as the girl sang.

Corey summoned the last of his strength, opened his arms wide and embraced her. She nestled her face against Corey's neck, but he felt no breath from her lips. Her pale skin turned silver and her hold on him tightened. Corey's eyes widened as Rachel became entirely reflective, both fluid and solid all at the same time. He saw himself, his reflection, in her as she held him tighter. The air in his lungs hissed as living glass dripped into his eyes and everything disappeared.

All senses blocked, Corey felt and thought nothing until gravity took him all at once. His torso suddenly slammed against the ground, and he felt his ribs crack. His moist palms met a cold ground that almost held no texture, like he had landed on solid water. All at once, light blinded him as it poured in from every angle in the room.

He rubbed his eyes hard as spots of pink and blue danced in his vision. Mirrors, bright and clean, surrounded him, the floor, ceiling, walls, at all different angles. He was trapped inside a disco ball with no doors. A thousand reflections of his own face stared about the room in confusion, infinite versions of him doing the very same thing. He clambered to his feet and blundered through the empty space in a furious search for the edges of the room.

'Oh, CeeCee! Don't leave me again!' Rachel's voice echoed.

Corey whipped his gaze around the room. Something wrapped around his ankles and, when he looked down, he saw that his feet were gone. He was sinking into the bubbling, mirrored floor, alive with grasping hands and fingers…all reflective, solid, and yet…

'You left me! You left me! He told me it was your fault. Stay here with us, never leave. Never.' Her voice sang out and the walls morphed into people, hundreds of shining people reflecting Corey's face on the curves of their bodies. Each of them reached out for him, swallowing parts of him with their limbs, and he took a deep breath and stared at the ceiling, helpless, until he was no more.

* * *

Corey opened his eyes. He was floating in mid-space. A solid glass ceiling loomed over him and looked into the mirrored room. Soft darkness cradled him.

Silently, one of the mirrored walls above opened and an old man stepped into the room. He held himself with a bird-like posture, his features sharp and aging. Corey raised his fists to the glass, but the old man simply passed through. As he opened a once hidden door on the other side, the two briefly made eye contact.

The man smiled slightly and disappeared through the door.

In that moment, Corey felt his heart stop. His eyes widened, and he sank deep down into the bowels of the house.

Chapter One

One Week Earlier

1. Brandis at His Desk

I stared at a blank screen.

It felt like I've been staring at it forever.

Everything was set up and ready to go; my laptop was warmed up, all of my files and tabs were open, and my browser was ready in case I needed to research anything.

Yet my screen was blank except for the little mouse cursor and a single, slim black line blinking at me against a sheet of white.

Blinking.

Taunting.

Daring me to try and write something.

I wish I could.

I had the very basics of a story worked out; the ghost of a main character, an idea of the setting, and definitely enough material to write the first draft of roughly three chapters…and yet…nothing.

The old me could've done it.

Not even two years ago, I could've typed *something* and at least gotten started, and would never be left staring at a blank screen after deleting an hour's worth of work in a fit of pique.

Even now, I'm struggling to justify *why* I did that. I'm humble enough to know when my writing isn't great or needs more work. Hell, I have a whole folder that's full of half-finished concepts, cut material, and discarded ideas.

Lately, though, something has definitely gotten lost.

I don't feel like myself.

I feel like the dark looming sense of doubt is controlling my arms in a mockery of productivity and that the words I type aren't *mine*. I read them back and it was as though I was reading someone else's thoughts; like that dark entity had smashed its claws on my keyboard just to mock me.

I felt sick, disgusted even, and instead of trying to salvage the work, I highlighted it all and deleted it forever. It was like I'd somehow wandered into the wrong flat and accessed a stranger's machine. Even my *Breath of Eden* folder seemed strange and alien to me, as though I had misappropriated it from someone else, changed a few things, and claimed it as my own.

That hadn't been *me*.

It was crazy. Of *course*, I was in my own flat; of *course*, the laptop and its files were mine...and yet I was continually met by this brick wall every time I tried to write. Frustrated, I slapped my hands to my face and ran my hand across my beard. As I did, my eye was naturally drawn to the small, stuffed bookcase beside my rickety desk. Admittedly, for someone who calls himself a writer, I'm not especially well read. Hell, my teachers had continuously lamented that I never really read real books.

Real books? What the fuck is a "real book"? All books are real? All the books I've read and own are "real"; if they weren't then their bent and faded spines wouldn't be glaring at me from my fuckin' bookcase!

One book, as always, taunted me most of all.

My book.

Breath of Eden.

My one minor claim to fame.

I started *Breath of Eden* when I was fifteen; barely old enough to know anything and yet determined to put this "talent" to good use. I'd written stuff before, mainly off-beat fantasy stories or shameless rip-offs of the science fiction and horror movies I watched as a kid. I had even revisited some of these for writing assignments at university. *Breath of Eden* was different, though. I wouldn't go as far as to say it was my *magnum opus* (I was fifteen when I started it, eighteen when I finished it, and twenty-six when I published it. I'm thirty-four now so it seems a little fuckin' early to have produced my *magnum opus!*) but it *is* the first full-length novel I've written. It's an experience I have little desire to recreate. When I proofread it the first of maybe twelve times, I noticed errors on every single page (from minor stuff like repeated or missing words to major stuff like character's names being wrong and ages getting mixed up), and that I'd repeated at least two anecdotes about a hundred pages apart.

The whole thing was tantamount to a nightmare. Considering I have a battered notebook in my bedside cabinet detailing the nightmares I've had over the years in the hopes of one day turning them into short stories, you can believe that I know a thing or two about nightmares…or, at least, I used to. It's been years since I have (or could remember) my dreams, whether good or bad, and so my notebook hadn't come out in the dead of night for some time, and those I had typed up were left to gather digital dust. I used to have nightmares all the time; generally vague terrors of shadows or monstrous creatures stalking me, tormenting me, usually tearing me apart in gruesome ways. Still, they were just dreams and, despite what those horror films tell you, dreams can't hurt you.

When you don't remember them, though, they can hurt you pretty bad…and maybe this is why I'm staring at a blank screen.

Or maybe I'm just not good enough.

It's not like *Breath of Eden* was a hit. The first, clunky draft had been a mess of clichés, conveniences, contrivances, and one-note characters. Still, I was happy to get it out of my system; and just in time, too, as I was a little busy reading and studying

(*and drinking*)

at university. Suddenly, refining my quirky novel about teenagers trapped in an abandoned mental asylum that's also, maybe, kind of a level of purgatory just didn't seem as important as boning up for my next essay or my next class.

Or my next lay.

'Back in t'day,' I smiled weakly.

After university, emotionally battered and bruised but nonetheless changed from my experiences, I applied everything I'd learned in those three, drink-addled years to *Breath of Eden*. Characters were merged, entire chapters were deleted or cut down to barely a paragraph, and new elements were introduced. I focused on trying to recreate the banter I'd had with my friends and some of our odd ways of pronouncing words. Lucy had always…

(*bludgeoned*)

(*crime scene*)

(*victims of a*)

Something warm and fuzzy bashed into my calf, forcing my eyes away from my blank screen. '*Mwrp?*' came a small cry as Bert nuzzled against my leg.

I adopted Bert after one of my neighbours had to move and their new place wouldn't let her have pets. He is the oddest cat I've ever known. He's extremely finicky and antisocial, rarely cries, hates being picked up and cuddled, and never sits on the sofa or on my lap. Thankfully, he's perfectly happy being in the flat; we're too high up for him to escape out the windows (we are nicely fenced off to keep him (or me) from plummeting to the street below), and I always lock him in my bedroom whenever I go out to keep him from dashing out the door.

It's not like I really have to worry about visitors or anything. Honestly, I couldn't really say why I even bothered staying in Northward after

(*Lucy*)

university. I guess I got used to being here; the rent is cheap, the place is familiar, and I feel like I owe it to Lucy to stay here until something positive comes from it all.

I stroked Bert's fluffy chin and he padded over to the doorway and stared at me with cold, patient judgement until I gave in and fed him. As he eagerly stuffed his face, I lamented the state of the kitchen: the wallpaper was noticeably peeling and faded, most of the cupboards were missing doorknobs, and the fridge whirred much too loudly to be safe.

Christ, when did I become such a loser?

Breath of Eden was eight years ago!

It was now as old as I was when I wrote my first story about a chaotic dimension filled with demonic forces. This writing fancy of mine just wasn't happening…and even if it *did*, what was the fuckin' point? No one would even notice if I wrote another book or not; even if I stuck with it and made Sam the star of his own story, it wouldn't bring him back and wouldn't mean anything to anyone.

As I shut down my laptop, I vaguely realised that I'd wasted my entire day. I could've been out, or reading Aster Callahan's new novel, or visited friends or Mum's grave. I could've tidied the flat or even messaged Dani, the super friendly and pretty girl from work who suggested that we should meet up some time. If I'd not wasted all my time on this pointless endeavour, I could've been dating her…maybe even living with her or trying to build a real life for myself.

'*Mmrowp?*' came Bert's cry.

I turned to look at him as he sat looking at me on my crumpled bed sheets. 'I know, Bert. I know,' I sighed and went to bed feeling more like a failure than ever.

2. *Mikhail in His Car*

The once-acclaimed author awoke with a sudden jolt; his searing headache exacerbated when his head thudded off the ceiling of his cramped, freezing little car.

'*Блять*,' he muttered wearily. His legs had seized up in the night and pins and needles stabbed through his tense, aching muscles. He kicked out involuntarily and heard the familiar clink of glass. A hiss of frustration escaped his lips.

Drinking.

Again.

Last night was such a blur that he struggled to remember who and where he even was. He peered out through the car's frosted windows at the deserted, mist-covered streets of Voronezh, where he had been born and raised (and, he had no doubt, would die).

'Mikhail,' he muttered, his tongue little more than sandpaper in his acrid mouth. 'Mikhail Orlov.'

Mikhail regarded the empty bottle of Белочка with disgust. Ordinarily, he wouldn't touch the swill, but a memory painfully surfaced of Rodion swiping it from behind the bar when the air-headed bitch took her eyes away. Suddenly craving the taste of vodka (even cheap, rancid vodka such as this), Mikhail brought the bottle to his lips and shuddered as a few tiny drops settled on his tongue. Nowadays, it seemed he could barely get through the day without at least one drink, and he found himself craving alcohol on a near hourly basis.

He dropped the bottle and winced as he wiped his lips. Not only were his knuckles grazed, but his jaw ached fiercely when he touched it.

Hey! A memory yelled. *Are you going to pay for that?!*

Mikhail groaned as another memory flooded back. Trevelyan's was a sports bar where he, Rodion, and Yuri often crammed their brutish frames into a small, sticky booth with pitchers of vodka and warm, frothy beer laid out before them, and cheered on FC Fakel Voronezh. This season had been insulting, however, and Mikhail had been especially angered at their performance last night.

'Сукин сын!' He'd been so pissed out of his head that he hadn't even noticed that he had knocked over a stranger's drink in his anger.

'*Hey!*' the man had barked angrily; he had been wearing a Spartak's shirt, and just the sight of those colours sent Mikhail's blood boiling. 'Are you going to pay for that?'

'Pay?!' Mikhail had literally spat. 'I should rip that shirt right off you and make you eat it!'

The Spartak had squared up to him immediately, and Mikhail had felt adrenaline rush through him as he sneered right back. The Spartak was stocky and had been a good two feet shorter where Mikhail was strong and tempered.

'Hey, *hey!*' the bargirl had called. 'Take it outside, guys. We don't need no trouble in here.'

'It's no trouble, darling,' Mikhail had scoffed before slapping the Spartak's face.

The Spartak supporter had reeled and swung a flailing punch that Mikhail had been too drunk to dodge. The punch had wracked his jaw, and the next thing he knew Rodion and Yuri were pulling him off the Spartak's prone body and hauling him out into the cold night air as he hurled abuse at Spartak and all who cheered their name

Rodion had hollered and slapped him on the back; Mikhail had shrugged him off, but his mood had cooled when Rodion handed him the bottle he had swiped. Mikhail had twisted the lid off and taken a deep swig. 'Fakel forever!' he had roared into the night sky.

'Come on, my friend. Let's get you home, yeah?' Rodion said as they stumbled to the cobbled, cracked pavement.

'No home,' Mikhail had yelled through a mouthful of the acidic, stale liquid. 'Jus' get me t'my car.' When Yuri had questioned if he was fit enough to drive, Mikhail had shouted: 'What am I? Some kind of idiot? Just…just get me t'my car!'

After he'd been bundled into his creaky Nissan Qashqai, Mikhail had passed out almost immediately and remained dead to the world until now, some eight hours later.

Mikhail fumbled the door open, spilling his empty bottle out onto the street where it shattered into thousands of tiny pieces. The cold air hit him hard as he lurched around to the driver's seat, slamming the door shut behind him and firing up the Nissan on the third try. It was temperamental at the best of times, especially when the weather grew colder. Voronezh normally didn't get below -9° but the thermometer had read -26° last night, and Mikhail seriously worried how he would be able to survive living out of his car with little more than a few blankets for warmth.

'How'd this happen to me?' he mumbled.

So far, he had been able to hide his current condition from Rodion, Yuri, and even Pavel, his agent, but it wouldn't be long before they realised that he was constantly passing out in his Qashqai rather than his apartment. Rodion's and Yuri's concerns mainly centred on whose round was up next, where FC Fakel Voronezh were in the league, and how to keep their mistresses a secret, but even they would begin to suspect something was amiss before long.

'This's what you get, you know,' he grumbled. 'If only you had not put all cards on *Смертельное Желание*, things would be different.'

Смертельное Желание (or *Death Wish*, as the Americans had rechristened it, much to Mikhail's dismay) had been a bestseller in Russia two years ago, and across some of Europe too, and Mikhail had become quite a celebrity for a while. He had treated himself and his friends to season tickets, bought his Nissan Qashqai brand new from a dealership, and even made appearances at bookshops around the city. It had been like a whirlwind of fame…until it had all inevitably come crashing down.

'People want to know when the next book is coming,' Pavel had said one morning. 'Competition is fierce, *Миша*, and this business is fleeting.'

Mikhail had laughed it off; he'd have plenty of time to write once the football season was over (and this time he would demand that the original, superior Russian title stay on the book!). He'd filled his days with excess, stoking his pipe with the finest tobacco and buying only the very best brand of vodka, all while handing over his credit card with a smile.

All too soon, the bills piled up. "Неуплачено," "Последнее," they read, and he threw them all away, fully believing that *Смертельное Желание*'s popularity would never wane. Then one day he had staggered back to his apartment, a squirming whore in his arms and his pipe clamped between his teeth, and the *Уведомление о выселении* notice stuck to his door had finally shattered the dream.

'Черт меня дери!' he'd snarled, pushing the woman aside and slamming a fist on the heavily padlocked door. He'd then barged into the landlord's office downstairs. The greasy, rotund little man had been shocked, but wore a face of condescending dismissal as Mikhail had raged at him while brandishing the eviction notice.

'You're six months overdue,' the landlord had said. 'You pay your rent, I give your apartment back.'

'I'm good for it!' Mikhail had insisted. 'When have I ever missed a payment?'

'Last month,' the landlord had replied as if addressing a child. 'And the month before, and the month before that. Need I go on?'

Mikhail had thrown his hands into the air in frustration and then dropped into an uncomfortable chair, his hands clasped together in a desperate plea. 'Please,' he whispered. 'Don't do this. I-I will get you the money…'

'Is nothing personal,' the landlord had insisted, though his eyes had told a different story, and Mikhail had been sorely tempted to choke the life from his flabby neck. 'I give you a week,' the landlord had offered. 'One week to pay me my rent, then I throw your stuff into the street, got it?'

And just like that, it was over. Without his apartment, Mikhail couldn't write, and he was too stubborn to work a menial job; the very idea of him, a once prolific author, lugging around furniture or driving lorries like his father made him sick to his stomach. All of his cards were maxed out, his pockets were empty save for a few torn notes, and he'd been left drowning his sorrows on the charity of others and desperately driving around town on fumes, parking up in a new side street each evening, and hoping to awaken to the same success he had once enjoyed.

3. Brandis Gets a Letter

My work is very boring. I've never really had a career goal, and quickly learned that studying English at university was a bit of a mistake when even my tutor had struggled to suggest a career path for the degree. Many were so panicked at having effectively wasted three years of their lives that they immediately signed up for PGCE courses.

Personally, I couldn't imagine anything worse. Not only am I not much of a teacher (or a very good communicator, judging by how many of my work emails are ignored…) but I'd seen how hard Shane's teaching course had been. It had taken him four years to complete rather than my three and involved getting a lot of experience with different age groups, classrooms, and schools. PGCEs, in comparison, saw students cramming all of that work into *one year*. As such, it kind of sickened me to see so many people from my course suddenly decide, literally at the last minute, that they'd wanted to be teachers all along.

I didn't sign up to become a teacher; I did it because I was bored and figured it'd be a good change of pace. Luckily, my dad's low income meant I was afforded additional loans for books and living that I didn't have to pay back, and my tuition fees weren't really an issue as I didn't earn enough to have to worry about making repayments. I'd been thoroughly amused when students had protested the raising of tuition fees. 'Rich kids,' I told Bert when it had flashed up on the news. Rich kids mooching off mummy and daddy and who hadn't worked a day in their lives.

I work a boring office job; it has next to nothing to do with my degree and basically amounts to data entry, maybe a bit of quality control, and making calls to clients about their policies. The pay wasn't great, but I have simple needs and few attachments. I tell myself that as long as I can pay rent and bills, feed the cat, and keep my car fuelled, I'm fine with that but...I hate my job. It's so tedious and everybody's so fuckin' uptight that you can't really talk to anyone (apart from Dani...). There's always some fucker waiting to hear something out of context so they can get offended by it, and the job is depressingly simple but ridiculously overcomplicated by lack of clear guidance, inconsistent standards, and seemingly endless emails and meetings.

My supervisor, Reginald, is a strange, mole-like man who drives everyone mad with his constant sniffing and who only cares about the numbers. Often, we simply doctored these so he would see only good things when he glanced at the stats. It was all a fuckin' joke. There were no guidance documents, half of what we were told was vague and wildly inconsistent, and the rest was hoarded by the more experienced staff who had no desire to share that information. Like most employees, Reginald had been there for at least ten years and wanted things done *his* way...but rather than actually specify what he wanted, he preferred to send pretentious emails and laud his holier-than-thou attitude.

Well, joke's on *him* because I created my own work guide that contains all kinds of reminders, templates, style guides, and guidance for myself, and so far this cheat sheet has kept me out of trouble. Ironically, Reginald once asked why I didn't share it with the rest of the team, but I had no intention of sharing it with anyone except Dani.

Yes, I fancy her but so what? Can't I still be nice as well?

Coming from a telesales background, Dani was fine with the emails and client calls and had a fantastic telephone manner but had been absolutely blindsided by the toxic atmosphere that hung in the office. 'You just hafta let it blow over,' I'd whispered to her in the lunchroom once, keeping my voice low so the snooty cow by the coffee machine didn't overhear our conversation. 'No one expects you t'pick it up after one week.'

This was partially true...but also a lie. I'd seen the company cut people halfway through their probation because they just weren't "getting it". 'It's not rocket science,' Reginald would say. 'We're not asking them to reinvent the wheel.'

What an asshole.

It's not easy working a nine-to-five you hate, coming home to a cat who judges you silently, and then finding that the one passion you have left in life is a veritable dead end. Lucy might have pushed me towards doing more but, without her, I don't really have the motivation. Bert had let me know with the slightest tilt of his head that I was simply making excuses.

So, suffice it to say that the last thing I expected to see when I came home (and after nearly tripping over the damn cat, who was being unusually affectionate) was a wax-sealed envelope amidst the usual junk mail offering to fix a conservatory I obviously didn't have.

Wax-sealed! What is this, the goddamn dark ages?

Not only was it wax-sealed, the envelope had a slight colouring to it (bone, or possibly an off-white eggshell) and my name and address were written in highly stylised calligraphy.

'*Mehp*,' Bert enquired as he rubbed against my ankles.

'Just some...'

LaVey House?

'Fuck off,' I scoffed into my empty flat.

But it was. The return address was printed in the corner of the envelope almost like a watermark:

LaVey House
Gilead

Where the fuck…? I wondered.

Geography was never my strong suit, but I recognised the name LaVey. And I should, considering they published many of the textbooks I'd read at uni, and even some of the horror fiction I owned.

I tore open the immaculately crafted envelope and beheld a letter written in a sweeping calligraphy that could only have come from a quill and inkwell.

LaVey Publishing was one of the biggest publishing houses in the United Kingdom. They did it all: research books, maps, biographies, *auto*biographies…but their speciality was horror. They published regular anthology books and frequently invited authors of all kinds to submit their work. I'd submitted at least three stories to them, but it was practically impossible to break their glass ceiling as they only accepted submissions from literary agents.

They were legitimate.

What the fuck are they writing to me for?

Dear Mr. Brandis,

I trust this letter finds you well. I am writing to you today to…

As I read, my eyes widened as I spied words such as *cordially invite*, *collaborate*, and *generously compensate*.

'*Meh-hep*,' Bert yawned at my feet. I could tell that he was hungry, but I'd reached the part of the letter that truly blew my mind:

Mr. LaVey is looking to host a writing circle at his stately manor, LaVey House, and would very much like to invite you to attend and collaborate from 18th February through to the 24th.

'I mean…why *wouldn't* he want me there?' Was this a scam? Nothing could be this…'*Five hundred pounds?!*' I screamed into my empty flat. Bert looked at me like I'd gone crazy.

They were gonna offer me £500 *a day* to be part of this writing circle. I'd heard of such things, but I thought the closest you got to a writing circle these days was angry comments online. 'Or a murder mystery…?' I shrugged. They were going to compensate my travel expenses and give me a further £1000, 'Upon completion of your piece…' I finished out loud.

Wait…my piece?

Mr. LaVey is looking to bring together some of the most accomplished authors in the field of horror, and some of the most promising up-and-comers, to contribute to an anthology piece to be titled Even Death May Die.

I frowned. That was a bit on the nose. There was also some preamble about how each writer would be further compensated with a percentage of the book's profits and that LaVey Publishing would personally market the book, and each of its contributors, and offer further publishing opportunities depending on the quality of the finished piece. But then my heart dropped.

Write a horror piece of at least…five thousand words? In just a week? All while locked up halfway across the country with a handful of other writers?

Hell, I was one bad day away from throwing my fuckin' laptop out the window and packing it all in for good.

I wasn't good enough.

It wasn't even a question.

A quick look online told me that the letter was legitimate. My Instagram was alive with people talking about it.

All very fascinating stuff but I was curious to know how they even knew about me. *Breath of Eden* was just one of thousands of books available; the first three most recommended titles attached to my book all had proper written reviews, and my e-books may as well not exist.

No.

Clearly there was some mistake.

I prepared to throw the letter away and forget about it. Then I would grab a beer, watch some TV, and maybe ask Dani out…

Five hundred pounds…

I unfolded the letter again.

Arklington.

Apparently, this town I'd never heard of was just outside of Gilead, a massive city full of bronzed up suburbanites obsessed with brands, fake tans, and botched boob jobs. Gilead was over a hundred miles from Northward. In my piece of shit car, it'd probably take three hours to get there (and that was if the traffic was good; that motorway was constantly stalled by road works and I vaguely remembered some drama about a bridge collapse a few years back).

No, come on, it was just completely out of the question. It'd cost me…

Nothing, because they're gonna pay your fees.

Right, but Bert…

You could drop him off at Dad's. Could even add the mileage to the bill.

I mean…yeah, I guess…but I have work to think about …

Excuses, Lucy tutted in my head.

I fiddled with the letter absent-mindedly and stared at my laptop. It had betrayed me the other day, and even more so recently, leaving me with nothing but heartache and rejection and disappointment. I couldn't break ground on my most recent idea, a tech-noir piece that cast Sam as a disgruntled detective in a society where androids were the norm. It couldn't have been a more played out genre and yet I couldn't crack it…but then, I wasn't being paid £500 a day to work on it.

I didn't even earn that at my job now.

Three thousand five hundred pounds for one week's worth of work. I'd have to work for nearly two-and-a-half months to earn that.

And the extra grand at the end.

And the guaranteed publishing incentive.

I let out a hefty sigh and glanced at Bert. He looked up at me wearily, as if sick of my bullshit. 'What would you do?' I asked.

4. *Mikhail's Last Chance*

Pavel's office hadn't changed since Mikhail had last been there about three months ago, when he had tried selling the idea of a hardback version of *Смертельное Желание*.

'Hardback is good,' Pavel had agreed. 'But it is not *new*, *Миша*', and the people need *new*.'

Easy for *him* to say. As an agent for Voronezh's largest publisher, Andreev House, Pavel didn't have to worry about being evicted from his home or shaming his family. Pavel's father co-owned Andreev House, after all, and would never see his eldest son in such a state. Pavel's father had also served alongside Mikhail's in the Russian Armed Forces, forming a bond beyond friendship, and this influence had allowed Mikhail to jump a long line of writers wishing to have their work published.

Mikhail marvelled at Pavel's ability to maintain a professional relationship. The wild child he had once absconded with to Amsterdam had died after he had joined his father's company and very few would ever suspect that the two had anything more than a mutually beneficial, professional relationship.

If Pavel's father knew what the two of them had gotten up to in those sordid back alleys…

Mikhail had started this day the same as every day, by parking his Qashqai and wandering the city centre, head down and hands stuffed into his coat pockets, stepping into shops for warmth and perusing the newspapers only to find nothing but doom and gloom. Inevitably, he would head to the library to check local job listings. Sometimes he found some that seemed worthwhile, but he just couldn't work up the confidence to make enquiries. The library closed at five in the evening on weekdays, forcing him to leave and try to find some food either by slipping what he could into his pockets while meandering through the market or foraging through bins, and then he would slink back to his car and start the whole thing over again the next day.

Today, though, Mikhail had taken advantage of the library's electrical supply to recharge his phone; it would only be a matter of time before his service was cut off due to lack of payments but, for now, he was still able to send and receive calls and texts. As his phone had vibrated to life, Mikhail had been shocked to see Pavel's name flash up on the chipped screen.

'Orlov! Can …make in …y office?' Mikhail strained to hear and yelled into the receiver a few times (which naturally didn't help) before stepping outside. It seemed Pavel had an important message for him and needed him at the office right away. Mikhail had been intrigued; Pavel hadn't been in touch for months, beyond the demand for more writing, so Mikhail had wrapped his coat around him and walked across the city centre to Andreev House. Mikhail was a tall, well-built man in his early thirties. He played football in his youth, making captain of his *kolledzh* team before he'd blown his knee out, and had grown used to spending his days walking around, so the trip to Andreev House took no time at all.

He stepped into Pavel's office to find his friend smiling broadly. 'A balm for the soul!' Pavel embraced Mikhail. 'You are going to be very happy with this news.'

Mikhail was wary; Pavel was never normally this excited, and he couldn't decide whether he should be happy or worried. Mikhail's eyes glanced towards Pavel's collection of spirits and glasses and felt his mouth water at the thought of a glass of vodka, whiskey…anything.

As if reading his mind, Pavel poured them both a generous measure of vodka; the two clinked glasses and toasted: '*На здоровье!*' Mikhail felt his worries settle as the liquid scorched down his throat. 'You have my attention,' Mikhail said, already thirsty for another. 'Now, tell me more.'

Pavel sat and pulled an envelope from his desk drawer. 'Apparently, I am your mailman now? This arrived here this morning; it seems they've had some trouble reaching you.'

Mikhail tore the envelope open and said: 'I've been…busy, lately.'

'Writing, I hope.'

Mikhail's desire to cave in his friend's face was momentarily quelled as he read the letter, but he glanced at his friend with suspicion. 'What is this LaVey House? I've never heard of them.'

Pavel laced his fingers together. 'LaVey House is one of the most prominent publishing houses in all of the United Kingdom. I met Mr. Howard LaVey at a conference a few years back; very charming, very respectable, *very* serious about his craft. This is not the first time he has extended such an invitation, and trust me when I say he is very…selective about who he works with and what submissions he publishes.'

Mikhail remained sceptical. 'Why would this…LaVey invite me? How did he even hear of me?'

Pavel looked at him sheepishly. 'I know things have been…stagnant for you lately. You're my client, and it's my job to look out for your best interests, but you are also my good friend. I sent a copy of your book to him a while back…as well as your acceptance speech when you won the Gogol Award last year.'

Mikhail tossed the letter to Pavel's desk and struggled to contain the seething anger welling inside of him. 'So, this was all some kind of charity, hm? Perhaps you think I am not good enough to sell myself, yes? Or was the percentage just too good to pass up?'

Pavel shook his head immediately. 'No! Of course not! I'm just doing my job. Frankly, you *need* this. My father is a patient and loyal man, but we can't keep printing your book when it's not making money.' Mikhail stewed in silence as Pavel continued: 'Besides, LaVey had asked about some of the more renowned authors I had worked with at the conference and your name was at the top of my list, alongside a few others to make it look good for Andreev House. Nikolai Morozov, Boris Volkov, Ulya Pasternak…the usuals that are right up there.'

Mikhail rolled his eyes. 'Любители.' As far as he was concerned, Nikolai and Ulya could both rot in hell, and Mikhail had no time for Boris's overly cheerful demeanour. It made him feel sick thinking about how someone could be so happy and optimistic all the time.

'None of them are as good as you, Mikhail,' Pavel insisted. 'And I mean that. You have real talent, and the world needs to see *more* of it, and something like this makes us all look good.'

'Right, right,' Mikhail huffed. As much as he hated to admit it, Pavel was right; he *needed* this opportunity, which almost seemed too good to pass up. This LaVey was willing to foot the bill, so he really didn't have much choice. Still…he hadn't written for some time, and sometimes, late at night with the alcohol burning into his brain, Mikhail wondered if *Смертельное Желание* had been some lucky fluke. No one would ever say that to his face, and his accomplishments spoke for themselves, but he was an intimidating man and people could just be placating him.

'Listen,' Pavel said. 'It is simple: you agree to go, take copies of your book, and spend a few days writing, get back to the old Mikhail who took this country by storm, and we can sign a new contract? Get your name back out there, where it belongs.'

Mikhail nodded thoughtfully. 'I'm going to need a few things first,' he said.

Chapter Two

Sunday – The First Day

1. Mikhail's Nightmare Flight

Mikhail had been embarrassed to ask Pavel for favours, but he couldn't afford to travel from Moscow to Heathrow dressed like a bum. In order to channel the man who had once had women falling over themselves to get to him, he needed to look and dress the part, and Pavel had come through beautifully. Since LaVey was covering the costs, it hadn't taken much to convince Pavel to book Mikhail a barber and tailor, and a refreshing hotel room, before taxiing him to the airport. Mikhail had hastily explained these luxuries by saying: 'I just want to be able to get up and go as quickly as possible.'

Pavel hadn't questioned why Mikhail needed a new wardrobe and had simply seen it as a worthy investment to furnish his client with three-piece suits for his journey. Dear, sweet, trusting Pavel. He had been so excited to confirm Mikhail's acceptance of LaVey's offer that he hadn't even noticed his old friend slipping an unread submission from his desk and into the inside of his coat.

As Mikhail flew in a comfy first-class seat, sipping a refreshing glass of gin, he almost felt bad for his friend.

Almost.

He did not, however, feel bad about rinsing LaVey's generosity. While others may be content to travel cheaper, Mikhail was determined to make the most of the entire experience. Plus, he needed the extra leg room and solitude afforded from first-class.

Mikhail pulled the stolen submission from the lavish briefcase he had insisted upon having for his trip and flicked through it. LaVey wanted a horror story, Mikhail needed the money, but nowhere in the invitation did it say that the work had to be *his*. Fortune had been in his favour; he had swiped quite the psychological horror courtesy of Sophia Novaskaya's *Mara's Secret*. Mikhail was confident that he would be able to cut the piece down into something suitable for LaVey's anthology in a day or so, leaving him plenty of time to indulge himself.

A content smile crossed Mikhail's rugged features for the first time in what felt like forever. In just seven days' time, he would have enough money to regain his apartment (or find a new one) and his reputation. No more living out of his car or scrounging around like a hermit...or drinking himself to death.

* * *

Папа! Папочка, I'm scared!

What? What is this?

Папа! Please, don't let her ...

Luka? *Мой Бог*...Luka, where are you?

Help me, Papa! Please, help!

Luka!! Where...

YOU'RE NOT TAKING HIM FROM ME!

Папа! Папа!!

'Luka!' Mikhail jerked awake so violently that the passenger across the aisle raised a pretentious eyebrow. Mikhail barely noticed; his heart was pounding like a jackhammer. 'Nightmare…nothing more.'

But it had seemed so *real*. He had *heard* Luka's screams, felt his anguish…but had been powerless to help him. Mikhail quickly flagged down the stewardess to order a double vodka and stared out of his window. Grey wisps of cloud hung in the night sky as the plane was lightly buffeted by turbulence. Mikhail eagerly sipped at his drink; it was the only way to stop the nightmares.

The memories.

He had heard Lia's voice, or a twisted version of it, at the end of the nightmare, and was grateful to have been spared seeing her face. She, like Luka, had been gone nearly four years now…how strange that these memories had surfaced when he was on the cusp of greatness once more.

Lia had been a skinny, shy wallflower when they had met at *kolledzh*; he'd been dancing rings around his peers on the football pitch, and she had been dragged along to watch by one of her friends (her name escaped him now, but he'd had no qualms about ravishing her in the deserted locker room the previous week). This girl, whatever her name had been, had been infatuated with him, but Lia had simply hidden behind her long, curly blonde hair and said barely a word.

Mikhail had been fascinated. Here was a girl who didn't swoon in his presence and who actually seemed uncomfortable around him. The challenge had been too tempting to pass up and, for the next several weeks, he had endeavoured to learn everything he could about her by systematically working through her friends. Soon, he knew it all: Lia Ivanov, the twenty-year-old daughter of Maxim, a common construction worker who worked himself to the bone funding her education. She was studying Marketing Principles and wanted to work in digital marketing. Her hobbies included reading and watching trash television, particularly American soap operas, and she longed to visit New York. Mikhail's desires had been sent into overdrive and he simply had to have her. While their social circles and classes couldn't have been more different, Lia loved to dance, and that was where Mikhail had made his move.

Had he known what she would turn out to be later in life, he never would have approached her in the smoky, blaring nightclub and bought her a drink. 'I know you!' she'd cried, clearly already very drunk. 'You're that футбольный everyone raves about!'

He'd smiled and ordered her a double shot of Beluga to toast her good health. Moments later, they were grinding and bumping against each other on the crammed dance floor. Two hours later, she was writhing beneath him, her fingernails digging into his back and gasps of ecstasy escaping her pink, full lips as he took her with an animal lust.

The next morning, she had made him some hearty колбаса sandwiches and black tea with lemon, just as he liked it, and he had found a satisfaction he had never thought possible. Being with Lia felt like being back at the old family home, on the days when his father had thankfully been at work and it had been just him, his mother, and his two sisters enjoying something resembling happiness. He'd always treasured the warm look on his mother's tired face, the playful giggling of his sisters, and hated his father for his brutish ways. Like them, he had been no match for his father (especially when he had been in one of his foul moods), but being with Lia reminded him of why he had so

38

often tried to defend his mother and sisters from his father's drunken outbursts.

Mikhail's injury had derailed his once-promising football career. Lia had helped nurse him through it and been the first to encourage his writing talent. 'You need to pursue this, *любимый*,' she'd said. 'This could be where you find your purpose.'

Mikhail had initially been sceptical but had been convinced to take it further after seeing his grades and feedback. Soon, he was winning writing competitions, his assignments were being recommended for serious publication, and he had dreamed up *Смертельное Желание* while lying naked next to Lia after she had collapsed from her orgasm.

After *kolledzh*, Mikhail worked as an intern for a local tabloid, and had been overjoyed when Lia had greeted his return to their small apartment with the news that he was to be a father. He had quickly pushed to legitimise the event and, though they couldn't afford much, and her father had vehemently disapproved ("He's going to drag you down to the gutter with him, *мой ангел*," Mikhail had heard him rant to Lia one evening. "Mark my words, that man is nothing but trouble"), Lia hadn't cared one lick.

Things had changed after Luka had been born, though. Lia grew moody and snappy. She put on weight, her skin became greasy, and she lounged around with little interest in cooking or cleaning. His attempts to push her into work were met with increasingly aggressive outbursts; Lia hurled objects at him, sulked in their bedroom for days, and had very little interest in caring for Luka.

It had tested him, and he had been disgusted to see how alike he and his father really were. His patience was exhausted when he had found Lia in the kitchen, staring into space, and holding a knife as Luka wailed on the floor. He'd thrown her out after that, only to face the condemnation of her father. 'You have done this to *мойя милая!* Is this how a husband treats his wife? You're a disgrace!' the old man had ranted, focusing only on Lia's black eye and limp, unconcerned to hear the truth.

'Sir?' a sweet voice roused Mikhail.

'My apologies,' he croaked at the stewardess. 'I was just...thinking.'

'Hot towel?' she offered.

Mikhail frowned. 'No,' he answered bluntly, and the stewardess wandered to the next passenger. Inwardly, Mikhail cursed Pavel. Why couldn't his friend have found a writer's circle in a city closer to home, like Vladivostok?

2. *Brandis and His Dad*

I worry about my dad sometimes.

He's lived alone ever since Mum died six years ago. It had been heartbreaking when we'd packed up his belongings into three separate piles (keep, car boot, and charity shop) to move him into a cosy little ground-floor flat. He'd resisted at first, mainly because he hadn't wanted to leave the old homestead or spend his days watching time ticking down. 'Still got plenty 'o life left in me,' he'd proudly proclaimed, completely unaware that he was only wearing one slipper and his shirt buttons were misaligned.

Eventually, he'd gotten used to it and fallen into a nice little routine. He'd potter about in the small garden, get on the bus, and go into town twice a week, play draughts or darts on Wednesdays, and take regular coach trips across the country, but he's never really gotten over Mum's death. She was a hard taskmaster who never depended on anyone, so it was soul-destroying to see her literally wither away as bowel cancer ate her from the inside out. A stubborn woman to the end, she didn't even go quickly; she clung to life and came back from the brink so many times that, when she finally passed, Dad and I had said our goodbyes more times than we could count.

Still, I worry about him. Not only is he by himself a lot but he's forgetting things. Nothing major just yet; his long-term memory remains as keen as ever, but we can talk about something one week and, a couple of weeks later, he'll argue until he's blue in the face that we've never mentioned that subject before. So far, it's not led to much more than a few easily resolved misunderstandings, but I worry that he'll leave the stove on or forget to lock the door…or forget where he lives.

Nevertheless, leaving Bert with my dad was the best option. I didn't like the idea of him being surrounded by strange people and cats, so I dug out his kitty carrier (it never ceased to amuse me how Bert got into his carrier so willingly) and made the relatively unspectacular drive down to Haverhill.

'Just need t'drop him off with you f'ra coupla days,' I said as I handed the kitty carrier over.

'*Meh-hewp!*' Bert whined.

'Eh?!' Dad grunted. Even with two hearing aids, he was still as deaf as a post.

'*Just droppin' him off with you f'ra few days!*' I repeated, louder.

Dad glanced at Bert. 'Is he stayin' here, then?'

Fuck's sake! I thought, but I replied as patiently as I could: 'Yes. Just f'r a week.'

'A week, is it?' Dad mused thoughtfully.

'Make sure he don't get out,' I cautioned as I brought in Bert's litter tray and food.

'He's not an outdoor cat, is he?' Dad asked as Bert sniffed the radiator.

'No,' I sighed.

Dad held up the bag full of cat food. 'Is this for me?'

'Yes!' I swear Dad does this shit on purpose. 'One in the morning, one in the afternoon.'

'Mmm?' he looked up. 'One in the…?'

'*Morning,*' I stressed. 'Another in th' afternoon!'

'Okay, okay,' he nodded repeatedly.

I spent another hour or so helping my dad with various household chores. Before leaving, Bert suddenly hopped up onto my lap and nuzzled my hand. '*Mrwep!*' he squeaked, a loud, rattling purr emanating from his throat as he padded warily on my thighs. Surprised at Bert's sudden affection, I scratched him behind his ear, which he always loved, before he shook his head comically and jumped down.

My dad shuffled into the room in a confused daze. 'What a friendly chap.'

'Yeah.' I was suddenly apprehensive about leaving my furry, unpredictable companion behind. 'Maybe I should write this down?'

'Write what down?' Dad answered, genuinely confused.

'We…We haven't changed the subject! About Bert…?'

'*Oh!*' he exclaimed. 'No, no, I think we'll manage. Won't we, puss?' Bert sniffed Dad's gnarled, arthritis-ridden hand

Exasperated, I left as politely as I could (despite Dad's assurances, I stuck a written reminder to the fridge after using the loo).

Dad had watched Bert for me before and he was very good at making sure the doors were shut to keep him from wandering off…but I still worried. It was out of my control now, though; I was already an hour into my trip. The finest hard rock of the late eighties blared out of my car's speakers (well, one of them; the passenger's side speaker had died ages ago). I had a bottle of water and an open packet of jelly beans ready, and was nicely cooled by the air conditioning as I trundled along the M25.

Yes, I had decided to go.

I honestly didn't think I would, but Reginald had been uncharacteristically co-operative about me swapping my holidays around—I can only assume that this will come back to bite me once the overtime is required—and any excuses I might've had died when Dad agreed to watch Bert. I was now too far along to consider turning back, even with doubts still nagging at me. I used to exorcise such dark thoughts with my writing, and actually welcomed them as they fuelled my creativity and imagination…but then Lucy and Sam had died

(*been murdered*)

and made my nightmares a reality. I'd tried to tackle these in a short story titled *Slain*, which was about an old knight who retired to a cave in a deep forest after many years of battle. One day, townsfolk begged him to slay a rampaging beast who fed on their children, and the old knight had sharpened his weapon, donned his armour, and ended the monster's threat with the sword of righteousness.

Slain was downloaded ten times when I ran a free promotion. It received no reviews, and I made no money from it.

Still…LaVey's offer was just too good to pass up.

I was gonna get paid to write…and be published in an actual book that people could buy in a shop!

I mean, that was the dream!

I figured I'd make the trip down there, see what's-what, and find out a bit more about the brief (it was probably in the letter they sent but…if I did read it, I don't remember what it said), get settled, and then do everything I could to bash something out.

On paper, it sounded so easy…but I still have my doubts. The letter seemed to assume that I'd be able to produce something worthwhile in the time frame. I'm sure the others would be fine with this, but…what if I get three days in and decide to scrap my project? What if LaVey decides what I've written isn't good enough? There was some mumbo-jumbo about additional consultations and such…but all the editing and rewrites in the world can't polish a turd.

I struggled to think of an idea for the assignment and kept drawing a blank. Besides, I was too busy concentrating on driving at the moment.

I like to think Lucy would have been impressed at how convincing that excuse was.

I've never really been one to wing it, but time was short, and my motivation and self-esteem were shot to shit. In the end, it came down to the money and the vague hope that I could get published in LaVey's book. Either way, I was going to get paid (as far as I could tell), so I abandoned any pretence of doing it for my love of the craft or the chance to network and focused on the money. For seven days, I would be generously compensated, and I could use the earnings to maybe justify just quietly walking away from this crazy dream of mine, which at this point sounded very appealing indeed.

3. Aster Boards Her Plane

'Flight number 3624 to London Heathrow is departing in fifteen minutes. If this is your flight, please make your way over to Terminal F, Gate 14. Thank you.' The announcement blared through Atlanta's airport, but I wasn't fussed as I had been waiting at Terminal F for two hours. When the plane touched down in Atlanta, I had made a beeline to Terminal F. I suppose it wasn't an urgent matter; I had a three-hour layover and would have plenty of time to get to the correct gate.

This was my first time visiting a foreign country. When some of my closer (and more well-travelled) friends found out I was heading to the United Kingdom, they weren't shy about making their opinions and suggestions known. I needed to check out everything London had to offer, take in the scenery in Edinburgh and, time permitting, make my way down to Brighton. However, when I informed them I would be spending the entire week outside of Arklington, I was greeted with several confused looks.

'Where's that at?' my best friend Alyssa had asked. 'You know, I've been over there several times and considered myself well-travelled—you could almost call me a secondary British citizen! I have never heard of Arklington!'

'See,' Walter had sneered. 'All the more reason it would be a bad idea for you to go. This place could be made up and you could be scammed out of thousands of dollars!'

I pushed the memory aside. I was excited, yet terrified. It might have seemed silly, but I was nervous about what the people would be like. If they were like anything depicted in movies and TV shows, I'd stand out like a sore thumb. My mannerisms and accent would be my giveaway as I could never pull off the sophisticated, posh way Brits seemed to carry themselves.

'You can start losing a little more weight for the wedding. Their food is too bland for your liking,' I murmured to myself. If "fish and chips" and "haggis" were as common as they were portrayed... let's just say I was looking forward to getting back to the states.

Doesn't hurt to be prepared, given how much of a perfectionist you can be! This is going rather well so far, I reassured myself as I made my way back from one of the terminal's shops, over-the-counter medication in hand.

The flight from Des Moines to Atlanta had taken four hours; nowhere near enough time for me to take a decent nap. Not that I would have anyway due to my crippling fear of heights, the result of a traumatic event from my childhood. While some viewed this fear as ridiculous, I didn't care. There were several events I had declined attending because they'd required me to book a plane ticket. If it wasn't for the lucrative offer and tremendous opportunity I received from LaVey Publishing, there was a good chance I would have passed because of the two flights I needed to take.

'Maybe these sleeping pills will help me get through this long flight.' Storing the medicine away, I pulled out the letter from LaVey Publishing and read through it once more.

Dear Ms. Callahan,

I trust this letter finds you well. I am writing to you today to discuss an incredible opportunity. Mr. LaVey is looking to host a writing circle at his stately manor. You are cordially invited to LaVey

House to attend from the 18th of February through to the 24th. Mr. LaVey is looking to bring together some of the most accomplished authors in the field of horror, and some the most promising up-and-comers to contribute to an anthology piece to be titled Even Death May Die. *For your time and contribution to this project, all travel expenses will be compensated, in addition to being paid $700 a day. Upon the completion of your piece, an extra $1,400 will be provided as compensation…*

At first, I thought it had been junk mail; it sounded too good to be true. *Probably some scammers trying to get my social security number or bank account information,* I'd thought. That was a lot of money, after all. It was when he mentioned all my books, including my current project, *Masquerade,* that had made me take it seriously. Of course, most of this information could be viewed on my Instagram page. I did a quick search online and found that some of the most infamous authors on that side of the world were published under LaVey Publishing, such as Jean Buerke, Christian Grainger, and Chantel Braxton. But there was still one thing that bothered me: why would some large UK publishing company want me, an author from the United States, to be part of their collaboration? To be fair, it said the best authors in horror, and it was safe to say I was one of the best independent authors in the field of horror…from the States. I had been on the bestsellers list at some point or another, and I made enough to write full-time. Walter, my fiancé, had not been happy with this decision initially; he saw it as a waste of time and berated me for weeks on making such an irresponsible career choice. He quickly changed his tune when *ReSpawn* became a bestseller for six straight weeks and earned me all kinds of accolades and money.

Still, this letter baffled me. There were so many other names to choose from. Why me? I wouldn't know who else had been invited until I arrived as no other names were mentioned. Nevertheless, I was curious to see who would be there, and I was excited for the chance to make new connections. Usually, I would have shared this all over my Instagram, but I had wanted to keep this on the down-low. I planned to share the news once I touched down in London, as well as drop hints until the collaboration came to an end. As much as I loved providing content and engaging with writers and fans, it was exhausting work, and there had been an increase in stalkers messaging me. Normally, I'd pay them no mind, but something about sharing details of me being alone in a foreign country didn't seem like a good idea, and I had no desire to become a statistic.

'Flight number 3624, London Heathrow, is now boarding.'

I shot Walter a text message telling him I would be unavailable for the next eight hours and shut off my phone. He would see this message later; Walter had recently picked up a third shift to earn some extra money and would be starting his shift as a security guard about now. *Hopefully the money can be for the wedding or a start to a down payment on a house. At least he finally got you a ring.* Looking down at my simple solitaire diamond, a surge of love and warmth spread through me. Despite his opinion on marriage and how anything associated with weddings was a waste of money, Walter still got me a ring and proposed to me.

Grabbing my luggage, I popped the sleeping medicine and waited in line to board. My mind began to wonder about this

49

collaboration event. What would this Mr. LaVey be like? Would my writing be good enough? *Of course it is! He* did *reach out to you about this! One of your books* must *have caught his attention.* Then I started to wonder which one it could have been. Was it *Only Come at Night*? Or maybe it was *Unholy Birthright*? *Does it matter, Aster? Howard LaVey chose* you. *Out of millions of authors out there, he chose* you *to be part of this. Just be grateful and recognise your talent and hard work. You earned it.*

Twenty minutes later, I made my way down the aisle, found my seat, and settled in for the long flight, selfishly relieved to find that I wasn't going to have a seat partner. I yawned as I dug around for my earbuds; classical music always helped with my anxiety attacks, and it would be necessary before take-off. *Wow, these pills don't mess around.* My eyes started to get heavy, and my mind was clearing out thoughts fast and slipping into a black void of nothingness. Closing my eyes and leaning back into my seat, my music began to play as I fell into a deep sleep.

4. *Rhiannon Makes the Drive*

The driving rain battered the windscreen of the classic Jaguar E-type as it snaked its way around the sharp bends of the English country lanes. The cold February winds were punishing the little car, forcing the freezing water through the minuscule cracks in the convertible's roof, which, in turn, made the driver of the car angrier, wetter, and colder by the minute. Rhiannon Hughes had started her four-hour journey in dry weather and relatively warm temperatures, but things had taken a turn for the worse nearly fifty miles ago. It was now dark and nearing ten o'clock at night.

Rhiannon loved her red Jaguar and had restored it to all its former shining glory. She had spent far more than it was worth on doing it up but, alas, the British weather was never kind. This beauty of this vehicle was made for summer days filled with glorious sunshine, cruising along country roads such as these with the top down, not this horrid weather in the middle of the wettest and coldest winter she could remember. The car usually stayed safely tucked away in her garage on rainy days as she preferred to take her normal, everyday BMW out to face the weather, but she'd wanted to take the Jag on a proper road trip for once, stretch its legs, as it were. Now she realised what a ridiculous mistake that had been. She'd clearly pushed her luck too far.

Rhiannon clenched her jaw as more rain splattered down into her already sodden lap. So much for the convertible roof being *waterproof.* She made a mental note to get the damn thing replaced after this escapade was over. She glanced at her phone, perched precariously on the dashboard in front of her, to check her route. Only two miles left until she reached her final destination. She'd just passed through the quiet town of Arklington and had not seen a single soul on the streets, which wasn't surprising due to the time of night, but it had seemed slightly odd to her at the time. Driving through the town at the recommended speed limit of twenty miles per hour had seemed to take forever even though no other cars had been on the road. Clearly, the local community knew better than to venture out when it was raining this heavily.

Glancing at the passenger seat, she quickly scanned the address that had been beautifully handwritten on an exceptionally expensive piece of paper that was now dripping wet and completely ruined. The ink was smudged and running off the page and onto the leather seat, but she could still make out the writing…just. The letter and the envelope it had arrived in were basically sitting in a puddle of water now.

LaVey House, 1890 Rosenberg Drive, Arklington, Gilead, MR12 5AH

She'd never even heard of Arklington before and had resorted to Google in order to find whereabouts it was located. It was in the middle of nowhere, a small town on the outskirts of Gilead, another place she'd never heard of, so she'd had to rely solely on her phone to guide her there.

These twisty, narrow roads reminded her vividly of those around where she'd grown up, a small village in mid-Wales. Rhiannon should have been used to these types of roads, but she hadn't been back to her home country for quite some time and had lived predominantly in London for most of her adult life. London didn't have tiny, dark roads that seemed to stretch on forever. No, it had hundreds of interconnecting roads, jam-packed with cars, lorries, and cyclists all hurrying along as fast as humanly possible, with no regard for any other life apart from their own. It could be worse. At least she hadn't encountered another car coming the other way …

'Foock!' she screamed as she slammed on the brakes, the wheels screeching in response as they attempted to grip the wet road. A huge 4x4 the size of a tank was barrelling towards her at an alarming speed, the driver seemingly unaware of the tiny convertible in its path. Rhiannon wrestled with the steering wheel (which lacked power-assisted steering) and forced the car off the road and into a small ditch as the 4x4 zoomed past without so much as slowing down, sending a tidal wave of standing water through the already leaking roof.

'You're fooking welcome, ya fooking prick!' Her expletives and Welsh twang were lost in the sounds of pouring rain and a sudden clap of thunder. It was days like this when she wondered why she'd even bothered getting out of bed.

Just two more miles… just two more miles, she thought.

She hoped to God that this drive was going to be worth the effort. She cast her mind back to the handwritten invitation she had received a week ago. It had been addressed directly to her and as soon as she'd spotted the LaVey Publishing logo embedded in the envelope's wax seal, she'd known it was important. She'd cast all her other post aside and absorbed the words as quickly as possible.

Rhiannon knew all about LaVey Publishing. She had worked with them, long ago, on *From Within*, her second traditionally published horror novel, but this was the closest she'd gotten to hearing from the owner himself. She'd never met the elusive Mr. LaVey in person, having only seen photographs of him usually sitting like he would for an oil painting, with not a hint of a smile across his thin lips.

The letter was an invitation to a writing circle at his stately manor as his honoured guest to collaborate with fellow horror authors on an anthology piece, *Even Death May Die.* It was certainly a once-in-a-lifetime opportunity, and she'd barely had to think about it before deciding to attend. She wasn't doing it for the money, of course; she had plenty of money. She had twenty-four full-length horror novels to her name, all of which had been best sellers at one time or another, having hit the charts and been featured in many writing journals and bestseller lists in newspapers. She was a widely renowned and respected author in her genre and had won numerous awards for her books.

Lately, however, she'd felt a bit stuck and unsure of where to go with her next book, which was currently untitled and sitting in a completely unfinished state on her laptop. Her literary agent and publisher had been hounding her daily to make a decision regarding the plot and were determined to keep her to a strict deadline as dictated in her contract, but her heart just wasn't in it. She'd had writer's block before, but this was different. It wasn't that she *couldn't* write, but that she didn't *want* to write. That's why she'd accepted Mr. LaVey's unusual proposal; she thought it would be good for her to get away from the busy streets of London and the stresses of everyday life and relax in the country for a week. Maybe she would meet some new people and do some writing without the threat of her agent and publisher breathing down her neck and reconnect with her passion for creating dark stories. Hopefully, this week away would ignite the writing spark again, which had been flickering so low lately it was on the verge of going out completely. She apparently had free reign on what her short story could be about, and she already had a rough idea in mind. Maybe she'd name one of the characters after her childhood crush. She hadn't thought about Owen in a long time.

She tried not to think about him because it always left her with a horrible taste at the back of her mouth and an upset stomach.

5. *Mikhail Makes an Impression*

Mikhail had to admit that LaVey certainly had a sense of style. Not only had his mysterious host arranged for a very comfortable limo to ferry him from the airport, but the vehicle had been equipped with a fully stocked mini bar. Mikhail had settled down into the leather seat, removed his jacket, unbuttoned his waistcoat, and loosened the top two buttons of the silk shirt he had convinced Pavel his suit required, and indulged himself. He gazed out of the tinted windows at the sprawling countryside, amazed at the traffic and construction works clogging up the motorways. Luka would have loved it; the boy always enjoyed trips to the old country, and his cars.

After two glasses of vodka, Mikhail dozed off, but was grateful to find his sleep uninterrupted by nightmares or twisted memories. He was roused from his light slumber to find LaVey's driver weaving the long, immaculately polished car up a twisting, overgrown path towards LaVey's estate, which had clearly fallen into disrepair. Still, as he stepped out of the limo and stretched his aching muscles, Mikhail was impressed, nonetheless. The driver carried his luggage inside, and Mikhail straightened his attire and followed, taking in the opulence of LaVey's home.

A strange old man with a slight hunch met him in the main hall. His eyes twinkled with the mischievousness of youth, but his face was lined with deep wrinkles and faint wisps of hair.

'Ah, yes. Mr. Orlov,' the old man spoke. Mikhail lamented the strange, drawling pronunciations of these Westerners who seemed incapable of grasping that words weren't always spoken phonetically. 'It seems you're the first one to arrive.'

Mikhail smirked. He was known for his punctuality, but fate was clearly on his side. His promptness would allow him to not only get the lay of the land ahead of his competitors, but also impress his host.

'Орлов,' he corrected, shaking LaVey's hand with a curt nod. '*Приветствия.*'

'Oh-ho-ho, Mr. *Орлов*,' LaVey chuckled.

'Pavel told me about you, but he failed to mention how grand your home is.'

'LaVey House may carry my family name, but it hasn't been *my* home for many years now, probably long before you were born.' He walked Mikhail into a nearby study, and Mikhail glanced around expectedly looking for the driver or some other member of staff to take his bags, before grabbing them himself with an irritated grunt. 'No, no,' the old man was saying, his voice echoing clearly. 'I like to use the old place for social events such as these. I find it creates a certain kind of ambiance.'

Mikhail lugged his bags into the study and set them down by a sofa. LaVey was oddly underselling the extravagance of his family home; just the fact that he owned such lavish grounds, however unkempt they were, indicated that he was from old money. As Mikhail pulled his pipe out and began filling it with tobacco, he felt a momentary pang of pity for the other writers; they were doubtless coming into the task far less prepared than he, and he felt reassured by his arrogance.

And why not? He had read through *Mara's Secret* twice now and was confident in his ability to cut the piece down in no time at all. It was lucky for him, he supposed, that Pavel primarily dealt in submissions of no more than ten-thousand words. Mikhail had highlighted parts to excise, characters to combine together, and had no doubt that he could easily transpose his notes into a suitable piece in a day, two days maximum.

Pavel would probably have been incredibly disappointed at such subterfuge, but his old friend wasn't here, was he?

'What's your poison, my friend?' LaVey asked as he helped himself to a small sherry. 'Seeing as you're the first, I'll make an exception and toast your good health.'

'Vodka,' Mikhail replied immediately as he took a match to his pipe and puffed out thick plumes of smoke.

'Naturally,' LaVey chuckled. He shuffled over with their drinks, struggling slightly with his cane, and Mikhail accepted the glass gratefully. 'What is it they say in your country? *На здоровье?*'

Mikhail raised an eyebrow and touched his glass against LaVey's. '*На здоровье,*' he said, swallowing some of the clear liquid. A cool, smooth sensation sent waves of pleasure rippling through his skin. '*Beluga,*' he commented. 'My compliments.' The very finest chilled vodka that his home country had to offer. Either this was all a happy coincidence, or LaVey had done his research.

'The old homestead may not look much from the *outside*, but I assure you that I have only the best *inside*,' the old man smiled.

Mikhail lazily made his way to the extravagant sofa, feeling how soft yet firm it was as he sat. A drink this fine had to be treasured. Picking up a stone coaster with an 'L' engraved in its centre, he took another sip of the Beluga before setting his glass down. He felt relaxed and satiated as he crossed one heavy leg over the other and sucked on his pipe, but his curiosity was piqued.

'So, who are the others you have invited? Pavel did not mention any names.'

'That was my intention,' LaVey clasped both hands to his cane. 'I find a little mystery is good for the soul, don't you agree?'

'*Tch*,' Mikhail muttered through gritted teeth. The old man was a playful one. 'As long as there are no Americans...'

'Oh, they come from *all* around, my friend,' LaVey mused, causing a ripple of disquiet to flutter Mikhail's heart.

Lia had been so obsessed with American culture; she'd quoted their movies, danced to their songs, and even dressed like them. Although he had been dismayed to find how much like his father it made him sound, Mikhail had found it decadent and needlessly excessive.

'I'm casting a very wide net this time around.'

Mikhail found himself itching for another shot of Beluga but kept his desires in check for now, content to enjoy the taste of his tobacco. 'And why is that? Surely it is cheaper to recruit writers closer to home, yes?'

LaVey rocked slightly on his cane. 'I don't do "cheap", Mr. Орлов. Besides...this time is...special, yes. You might even say it's the culmination of my entire life's work.' Mikhail smirked, unconvinced, but the old man simply said, 'Just be patient; you'll understand in time.'

It turned out that Mikhail didn't have to wait too long to get his answers. The murky blackness of evening soon settled in, bringing with it a wild storm of wind and rain, and he had been tempted to retire for the evening as he felt rattled from the vodka and the long journey.

LaVey had been regaling him with stories of his grandfather, evidently an opulent man who had travelled the world seeking knowledge and riches and returned with all kinds of artefacts that had made his fortune, when his attention had been drawn to a light sweeping through the study windows.

'Ah!' he exclaimed. 'It appears we have another guest!'

'Allow me,' Mikhail said immediately. He had no intention of waiting on LaVey's guest, but he wanted to size up his competition. He had once prided himself on being a good judge of character; he could tell almost instantly whether someone was a threat or an easy target just from first sight. At least, he *had* been good at it…Lia had, after all, turned out to be very different from what he first assumed. But that had been an anomaly…

As Mikhail stepped outside, he saw a bright red Jaguar pull up. Whoever this was certainly had impeccable taste. 'Someone with worth and value if they have a nice car like that,' he muttered.

However, when Mikhail saw that a woman stepped out of the striking Jaguar, he was instantly annoyed. How in all the hell did a *woman* come to possess such a beauty of a vehicle? There was no way it was hers; it had to belong to her husband. Mikhail was sure of this.

'Блять!' he barked, and the redhead sharply whipped her head towards him.

6. Rhiannon Takes a Drink

The weather was getting steadily worse. The rain was so heavy that Rhiannon could barely see beyond the car bonnet, but she knew the road was out there somewhere. It had to be. Two miles felt like one hundred, but somehow the wheels of the car found the concrete of the road and she kept driving forward, albeit slowly. The darkness was so thick that her headlights could barely penetrate it.

Finally, her phone signalled that she'd arrived at her destination, but she couldn't see any sign of the mysterious LaVey House thanks to the rain and darkness. There was, however, a very large driveway ahead, blocked by a set of heavy, intimidating wrought-iron gates, which looked so ancient that Rhiannon immediately assumed that they'd not been opened in decades. Twisted vines, which looked suspiciously like thin, skeletal hands, grew along the gates and the adjoining walls. She smiled to herself, knowing that her vivid imagination as a horror author always made her jump to the worst conclusions.

She decided to investigate. Without waiting for the rain to ease, she opened her car door and was met with a blast of freezing cold wind and torrential rain. Her raincoat was saturated within seconds of stepping outside. Her red hair flapped about in every direction, sticking to her face. Stepping closer to the gates she spied a rusty plaque fused to the outside of the rock wall that ran in either direction on each side of the gate.

LaVey House.

This was definitely the place, but how was she supposed to get in?

Rhiannon stepped closer to the gates, a constant stream of rain pouring off the end of her nose, and attempted to open them. A large, heavy chain encircled the handles of each gate, locking them shut, but upon further inspection she realised that the chain was a mere formality, as the padlock which held it in place was unlocked.

Due to the darkness, she didn't notice the small black box attached to the wall next to the gate; the intercom. She felt like she was trespassing as she unwound the chain. The gates, chains, and padlock were a clear deterrent and sent a strong message to the outside world: Stay Out!

Finally, the gates were free. She struggled against the elements as she pushed the gates apart. They creaked and groaned in protest. She didn't bother closing them again because she knew others would be joining her at the house later and she hoped to spare them the job of opening the gates.

You're welcome.

As Rhiannon drove her Jaguar through the gates and up the road, the rain finally began to slow, almost as if it was signifying the end of her long journey and saying *welcome to your destination.*

Fooking typical, she thought.

She was rewarded with a spectacular view of LaVey House, but it was nothing like she had expected. Did anyone even live here? It was hard to tell due to the lack of light, but she could just about make out the start of the grounds on either side, which were clearly overgrown and had fallen into disrepair, left to grow, rot, and die over and over.

The house itself was one of the largest she'd ever seen in real life, but it looked as if it had been derelict for decades. The walls were overrun with twisted vines of God knows what, covered in prickly thorns and large expanses of greenery. The vegetation seemed to be strangling the building, squeezing it of all life. The windows were filthy and wrecked by the bad weather, and a faint orange glow emanated from within the house that gave it the look of a typical haunted mansion.

The house took her breath away and not because she was in awe of it, but because there was something about the estate that didn't sit well with her. She immediately felt her chest tighten as she pulled up into the driveway.

She had no idea who else had received the invitation and she was mildly concerned as well as curious about who they'd turn out to be. The invitation had stated that there would be some novices among them, which alarmed her slightly. Why would Mr. LaVey want a novice to be part of his anthology? Rhiannon knew she'd been chosen because she was one of the best horror writers in the country, despite the recent setback on her new book. Her reputation needed to be upheld and she didn't want some arrogant newcomer stepping on her toes. At least the house was big enough that she hopefully wouldn't run into them too often.

It was time to go inside.

* * *

A loud booming shout echoed across the large driveway just as Rhiannon stepped out of her car. She slammed the door as a large and rather daunting-looking man trundled towards her. In the darkness, he looked like a looming shadow, a slightly startling experience given the situation. She hadn't even noticed where he'd come from, but she assumed it was from the house. Was this Mr. LaVey? No, it couldn't be. She'd seen a photo of the renowned man before and this cumbersome creature spitting insults at her was definitely not him. Who the hell did he think he was? This wasn't his house.

'*Ei, khoroshaya mashina, kotoruyu poluchil vas mouge?*'

Rhiannon raised her eyebrows, stuck her hands on her hips, and puffed her chest out as the large man stomped up to her. The light from the open doorway of the house provided just enough illumination for her to make out his appearance. He was younger than her, she guessed early thirties, and was rather rough-looking, but she could tell used to be attractive.

'Excuse me?' she asked him sarcastically. By the tone of his voice and red face she could only assume he wasn't being polite.

'*Dolzno byt priyatno imet bogatogo muzha!*'

'I've no fooking idea what you're saying, mun. Either speak English or fook off.'

The large Russian gave her what she assumed was a rude gesture and then turned and stomped back into the house, muttering words that she couldn't comprehend.

Rhiannon exhaled in relief before unloading her car. She'd packed light, never really needing much more than the bare minimum when she went away on trips. She wasn't a woman who wore an excess of makeup or changed her clothes several times a day. She'd brought her running kit, two changes of casual clothes, and something a little dressier for the banquet the invitation promised at the end of the week.

Underneath her raincoat, she was wearing figure-hugging jeans and a tight long-sleeve dark top that emphasised her toned, athletic shape. Although nearly forty, she knew she could give women half her age a run for their money in the looks department. Usually, her bright auburn hair was glossy and wavy, however, it was currently plastered to her scalp and face thanks to the rain. She'd hoped to make a better first impression. She hadn't even had time to have her grey roots touched up before she'd started her journey.

As she approached the large oak doors of the house, she glanced skyward. The dark clouds were looming overhead sadistically, threatening to unload again at any moment. She wanted to get the meet and greet over and done with and then get to bed so she could rise early and go for a run around the grounds. She hoped the rain cleared away overnight. It's not that she despised running in the rain, but it would make for a more enjoyable run if it were dry and clear.

The brutish Russian had left the doors cracked open for her, so Rhiannon pushed them the rest of the way. They creaked the way old wooden doors in horror movies did. She smiled to herself again, already imagining the house to be full of wonder and creepy things around every corner. This was the perfect location in which to bring a horror story to life.

It felt like she was on one of the exciting adventures that she wrote about, and here she was, in a real-life creepy mansion. There were no such things as ghosts, of course, but she expected that these walls concealed a great many secrets (and suspected that some of them weren't all that pleasant).

Standing in the middle of the extremely large entrance hall, she could smell the woody aroma of a burning log fire…and the earthy scent of proper Scotch whiskey. *Perfect*, she thought. It was exactly what she needed to warm herself up after freezing her ass off: a fire and a finger or two of her favourite liquor.

Rhiannon liked a tipple or two in the evening. She'd never been a big wine drinker or enjoyed those girly, fruity cocktails, but whiskey was definitely her go-to alcoholic beverage. Some would say that she drank too much on occasion, but those people were ignorant and had no idea of the real horrors she'd been through in her life. Alcohol was one of the things that dulled the senses and made her forget about those things that often kept her awake at night. That, and running, but it was too late to go running now.

'Ah, Ms. Hughes!'

Startled by the loud mention of her name, she turned to see a slim elderly man gliding towards her, his bony hand outstretched. *This* was unmistakably Mr. LaVey. He was smartly dressed in an impeccable overcoat that reached down to his knees; the sparkle of a gold waistcoat poking out. He easily looked as if he could be over one hundred years old, though Rhiannon knew from her research that he was closer to eighty, but the man certainly had a shocking ambiance about him.

Shaking his hand, his paper-thin skin felt cold and clammy, but he had a firm grip for such a frail-looking man.

'Mr. LaVey, thanks so much for your invitation. It's an honour to be here.'

'You flatter me, m'dear. The honour is mine to welcome you to my humble abode. I take it you had no trouble finding the house, hm?'

'Yes...I found it okay...just about.' She refrained from mentioning her escapade with the chained gates. 'My car isn't that waterproof,' she said with a laugh when the old man glanced at her soaking wet clothes with a raised eyebrow. It probably looked as if she'd walked here.

'Oh, that we could control the rising of the sun and the falling of the rain,' the old man chuckled. 'Please, make yourself comfortable. The others will be arriving soon, but do help yourself to refreshments.'

Mr. LaVey made no comment about her changing into some dry clothes, and Rhiannon felt that she couldn't raise the subject herself, so she politely smiled and followed the old man into a large study of sorts. She approached the bar, ensuring her bag was safely stored out of the way.

A vast range of whiskeys, gins, wines, and vodkas were arranged on the bar, along with an assortment of mixers and garnishes. Rhiannon, however, knew exactly what she wanted and poured herself two fingers of the Macallan whiskey into an extravagant glass tumbler and added two ice cubes. She knew how expensive and rare that particular brand of whiskey was, so she jumped at the opportunity to taste it.

She took a small sip and instantly felt a warm, fuzzy feeling float over her. The stresses of the journey seemed insignificant now.

'What you drink that shit for?'

Rhiannon turned to see the large, rude Russian casually stretched out on a lavish sofa. She struggled to keep her lip from curling in disgust. He was such a typical, dominant man, posing like that, ensuring that anyone who looked got a tantalising look at his body. Yes, he was in decent shape, but Rhiannon actually felt nauseous as she glanced at him.

'I happen to enjoy whiskey,' replied Rhiannon with a slight hint of annoyance.

'Vodka is better.'

'That's your opinion.'

'Ooh are you? You look familiar.'

'Rhiannon Hughes, and you are?'

'Ah yeah, I know you. You that rich bitch in those shiny magazines. You know ooh I am. Everyone has heard of famous Russian writer.'

'I haven't.'

The Russian snarled at her as he sat bolt upright on the sofa. 'Mikhail Orlov.'

Rhiannon nodded slightly to show that she had heard but did not reply straight away. She had indeed heard of the notorious man and had been warned by other authors and publishers to never cross paths with him. His arrogance and rudeness were never something she'd experienced from any other published author. How any publisher or agent had agreed to work with him was incomprehensible. The man was a thug, and she often had the suspicion that he plagiarised his work.

'You heard of me now?' he bellowed.

Rhiannon took a drink. 'Vaguely.'

'If you like, you come closer and get to know Mikhail much better.'

'I'd rather set myself on fire.'

Mikhail muttered more Russian words.

Rhiannon rolled her eyes and turned away to casually walk around the study. She wondered who the next two authors would be. Hopefully they would be more approachable and much friendlier than Mikhail Orlov, otherwise it was going to be a very long week.

7. Aster Makes a Landing

A glass shattered against the wall beside me, causing me to jump. My eyes were watching Walter carefully, his face an ugly shade of red. 'You aren't going to that writing...meeting...circle...thing! I forbid it!'

Crossing my arms, I narrowed my eyes at him. I was not about to let him deny me this. This could open more doors and prospects for me. 'That's too bad! Opportunities like these aren't just given freely! This is important to me!'

Walter gritted his teeth, his body shaking in anger. 'What did you say?' He closed the distance between us, gripped my shoulders tight, and got within a couple of inches from my face. 'Ya ain't going! End of discussion!'

'Honey, you're hurting me!' I tried twisting out of his grasp, but it was pointless. He towered a foot over me, his weight easily doubling mine. I didn't stand a chance. 'I'd be an idiot to not accept this! If this is about money...'

A loud crack filled the room, my cheek stinging hot with pain. A cry escaped from my lips as tears swam in my eyes. Walter released his punishing hold instantly and, like a switch, pulled me into a gentle but firm hug against him. 'Oh, baby. That was an accident. I didn't mean to...'

I went limp in his arms, unable to process what had just happened. Never in our five years together had he hit me. Tremors coursed through my body and I pushed away from him. Glaring at him, I tried to remain composed, reminding him I was going and that he would just have to be okay with it. His expression remained stoic, but I could tell he was not pleased. He said nothing and made his way to our bedroom door, slamming it shut behind him.

The memory startled me awake. That had been our last conversation before I left for the airport. I had meant to apologise before leaving, but his phone had been off when I tried calling. This wasn't uncommon when he was at work, but it was frustrating.

I wasn't sure how long I had been out and asked a flight attendant when we would be landing. She informed me it would be a couple of hours. Knowing I wasn't going back to sleep, I pulled out the book I brought and picked back up where I left off. The action was getting intense and maybe the protagonist would finally confess his wrongdoing to his best friend. It had been quite the interesting read, undeniably keeping my attention.

'Your attention, please,' the sound of the pilot's voice jolted me from reading. 'We will be landing in London Heathrow Airport in ten minutes.' Two hours had already gone by? It felt like I had just started reading. When I saw I had read about a hundred pages, it surprised me. Being lost in a good book was the best feeling and being interrupted annoyed me—until I remembered I was going to be with a group of other writers for a week. Oh shit! I needed to get ready.

Placing the book back in my carry-on, I took out the small compact mirror from my bag to give myself a quick look-over. I wanted to look my best before meeting Mr. LaVey and whoever else was present. My red hair was a fuzzy mess, which was nothing new…and nothing a little water and a comb wouldn't fix. My makeup was mostly untouched, but my glasses were missing. *Probably ended up in your carry-on; not like they're prescription*, I thought. I wore them merely as a fashion choice. It was safe to get up, so I made my way to the small toilet in the back, taking care of my hair and smoothing out the minor wrinkles on my clothing.

'We will land soon. Please remain seated until instructed,' the voice over the intercom spoke as I was returning to my seat. I gathered my items into my small backpack and padded my pocket for my phone. I was dreading checking it. Walter would have probably left several calls or texts by this point.

After gathering my duffle bag from the baggage carousel, I was told to be on the look-out for a man holding a sign with "Ms. Aster Callahan" at my terminal. Despite being handicapped by my short stature, it didn't take me long to see a bright sign with my name scrawled on it. Shifting my backpack more comfortably, I approached him.

'You must be my driver to Mr. LaVey's mansion, yes? I'm the Aster Callahan you're looking for.'

He studied me for a moment before giving a nod. 'Yes, Ms. Callahan,' he responded in a thick accent. 'Right this way.'

8. Brandis Gets Directions

Driving to Gilead had been simple enough before my phone died as I was blindly meandering through Arklington's roundabouts and intersections. Arklington was like something out of Shelley; the town was probably three times bigger than my hometown and seemed lost to the mists of time.

As I drove through the crooked, uneven roads, stopping at cracked and faded traffic lights, pedestrians shuffled about in a daze, their eyes glancing skyward as if expecting rain, and every other business was boarded up. The pavement was full of cracks, the trees were decaying and weathered, and a blanket of fog from the industrial district enveloped the horizon. It seemed like a town where industry had brought prosperity before its inhabitants were ready and had stripped it of all life and charm.

I drove around in circles like a tit in a trance and, desperately in need of petrol, begrudgingly pulled into a Teamos petrol station to fill up and get directions. I was met by a blast of cool, stale air conditioning that tasted like copper. I grabbed a chocolate bar and approached the weary-eyed cashier with a face full of freckles and acne. I paid for my petrol (keeping my receipt so LaVey could set me straight) and did the one thing I hated doing in shops: I asked a question.

'I'm lookin' for LaVey House?'

'U*h*m...' the boy croaked, puzzled. 'I *fink* that's on Rosenberg?'

'Right?' I said as patiently as I could, '*Where* is that?'

The boy blinked. 'From here?'

'Yes. From here?'

'U*h*m…' he pointed vaguely to his left. 'It's up t*h*at way?'

I tried to tell myself that he was just a kid stuck in a dead-end job, but the drive had been long, and my patience was wearing thin. 'Do you wanna be a bit more specific? Like, am I turning left outta here or what?'

Eventually, the boy stammered out some vague directions that, surprisingly, were accurate enough to steer me to a twisting, overgrown road outside of town and the looming grandeur of LaVey House. I beheld a massive iron gate swaying in the evening's downpour; I spotted a large chain and padlock in the grass verge as I drove up the winding, gravelled path towards LaVey House.

LaVey House loomed ahead as the path widened to encompass a magnificent stone birdbath held aloft by three slender figures. Even in the murky darkness, I could see that the house was like a gargantuan great stone stab flanked by rotting and overgrown foliage. The many windows were long and thin and laced with a diamond lattice. Very little light peeked behind thick curtains and the house was bookended by a shamble of a conservatory on the west side, and overgrowth on the east side that enveloped what appeared to be a garage. It was as though nature had tried to reclaim its birthright, done so, and then withered away and sat like a thorny, rotting corpse. The roof was completely flat but for a single, ornate growth in the middle that resembled a blossoming flower and housed what looked to be an attic. As I pulled up to the huge oak doors, I noticed some flaws in LaVey's magnificence: the brick work was flayed by a decaying twist of ivy that had snaked all around the exterior like the tentacles of some unspeakable beast. The windows were also greasy and smeared; some were even chipped or broken, as if something had been thrown through them.

…or out of them…

There was a bitter chill in the air that seemed to come from the house itself and I was suddenly desperate to get back in the car and head home. Sure, it was a long-ass drive and would have been a waste of time, but the house was too much. I'd just have to live off peanut butter sandwiches for the rest of the month to cover the expense.

'Boy!' a shout interrupted my thoughts. I snapped my head up and saw a burly man chewing on a pipe. *Who the fuck smokes a pipe?* 'Are you some kind of help or staff for LaVey? Fetch me another bottle of Beluga.' The man held up the near-empty bottle. 'This one's gone.'

'What? No, I was just…'

'You surely must be staff! Look at how you're dressed!' the stranger sneered.

I glanced down at myself; polo shirt, faded jeans torn at the knees, and frowned. 'Um…No?'

'*Tt!* Is insulting to have to wait for my glass to be filled,' the large man said. 'Someone would be shot for such inefficiency in *my* country.'

'Delightful,' I muttered. *What a prick.*

Still, it was too late to turn back now. I yanked my battered old backpack and laptop out of my car and made my way up the moss-strewn stone steps towards the warmth radiating from inside the manor. I entered eagerly—closing the door as gently as I could and yet still producing a rattling slam—and was immediately overwhelmed. The entrance hall alone was bigger than my childhood home! Lined with huge paintings of LaVey's ancestors, the hall was a striking brass glow

74

of opulence dominated by two central staircases that sported dark oak banisters almost as tall as me. The floorboards glistened as though freshly polished and they were covered by a series of patterned rugs. I was so awestruck that I scarcely even registered the doorways at either side of the entrance hall.

'A step up from whatever hole you crawled out from, no?' the brute puffed out thick rings of smoke amidst a condescending sneer.

I stumbled slightly as my backpack threw me off balance. 'So, you got a name or…?'

A look of disgust creased his face. 'Orlov. *Mikhail* Orlov.'

'Hi, Mikhail…'

'Михаил!' Mikhail said scornfully. 'Me-*hi*-elle.'

'*Mi-Kyle*,' I corrected. A scowl remained on the Russian's features. *Like it fuckin' matters.* 'I'm…umm…Frederick Brandis. Or just Freddy, if yah like.'

'*Ты идиот*,' Mikhail sneered. '*Вы наверняка потерпите неудачу!*'

Were…were those words? I had no idea how to respond so just offered an unconvinced smirk.

Mikhail shook his head dismissively and moved into the next room, a large study. A woman stood behind a bar across the room and was pouring herself a generous helping of whiskey, and an elderly man gazed at a wonderfully painted depiction of a gruesome battle between soldiers in tight, red uniforms and a legion of demonic entities crawling up from a pit. A selection of comfortable-looking armchairs faced this painting, which hung above the warm glow of the fireplace and was flanked by large bookshelves. I dropped my bags beside a large leather armchair and inspected the shelves. they looked like ancient tomes of long-forgotten Magicks that threatened to raise the dead with even a cursory glance.

Mikhail lounged on a sofa as though he were lord of the manor. 'Those are books, *дурак*. You do read, yes?'

I ignored him and approached the elderly gentleman who stood before the painting. He was dressed in a long frock overcoat, a buttoned-up waistcoat of shining gold, a knotted bow tie, plaid trousers, and he had his hands clasped behind his back. *I am so underdressed*, I lamented as he muttered, 'Seventeenth century.' His voice was like coal rolling over sand. 'They say the painter, Clarence Stoughton, spoke to God.' Mikhail scoffed behind us. The old man turned his grey, shimmering eyes to me pointedly. 'Mushrooms.'

What kind of fuckin' circus...

'Y'wot?'

'*Mushrooms*,' the old man repeated, as if this made things any clearer. 'Psilocybin fungi, if you will. Rotted his mind,' he turned back to the painting. 'Still...exquisite penmanship.'

I glanced at the painting. It was intricate and impressive and probably took hours to complete, but paintings weren't really my thing, even disturbing ones like this. 'Are you Howard LaVey?'

A smile briefly exorcised the years that were etched into the old man's face. 'Of course, m'boy!' He held out a wizened hand and I shook it cautiously. 'And you are...?'

'Brandis,' Mikhail called out. 'A *идиот* if I ever saw one.'

LaVey waved a dismissed hand. '*Psh*, pay no never mind to him, m'boy.'

'Still...' I hesitated. 'If I'm bein' brutally honest, I don't really get why *I'm* here, sir.'

'Less of the "sir",' LaVay admonished. 'I get enough yes-men at work. And, if you're *here*, you're here for a *reason*. Mebbe you don't *see* it yet, but I guarantee that you will…one way or another.'

LaVey returned to his painting, and I took this as my cue to step away towards the bar. I hadn't drunk alcohol for a long time, but a stiff drink was long overdue. The woman was still there, and I timidly asked her: 'What's on the menu?'

'Whiskey…and lots of it.'

I smirked. 'Well, save some for t'rest of us.'

'Excuse me?' She slammed her glass to the bar. 'I've had a long day, mun. I don't need a homeless-looking nobody telling me I drink too much.'

This is becoming a habit, I grimaced inwardly. 'Jeez, okay…I wasn't tryin' to imply…'

'No offence, but who even *are* you?' she fixed me with a glare. 'I know of most horror writers who are worth knowing and you don't strike me as very successful.'

'Uh-huh,' I scowled. 'And *you* are…?'

She straightened up and smoothed out her damp clothing. She did look a pathetic sight standing there all wet. 'Rhiannon,' she said with a dismissive sniff. 'Rhiannon Hughes.'

This was going to be a *long* week. 'Well, if it's any consolation…' I said as I grabbed a bottle of scotch and a glass, '*I've* never heard of *you*, either.'

'Maybe that's because you don't actually read any other author's books outside of your own.'

I briefly thought of my stuffed bookshelf back at the flat. 'Yes,' I mumbled. 'That *must* be it.'

I flopped into my chair with a hefty sigh. The scotch burned like a motherfucker but was smooth as silk. Suddenly, my hum-drum existence seemed oddly preferable to being in this house full of strangers, with Mikhail's abrasive barking and Rhiannon's ugly scowl. I was lamenting that I had missed my best chance to get away, that I had even made the trip, when Mikhail's latest tirade was interrupted by a cry from the doorway. I awkwardly turned in my armchair and felt as though I was struck by lightning.

9. Aster's Big Entrance

After loading my bag into the car, my driver—who I learned was named Heinrich—and I were on our way for the hour-long drive to Howard LaVey's estate on the outskirts of Arklington. I made small talk with Heinrich and, while he didn't say much, it was all right; I was using him as a distraction. That anxious energy was coming back again, crawling its way into the pit of my stomach. It was interesting considering I'd spoken in front of thousands of people with little issue many times, so why was this intimate gathering causing me to feel like a nervous wreck?

'You wouldn't happen to have the time, would you, Ms. Callahan?' Heinrich interrupted my thoughts. When I said I would check for him, I realised I hadn't turned my phone back on. *Shit*, I thought to myself. *Wonder how many messages and calls I've missed.* There were five text messages and three voicemails…all from Walter.

'It's 11:45 p.m., Heinrich.' I felt it polite to answer him as I scrolled through my fiancé's messages. I'd have to check the voicemails later since I had no service at the moment.

The first two text messages seemed nice enough with him being worried and wanting me to let him know once I landed. However, his last message bothered me:

I know you're there by now. If you don't let me know of your whereabouts in the next fifteen minutes, I'm calling the cops.

Not wanting to refuel the fight from last night, I sent him a text saying I was here and on my way to LaVey's. A *ping* told me the message would be sent once we were in an area with better reception.

Honestly, I knew he was full of shit; despite working in security himself, he wouldn't call the police unless it was a last resort. Walter didn't have the cleanest of backgrounds and knew dealing with the cops wouldn't go over well, no matter the circumstance.

Sometimes I wondered why I stuck it out with Walter. In the beginning of our relationship, his best friend Sawyer introduced us, thinking Walter and I would be good together. I could help him manage his stress and be a support system for him, and he could help me get out of my shell more. At the time, I had been grateful to Sawyer for introducing us; I had all but given up on love due to a horrid breakup with my ex-boyfriend of seven years. Walter had been shy at first, but started showing his sweet personality to me soon after. I hadn't seen that part of him in so long; there were times I wondered if it was a ruse.

He's just going through a time of stress, I told myself. *You should be able to understand that. We've all had our times of stress. When I have better service, I'll call him and tell him I'm okay and that I've landed safely. Surely, he can't be mad at me for that, can he?*

'We're approaching Mr. LaVey's property.'

Despite the darkness, I looked out the window and could see a colossal gate surrounding a large mansion. I was in awe. Sure, I had seen my fair share of large estates thanks to my book tours in large cities, but none of them held a candle to Howard LaVey's mansion.

'That's strange. The gate is already open,' muttered Heinrich.

This surprised me as I figured a place of this grandeur would have security or at least a lock on the gate to prevent any undesirables from strolling onto the grounds. Still, maybe it wasn't necessary. It appeared we were in the middle of nowhere (the last town I recalled seeing was Arklington) and it would be quite the trek for someone to come out here just to stir up trouble.

'How are you feeling, Ms. Callahan?' asked Heinrich, his eyes staring at me through the rearview mirror.

'I mean, I'm excited. This is an amazing opportunity, and I can't wait for…'

The car came to an abrupt halt at the large front doors. Heinrich cleared his throat and turned to face me. 'Things are not what they seem here. I am just glad I could get you here. Mr. LaVey would not have been pleased with me if that wasn't fulfilled.' He nodded towards the house, holding his gaze on it before turning back to me. 'He is expecting you. You better hurry.'

Nodding, I stepped out of the car and into the crisp late night air. It was still misting, which made the night heavy and damp, and I felt a chill run down my back. As soon as I retrieved my bag from the car, Heinrich took off in a hurry down the gravel drive and out through the large gate before disappearing into the darkness.

Staring at the large doors in front of me, I saw a sole light coming from inside. Not wanting to be rude, I knocked on the door and waited for someone to greet me. I waited for thirty seconds to pass with no answer before knocking again, this time a little harder. Surely my host would have staff to assist him with greeting guests at the door. Before I could knock a third time, the door groaned opened. Darkness greeted me and it was obvious there was no one there. While I didn't want to be rude and barge in, I was freezing my ass off in the wind and rain, so I went into the house and gently shut the doors behind me.

The inside of this place was huge, but there really wasn't much light to show me where I was or where I needed to go. Pulling out my phone, I turned on the flashlight, and shone it in front of me. There were two enormous staircases in the middle of the large room, its carpet a deep red that reminded me of my hair. Everything was clean and looked expensive. I was scared to touch anything.

'Hello?' I called out. I was met with silence. I decided to continue on, sure that I would run into someone and they could show me where I needed to go. As I walked further down the hall, there was a set of doors on both sides. One of them was ajar, and light poured from it. Getting closer, I could hear the murmurs of voices; a deeper male voice, followed by the voice of a female. I pushed the door open and saw three people, none of whom noticed my entrance.

'Hello? Is this the home of Mr. Howard LaVey?'

Three sets of eyes shot in my direction. 'Shit,' I mumbled under my breath. 'I'm surprised there wasn't anyone to greet me at the door when I got here.'

In my peripheral vision, I saw someone rise from an armchair, but my attention was on the older male. 'Here at LaVey House, we fend for ourselves, m'dear.'

Raising an eyebrow, I studied him. He looked as though he couldn't harm anyone; in fact, he reminded me of my late grandfather…but there was something about him that made me anxious. *Think it's jet lag and sleep deprivation.*

''Cuse me for my rude behaviour. Didn't mean to offend anyone.'

'Who the hell is this *сука?* Why are you here so late?' a bigger man said; his accent was thick and distinct, but I couldn't place where it was from. He was giving me a nasty scowl.

'I'm Aster Callahan, if you must know. The better question is, who are you?' A sneer flashed on his face as he pulled the pipe from between his thin lips.

'This is Mikhail Orlov,' LaVey interjected. 'Renowned author of *Death Wish*…'

'It is *Смертельное Желание!*' Mikhail cut him off.

A redhead stepped towards me, thankfully taking my attention away from this Mikhail. 'Hey, I'm Rhiannon. Ignore this guy…he seems to hate everyone. Bet this British weather is a bit of a shock to your system, huh?'

'Wait…*you're* Rhiannon Hughes? It is a pleasure to meet you!' I went to shake her hand. She hesitated at first, but a polite smile emerged as she placed her hand in mine and shook it firmly. 'I've read some of your work. You're incredible!'

Her face blushed slightly. 'Ah, thanks. I'm always surprised when readers from other countries know about me. I've heard of you as well. I have your first book on my shelf at home.'

I had to suppress a huge grin from exploding onto my face, so I quickly nodded before turning my attention to the last figure. He was standing further from the others, but before I could get a decent look at him, someone cleared their throat and I saw Mr. LaVey staring at me with a fiendish smirk on his lips.

'I'm so sorry if I'm late, Mr. LaVey. I don't mean any disrespect. Didn't mean to ruin anything by arriving at this hour—'

He held up his hands as if to show he was harmless. 'Oh, ho-ho!' he laughed. 'Nothing like *that*, m'dear. I'm just grateful to see you here. Now we can *truly* get down to brass tacks!'

'Wonderful, Mr. LaVey. I'm more than excited to get started.' A yawn escaped from my lips.

'Are we boring you?' Mikhail sneered.

'Oh no, Mr. Orlov. Just a long flight. Not used to the time change.' I was too tired to deal with this.

He responded with a scoff from the back of his throat before he turned his attention back to LaVey. 'You can't expect me to work with such amateurs!' Mikhail exclaimed. 'Is this really the best you could call on?'

I set my bags down on the ground and tried not to shoot Mikhail a dirty look. I could already tell I would need to avoid him. If he was this confrontational with everyone, this was going to be a long week.

'We all have a part to play, my friend,' LaVey answered calmly, before addressing the room. 'All I can offer are my services, humble as they are. The press would probably call this a publicity stunt…' He continued to drone on a bit more before his voice took a sharp inflection from his warm demeanour. 'I expect results by the end of the week!'

'And we have complete free rein over what we write about as long as it is horror related, right?' Rhiannon asked, crossing her arms.

LaVey replied, but I was too busy looking around the room and observing my fellow authors to pay more attention to specifics. Rhiannon was the only one I recognised so far. I had never heard of Mikhail Orlov and I still didn't know who the other guy was. Taking another quick glance over at him, I took in his appearance and tried to place him from anywhere: shaggy brown hair, casual attire, clearly keeping himself apart from the others. I wondered why that was. Maybe he and Mikhail had a confrontation and he was just trying to keep his distance. If so, I couldn't blame him.

'And what is objective?' Mikhail snipped. He was eyeing LaVey disdainfully, almost like he was ashamed to be talking to the very man who asked him to come here for such a prestigious, albeit mysterious, assignment. The nerve of this man! Who the hell did he think he was?

'The intention of Mr. LaVey inviting us here is one of honour and should be respected,' I interjected. 'He clearly saw something in each of us to invite us here, pay us handsomely, and include our works in his anthology.'

Ha, take that, douchebag, I thought.

Mikhail ignored me and kept his gaze on LaVey. 'I only work with the best,' he glowered.

'And you think you're one of the best horror writers around, do you?' Rhiannon shot back, glaring at him with such intensity that I was thankful it wasn't me on the receiving end of her contempt.

'Of course! Last year *Смертельное Желание* was top-selling independent publication across all fields!'

Rhiannon didn't reply directly, but I saw her roll her eyes while taking a big slurp of her drink. I, however, couldn't hold back the scoff in the back of my throat.

'Is that so? To be honest, Mr. Orlov, until tonight, I had never even heard your name, let alone the name of your book.' I could see him stiffen at my response, but he still hadn't looked at me. 'And not to be too much of a show-off, but I know quite a few indie and traditional authors by name. I have never seen your name come up at all.'

Mikhail slowly turned towards me. 'In my country, women know their place.'

I closed my eyes for a moment and took a deep breath. He may have been a respected author in his country, and perhaps what he was saying was true, but I would not allow someone to speak to me like that.

'I'll have you know, Mikhail,' I snapped, 'that all four of my books have been bestsellers and highly praised. I can work full-time as an author without working a second job to pay for my bills and have received several awards and recognition for my books. I have even made it to the top ten in a few other countries as well. I don't need some pretentious jackass telling me to—'

'The point is, Mikhail,' Rhiannon interrupted sharply, 'you aren't the only one who is a respected author. I, for one, have written over two dozen horror novels, all of which have won me significant acclaim! We all clearly deserve to be here...' I noticed her shift her eyes over to the currently unknown author in the corner as she continued, '... so you better get fooking used to it!'

'Is this supposed to impress me? Of everyone here, you're probably the only one who can hold a candle to me, unlike this *Американос*,' he pointed directly at me in disgust before turning away. 'As for this nobody—' Mikhail stopped mid-sentence, confusion on his face; LaVey's other guest was gone. 'Good. Seems like someone got the message to leave when they're not wanted.'

I rolled my eyes at him. 'Maybe he just got sick of you berating him and making him feel like he didn't belong here.'

LaVey finally turned around to see that Mikhail was indeed correct. 'I wonder where Mr. Brandis has gone? I'm sure he'll be right back.'

Finally, I got a name for the mysterious author. 'Mr. Brandis?' I questioned. His name rang a bell, but I couldn't place where I had heard it.

'Yes, m'dear. Mr. Frederick Brandis. He is—'

'Who? I've never heard of him.'

'Really, Mr. LaVey, why is this...Brandis even here'? Mikhail scoffed. 'It's clear to me he does not belong here...just like her!' He nodded in my direction, clear repulsion on his face. 'And don't get too full of yourself, Ms. Hughes; your *talents* are nothing compared to mine!'

I saw Rhiannon roll her eyes in annoyance before giving him a sweet, yet sarcastic, smile. 'I could show you a thing or two about my so-called talents.'

The room was uncomfortably silent for a few moments before I cleared my throat and did an overly dramatic yawn. 'Do you think you can tell me where I will sleep for the week, Mr. LaVey? I don't want to go around snooping in your lovely home.'

LaVey approached me and took my hand in his. 'M'dear, I appreciate your concern, but it will be alright. You will all be staying on the second floor. The stairs leading up there will be to your right when you go out these doors. You'll take the two flights of stairs and immediately turn to the left. The room you will stay in has an engraving of a helmet on the door.' LaVey dropped my hand and winked. 'You can't miss it. Hope you get a good night's sleep. It's going to be a busy week.'

10. *Rhiannon Calls it a Night*

It had taken two agonising hours for the others to arrive, and by then Rhiannon was ready to head to bed. She had consumed three large tumblers of whiskey and she was afraid she'd say something she would later regret if she had many more. She'd engaged in conversation and had introduced herself to the other authors, but there was already a strange tension in the air. The four of them were from completely different writing backgrounds and she felt like she didn't have anything in common with any of them. The only author she could see herself becoming acquainted with was Aster Callahan.

Aster was an indie author from the United States, but that apparently hadn't stopped her from becoming somewhat successful; several of Aster's books had competed against Rhiannon's in the horror charts. They exchanged a few pleasantries, but all Rhiannon wanted to do was strip off her damp clothes and curl up into a warm bed and sleep off the whiskey buzz that was threatening to turn into one hell of a hangover. She made a mental note to find Aster and talk with her tomorrow because she seemed nice enough, although her attire was somewhat odd and betrayed her unfamiliarity with the British weather.

The other writer was someone called Frederick Brandis. He looked completely out of place next to the other more well-known authors and she hadn't heard of him before. She knew she didn't have to worry about him writing anything better than her, so she gave him no thought other than feeling a bit sorry that he was here and was expected to write a story that was as good as the others. He'd barely said two words to any of them, so she assumed he was feeling as inadequate as he appeared.

Before anyone could engage her in further conversation, Rhiannon grabbed her bag and headed for the ornate staircase, as majestic as it was large, following the thick, red carpet that snaked its way up the steps to the first floor and pausing briefly to admire the intricate design of the dark oak banister. It appeared to have been painstakingly hand-carved into swirls and complicated patterns. At the top of the staircase, she was forced to look upwards at an exceptionally large painting of Mr. LaVey, dressed in a long, thick frock coat with large buttons running down the front, a dark blue silk scarf tied loosely around his neck, and one hand resting on a shiny cane with an intricate brass handle. His other hand rested on a thick, red leather book, and his face was one of stony, stoic implacability as he gazed off to the left, as if distracted. The man was slightly scary blown up to ten times his usual size and immortalised in paint.

Rhiannon shuddered as she turned to climb the next set of stairs to the second floor and followed the red carpet to the left, trying hard to remember the next set of directions that would lead to her room. The last thing she needed was to get lost in this place. It was past midnight and placing one foot in front of the other was becoming severely difficult now thanks to the copious amount of alcohol in her system. If she wasn't careful, she'd be forced to find a quiet corner to curl up in and wait it out until morning when perhaps all the corridors wouldn't look exactly the same.

Down every corridor she walked, Rhiannon saw numerous doors, all of which were closed. Each wall was laden with artwork, some modern photographs that looked completely out of place in such an old house, and some extremely old tapestries that could have easily been hanging there for hundreds of years. Rhiannon didn't stop to admire any of them, merely casting a quick glance over the ones that stood out the most, which were adorned with colour. She was bursting to have a wee since she hadn't been able to excuse herself all evening.

Soon enough, Rhiannon found herself facing the most fascinating door she'd ever seen in her life. It was at least twice the size of a normal door and made of dark oak with wrought-iron hinges that were easily three feet long to support the wood's exceptional weight. In the middle of the door sat a light-coloured piece of wood carved into a shape of a shield with fantastic decorations on the face of it.

This was definitely the correct door. Mr. LaVey had been very specific about whose room was whose, which no one had questioned, and Rhiannon had been given the shield room to stay in. She had no idea whereabouts on the second floor everyone else was staying because the floor was vast and the other rooms (sword, suit of armour, and helmet) could have been located anywhere. It appeared that, for the time being, she had this corridor to herself.

Rhiannon attempted to open the door while still carrying her bag, but it was impossible to shift it, so she set her bag down and leaned her bodyweight into the door, pushing as hard as she could. She felt the whole house turn upside down and spin around. The door creaked open in slow motion, revealing the most lavish room she'd ever set foot in. Rooms like this, she assumed, were only located in palaces or castles, however, here she was standing on the threshold of a room that could have been designated for royalty. She allowed her eyes to adjust as she scanned the area.

The main focal point was the enormous fireplace, which loomed over everything but the four-poster bed, which sat in the middle of the room like an island. Rhiannon had never seen such a strange layout for a bedroom before. The bed was enormous, with thick oak beams on each corner rising to the ceiling and velvet red drapes hanging over the top like a canopy. It could have comfortably slept five people. The sheets looked expensive and expertly laundered, not a crease to be seen.

On either side of the fireplace were mounds of logs piled up to above her height, as well as two large statues of dragons (or were they griffins or some other sort of mythical creature?) made entirely out of carved wood.

One element in the room held her attention for a few seconds longer than anything else: an old typewriter. It was a strange looking contraption. Rhiannon had never seen one properly before. Apparently, Mr. LaVey wanted them all to type out their finished manuscripts using the typewriter, which seemed slightly odd and excessive, but then, the old man was very eccentric. She just hoped she'd be able to figure out how to use the damn thing.

Rhiannon stumbled slightly as she peeled off her clothes and staggered towards the en suite. The woman who looked back at her from the mirror was someone she barely recognised.

'You're a fooking mess,' she said aloud to the reflection.

The woman in the mirror merely smiled as an invisible knife sliced across her throat. Bright red blood began oozing out of the single line…

Rhiannon gasped and clutched her throat, but there was no blood.

'Ya really need ta quit drinking,' she muttered.

After using the facilities and having a quick shower, it was finally time to sleep off the alcohol, so Rhiannon crawled beneath the lavish sheets and soaked up the warmth.

She dreamed about her ex-husband; the same dream she always had.

11. *Brandis in the Attic*

I found myself lost among the hallways of LaVey's grandiose abode and taking long swigs from a half-empty bottle of scotch.

It hadn't taken long to realise that I really didn't fit in with this group of strangers. I couldn't believe it when she had appeared in the doorway. Aster Callahan…in the flesh…and apparently dressed for an excursion to the North Pole! She had been wearing fluffy brown snow boots, a dark grey winter coat, a red stocking hat, scarf, and mittens. Her messy side ponytail had swept behind her as she had kicked up a storm in mere seconds, shutting even Mikhail's taunts down with a cutting edge, and I could scarcely believe my eyes

Aster Callahan!

I'd bought her first book, *Only Come at Night*, on a whim and been immediately captivated. I followed her Instagram page…which was intimidating, to say the least: she had about 13,000 followers, was showered with comments and likes, and her books averaged five-star reviews. She posts her newest acquisitions, flash fiction challenges, and even video clips on a daily basis, and it was like someone was always reading or recommending her books. I'd read them all, of course; I was currently trying to get through *Unholy Birthright*, her most recent release, and had even volunteered to receive an advanced copy for review purposes. Though I doubted that she would notice my eventual review, I felt bad that I hadn't finished the book yet…and, selfishly, I had hoped that posting a review of an Aster Callahan novel would help boost my own online following.

However, neither Aster's undeniable allure (with her flowing copper-red hair, full lips, and glistening blue eyes) or LaVey's money could ease the frosty atmosphere that had hung in the study as the others had boasted of their successes. I'd felt a rising panic as I realised that simply winging it wouldn't cut it here; they *knew* I didn't belong and probably considered me a fraud hiding behind the mask of obscurity.

I'd left the room as soon as I could. I didn't even have to be surreptitious about it as they were so engrossed in their own conversations that they barely even noticed I was there, much less that I'd left. If it'd just been Mikhail who was the problem then I'd probably be okay. The hefty Russian was probably the most self-absorbed man I had ever met, so it'd be easy to tune out his conceited opinions. I liked to think I was good at this particular trick; after all, this wasn't the first time complete strangers had taken an instant dislike to me or the first time I'd struggled with my communication skills.

I'd once tried to address this by meeting with the dumpy, wide-eyed woman from HR. 'So, what do *you* think the problem is?' she'd asked.

'Well... I don't really know...' I'd answered, surprised.

'Then why are you here?'

'Be-Because I was told it'd be a good idea to see how I could improve?'

'So, you don't actually *want* to be here?'

What the fuck is goin' on? I'd thought, confused. 'What? No? I just...I just don't really know where the problem is.'

'So, everyone else has the problem, is that it?'

'Well...I mean, I don't *know* because no one has *told* me.'

She'd twisted her face into an unimpressed expression. 'Sounds to me like you don't really want to be here so I think we should just end it there.'

And that was that. To this day I still have no idea what had happened there, and the whole debacle had come back to bite me in my next performance review. After a stern lecture about my "attitude," I decided that the hassle just wasn't worth it; similarly, I had kept my mouth shut as Rhiannon, Mikhail, and Aster had argued over each other barely keeping track of LaVey's words as he had clarified the expectations of the week, and slowly gotten more and more drunk. It didn't take much. Whatever LaVey stocked his bar with, it was potent stuff, and I had apparently lost my tolerance to alcohol over the years.

By the time I stumbled up the stairs, my vision was blurred, and my feet were unsteady; just reaching the first floor was a monumental achievement. The first floor was glaringly bright thanks to the white-hot lamps, and I suddenly felt a bitterness towards this affluent old man whose home was a maze of corridors and opulent luxury. Just one of his paintings could have paid my rent for the next five years!

As I ascended the next flight of stairs in a daze, I felt a pang of guilt. LaVey was the only one to show me any common courtesy, but it would take more than some kind words to quell my overwhelming feelings of disassociation.

Like Dani arriving at my workplace, it was too little too late.

I tripped up the last two steps. LaVey had said that our rooms were on the second floor, but I'd gotten a bit turned around. I looked over the balcony and heard my co-writer's voices echoing up to me:

'One hundred reviews in just two weeks...' Mikhail boasted.

'All of my books have been in the best sellers list at least once,' Rhiannon declared.

What did I have to offer compared to that?

I turned away and pushed open the door nearest to me and beheld a bedroom larger than my entire flat. A brass suit of armour was etched into the door; LaVey had said that we were staying in rooms with etchings such as these, but I was pretty sure that the armour room was assigned to Mikhail, and it looks like I was right. The hefty braggart had clearly arrived before me. Bags were dumped at the foot of his bed and his laptop was already sitting on charge. A thick, heavy book sat on the bedside table, and I grimaced when I saw the title. The self-entitled prick had actually brought a copy of his own book with him!

It took every last bit of self-control I had left to not wreck the room in a bitter tantrum. Such emotional outbursts weren't at all uncommon in my drunken uni days; I was always the first to kick off when things got rowdy, but I'd mellowed since then. It wouldn't do well to lose my shit at work. I'd already been reprimanded for my arguments with Reginald for no other reason than I was talking the loudest. While I was mostly pretty good about holding my tongue these days, it embittered me to repress my personality when the office was alive with chatter and banter all around me.

I left Mikhail's room intact and backed into the hallway. Even though the brute regarded me with utter disdain, I was certain he would pin any kind of disruption on me whether I was guilty or not. In the end, some people will find any reason to dislike you. Maybe it'll be because you've said something, maybe because you've *not* said anything. For instance, some of my co-workers snubbed Dani just because she started on a higher wage than they had, which had riled me up quite a bit. I could understand people not liking *me,* but Dani actually went out of her way to be nice to people and was still judged for circumstances entirely out of her control.

Speaking of Dani…

I fumbled for my phone, suddenly feeling like I should message her in a drunken stupor and was actually relieved to see that it was still drained of its battery. I pocketed it and padded along the carpet—almost tripping into one of many suits of armour that stood to attention against the walls—towards my room: the sword room, which was functionally identical to Mikhail's except for its more subdued, maroon-brown colour scheme. I dropped my bags and collapsed onto probably the firmest mattress I had ever laid on. I swept the pile of cushions and pillows from the bed with an annoyed huff and clamped my eyes shut but trying to sleep was a fool's errand. The scotch had done its work too well.

I sat up and ran my hands down my face. Was it really too much to ask to just sleep it off? I kept picturing Mikhail's sneering face, Reginald's dismissive scowl, Rhiannon's judgemental glare, and the way Aster had simply acted as though I wasn't there.

I *was* here, right?

The idea was ludicrous, but I found myself patting myself down and running my hands through my thick, shaggy hair just to be sure.

I snatched up the half-finished bottle of scotch and stumbled back into the hallway where I wandered with little rhyme or reason. I turned a corner down a corridor, half-tripped up a small set of stairs (they seemed to be everywhere in this damn place), before being met by a dead end. I swayed before a large door with a huge iron handle and a glistening keyhole. I lifted the bottle for another slug and a disappointing dribble teased at my tongue.

'Empty?' I glared at the bottle. 'Bah!' I tossed it aside and it clattered to the thin layer of snow at my feet.

Wait…*snow*?

I looked around, desperately trying to focus my eyes which swam in grey waves. A light sprinkle of snow was scattered on the carpet like sugar. Through the nearest window, I could see a torrential downpour outside and yet snowflakes danced before my eyes. I reached out for them lazily and gawped as they slowly melted on my fingers.

The snowflakes were carried on a slight breeze coming from behind that ominous door. A shudder ran through me. *Nope*, I thought, as I staggered away, already convincing myself that it was a result of my drunken state when a loud, piercing creak stopped me in my tracks.

I turned around slowly. The door yawned, lightly buffeted by a gentle gust. Curious, feeling myself drawn, I peered within and saw a staircase of exposed, scuffed floorboards that led up into the darkness of the attic and were covered with a light dusting of snow.

Still, I wasn't about to…

Ghnnnahk…

A throaty, gurgling sound echoed from the attic. I wanted to flee in a desperate panic, and yet found myself paralysed.

Gknnnhnnnahk…

The choking death rattle seemed to be coming from the darkest corner of the room.

The…room…?

Without even realising it, I'd wandered up those creaking stairs into LaVey's dark, musty attic. Cobwebs, thick layers of dust, and splintered rafters were everywhere, and the stained, chipped windows glared at me. The rain pelted relentlessly like thousands of tiny feet running across bare floorboards and I could see hanging ivy scratching at the glass as the storm raged outside. The attic was a dumping ground of treasures; more paintings were piled up against the wall, barely covered by sheets of cloth, and furniture was scattered all over. I peeked beneath the one nearest to me and caught a stench of damp and saw a skittering little spider and the top of a large piano. I glanced back at the stairs and wondered how LaVey had managed to lug a piano up here, before I found myself drawn to a large cabinet.

The shelves were askew, rotting, and all kinds of insects dashed away as I brushed aside years of dust. Upon it was a small silver tea set, stained and grimy from neglect; a cracked and chipped porcelain doll, one eye turned lazily towards me; a pile of dusty leather-bound books. I picked up a framed picture that showed LaVey shaking hands with a tall man in a military uniform behind a cobble-stone green grocer's in what looked like the late-fifties. LaVey was wearing the same outfit from earlier.

I placed the picture back on the shelf next to a smattering of ornaments: an upturned candlestick holder of solid silver, a curious rune stone marked with the crests of four families mostly likely long dead, a heavy piece of sandy stone upon which was carved an ominous hieroglyph, and a twisted dagger of the blackest obsidian that I was about to reach for when that croaking rattle bubbled up from a large camphor wood chest on the floor against this cabinet of curios.

The chest sat beneath a large, crooked painting of a grim, stone-faced man holding a sceptre and riding a rearing horse. It was a thing of beauty, and it seemed untouched by the ravages of the attic. The brass

99

brackets and clasps glistened; I couldn't help myself from stroking its intricate swirling carvings.

I dropped to my knees and flicked open the front clasp and immediately flew backwards and scrambled away in a desperate panic as a crooked, twisted ghoul lurched its way out of the chest like some warped imitation of life.

'*Gnnnarrrk!*' came its guttural wheeze as it tumbled to the floor in a bundle of skeletal limbs.

I crawled backwards frantically. My sleeve snagged on an exposed nail and ripped a gaping hole in my top, but I barely noticed. I gawped at the gnarled creature that was flailing before me, its gangly limbs whacking at the floor with a series of hollow thuds. The back of my head suddenly and painfully hit the attic wall and I clawed my way up, watching, with mounting dread, as the ghoul mirrored my movements. It thrashed wildly and I could see an ungodly muck slop to the floorboards as it staggered upwards. It jerked and convulsed in a mockery of life, and I saw that its slender, vaguely feminine form was covered by a long, torn frock dress. It was smeared with dirt and blood and shredded by claw marks, leaving tatters of cloth that hung loose around its gnarled wrists and talon-like hands.

Its face was obscured entirely by tangled, jet-black hair that seemed as slick as oil and stretched down to her knees in knots. Long, viscous fluid oozed from her locks and hit the floorboards with a sickening squelch, and I could tell that it was thick blood blackened by untold aeons of suffocating darkness. As this wreck of life shuffled towards me, I realised with fresh dread that it had effectively blocked my escape route. Even if my legs were capable of anything other than trembling, they'd only be able to take me further into the attic's darkness…or out the window to a surely fatal fall.

I stifled a cry as it lumbered towards me, arms outstretched, its contorted hands grasping at the rancid air.

'*Gkknnnrk!*' the ghoul moaned. The few fingernails it had were chipped and encrusted with disgusting dirt, grime, and blood, and its flesh was semi-translucent and glistened at me with a sickening, ethereal glow.

Before I could even think, let alone move, the grotesque apparition was upon me. I felt its bone-cold hands clamp tightly down on my collarbone and I let out a startled cry that was more of a blubbering bark. The stench was beyond revolting; I gagged, choking as the fetid, putrid stink of decay and rotting meat filled my nostrils.

'*Jesus, fuck!*' I bawled and coughed up bile as the thing's claws dug into me.

My heart skipped a beat and I panted, not wishing to inhale more of that foul odour but desperate for air, however rotten. This twisted, contorted girl-thing pinned me to the floor with surprising ferocity, and her straggly hair hung around my blubbering face. She stared at me through the tangled darkness, her face a gaping void. Her wide, bloodshot eyes mesmerised me with their black glare of hatred and revulsion. Her thick, split lips yawned open, revealing gums stripped of teeth, and another of those long, groaning death rattles blew into my face in a scream of anguish.

I flinched as the razor-sharp grip intensified and I saw *things* crawling at the back of the apparition's throat. I let out a shriek of my own as a writhing, gnarled insectile limb suddenly burst from its gullet and swiped at my face. I gagged as the spidery appendage thrashed around wildly, ripping at the ghoul's thin, taught flesh with an inhuman squeal that pierced my ears.

I could feel meaty, ice-cold thighs pressing against my hips, holding me tightly in place and forcing me to watch as the girl-thing's gruesome visage began to melt. Flesh ran like wax and its large eyes rolled back and dribbled down grey-tinted cheek bones. For one terrifying moment, I thought this bubbling goop was going to splatter on my face and I felt my mind teeter on the brink of sanity when, just as suddenly, its skin snapped back and its head convulsed with a bone-rattling growl, its grip tightening like a vice as its features contorted into a nightmarish visage.

My mother glared back at me, her eyes blazing as her skin rippled as though barely able to hold its shape.

'*Black!*' she barked through rotting, crooked teeth. '*The Black!*' she shuddered, the tangles of her hair whipping this way and that as she bellowed in anguish: '*The Black comes for you!*'

I screamed in frenzy. The thing that wore my mother's face thrashed in a convulsion of limbs and a dark, rasping laugh as it held me tight and I was forced to watch my mother's face boil before my eyes. Her nose decayed in a bubbling stream, and her features were eaten inside out as the thing's visage changed once more. I struggled desperately but the thing simply pressed its clawed hands to my chest and held me in place before drawing its putrefied lips close to mine.

I tried to turn away, but the ghoul forced me to face it with a push of one rough, skeletal hand.

Now it wore Lucy's face.

'Oh, you fuckin' bitch...' I whispered through quivering lips.

Lucy regarded me kindly, watching me with those same dazzling grey-green eyes. However, while her pert lips were turned up into a warm smile, I sensed that malicious spirit lingering behind her and that insectile limb still flailed from her throat. 'N-not...not real...' I mumbled, unable to draw my eyes from my dead friend's gaze.

'*Don't you miss me?*' the Lucy-thing gurgled with a helpless gasp. '*We can be together...in the Black...*' That disgusting hair left streaks of oil-like blood across my face as she pressed her warm lips to mine.

I struggled beneath the ghoul's inhuman strength and finally tore my face free with a yell of revulsion. 'St-stop...stop...' I panted, grimacing at the thing that'd stolen my friend's face, and I steeled myself for whatever chaotic tumult had birthed this nightmarish apparition.

A sneer creased Lucy's beautiful, cream-white skin and I felt her talons gouge bloody tracks in my chest, and then...

...Nothing.

Lucy's face twisted into a puzzled expression; her mouth worked silently, but I could hear the skittering of insects and the distant mutter of voices in my head. She looked down at me with such warmth before three more of those slender spider-like limbs burst from her throat. They flew up before the ghoul's face like a claw and a horrendous growl rumbled from within her throat.

'*He's for the Black!*' The insectile claw clamped itself to her face and ripped at it violently, shredding Lucy's face off with one sickening clench of its talons. The Lucy-thing quivered fiercely as her limbs snapped and bent into horribly unnatural angles. That demonic, spider-like claw gouged at her face and great, gory chunks of flesh dropped between its "fingers" like bloody ribbons.

Suddenly, the ghoul grabbed me by the tattered remains of my top and tossed me aside with a demonic shriek. I landed hard on my left shoulder and turned to see it thrashing around the attic in a haze of contorted, flailing limbs. It ripped at the insectile legs stuck to its face and snapped them off, throwing them to the floor, where they dissolved into the same ashy substance that covered the attic. With heavy, staggering steps, the ghoul stumbled back to the camphor chest, still wailing like a banshee; it whirled around towards me, one hand clapped to whatever remained of its face, a large, dark eye glaring at me furiously.

'*Get out!*' it roared.

I was again propelled by vicious, inhuman strength that hit me completely out of nowhere and sent me half-tumbling down the attic stairs. I snapped my arm out in a panic and grabbed at the weak banister, saving myself from a bad fall. I tripped down the last few steps and was flung out into the hall by a furious shove.

Groaning, aching all over, I rolled over, feeling my flesh scream from a dozen scrapes. The large door that led to the attic slammed shut with a loud, echoing bang, which was followed by the unmistakable sound of a lock turning, leaving me panting and scared out of my mind on the hallway floor.

Chapter Three

Monday

1. *Aster Makes a Friend*

Making my way up the stairs, I pulled out my phone to see what time it was. My eyes widened when I saw it was half past midnight. 'Shit! I should try Walter again.' As I went to dial his number, his name popped up on the screen.

'Hello?' I answered but received no response. 'Hey, Walter, are you—'

'So, ya did fuckin' go, didja?' he growled.

My face scrunched in confusion. 'Yeah…I told you this yesterday, despite what you—'

'How much of *my* money did you waste getting there?'

'Um…I had money saved up. We talked about this.'

'*Psh*, okay. Quite expensive to fly over there, 'specially round-trip. Who's even there? Better not be any guys there.'

Rolling my eyes, I couldn't help the edge in my tone. 'Well, there's the benefactor of the event, Mr. LaVey, but he's old and has no interest in me.' I took a deep breath. 'If you're going to be this way—'

'Dammit, woman!' A loud bang came through Walter's end. 'You're skirting the question! There is, isn't there? Tell me…' his voice dropped dangerously low. 'You screwed them, didn't ya?'

My jaw dropped and a lump formed at the back of my throat. Did he really think so little of me? He always had a problem with me having any male friends, but I wouldn't stoop so low as to cheat on him. Biting my lip, I kept my temper in check. Lashing out would only make the situation worse.

'You little whore...' he growled. 'Just couldn't wait to fuck another man, could you?'

Hot tears fell down my cheeks and any effort to hold back my emotions collapsed. 'Why would you even say that, Walter? I have been nothing but faithful to you! I love you; you're the only one I want to be with!'

Walter scoffed. 'You're only saying that because you're covering your guilt.'

'What guilt?! I've only been here for a couple hours at most since landing and the majority of that has been travelling to get to my destination! There wouldn't have been any time for me to do something like that!'

I could hear a barely audible but dangerous chuckle under his breath. 'Lying bitch...why else would it take you so long to call me back?!'

'Have you ever heard of shitty reception, Walter? I've barely had a signal since I arrived here!'

Another loud bang. 'You're getting awfully snippy, woman.'

I heard glass clinking together. The pain I had been feeling was slowly being replaced with anger. 'You're out with Sawyer and Kelsey again?'

'This is your fault, after all. I wouldn't have even bothered to go out—'

I quickly hung up and powered down my phone. Dealing with him when he was in a bad mood was awful enough, but if he was out with Sawyer and Kelsey...that traitor! Sawyer was all right, but Kelsey and I clashed too much. It wasn't a secret she liked Walter and had tried dating him years ago. Walter reassured me that's in the past and he doesn't see the point in me being jealous of Kelsey. Still...after what had happened with my ex, flirty women worried me.

As I reached the final step of the second floor, I dropped down to sit on it in a huff. Wiping the tears from my eyes, I took in my surroundings and noted just how truly beautiful Mr. LaVey's home was.

I let out an irritated snort. 'Why am I such an idiot to think he could change?'

'You need to give yourself a break, luv. Sleep is just what you need.'

I froze. Where had that voice come from? It didn't sound like that Mikhail guy. Was it the other guy...Brandis? *That's stupid.* I thought. *You're tired and hearing things...now where in the hell is the helmet room Mr. LaVey told you about?*

'Of course, going through six time zones and being on a plane for over eight hours would make me tired and grumpy as well. Your sleep schedule is going to be out of sync.' The voice sounded closer. Nope I definitely didn't imagine it...but who in the hell was it?

I felt a presence behind me and turned around; my eyes spotted a boy no older than nineteen, dressed in a white dress shirt and black trousers. He had a kind look in his eyes and wore a soft smile on his lips. I blinked several times and rubbed my eyes to make sure he was real and it wasn't my exhausted mind messing with me, but, sure enough, he stood there as clear as day.

'I'm so sorry,' I said sheepishly. 'I didn't hear anyone coming. You're so quiet. Are you one of Mr. LaVey's help staff?'

The boy chuckled. 'You could say that, Ms. Callahan. I'd been tending to some late-night duties when I saw movement down the hall and decided to investigate.' He gave me a slight bow. 'My name is Finley. Pleasure to make your acquaintance.'

Sighing in relief, I smiled at this formal gesture. 'Pleasure to meet you as well, Finley. Just curious…how'd you know my name?'

'I overheard Mr. LaVey mention you shortly after you arrived. When I saw you, you definitely stood out from the others,' Finley replied.

My cheeks heated up, embarrassed at this oversight. 'Oh, you were there? I only saw Mr. LaVey and the other authors.'

Finley quickly shook his head and said it wasn't anything to fret about before nodding towards my luggage. 'Heading to your quarters? What room is Mr. LaVey having you reside in?'

'The helmet room. Do you think you can show me the way there? This house is quite large, and I'm not great with directions on a good day.'

Finley gave me a nod and made his way down the hall. We casually chatted the rest of the way until we reached the very door Mr. LaVey had described. The design of the helmet etched into the door was incredible. I ran my fingers over it, admiring the time it must have taken for someone to craft this.

'Do you know what having the helmet room symbolises?' Finley asked.

I shook my head, and he proceeded to explain to me that it was a representation of the body's most valuable asset: our brain. 'It's the very place we hold all of our knowledge. Our hopes and dreams. Least that's what ancient mythology states.'

Before I could respond to his interesting fact, a large yawn escaped me and I had no time to properly cover it. 'I'm so sorry...I don't mean to be rude.'

'I understand Ms. Callahan—'

'Aster's fine. No need for such formalities.'

A small smile spread across Finley's face. 'Well then, Aster. It has been a long day for you. Mustn't keep you too long.'

Nodding my head, I turned away to grab the doorknob when a thought suddenly struck me. 'Hey, I had one final quest—' I was greeted with an empty hallway. Standing completely still for a few moments, I blinked in disbelief. *Where did he go?* I thought. *There's no way he would have been able to move that quickly or quietly.*

'Finley?' I called down the hall. I was met with silence. 'Finley...if this is some kind of joke, this isn't funny!'

More silence. My skin crawled, a pit of terror forming in my stomach. *Maybe he had to check on something and didn't hear me*, I thought.

'He would have definitely heard you the second time.' I replied.

Not necessarily, my thoughts snapped back.

'This is ridiculous,' I said. 'I'm just tired and need to get some sleep. I probably just missed seeing him off.'

Wasting no time, I pushed the door open into a room fit for royalty. The walls were a deep burgundy, giving the room a warm and comforting glow, and the plush cream carpet sported flecks of dazzling gold. There were several tiny shelves with lit candles placed on them, making the ambiance of the room warm and welcoming. A huge smile spread across my face when I saw the large four-poster bed with its exquisite design and rich gold shade that appeared to be shimmering. It looked so inviting and relaxing; I could tell it was going to be a comfortable, peaceful sleep.

Dropping my bags to the floor, I tossed my glasses from my face and collapsed face-first onto the mattress. It was firm but comforting…unlike the bed I slept on back home. It was too soft for me, but Walter refused to get a new mattress; he said that it was perfect, and that I would eventually grow accustomed to it. This bed was large, much bigger than the full-sized bed I shared with my fiancé who took up most of the mattress. I didn't mind too much; I didn't move around in my sleep and was accustomed to smaller beds growing up.

'I could get used to this,' I muttered to myself. Not bothering to change into my pyjamas, I shrugged off my winter coat and kicked my boots off before settling under the duvet. The last thing I did was set an alarm to get up nice and early to do a little investigating of the grounds. The struggle to write a piece wasn't present, but perhaps I could draw inspiration from this grandiose property.

2. *Rhiannon Goes for a Run*

Rhiannon awoke the next morning regretting having drunk so much whiskey the night before and falling asleep without drinking a litre of water (as was her custom to ward off potentially severe hangovers). As it was, she had to force herself out of bed at seven and don her running gear. Running always extinguished her hangovers, more so than the usual greasy breakfast or cup of strong coffee. Breakfast would have to wait. A run would sort her out, shake out any anxieties she'd had from the day before, and set her mind straight for the task ahead.

Rhiannon opened her bag and took out her running kit. She didn't bother to unpack the rest of her bag and could feel her heart rate increasing at the prospect of running around a new area, especially one as fascinating as this place. Her friends often thought her strange that she found such enjoyment from running. Her ex-husband had never understood it either. She'd once attempted to drag him out for a short run and had instantly regretted it. Not only had he bitched and moaned the entire time, but she had also found that she couldn't enjoy herself and hadn't been able to clear her head because all she heard was his droning voice. That had been the first and last time she had offered to take him out running. Even her daughter had never wanted to join her on a run. It was a lonely hobby for Rhiannon.

Finally dressed, she tied her hair back with a cheap plastic hair tie and paused before leaving her room, having felt a cold breeze behind her. She turned and glanced at the window, but it was firmly shut and looked to have been that way for many years. Where had the breeze come from? She saw the fireplace and instantly understood; sometimes the wind could blow down the chimneys in old houses. Without thinking anything more about it, Rhiannon left and retraced her steps to the main entrance hall, hoping to whatever God was up there that she didn't run into any of her fellow authors or the master of the house. She had no intention of stopping for a chit-chat. Her foggy brain was struggling to recall the correct way back to the hall. Last night was still a bit of a blur and nothing really made any sense.

As soon as she stepped outside, the rain returned but it didn't dampen her spirit. In fact, it invigorated her. When she ran, she didn't care about the rain, but when she was sitting in her car and it was pouring through the roof...that's when she cared. Or when she was waiting for a bus and there was no bus shelter. But not when she ran. It could snow for all she cared. She was just glad to finally be out of the large, creepy house. Yes, it was a fascinating place, but she'd only been under its roof for less than twenty-four hours and already she felt a sense of...unease, which was growing by the second. She couldn't explain why she felt that way though. It was only a house after all.

Rhiannon didn't even bother to warm up; she just jogged at a slow pace that others would have found fast. She never ran for sport or for a race, had never completed a marathon or even a half marathon. She didn't run to collect medals or impress people. She ran because it made her feel alive, and for those solitary minutes where her feet pounded the ground, she felt completely at peace and able to block out all the troublesome thoughts that would often cloud her mind.

It was the perfect way to clear her head before writing, and that's exactly what she planned to do. Once she was back inside, had showered and dressed, she'd find a secluded spot in the house. She didn't want to waste any more time. She was bound to find a place; the house was big enough. Surely the other authors would find their own corner to begin their writing projects. Mr. LaVey had made it perfectly clear that they could go anywhere they wanted, which Rhiannon was now taking full advantage of as she circled around an enormous stone garden ornament and turned down a long pathway shielded under a canopy of thick trees.

The trees themselves were ancient and formed a perfect shelter from most of the rain. The path was well worn and had several large holes, which she either hopped over or avoided completely. Clearly, there'd been no attempt to keep the grounds in good condition. She wondered why this was. She hadn't seen any resemblance of a groundskeeper or even a housekeeper, which made it all the more impressive that Mr. LaVey could handle things by himself in his frail state. Maybe he didn't really care about the gardens or the house that much, or maybe he didn't actually live here most of the time and had only brought them here as it was a decent setting.

Rhiannon found herself following the natural trail around the estate. It seemed that there had once been a proper footpath, but now it was exceptionally overgrown and uneven. She could hear her trainers crunching the small gravel stones beneath her feet as she ran, her arms pumping in rhythm with her steps, her breathing heavy but controlled. She ran across the long grass that veered away from the path…and yet could still hear the crunching sound.

Someone was behind her.

She briefly threw a glance over her shoulder, but there was no one there. The crunching had stopped, but she continued to feel dread flooding her body as she ran back towards the house. Maybe she'd strayed too far after all. It was time to head back anyway. She'd been running for almost an hour and still hadn't circled the entirety of the grounds.

Ten minutes later, Rhiannon stood puffing and panting in front of the estate, bent over at the waist, catching her breath. She performed a few leg stretches while she surveyed the many dirty glass windows, some almost completely covered in the twisty, creepy vines and thorns.

A dark, slim figure walked past one of the windows on the second floor. It startled her for a brief second before she realised that it must be one of the others.

It must be that Brandis dork, she thought. He was fairly tall and slim…or was he average build? Rhiannon tried to recall what he looked like. She'd only really glanced at him and by that time she'd had one too many drinks and was seeing double anyway. He'd been so unimportant and boring that she hadn't paid him any attention at all. His clothes had been baggy and old, his hair unkempt and shaggy, the same as his scruffy beard, and he seemed like a bum. Why was he even here?

Rhiannon finished her stretches, gave Brandis no further thought, and went inside to shower and change before exploring the house for a quiet place to plan her short story.

3. Aster Asks a Favour

The irritating buzzer of my morning alarm shattered my peaceful sleep. 'Is it 7:45 already? Goddammit.' I rolled onto my side, grabbed my phone, and shut off the alarm as I threw off the blankets. I dug around in my bag and found my outfit for the day: black leggings, a grey chunky knit sweater, and moccasins. I didn't want to bother with throwing on make-up and my hairbrush seemed to be temporarily missing so I tossed my frizzy hair into a ponytail. I decided against looking for my glasses and unlocked my bedroom door to make my way down to the ground floor.

The daylight peeking in through the windows helped me navigate through the house better, and also provided a better view of what I couldn't see last night. Mr. LaVey was a man of exquisite and fine taste. Everything was clean and in its proper place, there were several portraits on the walls, and the décor looked very expensive. Upon finally reaching the first floor, I took in the colour scheme: a vivid gold which made the already elegant space look even more refined. Finley wasn't kidding; one could easily get lost in this house. Who knows where you could end up—

Finley! A smile came to my face. I wondered if I would see him at breakfast? I wasn't sure where the kitchen was, but I was sure it wouldn't be too hard to find it. Within a couple of minutes, I came around a corner on the ground floor to see an open arch that led to a large, empty dining room. There was quite the assortment of food against the furthest wall of the room. I wasn't feeling hungry at that moment (I rarely ate breakfast as it was), but maybe in a bit there would be something for me to check out.

'Good morrow, Ms. Callahan.' Mr. LaVey was sitting in one of the chairs, sipping away at a cup of what I presumed was tea. 'Nice to see a morning person such as myself.'

'Morning, Mr. LaVey.' I took a seat across from him. 'No, I'm honestly not, but I had a hard time getting back to sleep around four in the morning.'

He stirred for a moment before setting his cup down. 'Oh? What was troubling you, m'dear?'

LaVey flashed me a quick smile, no doubt an attempt to reassure me. I didn't feel comfortable talking to this stranger about Walter or sharing the specifics of my dreams...I was tempted to ask after Finley, but hesitated. The last thing I wanted was for my host to think me mad for imagining his helpful staff vanishing into thin air.

An exasperated scoff broke me from my thoughts as I saw Mikhail standing in the doorway, glaring at me. 'Сука,' he muttered under his breath before skulking into the hallway.

'Don't let him bother you too much, m'dear. Mikhail is a bit of a brutish ruffian, but a valuable asset to the collaboration, believe me.'

I simply nodded. 'I'll try to keep that in mind. Honestly, I'm going to try to do my best to avoid him.'

LaVey looked as though he was going to reply, but the sound of the front door opening and closing caught his attention. 'I wonder who that could have been.'

As he got up to leave, I grabbed a plate and picked up a couple of muffins and a glass of orange juice. My stomach growled at that moment, causing me to hurry back to my room. Once there, I curled up on the plush armchair and started devouring my food. It may have been simple, but it tasted divine. The blueberry muffin was warm, fluffy, and full of flavour, and the orange juice seemed freshly squeezed and had a distinct tang that store-bought OJ could not rival. After finishing the other muffin (a delightful chocolate chip), I decided that starting my short story would be a fantastic idea. 'Best to get ahead of the game and not wait until the last minute.'

Pulling out my charger cord, I went to plug it in…only to realise that it wasn't going to work. 'Shit,' I said. 'What am I going to do?' I sighed dramatically. Maybe Mr. LaVey could help me, or perhaps there was a regular outlet in this house. I got up from the chair, grabbed my phone, and marched downstairs. *You're not in the United States anymore…not everything is going to be catered to you.* I really hated to admit it, but my inner thoughts were correct: I hadn't seen or experienced anything else outside of my country, and not everything was like it was in the United States.

Finding Mr. LaVey wasn't difficult. He was now seated in the study next to the fireplace, watching the roaring fire. 'Mr. LaVey? I don't mean to disturb you, but I have an odd request to ask of you.'

He took his attention away from the fire, a smile on his face. 'What is it, Ms. Callahan?'

'I didn't realise until now that my laptop charger won't work in your outlets here. Is there something I can use or some kind of adapter available so I can work on my laptop without it dying in a day?'

There was a long pause before LaVey chuckled. 'Yes, I think I can manage that. Unless you wouldn't mind working down here in the parlour.' He pointed to a spot on the other side of where he was seated.

'I had an American outlet installed there years ago,' he winked. 'Never know who will show up here.'

'Of course. From my research, you are very well known and prominent. Which reminds me…how come you chose me, someone from the United States, to be part of your anthology?'

His smile faltered slightly before answering. 'We can discuss that another time, but now that I think about it…' he got up from his chair, '…I think there might be an adapter lying around. Follow me, Ms. Callahan.'

LaVey led the way down another of his many hallways and to another office; though smaller than where we had come from, it was just as elaborate and massive as everything seemed to be in this house. *How the hell could one guy live with all this space?* I thought. I wouldn't know what to do with myself. As it was, I barely had enough stuff to even fill up two rooms in this house. I stood in the doorway while he ventured towards the oak desk and rummaged through the drawers. Within a minute, he pulled out an adapter for me to use.

'I can't thank you enough, and I'm so sorry for not thinking ahead on this.'

LaVey waved his hand dismissively. 'It's no problem at all, m'dear.'

I spotted a small, silver famed picture on LaVey's desk. He stood with a small boy before him and a thin, dark-haired woman by his side. *His family, perhaps?* Something about the boy seemed familiar. I was going to ask about him, but Mikhail came barging into the room and interrupted my thoughts. Mr. LaVey, ever the polite host, calmly excused himself to address Mikhail's concerns—an unreasonable, unintelligible Russian bark about the food quality no doubt—about the breakfast spread.

As I took my leave, adapter in hand, a lightbulb suddenly went off in my head. *Finley!* I realised, shocked. *The boy was Finley!*

4. *Brandis at Breakfast*

Suffice it to say that I had trouble sleeping following my incident in the attic. Every time I shut my eyes, I saw that warped creature wearing both my mother's and Lucy's faces. To make things worse, my head was absolutely pounding from the bottle of scotch. My brain felt like it was dissolving, and an acrid taste scorched my throat, and the smallest movement made me feel like I was going to pitifully melt away.

I laid in bed for hours, tossing and turning, unable to stop my head from spinning or banish that sight, that dreadful croaking moan, from memory. I was afraid to even leave my room lest that phantom spring upon me down one of LaVey's many dark and dusty corridors. The rational side of my mind that was becoming dimmer and dimmer these days begged me to pack up and leave, but I was too drained to do anything but drift away into a brief doze.

I was startled to life by the morning sunrise peeking through my curtains. I threw back my duvet and wearily stumbled into the small en suite and showered without much enthusiasm. Fetid water spewed from a showerhead that had been stained by rust and limescale and only exacerbated my pounding hangover. I quickly reconsidered trimming the thick bristles of my beard when I saw how badly my hand trembled as I brushed my teeth; the others would just have to deal with my unkempt appearance.

Lucy would've been unimpressed to see me throw on a t-shirt and baggy joggers, and with how wild my hair had gotten. Normally, I was quite strict about cutting it, but lately it just didn't seem like it mattered. It wasn't as if my appearance would change Mikhail's judgemental attitude or Rhiannon's curt side-eye; they didn't think much of me, and who could blame them? *I* didn't think much of myself.

Without much enthusiasm, I sat before the ornate desk and stroked my fingertips on the large, glistening black typewriter that had been provided with my room. "I believe in the old ways," LaVey had said last night. "So, you may use your technology, but your finished piece must be typed up in the old ways." I could tell the others had been surprised, maybe even a little insulted, at this suggestion, but I'd grown up using a heavy-duty typewriter to produce my earliest stories, which had actually impacted my typing style. Lucy had always marvelled at how quickly I was able to type using just my index fingers and, thanks to using that old typewriter, the closest I came to using any other digits was the odd press of a middle finger or a thumb here and there. Also, I found that if I typed too fast with too many fingers then I made more mistakes.

Accordingly, I was still planning on using my laptop to type the story up so I could catch these errors. I'd plugged in my laptop shortly after I'd dumped my stuff in the room and, when I lifted the slim, slightly cracked screen and bashed in my password with heavy, weary hands, my heart sank. I'd left open a document to begin my writing for LaVey's project. Thankfully, it wasn't blank but what *was* written was little more than a garbled mess. I rarely went into a story completely blind, but I often just let the words come to me as I wrote. This had always kept me in good stead...until recently, anyway. Still, I've always been amused at how quickly stories take on a life of their own. For example, when writing *Incredulous*, I accidentally forgot that the mother of one of the main characters was supposed to be a tertiary antagonist. Instead, the secondary antagonist grew to the point where this parental figure was not only rendered obsolete but wasn't even mentioned in the final text! I didn't even realise she was missing until I did my first proofread and I barked a laugh so hard that Bert had shot me an annoyed glance from his spot on the thin carpet of my flat.

Incredulous got a random one-star review with no context or feedback.

I lightly brushed my fingertips over the well-worn keys of my laptop and silently hoped for a sudden burst of inspiration…instead the thought of that twisted wretch clawed through my brain and I was suddenly convinced I could hear it scratching from

(*The Black*)

within my wardrobe.

I bolted up from the chair and wrenched open the wardrobe.

Nothing, of course.

'Fuck's sake…' I wheezed.

I was about to go back to my laptop (was tempted, in actual fact, to smash the damn thing to pieces against the bed posts) when my stomach loudly churned, and I realised that I hadn't eaten since gobbling that chocolate bar from the Teamos petrol station what felt like two ice ages ago. The allure of food cut through my hangover, my melancholy, and my fears of the primeval horror locked away in LaVey's attic. I slipped into my battered trainers without tying the laces and stepped out of my room, cringing as the door banged shut and with every creaking floorboard that was like knives piercing my exhausted head.

Somehow, I managed to make it downstairs without tripping head over heels, but I had to steady myself as I was suddenly hit with a wave of nausea and convinced that I was about to puke in LaVey's grand foyer. Trembling breaths escaped my lips as I fought to control myself when I saw LaVey and that Neanderthal Mikhail standing in a doorway opposite. They looked to be having some kind of debate, but the old man hailed me with a small wave of his hand and a hearty call: 'Good morrow, Mr. Brandis.'

Although annoyed at having to interact with anyone— especially Mikhail—so early in the morning, I did my best to appear pleasant and coherent and not completely rat-assed.

'Morning,' I croaked. I coughed and repeated the greeting before complimenting LaVey on his house. I mean, what the fuck else was I supposed to say? *Hey, d'you know there's a fucked up ghoul living in a chest in your attic?!*

'Oh, yes, it's been in my family for…oh, generations now,' he mused, a beaming smile of pride etched into the wrinkles of his features. Despite the early hour, the old man wore an immaculate frock coat and a bolo tie that looped through an exquisite jade jewel. 'Of course, business often takes me into the city, but I do like to visit the ol' homestead on special occasions, hmm.'

'*Ttch*,' Mikhail grunted and rolled his eyes; his hairy arms were tightly folded across his chest. 'In *my* country, staff would attend a master's will.'

LaVey tittered and shook his head lightly. 'I have no need for such frivolities.'

'Is wrong for guests to be wandering halls and carrying their own bags,' Mikhail scoffed.

'Aw, c'mon,' I said, already regretting speaking. 'Surely a big guy like you can carry a few bags?'

Mikhail loomed over me. 'Was I talking to you?'

A hundred responses flashed through my head in a blur but, in the end, I simply shrugged and turned my eyes away from his steely gaze. Although Mikhail's threat was pretty ordinary compared to what I'd witnessed last night, I was in no physical shape to get into a scuffle with him.

'*Tpyc*,' he scoffed. 'Just as I thought.'

With that, the thug barged past me with a shove of his shoulder. LaVey gave a cluck and shook his head. 'That man's ego will be the death of him.'

'We can only hope,' I muttered as I rubbed my throbbing shoulder and made my way into the empty dining room.

A breakfast spread was laid out across the far wall of the room. Although the others had clearly feasted, there was enough left to satiate my hunger. I grabbed some *pain au chocolat*, toasted and heavily buttered two thick slices of bread, and filled a bowl with crispy grains that looked like sawdust. I poured myself a generous cup of strong, dark coffee, and turned to see that ghoul suddenly before me. Gangly and crooked, it leered at me for the merest fraction of a second, that choking growl rising to a crescendo, and I almost sent my tray of food flying before realising that my sleep-deprived, alcohol-dazed brain was playing tricks on me.

'Are you okay?' Aster Callahan asked. She was standing in the middle of the room with a phone in one hand and looking at me with concern, apparently having wandered in as I was piling up my plate. She was wearing a chunky grey jumper, black leggings, and her shining red hair was tied back in a ponytail, and I could tell that there was no way she had simply rolled out of bed looking as good as she did even though she wasn't wearing any make-up this morning.

Still, I wasn't in the mood to socialise, no matter how alluring the company. I set my tray down on the nearest table and sat down with a grunt as I sipped my coffee. I'm not normally a big coffee drinker but I swallowed it gratefully.

'Don't mind me, I was just on the phone to my fiancé,' *Oh great,* I thought, *now I get to hear all about "Mister Right."* 'Not the greatest reception, is there? I was down here earlier and saw the spread, but wasn't feeling it at the time, ya know? Now that I've woken up a bit, I thought I'd give it a try this time.' I

was happy to see that Aster had moved over to the breakfast spread (but not so hungover or gentlemanly to keep myself from checking out her ass) but my patience frayed as she took the chair opposite me and started eating a crumpet. 'I mean, what is this? It's like a cake, maybe? It's very dry and chewy...'

I threw a quick, blasé glance at her. 'It's a crumpet, and you're eatin' it cold an' without anythin' on it! Stick it in the toaster and put some marmalade on it or summink.'

Aster swallowed a chunk of the uncooked crumpet with a grimace and a puzzled look came over her features. 'It needs to be toasted? Like...grilled?'

I sighed and nodded.

Fascinated, Aster moved away from the table. I could hear her loading the toaster behind me, and then she was hovering nearby. I turned to her, and she asked: 'What'd you say? "Marm'laid"? What's that?'

Seriously? I bit my tongue. Her face was glowing red, and she was clearly embarrassed, but I wasn't really in the mood to catch her up with the history of British food. 'It's like jam. Should be an orange jar somewhere over there.' I waved vaguely. She busied herself behind me, tittering away about something or other as my thoughts wandered back to that ghastly sight from the attic with its tar-like hair and...

'*Oh. My. Lawd!*' Aster squealed, the sound cutting through my ears like the needles that had scarred her pale, silky flesh with tattoo ink. I felt my life ebbing away when she sat opposite me once again and wiped an errant drop of marmalade from her chin. 'Oh, my lawd!' she repeated, astounded. 'This..."marm'laid" is quite yummy! Wonder if I could sneak some back home before I go...'

After my run-in with Mikhail, I decided it'd be better to say nothing. Plus, I thought she would leave me in peace if I didn't indulge her, but my hopes were dashed as she asked: 'You're...Brandis, right?'

'Last time I checked,' I mumbled as I ate my toast.

'I thought so, yeah. I didn't get to talk to you last night,' she finished off her crumpet and wiped her hands with a comic exaggeration that I might have found amusing on any other morning.

'Uh-huh,' I swallowed the last of my coffee.

My head continued to throb excruciatingly as she prattled on. 'So, I'd like to know what you've written. I'm fascinated by the current company of LaVey and Rhiannon, not so much that douchebag Mikhail, and I came to realise I know nothing about you...'

'Look, I...'

'You must also be someone else who is amazing and has written a lot of books! I mean, I've only written four, currently working on my fifth, but suppose that's still not terrible considering there's people who don't even try to pursue their hopes and dreams...'

'Ye...No? I dunno! Look, I really ain't...'

'Oh, I'm so sorry for rambling on and on like this. I had just gotten out of a nasty phone conversation with Walter...not that you know who that is, of course. He's my—'

'Okay, honestly, I ain't in the mood for...*this*,' I waved my hand back and forth between Aster and myself. 'I didn't come down 'ere for a chat, or t'hear all 'bout your life story. I jus' wanna write my fuckin' story, get paid, an' get th' fuck outta here, okay?'

Aster looked at me, stunned, and I felt a pang of guilt. It wasn't *her* fault that I was a complete fuck up, or had been harassed by that wretched ghoul, or that I had gorged myself on that bottle of scotch. I opened my mouth to apologise but snapped it shut. What was the point? I'd just make things worse. Instead, I simply uttered a frustrated grunt, shook my head, and stormed back to my room in disgrace.

5. *Aster at Breakfast*

I left LaVey's office and was about to head back to my room when a loud clatter from the dining room caught my attention, and I turned to see it was…Brandis, I think LaVey said his name was. Something appeared to have spooked him, or he could have tripped over something I didn't see. Either way, I called out to see if he was all right. He must have just gotten out of bed: his hair was a dishevelled mess, and he was sporting a simple white t-shirt, black tracksuit bottoms, and worn-out tennis shoes. He must not have heard me, as he took a seat and started sipping at his drink.

I tried making small talk, but either he wasn't in the mood or was still waking up and needed a coffee fix before getting started for the day. Picking up a squidgy cake peppered with small holes, I took a bite and couldn't help but scrunch my face in disgust.

'I mean, what is this? It's like a cake, maybe? It's very dry and a bit chewy…'

Brandis muttered a response about it being a crumpet and that I'd need to toast it and add something called "marm'laid" to it, whatever the hell that was. Must be some British delicacy.

'It needs to be toasted? Like…grilled?' I loaded the crumpet into the toaster. 'What'd you say it was called? Marm'laid? What's that?'

He did not look amused by my question and I felt my cheeks flush in embarrassment. Turning away, I muttered an apology. Brandis explained to me what it was ('it's like jam…should be in an orange jar somewhere over there'). I found the jar he was referring to; it just looked like orange jam to me. What was so special about marm'laid? I stuck my finger into the jar and popped some of the sticky concoction into my mouth. The taste that hit me was unlike anything I had ever experienced before.

'Oh. My. Lawd!' I exclaimed with the giddiness of a child. I added this wonderfulness to my now toasted crumpet and took a bite. It was like tasting a slice of heaven. Taking a seat across from Brandis, I attempted small talk once more; he seemed more awake now after finishing a cup of coffee. Usually, I was not a fan of making chit-chat with strangers, but the conversation with Walter had left me a bit on edge, and whenever I got nervous, I started chattering away like a drunk. As I babbled away about Rhiannon and LaVey being wonderful and about wanting to get to know Brandis better, I hadn't noticed that he was trying to interject himself into the conversation. The floodgates had already been opened and even though I could see when I glanced up that he was not amused, I kept talking, thinking this would solve the issue. It never did, but I seemed unable to stop. The moment I mentioned my fiancé, however, Brandis slammed a palm onto the table and snapped in an irritated huff. As he went off on one, all I could do was stare at him with wide eyes. I hadn't meant to aggravate him.

'…and get the fuck outta here, okay?'

I tried opening my mouth or reacting, but nothing came out; the only thing I could do was stare at him, his face immediately flickering to an expression of guilt. He opened his mouth to say something, but snapped it back shut before storming out of the room.

I sat there, my crumpet forgotten. If I had known he was in a foul mood, I would have left him to his thoughts. Stupid me. *Not everyone wants to be friends*, my inner voice reminded me. Tears fell from my eyes as I stood up and made my way out of the room, up the two flights of stairs, and back to my bedroom. Quietly shutting the door, I plugged the adapter into the closest outlet and hooked up my laptop. I set to work on my story, but nothing was coming to me. I was still worked up from my conversation with Walter and Brandis going off on me. I was suddenly overcome by a wave of nausea, and I rushed to the bathroom to spew out a sudden burst of bile. *Must be due to not eating much in the last twenty-four hours*, I thought. It wasn't uncommon for me to get sick when under significant stress.

Fifteen minutes later, I crawled out of the bathroom and instead of going to the armchair to work on my piece for Mr. LaVey, I climbed into the comfortable bed and wrapped myself in the comforter. There was still a bit of nausea, so I popped a couple of ibuprofen and focused on my breathing.

'I need to write, but five more minutes won't hurt,' I said, trying to ease the guilt that was consuming me. At least I had an idea for a story: mysterious events plaguing a tiny town, and the police being clueless as to how to help. I thought it would be fun to name the town after a neighbouring town to my own as a nice throwback to the area I grew up in.

My eyes were getting heavy, and I repositioned myself onto my side. It was so comfortable here. I would get started soon enough. I just needed a little nap first to calm myself down and forget about Walter and Brandis.

'Men are such assholes.'

6. *Mikhail's Scheme*

When Mikhail snorted awake, he could still hear Luka's cries ringing in his ears. The nightmare had been so much more intense compared to the one he had suffered on the plane ride.

He had been in an infinite void of swirling mist, a child's footsteps echoing around him. Sure that they must be Luka's, he had given chase, only to find the ground slimy and sticky with blood. Try as he might, he only succeeded in slipping deeper into the quagmire, all while Luka screamed for his father. The last thing he had seen was the glistening reflection of a knife and then he had tumbled painfully to the hard floor of LaVey's study.

Mikhail muttered a curse and absently slapped at his aching thigh. He stretched, yawning, as the mid-morning sun pierced through the smeared windows. The fireplace was long dead, and the room was empty. He vaguely recalled that he had lounged on the sofa, sipping his Beluga and analysing LaVey's guests with both scrutiny and dismissal, until one by one they had retired for the evening, leaving him alone with his elderly host.

'You're quite the character, Mr. Орлов,' LaVey had commented; he had been sitting in a large armchair directly across from the flickering fireplace and watching Mikhail with eyes that seemed to glow with flames. *A trick of the light*, Mikhail had mentally shrugged. 'Of course, Pavel told me all about your…' LaVey paused and cast a curious eye over his guest. 'Your *quirks*, shall we say, but I find you can never really judge a person until you meet them face-to-face, don't you agree?'

Mikhail had jerked upright at the mention of Pavel's name and topped up his glass. He had wondered what stories his friend had told his host; Pavel did also have a tendency to be an idiot. "You are like chatterbox," Rodion had said when Pavel joined them for drinks one night. "Talk too much but say very little!"

'I shall retire to bed soon,' LaVey had continued, suddenly looking fatigued. 'But first, now that's it's just us and I can see your thoughts whirling away in that head of yours, tell me what you think of my guests.'

Was this a test? Mikhail thought, the alcohol fuelling his paranoia. *What if this whole thing is some big joke. Was Pavel trying to rub it in by having me surrounded by the ignorant and foolhardy and tricked into being kicked out?* The idea was ludicrous, of course. Pavel was well off but even he couldn't have organised such a journey just to play a joke on his friend when he was at his lowest.

Mikhail pulled out his pipe and filled it back up, dragging on it as he chose his words carefully. 'I am unimpressed,' he said bluntly, which caused no reaction from LaVey. 'This Rhiannon woman speaks with an impudent tongue; the Америкос is as ignorant as she is disrespectful; and as for that degenerate, Brandis…'

He could have gone on but chose to hold his tongue. The redhead, Rhiannon, wasn't much to look at; she carried herself with an irritable arrogance and he doubted if she could relate to losing a child, much less being forced out of her home. He had delighted in teasing her with his native tongue but had struggled to pierce her thick accent. In fact, each of his peers had an odd brogue that he found incredibly irksome. Still, his surprise to learn of her name was almost as great as his disgust in her taste in alcohol. Although he largely avoided social media on principle, Pavel had insisted that he have some online presence and Mikhail had seen Rhiannon's sponsored ads appear from time to time. Not only that, he had been reading *From Within* at the library just the other week and, as much as he hated to admit it, she had talent and was clearly a better writer than she was a conversationalist.

Equally, he had been grateful when the dishevelled Brandis had slipped away before the night's conversation could really get under way. Mikhail had been vexed at the boy's assumption that he was a mere *слуга* and insulted at his unkempt appearance. He was just like all of these ignorant Westerners, apathetic with the spoils and charity of his country, and Mikhail had struggled to not simply drive his fist into the boy's smirking, puzzled face.

Mikhail had kept all of this from LaVey and had simply sat, seething quietly, and puffed away on his pipe. Still, the old man seemed to read his thoughts, for he leaned back in his armchair and said: 'I find discord a veritable breeding ground for creativity. That, as much as your clear talent and my wish to extend my business further overseas, is the reason *you* are here.' LaVey had struggled to his feet, his gnarled hand gripping his cane as he mustered the strength to stand. 'You may not like your peers, my young friend, but consider this: each of them, even young Mr. Brandis, has far more publications under their belt than you.'

Mikhail had glared at that. *Fucking ignorant old bastard!* he thought, rage clawing under his skin. He saw himself knocking away the old man's cane and kicking at the decrepit fossil's body until he heard his ribs snap like dry twigs. 'I mean no disrespect, of course,' LaVey had said with a small wave of his hand that only riled Mikhail up further. Clearly, LaVey *had* meant to disrespect him, and he had invited him simply to sow dissension. 'And I have nothing but faith in you. *All* of you,' the old man added as he shuffled away. Before he left, he turned slightly over his shoulder and said: '*Спокойной ночи, Михаил Орлов.*' With that, LaVey had left Mikhail to his thoughts…and his drinking.

Now, his mind addled by his hangover, Mikhail felt nothing but disdain. Pavel may not have set him up to fail, but LaVey was clearly toying with him…with *all* of them. Mikhail considered telling the others but remembered the ignorant way they had addressed him and immediately dismissed the idea. Those *мудаков* didn't deserve his help, that much was clear, and he reminded himself that he didn't really need to be envious of them for none of them were as prepared as he.

A sly smile crossed Mikhail's face as he straightened his wrinkled clothes and slipped on his jacket. He spotted a brass key with a suit of armour etched into the head and recalled that LaVey had told him that the second-floor armour room was to be his quarters. Despite how poor his sleep had been, however, Mikhail had no desire to get comfortable just yet; his primary concern was eating, and *then* he would set himself up in his room.

* * *

Mikhail had actually been disappointed to find the small dining room empty, since he was itching to bombard someone with his contempt. By the looks of the chairs, someone had been in there, but there was still plenty of food left. Mikhail guzzled down some blood orange juice and quenched his hunger with a generous helping of scrambled eggs, black pudding, and grilled tomatoes.

He left his dirty cutlery and plates behind, grabbed his luggage from the study, and headed upstairs. As he passed by a window, he saw the fleeting shape of the redhead with the odd accent jogging through the dew-drenched grounds. *корова*, he thought with a glib sneer.

The bedroom was huge and full of little conveniences, including a small bar stocked with Beluga. He showered and then, with a thick towel wrapped around his waist, he unpacked, carefully folding and arranging his clothes on the hangers and in the drawers. He also found an ironing board and iron and made a mental note to smarten his attire before venturing out again. Unlike Brandis, Mikhail intended to make an impression at every opportunity. If LaVey had brought him there to cause friction, then he was going to do it in some style.

Mikhail grimaced at the sight of the huge, foreboding typewriter; it made the laptop Pavel had graciously furnished him with completely redundant and he questioned LaVey's reliance upon such antiquated resources. He muttered as he sipped from a fresh glass of vodka, swapped his towel for a long, thick bathrobe, and pulled out *Mara's Secret*. Mikhail tore up the first page; he then did the same to Sophia Novaskaya's acknowledgments and, since Sophia had neglected to put her name on every page, completely stripped her name from the piece.

Mikhail dropped the manuscript on the desk and swallowed the last of his drink, wiping a small trail from his chin with the back of his hand. Before he could start working, he would need to dispose of the evidence of his plagiarism. He slipped into a fresh pair of trousers, some comfortable moccasins, and a corduroy shirt and swept out of his bedroom with the crumpled pages in hand.

A strange sense of satisfaction crept through him as he bounded downstairs to the study to toss the incriminating papers into the smouldering remains of the fireplace. It was exhilarating snooping around knowing that neither Pavel, LaVey, or anyone else would realise that he had so completely fooled them. He would enjoy rubbing this in their faces. Let them think him a lackadaisical braggart; let them sweat and stress in their rooms desperately trying to claw together something worthwhile, all while he enjoyed the comforts of LaVey House. And if they should question or confront him, they would soon learn what Mikhail Orlov really thought of them and their so-called talents.

7. *Rhiannon in the Library*

Rhiannon clutched her notebook against her chest as she descended the huge staircase, her laptop bag slung over her right shoulder. The notebook was the primary tool that she always used at the very beginning of writing a brand new story. She couldn't just sit down and type away for hours on end, letting the words flow and lead her in different directions; she needed to plot and plan the story in black and white on an actual page in proper ink. She had her expensive ink pen in her pocket, the same one she had planned all of her novels with. It was her good luck charm. She never went anywhere without her pen and notebook because she never knew when the writing bug would strike, or when she'd be inspired by a random occurrence or a chance meeting, and she'd need to get it down on paper as soon as possible or else she was prone to forgetting it.

At the bottom of the stairs, she heard footsteps behind her. Whoever it was had most likely seen her. She didn't attempt to hide but she did mutter a few curse words silently to herself, annoyed that she'd have to engage in conversation. She just hoped that it wasn't Brandis (too boring) or Mikhail (too rude). She was pleasantly surprised to see it was Aster, her hair still a fluffy mess (though, maybe that was just her style). She wasn't wearing her signature glasses but was now dressed in much more appropriate attire: a maroon long-sleeved shirt with dark wash blue jeans, and black and white Converse trainers. She, also, was carrying a small, black laptop bag.

'Rhiannon! I'm so glad I ran into you.'

'Hi, it's Aster, right?'

'That's correct.'

Aster reached the bottom of the stairs and shook Rhiannon's hand, smiling politely.

'How are you settling in?' asked Rhiannon as she flicked her eyes to the hallway on the left, silently indicating that that's where she wanted to be.

'All right enough. This place is huge! Just taking a bit of time to explore before getting going on my piece for Mr. LaVey. Did I see you go for a run earlier?'

'Ah yeah, it's one of the first things I do when I get to a new place. It settles my nerves, and I like to explore.'

'I used to run as well, but after a bad knee injury I had to stop.' Aster paused for a moment, as if recalling a distant memory, before glancing back with a smile. 'What are the grounds like?'

'There's not much out there, really. This place is really run down on the outside. It's strange that the inside is so lavish.'

'That is strange, indeed. I was planning on going to explore the hedge maze that's out back at some point. I've never seen one before! Have you started writing yet?'

'No, not yet,' Rhiannon answered, wondering why she hadn't spotted a hedge maze earlier on her run. 'In fact, I'm on my way to find a secluded spot to begin now. How about you? Congratulations on your success with *ReSpawn,* by the way.'

'Thank you so much! I don't mean to be selfish, but have you heard of my other books as well?' she looked slightly embarrassed.

'Yeah, I've read a couple of your books actually. As I said I have your first book, *Only Come at Night,* on my bookshelf at home. It's one of my favourite horror stories.'

'Aw, thanks! *Only Come at Night* was honestly one of my favourites to write. I hope to be as successful and well-known as you someday,' she said, flashing Rhiannon a friendly smile.

'Thank you,' Rhiannon smiled, glad that there was someone actually worth speaking to in this house. 'I'm so sorry, but I really must get on and begin writing,' Rhiannon said as she inched away. In different circumstances, she would have been happy to talk more, maybe swap writing stories and share publishing tips, but she was on a mission to start writing and once she got it in her head that she was going to write, then nothing would stop her.

'Oh, of course,' said Aster. 'Hope we can catch up over a drink later.'

'That sounds perfect, actually. I'll see you later.'

'Catch you later.'

Aster turned to leave but a thought suddenly jumped into Rhiannon's head: 'You don't happen to know where the library is, do you? I'd like to check it out.'

Aster turned to her, a bewildered look on her face. 'Of course Mr. LaVey has a library. I bet it's massive with all kinds of first editions.'

'So, that's a no?'

'Unfortunately,' said Aster as she shook her head.

'No worries, thanks.'

Aster smiled as she walked towards the large study down the hall. Rhiannon sighed and straightened her laptop bag on her shoulder. Her next mission was to find the library. It would be the perfect place to begin writing, as long as no one else had claimed it first.

* * *

After searching for a good twenty minutes, Rhiannon had basically found every room on the ground floor except the library. She'd even seen Mikhail wandering about and had made a swift exit to avoid a confrontation. She was about to give up and go back and find the small sitting room she'd walked into earlier when she spotted a long corridor that she hadn't noticed before. She headed down it, quietly hoping that it would lead her somewhere different. Forget the hedge maze outside…this *house* was a maze.

The walls were extremely narrow and felt as if they were closing in around her. She knew old houses like this often had narrow corridors leading to different areas and she was right. Upon reaching the end of the constricted corridor she found herself in another large hallway with many doors leading from it.

Here we go again, she thought.

Rhiannon pushed the nearest door open. It was stiff and very heavy. In fact, it appeared that it hadn't been opened in a long time because thick grey cobwebs clung to the corners of the doorframe and around the handle. With one last shove the door creaked open and there it was: the library. Finally!

And what a library it was.

Rhiannon's mouth fell open in amazement and she trembled as she entered the enormous room. She was momentarily stunned by its sheer size and beauty. Thousands upon thousands of books adorned the walls on hundreds of wooden shelves, all of varying levels and lengths. They weren't new books either; they were ancient and degraded, covered in dust and decay. It was obvious that no one had set foot in this library in many years. The library reminded her of a particular scene from *Beauty and the Beast,* her favourite Disney film. There were old wooden ladders on rails that spanned the length of the shelves, some of which reached right up to the ceiling, easily twenty feet above her. Under her feet was a lavish, thick, blood-red carpet that had seen better days as it was torn and faded all over.

An enormous fireplace was situated at the far end of the room and two brown leather chesterfield armchairs sat on either side of it, both of which had also degraded over many years, especially on the arms and seat areas. Rhiannon shivered, suddenly realising that this room was freezing cold. It probably wasn't the best place to write, but she felt an overwhelming sense of familiarity within these walls lined with books. This was where all the forgotten stories were hidden, and it was the perfect place to bring a new story to life.

Ignoring the cold, she placed her bag and notebook on the floor next to one of the armchairs before wiping the dust off with the palm of her hand. She sneezed. Maybe later on she'd ask Mr. LaVey if the fire could be lit in here to make it a little cosier, although from the looks of the fireplace she reckoned it hadn't seen action in decades. Why would Mr. LaVey not want to use this room? It was morbidly fascinating.

Out of curiosity, she approached one of the nearest shelves and tilted her head to read some of the book titles. Shakespeare, Dante, Blake, Shelley, Dickins, and other copies of all the classics (no doubt first editions) lined the shelves alongside battered volumes of philosophy, encyclopaedias, meditations on the soul and evolution...and even books as black as charcoal whose spines were illegible. She was impressed with the range of books on display. There was even an entire shelf dedicated to different versions of the Bible, each one barely used but exceptionally old.

Her curiosity satisfied, Rhiannon sat in the musty armchair, which groaned under her light weight; the chair had likely not had someone sit in it for many a year. She opened her laptop, switched it on, and waited for it to spring to life. She had considered switching off all her devices, but a part of her that knew that she couldn't function without her phone (though she planned to do her best to ignore it).

Just to ensure her mind was clear of distractions, she quickly checked it – no signal. *Figures*, she thought. Not even one measly bar. She checked for a Wi-Fi connection, although she very much doubted that Mr. LaVey had splashed out on fibre-optic broadband in this place.

No connections at all.

Rhiannon sighed and switched off her phone. It looked like she was going cold turkey on all her devices after all.

Once her laptop was finally up and running, she quickly checked her emails out of habit and cursed herself out loud for her mistake: 'Fook.' She scanned a few old emails. There were a couple of junk ones which she deleted immediately, an email from her agent regarding their upcoming meeting next week, and one from her ex-husband, which she had purposefully ignored when she'd received it yesterday. Her stomach performed an unnatural lurch when she saw his name: David Evans. She'd barely spoken to him in years, only ever exchanging very short and boring emails (she hadn't given him her new phone number), which were usually to do with their grown-up daughter Sioned.

Rhiannon's finger hovered over the email for a few seconds, contemplating her next move. The subject line read: *We Need To Talk*.

That was never a good sign, so she chose to ignore it and closed her laptop. It was time to write, and she wasn't going to let her ex-husband ruin her writing flow, like he had done so many times during their marriage.

The light in the room was very dim. The weather outside had turned overcast, and a downpour seemed imminent. It certainly wasn't the cosiest of rooms to set herself up in, but she felt strangely at home among the books. They seemed to call out to her.

With the laptop now off and on the floor, she took out her notebook and pen and laid them across her lap and waited for the creative juices to begin to flow…

But it never worked quite that way.

Her mind drifted to her daughter and the last time she'd seen her. Three years was a long time to be apart from someone whom she loved with all her heart. Sioned was twenty-three now, a grown woman with a life of her own, possibly a boyfriend and a career that she'd never heard about.

Rhiannon had become a mother at age seventeen. She hadn't been ready, but David had stood by her only for the sake of their daughter. A year later they'd been married, but eventually Rhiannon had reached the end of her tether; fed up with David's affairs and his lies, she had left him.

That was ten years ago, and she'd been single ever since, but at least her writing career had evolved and given her the life she'd always craved. Unfortunately, Sioned had turned to drugs and alcohol somewhere in her late teenage years and at age twenty she'd almost overdosed, leaving Rhiannon to nurse her back to health. Rhiannon had given her money to get her back on her feet, offered to pay for her rehab, but Sioned had taken off with the money and severed all contact. David was in contact with her now and thankfully kept her up to date on their daughter's life. She was doing much better, but apparently Sioned blamed her mother for her addiction, because she'd left her father and torn their family apart.

Rhiannon was suddenly startled by a loud scream that seemed to emanate from the walls, snapping her out of her thoughts of her family troubles. She was grateful because no good story came from dwelling too much about a dark past...or did it?

* * *

Rhiannon had scribbled away for an hour and all she'd come up with were a few character names: Owen, Ceris, and Gethin. They were all Welsh names, of course. She had a vague idea that she wanted to write about the little Welsh village she grew up in, or maybe not the exact village, but the one that was only a few miles away from where she'd lived. Names were important to her, and she always tried to give her character's names which meant something, or at least the main character.

Owen.

She'd not thought about him properly for a while, but for some reason he'd popped into her head during her miserable drive. He'd been her childhood crush many years ago. She could still see his handsome face so clearly in her mind; he'd been tall...very tall, well over six foot even as a teenager. She smiled as she rested her head against the soft leather of the chair and recalled the memory of their first kiss while they'd been exploring the local graveyard. It had been magical, if slightly awkward and embarrassing, but it had stayed with her ever since.

Owen was dead now. He'd fallen to his death climbing down into a local mine, but his body hadn't been found for nearly six months. He had been there alone (for what reason she didn't know) and he'd entered a restricted section where there were loose rocks and steep drop offs. A tour guide had found him, and it had been the talk of the village for weeks, months, years even. After Owen had disappeared, everyone thought he'd run away; even Rhiannon. She'd blamed herself that maybe he was trying to run away from her, that she'd done something wrong and pushed him away.

Rhiannon suddenly felt a surge of inspiration and began to scribble some bullet points and notes on the page:

Graveyard, Owen, the devil, death…

The air in the library turned icy cold, even colder than it had been when she'd first arrived; she shivered and looked up from her notebook. She could see her breath dancing in front of her, swirling up towards the ceiling. The temperature had definitely dropped several degrees in the space of a few seconds. It felt…unsettling.

I could really use a roaring fire right about now, she thought.

A loud crack echoed around the room, causing her to jump in her chair and emit a small shriek. She wasn't usually the jumpy type, but it had been so sudden and so loud that her body had reacted instinctively. She couldn't even work out where it had originated. The sound had filled the room, spiralling from every corner. The shelves shuddered and layers of dust floated to the floor.

What the fook…

Without warning, a flume of fire erupted from the fireplace and her chair tumbled backwards. Rhiannon's head thumped hard against the floor. Before she could regain her composure and figure out what the hell had just happened, she was forcibly dragged to the ceiling. She slammed into ornate plaster with a loud thud and the air was expelled from her lungs. Her arms and legs were pulled tight in different directions as an invisible force held her against gravity.

She opened her mouth to scream, but no sound came out. It felt like a hand was covering her mouth, snuffing out any sound she dared to make. The flames were still burning hot below her, billowing out of the fireplace in huge waves and engulfing the entire area, and she was completely helpless. A massive gust of wind came from nowhere and hurtled around the library, pouring books off the shelves like a cascading waterfall. They tumbled to the floor, sending up clouds of grey dust. Piles of books and shredded paper of varying colours and sizes all littered the floor so that not a single shade of red from the thick carpet was visible.

The library abruptly fell silent, as if someone had flipped a switch. Rhiannon trembled involuntarily, tears streaming from her eyes as she waited for something else to happen. She was still being held in suspension on the ceiling but now everything was quiet, and the fear of the unknown filled her with dread.

Minutes ticked by…

Minutes of nothing but silence…the vice-like, cold hand still gripping her mouth closed.

Then…the wind started blowing violently again, books were tossed at the walls, the chairs span in circles, and Rhiannon's clothes were ripped from her body as if they were mere tissue paper. The invisible hand stifled her screams as she was stripped completely naked, her clothes falling in shreds to the floor.

The pain began as an invisible assailant pummelled her body over and over. No blood was drawn, but she felt every single blow with mind-numbing clarity. She didn't know how long it lasted, but to her it felt like an eternity as unseen hands violated every part of her body. A memory suddenly flooded her thoughts, powerful and vivid...

David had her pinned down, heaving and insistent, as though he couldn't hear her agonised cries. He'd taken her, defiling her against her will, more focused on his own gratification than her feelings...or dignity.

Beneath her, the library was being demolished but Rhiannon couldn't even close her eyes. Even when the noise and wind finally died down, her bare, trembling body remained pinned to the ceiling. As quickly as it had begun, everything started to reverse itself. The pain in her body vanished and her clothes floated up and magically mended themselves as they covered her body once more. The torn books were repaired before her eyes, taking up their usual residence on the shelves. The chairs stopped spinning and came to a halt in front of the fire, which died down and the room became icy once again.

Rhiannon felt the invisible force relinquish its control and slowly dropped her down to the floor. Her legs were too weak to hold her upright and she collapsed in a heap, shivering uncontrollably.

Chapter Four

Tuesday

1. Rhiannon's Painful Memory

Rhiannon laid helpless on the floor in a foetal position, not daring to move for fear of *whatever it was* happening again. Even now, she could scarcely believe what had happened. *Maybe I dreamt it*, she thought without much conviction. She hadn't been hurt and her clothes were intact, and even the library had returned to the way it was when she'd entered…but it had *felt* real. She'd felt a cold, strong hand covering her mouth and muffling her screams, and her clothes being ripped away, and her body being pummelled and violated. It had been real…*it had been real.*

Minutes ticked by before she was finally able to stop shaking enough to sit up and take in her surroundings. Her mouth felt like sandpaper and every breath caused her to wince in pain. She was desperate to get out of there, but her brain and legs refused to co-operate and didn't seem to be connected to each other properly. A combination of shock and fear forced her to stay put and caused an unwanted, horrible memory from her past to lodge itself in her mind…

* * *

Rhiannon and David were arguing again. It was a daily occurrence now, but then he was determined to drink every day and not lift a finger when it came to the housework, so she thought she was well within her rights to confront him on it. David didn't see it that way, though. He made the majority of the money that was keeping them living in relative luxury, so he didn't see it as his job to do menial household chores.

'Maybe if you actually got a proper job and helped with the income, we could afford a cleaner! Then you wouldn't have to do it,' shouted David as he took another swig from his bottle of beer.

Rhiannon hated when he talked badly about her writing career. She'd written two successful horror novels that had both been best sellers (if only for a few weeks) with professional publishing houses, and she'd just signed a contract with her agent and a new publisher for another six books. Her career was taking off, but David didn't see it.

'Writing is a proper job, David,' said Rhiannon quietly, more to herself than to him, but he still heard it.

'Oh yeah? Then where's the money? What you spent it on now? How come I don't see no fucking money?'

'I used it all to pay off your gambling debts, if you must know, so now at least we're in the clear.'

Rhiannon watched her husband's eyes light up at this statement and a smirk of a grin spread across his face. His whole manner changed in an instant. Setting down his bottle, he staggered towards her and brushed a strand of her auburn hair out of her eyes. She suppressed a shudder at his touch; she was no longer aroused by his caress but disgusted by it. She didn't know the exact moment she'd stopped loving him, but it had been a long time ago.

'I knew I married ya for a reason,' he whispered in her ear. David drunkenly began to grope his wife's body, kissing her neck and grinding himself up against her.

'No, David. I don't want…'

'Course ya want it.'

'No. Please stop it. I don't…'

David pulled away and slapped her hard across the cheek. 'Don't say no to me, bitch!'

Rhiannon grasped her flaming hot face, but he was upon her before she could react. His body was hot and heavy as he pinned her to the floor with his weight. Her breath was expelled from her lungs as her husband yanked up her skirt, his rough, callused hands grabbing at anything he could. Her underwear was ripped away, and he punched her again, this time in the stomach. She automatically curled into a ball to try and shield herself, but David easily flipped her over onto her stomach and pressed her face to the floor while he defiled and humiliated her, taking her as hard and as fast as he could. Rhiannon could barely let out a horrified cry as tears streamed down her cheeks and soaked into the carpet.

When it was over, Rhiannon laid trembling on the floor while David stood up and sorted himself out.

'Now,' he said. 'How much money you got left?'

Rhiannon shook her head as she attempted to cover her modesty. Her clothes had been torn away and left in tatters on the floor.

'I…I don't…' she began.

'You don't what?'

'I…don't think there's any left. I was going to put some in Sioned's savings account.'

'Don't bother. She don't need it.'

With that, David exited the room, leaving his wife to cry for three hours. When she finally peeled herself off the floor, Rhiannon decided that she was leaving him. She loved her daughter, but she knew she could never tell her the truth of what her father had done. It was Rhiannon's burden to bear.

* * *

After she finally left the library, Rhiannon struggled to remember the way she'd come. Every corridor and every door looked the same, her legs were wobbly, and she felt sick to her stomach as she clutched whatever stable surface she could find for support as her laptop bag dragged across the floor behind her. She didn't have the strength or will to pick it up properly. She was consumed by the need to get back to her room before she ran into anyone; she couldn't face a confrontation with Mr. LaVey or any of the other writers. What would they think of her in this state? It wasn't like she could tell them of her brutal attack, and there was no physical injuries or evidence to back up her claim, which either made her a complete liar or a delusional crazy person.

After what felt like an eternity, she finally stumbled back to her room in utter relief. The fire was lit (she had assumed this was Mr. LaVey's doing) and bathed the room with a warm, ambient glow. Rhiannon slammed the heavy door shut and locked it by sliding the huge iron bolt across, fixing it in place before tearing off her clothes and inspecting her bare body in front of the fire. There was not a single mark on her apart from a tiny bruise on her shin, which she knew was from accidentally running into her coffee table in her haste to leave for her journey. That seemed like a lifetime ago now. This house, she felt, had a way of swallowing time as if it were merely a drop of water in a bucket. She could barely remember what day it was. What was the time? Realising she didn't care, Rhiannon crawled under the thick blankets of the extravagant bed and pulled them over her head, shielding herself from reality.

* * *

An hour passed. Then two, then twelve, and finally twenty-four as Monday bled into Tuesday.

Rhiannon eventually woke to hear a loud banging echoing around the room. Her head thumped with such pain she thought for a moment that she must be severely hungover again, but then the horror of the library incident came flooding back, sending almighty shivers up and down her spine. Her mouth was dry and her stomach achingly empty.

A light rapping came at the door, and she whipped her head around in a confused panic. 'Hullo?' came a faint voice. 'Are you in there, Ms. Hughes?'

Mr. LaVey's dulcet tones seemed to surround her. It was as if he was standing right next to her... Rhiannon sharply pulled back the covers, but to her relief found no creepy old man standing beside her bed.

The rapping came again, louder now; the old man must have switched from using his knuckles to his cane. 'Ms. Hughes? Hullo? Would you be so kind as to open the door?'

Rhiannon grabbed the thick blanket and used it to cover her naked body before stumbling towards the heavy door. Her legs were barely strong enough to support her weight, but she managed to open the door a crack and peered out at Mr. LaVey.

'Ah, there you are!' The old man was resting on his cane with one gnarled hand while holding a rusty old oil lantern in the other. A look that was equal parts concern and affection seemed to wash over his features. 'We've been most worried about you, m'dear. You missed a most delectable dinner last night; pan-roasted duck, don't you know.'

'Last night? What day is it?'

'Why it's Tuesday, m'dear. Have you misplaced a day somewhere? Why don't you come downstairs for some food? It's quite wonderful.'

'Uh, yeah, I'm not hungry.' That wasn't true, of course. She hadn't eaten since…she couldn't even remember. It was Tuesday? She must have been asleep for nearly a whole day.

'It doesn't do t'miss a meal, m'dear,' Mr. LaVey cautioned in a grandfatherly tone. 'Also, I'm not as young as I once was, believe it or not, and can't be traipsing around looking for runaways,' he sighed with a small shake of his head. 'Would you like me t'have something brought to you instead?'

'Yes please, if it's not too much trouble,' she squeaked. Her voice was weak, and she was beginning to shake again.

Mr. LaVey seemed to notice; he frowned and switched the lantern to his cane hand so he could tentatively reach out for her, but Rhiannon quickly flinched away.

'I hope you don't mind my being candid, m'dear, but you look awfully pale. Should I call a doctor? Loomis might be a left-wing braggart, but he does wonders for my rheumatism.'

'Fook no!' she said quickly. 'I'm fine…honestly…just…I think I'll stay in ma room for a bit to work on my writing.'

Mr. LaVey switched the lantern back to his free hand and held it up with a slight wince to get a better look at her face. Rhiannon squinted from the burning light and was grateful when he finally lowered it.

'As you wish,' he said, seemingly satisfied. 'I trust your writing is going well? Again, to be candid, I was of two minds about offerin' such freedom t'you all, but…'tis for the best. We don't get many freedoms in this world, after all, and it's best to cling t'those we *do* have.' He regarded her with a strange, vacant look. 'I know you understand. I'll bring you some refreshments anon and do let me know if you need anything more.'

Rhiannon watched intently as the old man turned and slowly walked down the long corridor. It was nice of him to have checked up on her, she thought, but the man gave her the creeps. There was something in his mannerism that made her feel uneasy, and despite his gentle and welcoming intentions she didn't trust him, nor did she particularly like him.

* * *

Mr. LaVey made good on his word and, upon exiting the shower, Rhiannon found a lavish spread of culinary delights laid out on her bed: pastries, pots of tea and coffee, bread, jams, cured meats, and cheese.

Rhiannon devoured it all, only pausing when she realised that somehow the old man had been in her room to leave this all here, but how? She'd bolted the door when she'd said goodbye to him. Was there a secret door into this room that she didn't know about? Now that she thought about it, she still hadn't seen any staff or helpers around the estate since she'd arrived. Surely, the elderly man hadn't prepared all this by himself...also the fire was fully stoked again and piled high with new logs, filling the space with warmth and the unmistakable aroma of burning wood.

Rhiannon shuddered again. She didn't feel safe and was now beginning to think that coming here hadn't been such a good idea after all. She was clearly losing her mind and becoming paranoid, and the sooner she left the better she knew she'd feel, but the only way she could do that was to hurry up and finish her anthology piece, so that was what she was going to do.

2. *Mikhail's Recurring Nightmare*

It is truly my finest work, Mikhail heard himself thinking. Sure, Kirill was a thinly veiled facsimile of his father (they shared temperaments and first names, and many physical characteristics, but Mikhail cared little for this considering his father, the *real* Kirill, was long in his grave) and he had taken some creative liberties with the ruble crisis, but that was all part of the process.

The part that recognised that this was a dream noticed that the computer monitor was completely blank except for a turquoise glow, that the small study in the old family home wasn't quite as it had been and seemed to bleed in and out of reality as elements of his grotty little apartment in Voronezh seeped in, and the Cyrillic of his keyboard floated like an ethereal mist.

His dream-self was completely oblivious to any of this, however. *Finally, my long toil is over.* His dream-self's thoughts were like distant memories, and Mikhail could only watch as his broad-shouldered form shuffled the printed pages into a neat stack with a relieved pride.

It was a good memory, if skewed from reality. For starters, he had completed the final draft of *Смертельное Желание* in the dead of a bitter winter night, wrapped up in blankets as the smouldering flames of his old wood-burning fire bathed the room with heat. His dream-self had finished up on a bright summer's day. Mikhail saw a forest of rowan trees stretching across verdant fields just outside of the patio windows, two things that told him where he really was (besides in a dream): the old family home, just outside of Kolomenskoye.

Хорошо ли это, nana? Mikhail's heart broke as Luka's small, chubby form pattered across the bare floorboards towards his dream-self. The boy was clutching that same old tattered rabbit he loved to carry everywhere, and his brown-blond hair hung over his wide, doe-like eyes.

It is my masterpiece! his dream-self declared, scooping the boy up with his strong, thick arms. Luka giggled with glee as he was whirled around in a circle. Mikhail, growing more conscious with every second, envied the happiness of this distorted memory; he could almost *smell* Luka's hair, and the loss he felt drove him into a frenzy.

Mikhail mentally pounded his fists against the invisible cage he was trapped in. While he could no more interact with this dream world than he could capture the sun, he noticed his dream-self look around sharply, as if hearing a distant noise. Mikhail suddenly found himself not trapped within a prison of the mind, but in his own body! He now inhabited his dream-self, but was merely a passenger, unable to keep him from stepping away from his son to investigate the noise. *No, you fool!* Mikhail mentally screamed. What he wouldn't give for one more moment with his son and this fool was ignoring the boy!

Папа...?

Mikhail's dream-self turned to reassure the boy, his son...and he felt an awesome wave of terror rush through his body. *No!* he screamed soundlessly. *No, no! Not again!*

Dark, viscous blood bubbled from Luka's small, pale lips. His eyes, once so wide and innocent, were blemished with a creamy translucency and robbed of all their vigour. The skin on his face was cracked and peeling, like a porcelain doll haphazardly pieced back together, and his hair was plastered to his head in matted clumps.

Ilana? the boy mouthed and reached for his father; Mikhail wept as the boy's fingers crumbled to dust. *It hurts...* Luka wailed as his tiny body shrivelled from the inside out until all that remained was a dirty, ragged pile of clothes where a sweet, harmless little boy had once stood.

Luka! Mikhail's dream-self fell to his knees and grasped pitifully at the boy's remains, which slipped through his fingers like water. *Just a dream!* Mikhail screamed. *A dream! It's just a dream!* His dream-self wept uncontrollably, oblivious to the pleading screams coming from the back of his mind.

Mikhail felt himself clawing and thrashing as he frantically tried to wake himself, but it was as though his mind delighted in tormenting him with this twisted version of the past.

Urk! his dream-self gagged as a heavy, piercing weight stabbed into his back. Mikhail felt himself collapse, numb from the waist below, and frozen to the core. Black spots danced before his eyes as he finally, gratefully, drifted awake, but a slender form in a long, eggshell-blue dress held him firmly in the nightmare for a few more agonising moments.

Lia... he whispered. She looked just as she had that day. Her hair was wet and ragged, as though she had torn great chunks out of it; her hands were seeping sickening pus from the gaping wounds where her nails had once been. A slash, cruel and deep, ran diagonally across her face, causing tears of blood to run down her cheeks. Her lips were bruised and puffy, and dark purple-red blisters and bruises were around her misshapen neck.

She held a long, sharp knife that dripped with his life's blood; it quivered in her grip as her spindly, corpse-like arms struggled to hold it over his mangled, feeble, dying form. *Just a dream*, he yammered, icy dread clutching at his skin. *Just a dream…*

Lia hissed and darted at his face, knife at the ready, and Mikhail's eyes finally snapped open to behold a strange bedroom shrouded in darkness.

Mikhail clutched at the thick duvet that surrounded him as his fear-addled brain caught him up to speed with his surroundings. He was in one of LaVey's luxurious bedrooms in a part of the world that was alien to him, far from anything and anyone he had ever known and loved. Lia was gone…Luka was gone…and dreams were harmless.

And yet he dared not turn over lest he spy Lia's mutilated corpse lying beside him; he dared not keep his eyes open a second longer, lest Luka's quivering hand settle over his; and he dared not turn on the light lest the shadows be angered. Instead, he simply laid there, huddled under the sheets, with his eyes clamped tightly shut, whimpering as Lia's words pierced his brain like needles.

Ты не отбираешь его у меня! she'd screamed, her words hot and black and choking. *You're not taking him from me!*

* * *

After what felt like many torturous hours, Mikhail felt the warm glow of the sun's rays and lurched out of bed to bask in their calming radiance. He found himself grateful even for the dismal British weather (it was constantly dreary, overcast, and rainy), and he spent a good fifteen minutes enjoying a hot shower before finally leaving his bedroom.

LaVey House was even bigger than he had first assumed. Its twisting, narrow hallways seemed to go on forever and held many locked doors, bedrooms, or rooms whose functions had long since been laid to rest. *It is impossible that the old man survives here alone*, Mikhail thought stubbornly as he toured the first-floor corridors. Despite feeling famished, he decided against breakfast and had only barely gotten dressed before leaving his room and wandering around like a zombie in a long, warm dressing gown and thick slipper boots, his pipe firmly clamped between his teeth.

The architecture and construction of LaVey's estate fascinated him. There seemed to be little rhyme or reason to its furnishings and barely anything resembling an overarching aesthetic theme beyond "Gothic" and "antiquated". He told himself that he was searching for treasures to sell for an additional profit (LaVey certainly made no attempts to hide his finest silverware and expensive-looking ornaments), but he knew, deep down, what he was really doing...

'Hiding?'

'Блять!' Mikhail hollered, spooked. He whirled around, his dressing gown flapping open to reveal his striped pyjamas, prepared to launch into a verbal tirade...only to find LaVey standing in the doorway.

'Give you a little fright, did I?' LaVey chuckled, the sound doing little to quell Mikhail's anger. 'I was simply enquiring what you were doing hiding up here in the old drawing room?'

Mikhail lowered his balled fist and hissed a curse; his host may be eccentric, but he had no desire to cheat himself out of the money he was due. Begrudgingly, he wrapped his dressing gown around his tense body and folded his arms across his broad chest.

'I was merely seeking…inspiration.'

LaVey stepped into the magnificently ornate room, his buckled boots padding softly over the gold and ochre rug that dominated the floor space. 'You'll find plenty of that in here, my friend,' he said, shuffling past three cream-white cushioned chairs arranged around a glass table and sitting before a piano that had probably once been bone-white but was now stained yellow and caked in dust.

The old man tapped his fingers softly to the keyboard and Mikhail watched him curiously. 'Tchaikovsky,' he muttered after a few strokes. Another coincidence, like the Beluga? Or did LaVey know of Lia's appreciation for the classics?

'My father…well, my *grandfather*, as well…would entertain the social elite right here, at this very piano,' LaVey mused as he played. The piano was off-key, but the music was still soothing (if a little disconcerting). 'I used to sit right over there…' LaVey gave a gentle nod towards two faded, tattered crimson chairs that sat before a long-dead fireplace. A large, dust and cobweb-encrusted mirror hung above it and Mikhail turned away from his dishevelled appearance. 'Just…listening,' LaVey continued, 'as the adults talked business, or politics. Not really understanding, of course, but attentive, nonetheless.'

'It is…' Mikhail struggled for the right response, '…a beautiful room.'

A mischievous smirk wrinkled LaVey's features. 'Don't stand in ceremony on my account, Mr. Орлов. I know the old homestead's not what it once was.' He stopped playing and shifted to face the large Russian with a wince. *Arthritis, most likely*, Mikhail thought without much interest. 'But you'll come to find that even relics have their uses.'

'I should go get dressed for the day,' Mikhail murmured after an awkward silence.

LaVey stopped him before he was even halfway across the room with a simple query: 'Bad dreams?'

Ты никогда не заберёшь его у меня!

Mikhail scowled. Had LaVey heard him in the night? He didn't recall making any noise (Lia had always marvelled at how deep he slept: "I sometimes have to poke you just to be sure you're still breathing!" she'd once laughed), but, then again, he wasn't used to being tormented by such vivid nightmares.

You'll never take him from me!

'*I* used to have them when I grew up here,' LaVey continued, gazing out of the window. He seemed transfixed by the topiary animals that guarded the large hedge maze out amongst the overgrown wildness of his grounds. 'Every night of my childhood. Vivid, intense nightmares that left me trembling in my bed. It didn't matter which room I slept in, or how many spoonfuls of brandy my father forced down my throat, the nightmares would persist.'

LaVey gave Mikhail an apologetic look. 'You'll have to forgive the rantings of an old man, I'm afraid,' he struggled to his feet and Mikhail noticed for the first time that the old man was walking without his cane. 'Frankly, it was a blessing when my parents shipped me off to boarding school out in the city. I slept like a babe every night I was there and, by the time I returned home, I had long outgrown such foibles.'

Mikhail pressed his lips together and fumed silently. He was tired, hungry, and aching for a drop of alcohol, and now his decrepit host was accusing him of being a child! He had half a mind to demand a higher fee as compensation for such insolence and disregard.

'Houses have a way of...remembering things,' LaVey continued undeterred. He had his back to Mikhail, and the seething Russian remarked how easy it would be to strike the old man from behind and explain it away as a bad fall. 'I always felt at home here, despite those bad dreams, *heh*. And whenever I came back, it was as though I was returning to a part of myself I had long forgotten. Perhaps *you* understand that in a way the others don't, perchance?'

Mikhail found himself growing tired of the old man's riddles and games but controlled himself enough to mutter: 'I have no bad dreams.'

'Of course, of course.' LaVey nodded as though he had expected nothing less. 'Do let me know if you do; I would very much like to hear about them.'

With that, the old man shuffled out of the drawing room and left Mikhail standing there in his dressing gown and pyjamas, more confused than ever. '*Сволочь*,' he growled. Maybe he would switch rooms tonight to avoid having LaVey hovering outside his door, as he had clearly done last night, or maybe he would find the old man's room and show *him* what it felt like to have his sleep listened in on.

Mikhail's stomach gurgled painfully, and he decided that, for now, he would console himself by taking advantage of the old man's hospitality once more. He even decided to stay in his night clothes just to see how the others would react so he could give them a piece of his mind.

3. *Aster Follows the Light*

The sound of glass breaking woke me, and my eyes burst open in the darkness. Terror seized me and I buried myself under the duvet. *Fuck. What was that?* I remained as still as possible, straining to hear any more unusual sounds. *Yes, hide under the duvet. If there's a serial murderer out there, you're making it too easy for them.* I did have to agree; hiding in bed was not a great idea. As silently as I could, I pulled the covers back and slipped out of bed.

'Are you sure you didn't dream that?' I quickly scoffed at my question. 'Of course I didn't. That sounded too real, but…I am a little curious where it came from. It can't be too far from my room if I could hear it that well.'

Well, are you going to go investigate, or just make sure the lock on your door is done so no one can come murder you while you sleep?

I rolled my eyes. 'This is nuts. I'm going to go back to sleep for a little longer—'

The sound of glass breaking a second time stopped me mid-sentence. 'Okay, I definitely didn't imagine that…but I'm not brave enough to go check it out.'

I locked both sets of locks and double-checked them before hurrying back to bed and pulling the covers over my head so I could fall back asleep. *There. Now they'd have to climb up three stories and break their hand trying to bust through this door.*

Thirty minutes passed, but still sleep eluded me. I tried to get myself under control; those sounds had scared me, but I was safe now…I had locked the main way in or out of my room and there was nothing to be afraid of. I'm sure that if I asked Mr. LaVey about it, he would explain that...

A flicker of light in the corner of my eye caught my attention. 'Hm? What was that?' I turned to see the large window on the far wall, its curtains mostly drawn. I stared at them to make sure, blinking a few times. I was just chalking it up to my fatigue when it suddenly reappeared, but this time it was closer and brighter. It didn't scare me, though. Rather, I was intrigued by what I saw. 'What the fuck?'

Flinging the covers aside, my feet hit the plush carpet and I approached the window. Throwing the curtain back, I stared out at the curious structure that had captured my imagination since arriving. It was made entirely of long, wide shrubbery and hedges, and was beautiful. I had never heard of a hedge maze, much less seen one, before coming to LaVey House and now I was curious to go check it out.

Or you could wait until morning, like a sane person?

'No. My curiosity is getting the better of me.'

And what about the noises you heard? Are you going to dismiss the fear you were just feeling?

'This light is calling to me.'

You're such an idiot. This is what all the heroines in books and movies end up falling for...and do you know what usually happens to them?

Ignoring my logic, I pulled my boots on and threw on my coat before making my way back to the door. Unlocking it and slowly pushing it open, the hallway was pitch black. Flicking on my phone's light, I shone it down the wall, making my way towards the direction of the staircase. I would be lying if I said there wasn't any fear lingering in me. I kept peeking over my shoulder to be sure I wasn't being followed; but I'm sure I would have heard them before I'd see anything, even with my flashlight. The thing about old houses—even with work done to them—was that there were always spots that creaked or were extra loud when walking over them.

'Ms. Callahan, what are you doing up?' a voice said from the darkness to my right. Jumping out of my skin, I pressed my hand to my mouth to cover up the shriek threatening to come out. My eyes turned to see Mr. LaVey, carrying a small oil lantern in his hand.

'Mr. LaVey,' I whispered, my voice a little shaky, 'it's just you.'

'Of course, it was me, m'dear. I was coming back from getting myself a glass of water when I saw a light and decided to look into it. Not that it was a break-in, but one can never be too careful.' LaVey smiled reassuringly, but it made me feel uneasy.

'Too true, but I'm so sorry, Mr. LaVey—'

As I turned to leave, I was stopped by LaVey grasping my shoulder in a surprisingly tight grip. 'You never answered my question. How come you're up and about? Is something troubling you?'

I wasn't sure if I should say anything. Saying I saw a ball of light beckoning me might make me sound crazy, which was the last thing I needed. 'I was just…looking for the bathroom,' I quickly lied, making myself sound as convincing as possible. 'You know, still getting used to the layout of the house.'

I turned to face him, but I wish I hadn't. His eyes were narrowed as he studied me. 'You have one in your quarters…were you not aware?' he asked sceptically.

'It…wasn't working when I went in there,' I lied again. 'And this was an urgent matter. You know…womanly matters.'

Even in the faint glow of the lantern, I could see LaVey's face remained unchanged. 'I shall have to have someone look into the matter in the morning. You were able to find it, yes?'

'Yes, sir. Just coming back from there.'

He nodded slowly, releasing my shoulder from his grip. 'Best get some sleep. Don't want you to lose your creative spark, now do we?'

Before I could answer, he spun on his heel and walked back the way he had come from before disappearing around a corner.

I exhaled the breath I didn't know I was holding in. Mr. LaVey was quite the eccentric man, indeed. Why did I feel so uneasy around him? He had done nothing to prove his untrustworthiness.

You're just sceptical about strangers in general. 'That's a fair point. Being in a foreign place with unfamiliar people at night wouldn't exactly be the best time to indulge my interest in exploring this hedge maze, but I am curious what that light was.'

Worry about it in the morning.

Interval One

Mikhail at the Banquet on Saturday

Mikhail had been the first to arrive in the banquet hall. He had washed and cleaned his scuffed knuckles as best he could and wrapped a rudimentary bandage around them to hide the damage. He was dressed in a freshly pressed suit, and he relaxed with his pipe before the sweltering fireplace.

LaVey had definitely saved the best for last with this room; it was enormous, far too big to house just one dining table, even one as long and extravagant as this. This was a room made for large functions, the hustle and bustle of distinguished businessmen and honoured guests with waiting staff busying themselves to and fro. The walls were high and wide, dominated by LaVey's entire lineage stretching back to the 1920s. Suits of armour stood guard around the perimeter and the room was filled with the ominous, relentless ticking of a large and ornate grandfather clock. It was, quite possibly, the finest room Mikhail had ever stood in.

He puffed on his pipe as he wandered across the shining, bare floorboards, taking in the echoing sound of his footsteps and the great, sparkling chandeliers that loomed overhead. The table was set for five, with LaVey obviously at the head in a startling throne-like chair, and Mikhail made sure to place his finished manuscript at the place closest to his eccentric host. He wanted to go first, and he wanted to be front and centre for all to see.

The most impressive feast was laid out across the length of the table. Meats, vegetables, and well-roasted sides sizzled away on serving trays amidst the flickering candles; fine, bone-white plates with gold trim sat at the four places alongside an array of glistening, silver cutlery. Bottles of wine and champagne were laid out and Mikhail helped himself to a snifter of the red, marvelling at how fruity and delicious the aftertaste was.

'Please, make yourself at home,' LaVey's voice echoed across the huge room. The old man shuffled in dressed like a Victorian aristocrat; he wore a golden pocket watch and chain, a silk waistcoat beneath his dinner jacket, and his cane clacked across the floorboards as he came close. 'From my personal cellars, of course.'

Mikhail poured a generous helping into LaVey's glass and handed it to him; the old man took it gratefully and they toasted each other's good health. 'I trust your writing went well?'

Mikhail swallowed, placed his glass down, and puffed on his pipe. Even after everything, a smug sense of satisfaction coursed through his veins as he answered: 'I think you will be most satisfied.'

'Good, good,' LaVey mused, pleased. The old fool has no idea, *Mikhail thought smugly. 'This project is most dear to my heart,' he rambled on. 'Of all the circles I've hosted, this is the one that will have a lasting impact.'*

The fire cracked and blazed behind them; Mikhail felt his skin boiling from the heat beneath his suit but after being subjected to the British weather for a week he was hardly complaining. 'Why?' he asked bluntly. 'What's so special about this one?'

LaVey's eyes sparkled (or did they glow?). 'Let's just say that time catches up with us all, my friend.' The old man sipped his wine. 'One day, all this will be gone, along with me, but words can live on. Words can be powerful. What we do with them can define us, wouldn't you agree?'

More games, *Mikhail rolled his eyes internally, but said nothing. He simply enjoyed his tobacco and left the old man to his cryptic rambling. Soon enough, the others wandered in; Mikhail scoffed at their tardiness but held his tongue. At least they had dressed appropriately. Even Brandis had thrown on some respectable clothing for a change, but Mikhail had no interest in engaging with any of them.*

Thankfully, however, conversation was minimal. Each of them greeted LaVey, with Rhiannon especially engaging with their host, but there seemed to be a tension in the air between her and the Америкос, who seemed strangely interested in that fool, Brandis. Mikhail cared little for whatever dramas had occurred between them all. Frankly, he was weary of all of them, and the entire thing by this point, and just wanted to get his money and his credit.

Presently, LaVey motioned for them to sit. Mikhail took his seat next to Rhiannon, who glared across the table at Brandis and the Америкос, but Mikhail was too busy drooling over LaVey's impressive spread. 'A toast, my friends,' the old man said; he stood at the head of the table holding his wine glass. Reluctantly, Mikhail stood, his stomach growling. 'My thanks to you all. I owe it all to each and every one of you, and wish you every success...and long life. I've hosted these writing circles before—heh—more than I can remember, let me tell you, but none have meant more to me than this one, with all of you. It is no mistake that I called you all here and let me say that you've made an old man happy just by being here'. The ghost of a sorrowful frown briefly passed over his wizened features before he tipped his goblet to them. 'Choices are made not being free', he toasted. 'Another pull and give as if to need...The ones that speak of what is me'.

They each raised a glass (that idiot Brandis fumbled to pour his wine and the Америкос had to help him; God, it was pitiful!) and drank. As LaVey sat, he advised: 'I recommend the scallops; they're to die for.' Mikhail took his host's recommendation under advisement and was thoroughly satiated. The quality of the food was excellent, especially given the state of the kitchen...

But Mikhail had no desire to dwell on that *particular subject. As the others cut into stuffed potato skins or prawn salads, Mikhail dabbed his lips with his napkin and shuffled his papers. 'With your permission...?' he motioned to LaVey.*

The old man looked up from a bowl of minestrone and nodded. 'Oh, by all means!'

Mikhail stood, straightening his shirt with a sharp tug, and cast a scornful look upon those who fancied themselves his peers.

For Luka, he thought, and began his tale...

Mikhail's Submission:

это все в вашей голове

(It's All in Your Head)

'Stop!' I screamed. 'No, stop!' The monster came closer and closer to me. It had a large round body covered with sharp, prickly-looking hair. The hair looked a lot like needles. The red glow from its beady eyes was enough for me to see it. I watched it move closer and closer towards me. It had eight spindly legs, thin as willow branches, and I didn't know how legs like that could hold up such a fat body.

What did a monster eat to get so fat?

Maybe it wanted to answer my question, and I watched frozen in fear as it slowly opened its mouth into an evil grin. The grin didn't last long, and soon it was snarling. Its sharp teeth were shiny with blood. I wasn't bleeding yet. What other child had it eaten? I tried to kick it, but my legs wouldn't move. My nightie was hot and sticky, and tangled around my legs. I was like a fly struggling in a spider web. I never thought about how scared the flies must feel before the spiders killed them.

I tried again to kick or move, but I couldn't. I couldn't even wriggle my pinky toe. My legs were too heavy and felt like a big bag of rocks. The monster was closer to me now. I kept screaming, but I couldn't scare it away. I wished it was only a spider, and maybe I was jealous of the fly. The spiders killed quickly, but I didn't think this thing with its sharp teeth would kill me before eating me. The darkness confirmed my greatest fears.

The darkness whispered to me about what the monster wanted.

It was hungry. It wanted to taste my blood.

'Josephine-Claire, it's okay. Wake up, sweetheart.' The voice was far away and didn't feel as real as the evil whispers.

'Josephine-Claire,' the monster said, and there was no denying that it was inches away from me. Its hot breath coated my face and blood dripped down onto me. I desperately wanted to turn away. *Somebody help me*, I silently cried.

How'd the monster know my name?

'It's not real.' Gentle but firm hands shook my shoulders, and the soothing voice pulled me away from the monster and its sharp teeth.

'Momma,' I said, sitting up slowly and blinking my eyes. I wanted to blink away the bad things, but I could still see them. I could feel the teeth. They bit me and my arms bled everywhere. Momma wasn't there. There was only blood.

'I'm real,' the monster growled. So much blood dripped from its mouth, and I didn't know how much more I could scream. What if the screams only fed the monster? Did my fear taste as good as the blood? I couldn't stop screaming. I was too scared.

'Josephine-Claire.'

Finally, I was able to wake up and see Momma. She turned on my lamp and the warm yellow light scared the monsters as much as they scared me. I tried to keep them away with my nightlight, but it was too little and sometimes they snuck around it. I wished I could sleep in a room with all the light, but Momma said I needed some dark to sleep. How could I sleep when the monsters always came?

'Momma,' I said again. I didn't know if I was really awake. It was easy to fall back into the dark place.

'I'm here, sweetheart. You're okay.'

I wanted to hold up my arms and show her the blood. Blood meant I was hurt, but this was a kind of hurt no one could see.

With the lamp light, I could see the nightmare blood was all gone, but I still felt the sting. When I got hurt during the day, Momma would kiss it better. She'd pour some stuff on the sore spot. It made it sting, but it stopped it from getting worse. Then she'd get me a big butterfly bandage. It would cover up the entire scrape, and it made me feel better.

That was only possible to do when I was hurt in a way she could see. Momma couldn't see the bad things the monsters did.

'You're okay,' Momma said again. 'It's all in your head. I promise. It's not real.'

'It hurt,' I cried. I looked down at my arms and wished again there was something she could see.

'Do you want to tell me about the bad dream?' Momma asked. She tried to hold back a yawn but didn't do a good job.

'It's okay.'

'No, if you can't sleep, I can't sleep either.'

'It was really scary,' I said.

'I know, and if you tell me about it, then it won't seem as scary.'

'It was about a spider, but it wasn't really a spider.'

'You like spiders. You always beg me not to squish them and to put them outside.'

'Those spiders are nice and won't hurt me,' I said. I tried to swallow, but it was like there was a frog in my throat.

'What did the bad spider do?'

'It bit my arms with all its teeth.' I pointed to my arms and the invisible wounds once again. Tears welled up in my eyes. I didn't want to cry anymore, but it was scary. I wanted to go back to sleep, but sleep was dangerous.

'It's all over now. I wish I could make it all better for you, sweetheart. Little girls shouldn't have such bad dreams.'

'I'm five,' I said.

'Yes,' she laughed. 'I don't care how old you are, you're always going to be my little girl.'

'I love you,' I said.

'I love you even more. Do you think you can go back to sleep now? Do you need some water?'

'I'm okay.'

'All right. Do you want to come sleep in my room?'

'No,' I said. My stomach hurt as I thought about what would happen if one of the nightmare monsters hurt her.

'Are you sure?'

'Yes, Momma.'

'Well, you know, I'm all alone in that big bed.'

'Daddy will be home soon, right?'

'Yes, only five more days.'

'Yay,' I said. I wanted to sound happier. I missed Daddy a lot when he went away on business trips, but it was hard to be happy in the dark. The dark had too many shadows and bad things lurking everywhere. There wasn't enough light to keep them all away.

Momma left and after what felt like a very long time, I fell back to sleep, but not before I saw what looked like a woman standing in the corner of my room. *Momma*, I wanted to say to her. It was a silly thought and only something I wished was true. I knew whatever that thing was, it wasn't Momma. I tried to wake up, but it was already too late.

* * *

The sun poured in through my window, warming my face, and scaring away any lingering monsters from the night. I wished it could be daytime forever, and I also wished people would never ever have nightmares. Even bad people didn't deserve nightmares. At least I thought they didn't. I'd never want anyone to see what I saw in the dead of night. Well, maybe I wanted Momma to see it, but that was only so she'd know the nightmare monsters were real. If she saw what I saw almost every night, it might be bad. She might have her own nightmares, and then I don't know what I'd do. I couldn't save her. I couldn't even save myself.

No, I thought. *No one should ever see the nightmare monsters.*

At least during the day I could pretend they didn't exist. I got up and went over to my window. It was going to be another beautiful sunny Georgian day. My room overlooked a nearby orchard of peaches and a lake. I was sure I could get Momma to take me swimming. I slipped on one of my pretty yellow dresses and went to go find her.

She was in the kitchen cooking up a storm, as Daddy liked to say. She'd cut up fresh fruit, made toast with her homemade raisin bread, and there was a tofu scramble with veggies from the garden. There was flour and batter all over her apron as she furiously whisked up pancake batter.

'Morning, Momma.'

She turned to look at me with a smile brighter than the sun itself. 'Good morning, sweetheart. You're up just in time. Do you want blueberry or chocolate chip pancakes?'

'Chocolate chip,' I said quickly.

'Why do I even ask?' Momma said as she pulled out the chocolate chips. 'I know what my girl likes.'

She served me a full plate of food, and we had a perfect breakfast. Everything tasted so good. Momma was the best cook in the world.

'What do you want to do today?' she asked.

'Could we go swimming?'

'Absolutely. We'll wait awhile so you don't get cramps. We don't want that, now do we?'

'No ma'am,' I said.

It was Monday, and I'd usually have to go to school all day, but since it was summer holidays, it was me and Momma all day. Daddy would be home soon, and then we'd all have fun together. If only it could be daytime all the time.

I kept eating even when my tummy felt full. The food was too good.

'You don't have to eat it all.'

'It's really good. You're the best Momma ever. I love you.'

'I love you too, sweetheart.' She gave me a big hug and wiped some syrup off my face. While we waited for my food to settle, she helped me get my hair pulled into a bun. I had long black hair, just like her. It was almost down to my waist. Momma said I was her little Rapunzel.

I loved having long hair, but what I loved more than anything was looking like a little copy of Momma. We had the same dark hair, big round eyes, and fair skin that turned as red as a tomato if we were out in the sun too long. I wanted to be just like her in every single way.

'I love you,' I said again.

'And I love you more.'

'I love you more than that. Am I your best friend?' I asked.

'You and Daddy are my best friends.'

* * *

The day went by too quickly. Swimming. Playing outside. Lunch. Supper. After we finished supper, we watched *Tangled*. When the credits rolled, I was sure Momma would send me off to bed, and I wanted to delay the inevitable.

'Can we watch one more movie? Please.'

'How about a story and then off to bed?'

I wrinkled my face up, the same way people who just ate a lemon did. Bedtime. My least favourite word in the world.

'I don't want to go to sleep,' I said. 'Please, can I stay up?'

'You have to sleep eventually.'

'Please don't make me. The monsters will eat me,' I cried. Tears welled up in my eyes and spilled down my face.

'The monsters aren't real.'

'Yes, they are.' The spider monster from last night was one of the worst ones I'd ever seen. Then, when I fell back to sleep, I saw that woman. I didn't know what she wanted, but if I went back to sleep, I was sure she'd tell me. I didn't want to see her again. I never wanted to see any of them ever again.

'Josephine-Claire, please. I'll read you one story and you need to go to bed. You need to sleep.'

'No, I don't.'

'You're going to bed right now,' she snapped. Her voice left no room for argument.

My feet were heavy as I followed her off to my bedroom. It was the den of the monsters.

Momma tucked me in tightly. Snug as a bug in a rug. I'm sure that's what the spider said to the fly as it wrapped it up in a silky death blanket to make sure it would never get away. Would I die in bed? Maybe.

'They're going to eat me,' I sobbed.

'Josephine-Claire. No monsters are going to eat you. I promise you, it's not real. They're all bad dreams. You've always had them, and you're always okay.'

Maybe the nightmare monsters would eat me. I almost wanted them to. Then Momma would feel sad for making me go to sleep and not letting me stay awake forever.

Maybe it wouldn't be as bad if I didn't have to sleep alone. Teddy bears didn't make good night-time companions. I needed something that was really alive in my room. I wanted a dog.

A lot of the kids in my class had dogs and I always asked Momma and Daddy to get me one, but the answer was always no. Momma was deathly afraid of them. When she was a little girl, she was out for a walk with her brother Johnny, who was only a teenager. They were on my grandparent's farm when they came across a huge black hound. It might as well have been a hellhound.

Momma said it reeked like a dead thing, and there was thick white foam dripping from its mouth. Before they could do anything, the dog attacked her brother. All she remembered was screaming, and Grandpa had to shoot the dog over and over before it stopped. They rushed Johnny to the hospital, but it was too late, and he didn't make it.

There would never be any dogs in our house.

I understood Momma was scared, but I still wanted one. I wanted it to be there to protect me at night.

I needed to be more careful of what I wished for. I'd always need to sleep, and I was sure I'd always have nightmares. Momma tucked me in and said to have sweet dreams. What were sweet dreams? I wondered. Maybe I'd had sweet dreams when I was a baby, but I didn't remember what they were.

I tried to stay awake for as long as I could, but soon I was too tired to keep my eyes open. *Sweet dreams*, I thought. It sounded like a fairy tale.

I tossed around and got my legs all tangled up in my blankets. My hair was stuck to my face with sweat. The wind howled angrily outside. Then I heard something over the sound of the wind. It was low and deep. Growling.

I sat up and looked around, trying to find where the sound was coming from. There were too many shadows, and I couldn't see anything. The growling got louder and was closer. I tried to turn on my touch lamp, but no matter how many times I hit the base of it, the light wouldn't turn on. I tried the switch, and it still wouldn't work. If I wanted to turn on my other light on the other side of the room, I'd have to get past the growling thing first.

The shadows grew heavier and heavier. When I opened my mouth to cry out, no sounds came. This time I couldn't call for help. I could taste the evil in the air. It tasted like blood. I backed myself up against the headboard and kept trying to get the lamp to turn on.

Please, I thought. I needed any kind of light. I was crying and shaking like a leaf. The sound of the growling was almost as loud as my heartbeat. My lamp wouldn't work, but the growling monster had a plan of its own. I heard loud, heavy footsteps, and red light filled the centre of the room.

The nightmare monster was a big black hound. It looked like how I imagined the hound that killed Momma's brother. What if it was the ghost of that dog? Maybe it wanted to kill me too.

It was hard to tell with the red light surrounding it, but it looked like there was blood dripping from its mouth. It walked slowly over to my side of the bed, and the light followed it like some kind of glowing shadow.

I whimpered and tried to move away, but there was nowhere for me to go. The hound tensed its legs and just as it looked like it was about to leap onto my bed, I heard a woman say, 'Stop.'

'Momma,' I said, finally finding my voice. She was unable to save her brother from being killed by the dog, but maybe she could save me.

'Oh child,' the woman said, still hidden in the shadows. 'Last night, you were wise enough to know I wasn't your mother. I have no children of my own. I only have my pets.'

The hound growled and barked loudly.

It spooked me, and I screamed. Now, I hoped Momma didn't hear me because I didn't want her to walk into the nightmare.

'What do you want?' I cried.

'I want you to whisper. Then ask your question again.'

'Sorry,' I said as softly as I could. 'What do you want?'

'That's better, darling,' she said. She stood beside my bed, and I was able to see her with the red light surrounding the dog. She had hair that was just as long as Rapunzel's and dragged on the ground. The main difference was her hair was pitch black and full of knots. She certainly wasn't a princess. Her eyes were empty and cold, and when she smiled at me, I didn't think she looked happy. Instead, she looked like she wanted to eat me just as much as the dog did.

'I want to be your mother.'

'I already have a momma,' I said, emphasising the last word.

'Oh, and soon you'll have me. I'll take good care of you.'

'No,' I said, the tears streaming down my face. 'I don't want you.'

'It doesn't matter. I want you.'

* * *

I couldn't bring myself to tell Momma about what the nightmare woman said. I didn't think Momma would believe me.

She took me shopping and even bought me a new pink dress. It was perfect, but for some reason it was hard to even thank her.

'Has the cat got your tongue today?' she asked.

'No,' I said.

'You're awfully quiet.'

'I'm okay,' I said, sounding angrier than I meant too.

'Well, maybe you should go to bed early tonight, and it will help you get a better sleep.'

I wanted to protest or argue, but I didn't have the energy to put up a fight. The only thing that escaped my mouth was a yawn, and it confirmed Momma's point.

I went to bed an hour earlier than usual. Momma read me two stories, but her voice sounded far away. The only thing I could hear was the nightmare woman telling me she'd be my mother. Did she want to hurt Momma? Was she going to kill her? Eat her? Do something else terrible to her?

There were so many questions, and no answers at all.

Sometimes the monsters made sounds, and other times they were quiet with their attacks. Then there were times when monsters didn't look like monsters at all.

I first heard faint mewing sounds and followed the sound until I saw an all-black kitten. When I picked it up, it was small enough to fit into one of my hands. I knew right away it shouldn't be all alone, and it needed its momma still. The little ones needed milk.

I looked around for help, but there was no one there. It was only me and the kitten. I started walking as quickly as I could, desperately seeking someone to help me. My stomach twisted into knots as the kitten's crying became louder and more insistent.

It was too little to be on its own.

I kept walking, trying to find someone. Anyone.

My heart was pounding, struggling to beat as the sound of the kitten's crying tore it into shreds. I could also hear a clock, ticking louder and louder. I was running out of time.

The wind started wailing all around me and blew icy sheets of rain at my face. I tried my best to cover the kitten and keep it warm, but soon my nightie was soaked right through. It couldn't keep me or the kitten warm.

A large, dark building appeared in front of me. The door wasn't closed properly, and it looked like I could slip inside. Who knew what was inside? Maybe there were more monsters, or maybe I could find someone to help me. All I knew was I needed to get out of the cold rain, and the building felt warm.

I wandered the halls and walked past countless hospital beds. *It was a hospital*, I thought happily. *I could find a doctor, and then they'd help the kitten.*

I looked down to tell the kitten I'd have help for it soon, but it was gone. *No*, I thought. *No, no, no.* I was sure I hadn't dropped it. I retraced my steps and kept my eyes glued to the floor, searching for it. *Please be okay*, I thought. *Please.*

I started to cry as the floor in front of me turned red. There were bodies in the hospital beds. I turned and ran. My thoughts were only on saving myself.

I ran into the first empty room I found and slammed the door behind me.

I walked backwards, keeping my eyes glued to the door. I could see a shadowy creature roaming the halls and heard screams in the distance. Was I safe in that room? Could I lock the door? I didn't think a locked door would do much good if the creature was made of shadows.

I wasn't looking where I was going and bumped into a hospital bed.

A woman grabbed my wrist with her long bony fingers. The nightmare woman.

'Josephine-Claire,' she said. 'I missed you. You look so pretty in your dress.'

I thought she was talking about my nightie, but I looked down to see I was wearing the new pink dress Momma bought me.

'Thank you,' I said, only because I didn't know what else I should say.

She reached towards me, and my first thought was she was going to tear the dress from me. Instead, she pulled off the tags. 'Did Momma buy this for you?' I could hear the sneer in her voice.

'Yes,' I said. I remembered to speak quietly. 'Who are you?'

'My name is Mara,' she said. 'Soon you can call me Mother.'

I woke up soaked in sweat, my heart about to beat out of my chest. 'Momma, Momma, Momma,' I said. I didn't call for her, because even though I couldn't see Mara, I could feel her presence. I knew she was watching me.

* * *

On Wednesday I was tired. More tired than I'd ever been in my whole life. I hated it when adults said kids didn't know what it was like to be tired. Most adults I talked to said they didn't even have dreams, and they didn't have nightmares. If they had nightmares like mine, then maybe they would understand why I was so tired. I thought the grown-ups should be more awake because they got to get a good sleep with sweet dreams. I thought of having no dreams at all as the same as having sweet dreams. Anything was better than having nightmares.

I tried to help Momma make apple pies, but when she cut into one apple, it was full of worms. I'd seen worms before, but I started screaming and crying. Something about the sight of their squirming bodies hidden away in the perfect apple was too much.

Momma let me watch TV for the rest of the day until it was time for bed.

I didn't even remember her tucking me in or falling asleep. I only remember Mara appearing beside me.

'Why were you so upset about the worms?' she asked.

'I-I-I don't know,' I stammered. I didn't know earlier, and I still didn't know at the moment.

'You shouldn't be afraid of my pets.'

'They're your pets?'

'Yes, darling. Soon they will be your pets.'

'No,' I said.

'You'll learn to stop saying no to me,' she said in the cruellest voice I'd ever heard. Momma never ever talked to me like that, even when I was really bad.

Mara held out her hand to me, and at first it was difficult to see. I thought she had a handful of dark mud, but mud didn't move like that.

'Leeches,' she said.

'No!' I cried without thinking.

'I told you, you'll learn to stop saying no to me. You also need to keep your voice down.'

'Please, don't hurt me.'

'My pets need to eat. Give me your arm.'

I shook my head and pulled my blankets up to my chin. I don't know how I thought blankets could protect me.

'I'm going to tell you once more to give me your arm.'

All I could do was cry and try to hide behind my blankets.

'You will regret this,' she said.

* * *

Thursday passed by in a haze. All I remembered was Momma watching the news. Usually the news was boring, but there was one time it wasn't.

I remembered a news story about rats who ate a baby alive. I'd only seen a rat one time while I was awake. Momma was in the kitchen, and she started screaming like she'd seen one of my nightmare monsters. I didn't think the rat was that scary. Daddy was able to chase it out with a broom, and we never saw another one.

I didn't think rats were scary when they were on their own, but a pack of them was a real-life nightmare. A nightmare that could eat a helpless little baby.

I wasn't a baby, but weren't we all just as helpless as babies when we slept?

When it was bedtime, I couldn't keep myself awake and fell asleep quickly.

There was no warning, no sounds, no growling, nothing. I felt their furry bodies on my face, and then heard their squeaking. When I opened my mouth to cry out, a long tail slipped into my mouth, and I almost gagged on it.

Rats.

And I was covered in them.

There were hundreds of squirming, writhing bodies on top of me. I struggled to sit up and push them all away, but I couldn't move. There was an immense weight on my chest, and it was difficult enough to breathe, let alone move.

I couldn't scream because they'd get in my mouth. I thought since I was holding still, they wouldn't notice me, but movement wasn't necessary to get their attention. As soon as I started to cry, their squeaking grew louder, and they started biting me. Little nips soon turned to full on bites as they ripped chunks of skin out of my face.

I started wailing, and they began to feast on my tongue. Others tore through my nightie as if it was as thin as paper. Next was my stomach. Their teeth were like hundreds of knives. Gnashing, biting, and clawing. They ripped into my stomach and the burning pain made me want to die. I didn't care about anything else. I didn't try to get myself to wake up. It was real, and they were eating me alive. I only wanted to die and for the pain to stop.

I'd once tried to imagine how that baby felt being eaten alive, and now I had my answer. The rats in my throat blocked the worst of my screams and muffled any sounds I could make. They were frantic and eating as fast as they could. Their hurried movements caused them to fall, and other rats dove inside me. There was a huge hole in my belly, and one in my throat.

Soon, the tearing pain stopped, and it only burned. They'd ripped most of my skin open. When I thought they'd never stop, and I'd be their meal forever, they scurried off.

'Help me,' I tried to say to no one in particular. The words didn't sound anything like help me, and I didn't think anyone would understand me.

'Hush, child,' Mara said. I couldn't see her because my eyes were too damaged. The next thing I felt was a hand on my hair, and I flinched because I thought the rats were coming back.

'*Shhh*,' Mara said. 'I'm not going to hurt you. My pets were hungry. They need to eat as well. You could have made this so much easier by feeding the leeches. Don't worry, it's all over now.' She ran her long skeletal fingers over me and healed my body. It was as if the rats had never eaten me. Once she was done, I could see again, and she was holding the rats.

I was able to scream as loud as I possibly could.

'Josephine-Claire, you better be careful. You're going to wake your momma up.'

This scream did bring Momma. She ran in and held me tightly.

'It's okay,' Momma said. 'It's all over now.'

Momma was there, and I was sure I was awake, but it wasn't over. The woman still stood there, her long fingers beckoning to me and Momma.

'I'll be back for her, Josephine-Claire. Then I will be your mother,' she said in a voice as horrible as nails on a chalkboard.

* * *

Daddy would be home on Saturday, but I was too tired to feel excited. Momma said we were going to go to the store, but she took me to the doctor's instead.

'Why do I need to go to the doctor?' I asked. 'I'm not sick.'

'Sweetheart, your nightmares are a sickness and I want to help you with them, but I don't know how.'

'Doctors give you needles,' I said.

Well, Doctor Jones isn't going to give you a needle. He's going to give you some medicine, and the name of another doctor to talk to. This is to help you, not to hurt you.'

Sure enough, Momma was right. There were no needles involved, only medicine to take at bedtime, and the name of another doctor. Doctor Jones said it was all to help me, but I didn't know if I believed anyone could help me.

I took one nice white pill before bedtime. It was supposed to keep the monsters away. When it started to work, I felt sleepy, and my arms and legs were heavy. I started to worry I was going to never wake up.

'I'm tired,' I told Momma, as she tucked me in.

'Yes, honey. That's what the pills are for.'

'Will I wake up?'

'Yes, of course. You'll wake up in the morning and feel bright-eyed and bushy-tailed.'

'Are you sure?'

'Yes,' she said, but even though she tried to sound brave, I could hear the fear in her voice.

I didn't feel like I fell asleep. It was more like I was dragged down into darkness. When the images began to appear, the first thing I

THE SUMMONING

saw was the lake where Momma always took me swimming. It wasn't night-time, and it was a beautiful sunny day. I saw Mara standing in the lake with the water coming up to her waist.

'Come swim with me,' she said.

I looked down to see I was wearing my favourite red bathing suit. It was warm, and the water looked so tempting.

'Come on,' she called to me.

She looked nicer than usual, and I wanted to go in the water. I waded in and went deeper so I could swim. Mara picked me up and held me close.

'I told you I could be your mother.' She hugged me, and at first it was okay, but then it got tighter, and tighter. I felt my ribs crack.

'Stop,' I gasped, unable to say more.

She forced me under the water, and when I tried to swim to the surface, heavily watered-down fabric threatened to drag me down. I couldn't make my way back to the surface. My lungs screamed for air. At the last moment, Mara pulled me back up.

'Now, I want you to scream,' she hissed. 'Scream as loud as you can.'

I was coughing up water, but I still screamed in terror. I kept screaming and screaming. At some point, Mara let me go, and I slowly waded my way back to shore. I was freezing cold and couldn't stop shaking.

I saw the lights turn on in the house, and only then did I realise what I was luring Momma into. I wanted to run back to the house, but all I could do was collapse upon the bank of the lake.

'She's coming,' Mara said in a sing-song voice.

'Josephine-Claire!' Momma screamed. She ran towards me without any idea what she was running into. Mara was still there, waiting for her.

Momma dropped down beside me, pulling off her housecoat and wrapping her arms around me.

'Go back,' I said, struggling to get the words out.

'Baby, what happened?' she sobbed.

No, no, she wasn't listening to me. It was already too late. Mara floated over to us and grabbed Momma. There wasn't a fight, and Momma didn't even have time to scream.

Mara lifted her up off the ground by the neck and then tossed her aside like she was nothing.

Mara grabbed my arm and pulled me to my feet. 'I'm your mother now, and Daddy comes home tomorrow.'

Chapter Five

Wednesday

1. *Brandis and his Guilt*

My shame was so great after my run-in with Aster that I shut myself away in my room. Honestly, I was tempted to up and leave. Whatever that fuckin' thing in the attic had been should have been enough to convince me but snapping at Aster was somehow worse. She hadn't deserved it; while she hadn't exactly been the most welcoming of the writers, she had at least tried to engage me in conversation, but I'd been too fucked up from that *thing* to be civil.

Not that it was an excuse.

So, I wallowed in self-pity in my room longing for the days when things were simpler. LaVey's house was certainly grand and impressive, but it didn't feel like home, and right now I was feeling very homesick for my pathetic, normal life. I thought of my cramped flat and my simple, flat-pack desk, neither of which could hold a candle to LaVey's grandiose quarters, and yet I longed for their familiarity and security…and the pictures that hung on the wall above my desk. Two were canvas prints of film posters, another was (quite arrogantly) my graduation certificate, and the third was one of the few pictures I had of my university friends. I could picture it in my mind's eye even now: me, looking much more toned and with much tidier hair; Shane, wearing that same damn flannel shirt; Sam, eating, as always; and Lucy, slender, curvaceous, and with the brightest, most dazzling eyes I'd ever seen—all on a random night out like we always were.

All of us (except for Shane, who was studying to be a teacher and often away on placements) had been on the same course, English BA (Hons), at Northward University. It had been a decent enough campus; nothing special or out of the ordinary, but we'd had fun. We'd all lived on campus in that first year, but, while Shane and I lived over in the fancy new Sovereign Hall, Lucy and Sam lived in Accolade Tower, a squalid block of flats that wasn't a million miles removed from the one I lived in now. The lift often stuck, the windows were filthy, the rooms were small and cold, and they had to share the dirty little showers and kitchens found on every other floor.

I'd been at home when...*it* happened.

For a fuckin' stupid reason, as well. I'd offered to drive

(*Lucy*)

everyone up to the Teamos for supplies (mostly crisps, snacks, and alcohol; y'know, the essentials), but the key had snapped in the ignition when I'd tried to start the car.

Lucy had found it hilarious. She'd giggled so hard that her face had turned a deep, beetroot red and tears had streamed from her eyes.

I'd been so fuckin' embarrassed!

Of course, my first thought had been to call Dad. I had breakdown assistance and all that jazz but, in times of crisis, I always called Dad.

He'd also laughed himself silly and said to call the breakdown people. I had, and had waited for over an hour for this weird little bloke to show up, rip apart my steering column, and get my car started so I could make the thirty-odd mile trip back home to Haverhill where my spare key was…only for Dad to then ask why I hadn't just manually locked all the doors and have him post it to me!

'You're about as much bloody use as a chocolate teapot!' I'd exclaimed, mortified beyond belief at my own stupidity.

It'd been a massively humiliating experience but still…far better than what happened to Lucy and Sam, just two victims of a brutal and unexplained massacre that'd swept through the campus while the students slept, and I had been stewing in my old childhood bed.

They'd only been nineteen.

Nineteen and hacked to death while she slept.

The campus had closed for two weeks, and we'd been offered "mental health counselling," whatever the fuck *that* was supposed to be, but Shane had never been the same. In fact, I hardly saw him at all for the rest of that last year of uni. It'd been a bittersweet end to it all, but I felt like I owed it to Sam and Lucy to graduate. When I submitted *Breath of Eden* for publication, I dedicated the book to them.

It meant a lot to me.

I submitted it (alongside a reasonably customised cover letter) to seven publishers, including big names I had no chance with and smaller publishers who put out a few select titles per year, and nine literary agents. Most said they would respond within six to twelve weeks, which was a pretty outrageous timeframe, but it wasn't like I had anything else to do, so I sent them off and took to my Instagram page.

The first thing I learned about trying to advertise my book online was that I was one voice screaming into an endless, suffocating void. The second was that it was damned expensive. I was fresh out of uni and, although not really in debt, I was still out of pocket from all the books…and drinking. Designing a professional book cover, banners, and paying for adverts quickly became expensive so I resolved to do the best I could by myself. It wasn't like I was computer illiterate (I got a double E in Advanced I.C.T. at secondary school, after all…which doesn't sound impressive, but no one got above a C grade that year), and I was reasonably sure that I could try and stir up some interest.

I was wrong.

To make things worse, my submission was summarily rejected. Only one of the four rejections actually referred to me by name, and another was one of the longest and most pretentious emails I'd ever seen. The guy claimed that he liked my book but "didn't love it" because, according to his vaunted expertise, it didn't have a "wow factor." It was so scathingly harsh that I'd laughed myself stupid and it had taken everything I had to not send a bitter, sarcastic response of my own.

Luckily, I'd been prepared for rejection. I'd figured breaking into traditional publishing was extremely unlikely, and that even the few that manage it probably have to bow to all kinds of demands and compromises from editors, sub-editors, and other parties just to get published. Vanity publishing also wasn't an option; if I refused to pay hundreds of pounds a month for a primo advertisement then I was never going to pay up thousands on the off chance that some strangers would be able to get my book published. It sounded like a scam, reputable author websites *said* it was a scam, and I couldn't afford it anyway.

So, despite the fact that I (like Lucy…) was a purist for traditional physical books, I invested in a tablet and began formatting *Breath of Eden* into an e-book. In the process, I found even *more* errors.

It was crazy how much I had half-assed some of it and I remembered wishing that Lucy had been there to help proofread it. Her meticulous eye would've spotted right away that I'd changed one character's name from "Mark" to "Andrew" and been left with annoying and amusing errors such as "he was Andrewed" and "I Andrewed him." Still, after much procrastination and a lot of self-deprecation, *Breath of Eden* was as ready as it would ever be. I made my own cover, read through it again (by this point I was sick to fuckin' death of it), and began pushing the big release day.

I got some likes. I got some followers. I got some shares. Friends, most of them from uni, helped to spread the word online. I even put my hand in my pocket and invested a cool hundred into an ad campaign (which ran for ten days, reached under two-thousand people, and attracted eighteen clicks…basically proving that advertising only pays off if you have the money to invest in it). When the day came, I offered the e-book at a reduced price for the first week to try and attract downloads and that was, coincidentally, the most downloads I would ever get.

In total, I sold thirteen copies in two years, and that was including physical copies that were produced per order.

I quickly learned that likes and shares did not equal sales or reviews or actual interest in a work. I had hoped that the more I plugged it, the more people would like and share it, that the more likely it was that *Breath of Eden* would find its audience. However, that never happened, no matter what I posted or offered.

Nearly twenty years of effort…all for nothing.

I'd bought myself a copy of the book, of course, but I hadn't dared read it. I was reminded of when I'd spent about two months refining and checking and double-checking my final assignment for uni and, the day I got it back, opened up the spiral-bound document and saw an error screaming at me on page one.

Page one! Jesus!

I did manage to cobble together a few short stories between work, life, and *Breath of Eden*. The longest was about three-hundred pages but most were one-fifty to two-hundred. I published them all as e-books at the cheapest price possible, but my experience with *Breath of Eden* had left me disillusioned and I didn't put half as much effort into marketing these written works, which ended up with no reviews and maybe two downloads between all eight of them. I tried bringing them together into themed collections and offering them as physical copies but, again, there was little interest.

For Lucy and Sam.
I wish you could've seen this.

Page ten (technically page *x*) of *Breath of Eden*.

How spectacularly I had failed her...*both* of them. I'd graduated with a 2:1, which was perfectly acceptable and exactly what I wanted (Lucy had been on track for, and definitely would have gotten, a First), and I'd always gotten good feedback from my tutors and such. In my final year, I jumped at the chance to write a piece of fiction for my final assignment and had dusted off a short story from my youth about a post-apocalyptic future where, somehow, all of the world's oceans had dried up and left the world an arid desert—which I later published (to little fanfare) as an e-book titled *The Dried Earth*. It'd been fun, especially after two-and-a-half years of the usual boring assignments and, thankfully, I was all but finished when that maniac cut up all those students with a blunt axe.

Still…Lucy never got to read it, or *Breath of Eden*. I'd shown her bits of it, even read some to her, and she'd been enthusiastic about it. She loved to read; she'd been fastidious, laser-focused, and absolutely committed to every single lesson and assignment. She left the club at a reasonable time, always knew when she had reached her limit, and my God could she argue her point! She'd been writing her final assignment on a detailed comparison of three prominent pieces of feminist literature and had practically lived in the library that year with stacks of books piled up around her.

God, I'd admired her.

I had been so besotted with her. Everyone knew it (I suspect even *she* knew it), but I'd never said anything. In the end, I just couldn't work up the confidence. I was just too afraid of rejection…and of losing her.

Then I lost her anyway; stupidly, violently, unfairly, and the one thing I had left to honour her was met with nothing but rejection. My first instinct after what had happened to Sam and Lucy was to try and vent my feelings into a violent short story titled *Mania*. It was a disgusting piece full of sexually charged brutality and a cruel spite that even I couldn't really bring myself to publish.

'Maybe in an anthology…' I'd mused, knowing it was a lie.

One positive thing to come from *Breath of Eden* was meeting other struggling independent writers online. Many wrote romantic smut or cringe-worthy dramas that I wasn't interested in, so I sought out writers of horror, science-fiction, and fantasy. It had been humbling to see other writers, even those who paid for professional services, were facing similar troubles. Exposure, advertising, marketing, just getting your work *noticed* in a meaningful way was almost as hard as breaking into traditional publishing and I often wondered why the fuck I even bothered.

I guess that was about the time when my motivation for writing really started to falter. Sure, I'd limped along as best as I could, but I'd known, deep down, that I was kidding myself. LaVey's invitation had been my one last, best chance at honouring my friends, and I couldn't even make it one hour in this godforsaken house without getting on the wrong side of someone.

It'd be funny if it wasn't so depressing.

2. *Mikhail Taunts His Peers*

Thanks to LaVey's insistence on the four of them using the archaic typewriters, typing his new version of *Mara's Secret* had taken Mikhail longer than he had first thought, but not by much. He was fortunate that the original author had wasted copious words on character and world building. Mikhail had filled the nearly three-hundred-page document with his own thick, scrawled notes and words like "*повторение*" and "*ненужный*" were slashed through entire paragraphs as he had streamlined the text.

He had spent most of the day lounging around in LaVey's many comfortable and luxurious ground floor rooms, specifically to be closer to the alcohol and because the others frequented this floor and he delighted in riling them up. Earlier that morning, he had been reclining on a long, copper-red sofa with a bottle of Beluga sitting in an ice bucket on the floor, enjoying his drink and sharing stories of his success with Rhiannon, who had grown increasingly infuriated at his purposely relaxed and condescending tone.

'There was I,' he'd said, one large arm resting behind his head, 'a simple man from the old country, standing before two-hundred willing eyes and ears. I was the toast of the event. The host said that, in all his years offering the Gogol Award to aspiring writers, none had captured the hearts and minds of my peers as I.'

'That's nice,' Rhiannon had murmured, clearly growing more aggravated with every word. The arrogant bitch had probably never won a writing award in her entire life; how annoying it must have been to hear of his great successes.

'My Lia had never been prouder,' he had continued, now blatantly lying. Lia had never seen him receive his award, and when he had next seen her, the last thing that had been on her mind was congratulating him on his achievements. *Oh, but don't think about that*, he had thought, swigging a large gulp of his vodka before continuing: 'We made such passionate love that evening that you wouldn't believe. I find the touch of a good woman a fitting reward after such an accomplishment.'

That had definitely riled Rhiannon up. She had shot him a look of such disdain that he couldn't help but allow a large, smug smile to cross his features. 'You're disgustin'!' she shook her head and turned back to the dusty books arranged on the far side of the lounge.

She had been standing on a small wooden stool to reach the ones she needed, and Mikhail had briefly wondered why Rhiannon was poking around for reference materials in here when LaVey had an extensive library just a few doors down. Mikhail had wandered in there the other day, but the room had been freezing and the bulbs had blown when he had switched them on, so perhaps those same things had forced the *сука* into his presence.

She had left shortly after, leaving him to mutter a low chuckle; these Westerners were so *serious*, and he delighted in feeding off their scorn. He had finished his Beluga and wandered into the main hall, where he had spotted that idiot Brandis heading to the first floor. 'Running back to bed?' Mikhail had called, his speech slurred and his vision hazy.

Brandis had stopped halfway and muttered something under his breath, but Mikhail hadn't been able to hear it. 'Did'ju su-say somethin', *мудак*?'

'You're drunk,' Brandis had stated, a grimace on his face.

'I say *merry!*' Mikhail had exclaimed, throwing his arms wide. 'An' why *shh-udn't* I be?' he had half-tripped up the stairs, clinging to the banister for support, and was delighted to see Brandis back away. 'Yuh-you're all *жалкий* compared t'*me!*'

'Yes,' Brandis had scowled. 'You've made *that* abundantly clear.'

'Hu-who d'you think you are, tuh-talkin' t'me with such *дерзость*', hm?' Mikhail had clumsily jabbed his finger into Brandis's thin chest, which rag dolled under his lightest touch. 'I spit on your words, your…your books!' Mikhail had spat more air than spittle to drive home this point. 'Whatare*you* next to *me*? A *червь*; less than dirt! And…and whatever you write, if you even *can* write, will be *chush'* compared to me!'

'Right, well…thanks for the encouragement. Why don't you go take a shower or summink?' Brandis had grumbled.

Mikhail had wanted to throw a punch, but he had barely been able to stand by that point, so he had let the boy scuttle away and called out a few more insults as he walked away. As for Mikhail himself, he had somehow got back to his own room and been sorely tempted to pass out on the bed but, recalling his nightmare from the previous night, had thought better of it. 'Little shit…' Mikhail had rumbled before showering and then finally setting to work at the bulky typewriter.

All he could think about was the dream from the other night. Normally, the alcohol kept his night terrors at bay but, since arriving at LaVey's house, they had only increased in their frequency and potency. *Just as the old man had said*, Mikhail thought, as he tried to shake the lingering image of Lia shoving handfuls of Luka's guts into her gibbering mouth.

Working on *Mara's Secret* helped to banish those dark images; it had been so long since he had written that he had almost forgotten the exhilaration it brought him. Granted, plagiarising someone else's writing wasn't the way he usually worked, but he felt a gratification, nevertheless. He was fascinated by the imagery in *Mara's Secret*. It was far from anything he would have ever thought up or written, and he didn't recognise some of the words, but he simply excised them for a few of his own. Clearly, whoever had worked on this was someone with an overactive and vivid imagination, one perhaps touched by trauma, and he could certainly relate to that.

He worked long into the evening, cursing every time his wide fingers stabbed at the wrong keys or the paper got twisted on the platen. Hampered by having to use the unwieldy typewriter, the process was long and painful but the more he typed, the more he pushed away those dark images, and he focused entirely on completing the piece so that he could wave it in the face of that личинки.

Mikhail doubted that any of the others would be able to match his dedication. While Rhiannon gathered her research, Aster wandered around with her head in the clouds, and Brandis shuffled about pathetically, Mikhail Orlov was trumping them in one long, alcohol-fuelled writing session. The thought spurred him on; he relished the look on LaVey's face when he presented the finished piece—and knew that it would be all the leverage he would need to ensure that *his* name came first on the front cover, and *his* story the first that LaVey's readers would see when they opened the book.

Mikhail rubbed his eyes wearily as he glanced through his hastily typed, heavily plagiarised document, pausing here and there to note minor amendments. Although his body felt numb and physically spent, he dreaded the thought of witnessing what his dreams had in store for him. Luckily, his stomach begged for sustenance and, after shuffling his papers into a neat pile, he swept out to raid LaVey's larder.

3. Aster's Troubled Relationship

'Walter? Where are you?' I called out. Everything was dark save a small light which was hanging above me and following my movements. Looking up, there was nothing there, and yet the light remained. 'He was right here! Walter!'

A deep voice responded but the words were indecipherable to me. It sounded like my fiancé; why wasn't he coming? Was he in trouble, or trapped and couldn't get to me? This time, I screamed out his name. Silence. A chill ran down my back as I continued to walk further in the dark…room? Area? The only sound I could hear was the squeak of my trainers on the floor. Suddenly, the light went out, plunging me into darkness; I went still and tried to focus on my breathing. A low growl sounded behind me and I began shaking. Should I run or should I stay put?

'*Aster!*' someone shouted, but the voice was unfamiliar to me. It was deep and raspy, almost unnatural. The voice went on to shout my name three more times, growing closer each time. Squeezing my eyes shut, I waited for the owner of the voice to attack me.

'Aster?' That was Walter's voice, and he was behind me…but that wasn't possible because he didn't have that deep or gruff of a tone. 'I don't know what you think you were doing.'

The very sound of Walter's voice compelled me to turn, and a pair of yellow eyes greeted me and advanced on me quickly. As I screamed, I could feel myself "leaving" the room, and the next thing I saw was the golden walls of my temporary bedroom. *It was just a dream. It was just a dream. Thank God*, I thought, relieved. It was rather bright in the room, and I wondered how long I had slept in.

'1:19 p.m. Ugh, fuck.' I had basically wasted the day away sleeping in! My phone suddenly went off. Walter's name displayed on my screen, and I sucked in my breath. Remembering our earlier conversation and how shitty it had gone, I had to admit I was nervous about answering my phone.

Was he still mad?

Was this him breaking up with me?

Just answer it! my mind screamed at me. *He'll keep calling until you answer!*

I pressed my screen to answer and the sound of wailing and crying came through the line. The hair on the back of my neck pricked. 'Walter?' I carefully asked. The crying and howling continued for another thirty seconds before going silent and I heard my name softly on the other end.

'I'm...so sorry, my love.' I could barely hear him. 'I haven't been the most supportive partner to you. I should have respected you more.'

Words failed me as he continued to apologise and make beautiful declarations of love and adoration, but something about this seemed suspicious. One thing I liked about Walter was that he didn't beat around the bush; if something was bothering him, he'd let you know straight away (and usually without a filter). While he could be sweet and romantic, it had never been his starting go-to.

'What's up, Walter?' He stopped crying, but I could hear his heavy breathing on the other end. 'Walter, what's up? I feel bad about how things ended between us before…and isn't it a bit early for you to be calling?'

'You better be sorry! What the hell was that?!' he snarled. 'I had to call out of work because of you!'

'I don't understand…why would you call out of work?'

'You hung up on me! It was upsetting and I needed something to take off the edge!'

A noise of disgust left my lips. 'You were already out when I called you! Don't try lying to me!'

'Heh,' Walter chuckled lowly. 'You don't know what you heard. You always think so horribly of me.'

'I know you were out! I could hear Steve in the background! Why are you trying to lie to me? Am I not worth being honest with?' As I tried collecting my thoughts, I saw something in the corner of my eye on the desk. It was a typewriter. Where did that come from? Had that always been there? Walter continued to yell, but my attention was taken away. If I remember correctly, Mr. LaVey did mention something about our work needing to be done on the typewriter. Of course, that detail must have slipped my mind and I had already started working on my laptop. No matter, I could finish it there and then type it out on paper. My hand ran over the ancient piece. It was in immaculate shape.

'*Hey!* Are you even there? Stupid, spacy bitch…' Walter's insult snapped me from the temporary trance I was in. Clearly, things weren't going to get better…I could always try again once he'd had some sleep.

'If you're going to continue to berate me, I can just let you go until you sleep off your hangover,' I quietly said and I could still hear him ranting and raving away as I hung up on him for the second time. It was time to get to work on this piece. I mean, this was why I came here, right?

4. Rhiannon Takes a Smoke Break

Rhiannon was ashamed to say that she had barely made any progress on her writing at all. She'd spent the entirety of Tuesday night awake and flinching at every sound and scuffle that appeared, convinced that Mr. LaVey would creep into her room while she slept and…do things to her. It was preposterous, of course, but her mind continued to create complex and seemingly very real versions of events, none of which made any sense to her. At one point during the night, she thought she heard her ex-husband calling her name through the walls.

Writing was the last thing she really wanted to be doing now. What she really needed at this precise moment was a strong drink and a cigarette. She hadn't taken a puff since before she'd arrived, and her addiction was slowly starting to creep over her like a dark shadow. She needed a smoke…and she needed a drink, then maybe she'd be able to write. However, when she stepped foot outside the relative safety of her room, she was filled with anxiety and felt her heart doing palpitations.

She took a deep breath and held it as she peered into the hallway, scanning the area with all her senses for signs of life. There were none. The house was eerily quiet, something that didn't exactly fill her with confidence either.

With her cigarettes and a lighter in hand, she donned her rain jacket and practically jogged along the corridor and down the stairs to the main hall. She passed by Aster on the way. Rhiannon was tempted to ask Aster if she'd experienced anything *weird* while being here, but then thought better of it. Not only did the American seem a bit rattled herself, but Rhiannon thought that maybe it was best that she kept her stories of invisible entities and haunted libraries to herself. The last thing she wanted was the other writers getting a whiff of weakness from her.

So, Rhiannon turned her collar up against the cold, found a secluded spot overlooking the grounds, and finally treated herself to the sweet drag of nicotine. On the way back from her smoke break, she made a quick detour to the bar in the hopes of finding a random bottle of something lying around. She was in luck. It appeared that Mr. LaVey liked to showcase his wide array of liquors and spirits, so she grabbed an almost full bottle of whiskey, hid it under her jacket, and then scurried back to her room, feeling like a naughty teenager robbing her father's alcohol cabinet.

Upon entering her room, Rhiannon immediately unscrewed the bottle and took a quick drink. The liquid burned, but in a good, soothing way. With her addiction quenched, she sat on the bed, pulled her laptop onto her crossed legs, and clicked on the email from her husband. It was time to face him…then she wouldn't have to constantly wonder what he'd emailed her about. It was one of those annoying thoughts that buzzed around her head which needed to be eradicated.

Rhi,
We need to talk. I need money.
David

'What the fook!' she shouted, slamming her laptop shut and kicking it off the bed. She should have known better than to think David actually wanted to talk about something serious, like maybe their daughter. He merely needed money, probably either to pay off his gambling debts or to place a large bet. Ever since Rhiannon had started making big money with her novels, he'd been trying to scrounge off her. Luckily, she'd divorced him before she'd become extremely wealthy, so she didn't owe him anything. She did give him money from time to time, but usually only when it involved their daughter, but she knew that David was the type of man who could easily use his daughter as an excuse to ask for money. Never again. Never…again.

She sighed as she picked up her plain old notebook and resumed her position on the bed. She began to scribble a few words on the page and then…the ink in her favourite writing pen ran dry.

'Fooking hell!' she screamed as she hurled the notebook and pen across the room. She watched in horror as her notebook took on a life of its own and flew into the fire where it began to shrivel and burn. 'Noooo!'

Rhiannon leapt off the bed and attempted to retrieve her precious book, but there was an invisible shield. Something wasn't letting her put her hand in the fire, but Rhiannon didn't know if it was out of spite or to protect her from being burned.

Rhiannon knelt on the hearth rug with tears streaming from her eyes as she watched helplessly. Why was this happening to her? What was it about this house that seemed determined to ruin her life? She wished she'd never come. She didn't even need the money or the fame. Why had she *really* come? She didn't know the answer.

Eventually, she admitted defeat and left the embers of her notebook to sizzle away. She glanced at the typewriter in the corner of the room. Most of her notes had been in the notebook but, luckily, she had also made a start on her laptop, but she didn't want to open that damn thing anymore. She wanted no access or glimpse of the outside world. It was time to write…the old-fashioned way.

Rhiannon dragged the single wooden chair across the room and made herself comfortable in front of the strange machine, the bottle of whiskey perched next to it. The banquet was looming; on Saturday evening at six o'clock, Mr. LaVey would expect them all in the lavish dining room to reveal their work and discuss the larger piece. She'd be damned if she was going to turn up unprepared. If she had to, she'd work all hours of the next two and a half days to get this story written.

She fiddled with the paper and the knob on the side of the typewriter for a few minutes and then, finally, began to type freestyle…for the first time in her life.

Interval Two

Rhiannon at the Banquet on Saturday

Rhiannon drew in a deep rattling breath (she really needed to stop chain smoking when she was stressed) as she clutched the reams of paper against her chest. She'd just listened as Mikhail had read his story aloud, trying to ignore the annoying arrogance and condescension in his voice. It had been an amazing and riveting story, brilliant, and haunting...and that's why she knew, without a shadow of a doubt, that it hadn't come from the mind of Mikhail Orlov.

There was an evil part of herself that toyed with the idea of releasing this information to the entire group so she could watch as that cocky smirk was wiped off his face, but she held her tongue as she listened to Mr. LaVey praise him for his original and splendid writing. Rhiannon rolled her eyes as she adjusted the papers on her knees. She didn't know who would be next to reveal their story, but she hoped it would be herself. She'd put her heart and soul into this piece, and she knew that because of this it would likely reveal the inconsistencies in Mikhail's story.

Her stomach ached; not with nerves, but because of the overconsumption of lavish food. Her favourite course of the evening had been the starter: succulent scallops fried in garlic oil and topped with fresh salad leaves and a fresh, zingy dressing. Rhiannon knew that she'd also been slightly heavy-handed with the whiskey again tonight and could feel the alluring buzz all over her body, gently lulling her into that happy, relaxed state. She just hoped she didn't slur her words too much when she finally read out her story.

As luck would have it, Mr. LaVey revealed that she would be reading hers next. She glared at each of the authors in turn as she stood and then began to speak...

Rhiannon's Submission:

The Devil's Graveyard

There was a small, quaint village situated in the heart of the Welsh countryside that was surrounded in mystery, its name unpronounceable to everyone who was not Welsh. The village only had a population of less than eight hundred souls, most of whom were born and raised there and had never travelled further than a few miles in either direction.

At the centre of this village was an ancient grey stone abbey, built in the year 1164. The spectacularly high walls were long gone, having crumbled away into dust—or having been pillaged by the local community to build their own establishments and the local chapel—leaving only the stone foundations on which the magnificent abbey once stood. Many visitors to the village would often stop by the abbey to learn about the history or to stretch their legs while passing through. Dogs and children were welcome but were advised not to climb on the delicate structures.

The abbey, however, was not the main attraction to the local teenagers. They flocked to the small chapel within a large, irregular-shaped graveyard, flanked by roads on the north and west, with the abbey on the south side. It was the perfect place to hang out after school or at the weekend, basking in the warm sun during the summer or huddled under the massive trees in the colder months. The graveyard

216

housed both new and old headstones, which varied wildly in their appearances. Some of the older stones were merely a solid lump of rock, unrecognisable as a headstone, without any visible engravings, while the newer stones were constructed of gleaming black marble, the gold writing sparkling whenever sunlight touched it.

The original chapel building was thought to have belonged to the abbey and had been rebuilt and restored several times over the past two hundred years. The double doors that marked the chapel's entrance were made of solid yew from the nearby trees and bore the scars of age, but their ornate wrought-iron hinges were still solid and strong. The large door handle was situated in the centre of the doors and was accompanied by a heavy, rusted iron knocker.

There was a legend regarding the chapel known by everyone in the village and not freely shared with tourists or outsiders. If a person moved to the village, they would have to prove themselves worthy before being told of this legend. It, of course, was merely a legend; an entertaining myth. No one knew how or when it had originated, only that it had.

For the longest time, there was no one alive that had ever been brave enough to challenge the legend's validity. Usually, the person attempting it would lose their nerve at the last minute, but that all changed when a certain boy moved to the village.

That boy's name was Owen Davies.

* * *

Owen was the new kid in the village, having recently moved there from further afield in North Wales. At sixteen years of age, he was turning into a very handsome and strong young man, eclipsing other boys of his age in both height and size. He was already the talk of the village school and was especially popular among the girls, who had immediately plotted ways to catch his eye or get his number. He'd only been at the school three days and the rumours had started circulating almost immediately: *Owen Davies has already lost his virginity*; *Owen Davies slept with his previous teacher and that's why he's moved schools*; *Owen Davies punched a teacher in the face.* None of those rumours were true, but Owen rarely did anything to silence them. He enjoyed the attention, and it was better than having everyone know the real reason why he'd left his previous school and had to move halfway across the country.

Owen was a bit of a loner and he often found it difficult to make friends. Due to his exceptionally good looks, he found that most boys avoided him out of fear of being labelled his ugly friend and most girls turned into gibbering loonies whenever he tried to speak to them. He'd never found anyone he could connect with…that was, until he'd met Luke, but Luke was now gone, and Owen doubted he'd find anyone like him ever again.

Owen was sitting by himself and eating his lunch in the corner of the schoolyard when he overheard two of his classmates talking about a local graveyard. His ears pricked up at the mention of the word *devil.*

'Yeah, mun. We're doing it tonight. We're spending the night in the devil's graveyard and doing the ritual.'

'You're serious? You're actually gonna do the whole thing?'

'Yeah, mun; and when I do, I'll make history as the first kid to have actually done it. You're in, right?'

'Na, I can't. I'm babysitting my little sister tonight.'

'Get outta it.'

'I'll try.'

'You have to! Ceris is coming and you know what that means.'

'That one of us might get to second base?'

'Exactly.'

Owen lost interest when the boys began to discuss Ceris' body parts and who had already seen or touched what. He continued to eat his lunch, but the mention of "the devil's graveyard" intrigued him. He'd always had a slight morbid fascination with anything to do with the devil, demons, or ghosts, though he didn't know where this interest had originated. His mother hated that he read so much on local ghost stories, but this one sounded like the perfect opportunity to distract him from missing Luke so much.

The boys he had overheard began to walk away, so Owen quickly jumped up and jogged after them.

'Hey!' he shouted. 'Wait up.'

The taller of the boys (although he was still a couple of inches shorter than Owen) spun around. He had very shaggy brown hair that almost covered his eyes and was in dire need of a decent trim. The other boy was much shorter and had a buzz cut all over, which gave him a very sharp and severe look.

'Who the hell are you?' the taller boy demanded.

'My name's Owen…Owen Davies.'

'Ah, the new kid,' the shorter boy said with a laugh. 'Did you really have sex with your teacher? Was she hot? What did her boobs look like? Were they big…D cups?'

Owen frowned. 'Um, no, it's not true.'

'Sure it isn't.'

Owen ignored the shorter boy and turned to the taller one, who was eyeing him suspiciously. 'What's this about the devil's graveyard and a ritual?'

'What's it ta you, new kid?'

'I'm curious.'

'You're an outsider. You need to prove your worth first. The legend is legendary, and we don't tell just anybody.'

'How do I prove that I'm worthy?'

'Tell us what your teacher looked like while you was banging her.'

The boys laughed and high-fived each other.

Owen sighed. 'If I tell you then you'll tell me about the devil's graveyard?'

'Sure.'

Owen spent the next two minutes describing the female body, drawing primarily from a hazy memory of the time he had accidentally discovered his father's porn collection on the computer a couple of years ago. He'd only watched it for a minute before he knew he didn't want to see any more, but he explained the scene as best as he could, feeling himself blushing as time went on. Apparently, to these boys, a vivid explanation of a fake sex scene was enough to prove that he was worthy.

The boys stood with their mouths open, their eyes wide with shock and awe. Owen finished and waited while they whispered back and forth to each other.

'Okay,' the tall boy finally said. 'We deem you worthy.' He beckoned Owen to come closer and lowered his voice to a whisper.

'Apparently, the devil himself lives in the small chapel in the middle of the graveyard. The legend says that if you knock three times, run around the outside three times counter-clockwise, and then knock three times again, the devil will open the door and welcome you inside.'

'How did the legend start?'

The tall boy shrugged. 'Dunno. No one knows, but it's been passed down from generation to generation. All the local families know about it, but there's no one alive who knows why it started, plus everyone is too chicken ta actually do it.'

Owen laughed. 'Wait, so no one has even attempted ta do it?'

'Yeah, they've tried it, but they've always chickened out at the last minute or only done half the challenge, and nothing has happened. I'm gonna be the first person in living memory to do it.'

Owen's eyes grew wide with excitement. 'Can I join you?'

The taller boy narrowed his eyes and looked him up and down again. 'Sure, but don't you be stealing any chance I have at getting into Ceris' bra again. You and your pretty boy haircut can stay away from her, you hear? Besides, after what you did with your teacher, I doubt you'd be happy with Ceris' assets.'

'Don't worry, I'm not interested in...I mean...I have a girlfriend, so...' Owen felt himself blush bright red and his skin heat up.

'Your teacher, right? You still seeing her?' the shorter boy joked.

'Yeah,' laughed Owen. 'Something like that.'

'Cool. I'm Rhys, this short arse here is Gethin.'

All three boys shook hands, confirming their newly formed friendships.

* * *

Owen joined Rhys and Gethin later that evening at the local village shop, which was so small that only a couple of customers could enter it at once, so Owen and Rhys stood outside while Gethin went in for snacks and other supplies. The boys had brought a few blankets, too. Rhys was chewing on a long piece of grass; every few seconds, he would spit bits out directly in front of Owen, who was growing more disgusted by the second.

'So, why'd you really move here?' Rhys asked.

Owen shrugged. 'No reason really. Ma mam just fancied a change.'

'Uh-huh…I don't buy it.'

'Why not?'

'Cos you look like the type who has something ta hide.'

'What's that s'posed ta mean?'

'Means I'm watching you, new kid.'

Owen wrinkled up his nose in annoyance, but decided against arguing with Rhys, especially since a very attractive girl was now approaching them from across the street. She broke into a jog, which caused her ample young breasts to bounce up and down. Owen suspected that she'd either developed extremely early or had somehow managed to stuff her bra. She was wearing very few clothes; a tiny pair of denim shorts and a black crop top that showed off her toned stomach. Her long blonde hair danced in the breeze as she came to a halt in front of the two boys, both of whom made no attempt to hide their fascination with her breasts, even if they were for different reasons.

'Hey Rhys, what's up?' she asked coolly.

Rhys managed to wrench his eyes away from her bra area for a few seconds. 'Hey Ceris...this here's Owen Davies.'

Owen looked into her eyes and gulped.

'Ah, the new kid...I've heard all sorts of stories about you,' she said with a cheeky smile, followed by a wink.

Owen felt himself go hot all over again. 'I'm sure not all of them are true.'

'I hope they are.'

Owen held her gaze for a few moments. She fancied him; he could tell, but she wasn't his type at all. Sure, she was very attractive and would no doubt grow even more beautiful as she developed, but she was trying too hard in his opinion. She clearly knew the effect she had on boys of her own age and that was proven when Gethin walked out of the shop and saw her.

'H-Hey C-Ceris,' he stuttered, again attempting to stare at her breasts while trying not to be too obvious. Then he dropped everything he was holding; luckily none of it was breakable.

'Careful, you fat arse,' scolded Rhys. 'Where's the booze?'

'Old man Jones was in there.'

'Ah, shit.'

'It's alright boys, I've got us covered.' Ceris grinned as she pulled off her rucksack and opened the top compartment.

All three boys leaned closer and spotted an almost full bottle of cheap vodka in her bag. Things were about to get interesting.

* * *

The graveyard itself fascinated Owen immediately. His wandering eyes scanned the area in awe while the others laughed and chatted amongst themselves. He took a few moments and explored by himself, scanning each headstone, and soaking up the history and the atmosphere.

The headstones were not laid out in neat rows, but sparsely and unevenly placed in the ground, which made it difficult to read each inscription in turn. Most of the engraved stones had faded long ago, the bodies now no longer known by their names but merely by a rough piece of stone to signal that they lay hidden beneath.

One stone caught his eye, the writing barely visible. He crouched down and read the inscription. It seemed that some poor soul had lost his left leg and part of his thigh, which was buried here while the rest of his body was interred elsewhere in the United States.

He wandered around the perimeter of the graveyard and came across a flat stone near the north wall, which simply read:

Unknown.
He died upon a hillside drear,
Alone where snow was deep,
By strangers he was carried here
Where princes also sleep.

Owen stopped and bowed his head in respect to the anonymous soul.

'Hey, new kid! Over here!' Rhys' voice echoed around the graveyard, making Owen wince. He hoped they weren't disturbing the dead.

He felt a chilly breeze, despite the August warmth, as he made his way cautiously across the graveyard, following the paths, towards the small oblong chapel where the other three had set up camp. The building itself was fascinating and he read a small plaque that was propped up against the outside wall.

The chapel had been rebuilt from the ground up in 1815, which consisted of a nave and chancel and west bell-cote. It was restored again in 1875 and yet again in 1914 after falling into disrepair. It housed four stained-glass windows, which dated back to the 1960s, that had been donated by a local man.

Owen glanced up from the writing and took small steps towards the front doors. His heart rate began to increase; for what reason he didn't know, but something was drawing him in, something exciting and unknown. He held his breath as he grasped the cold iron of the door handle and pushed...

Locked.

'Hey, new kid! They locked the doors when a bunch of morons broke the pulpit a few years ago. No one's been in there since.'

Owen turned to look at the trio; they had taken refuge from the sun under the nearby yew tree, only a few feet from the front door. The bottle of vodka was already out of the bag and being passed around. He had a sneaking suspicion that it had been those three that had broken the pulpit.

Owen joined them under the tree. 'So, what now?' he asked.

'Now we wait,' said Rhys, who grimaced as he took a big swig of vodka.

'Wait for what?'

'Midnight.'

'Why? What's so special about midnight?'

'Nothing…just seems like a good time ta do the ritual.'

'Why can't you do it now?'

Rhys threw back his head and laughed. 'Cos I don't know about you, mun, but if you were ta face the devil…wouldn't you want ta be shitfaced first?'

Owen shrugged his shoulders. 'I guess so.'

'Well…drink up then, mun!' Rhys handed Owen the bottle, which he took apprehensively and then proceeded to take a slow drink.

Ceris winked at Owen and began to inch herself closer to him. She moved her bare legs so that they were touching his. He attempted a weak smile, his breath catching in his dry throat.

'Ya scared?' she asked.

Yes, he thought, *but not about meeting the devil.*

'N-No,' he stammered. 'I'm not scared.'

'You look scared,' she added. 'Don't worry…I don't bite…unless you ask me too.' She winked at him before snatching the bottle from his trembling hands.

'Hey, new kid…watch yourself with that *slebog*,' warned Rhys.

'Excuse me! Did you just call me a slut?' laughed Ceris, but from her tone of voice she didn't appear to be offended.

'If tha shoe fits!'

'*Coc oen!*'

'*Ast!*'

'*Pen dick!*'

Then all three started rolling about on the grass in fits of laughter. Owen smiled and began chuckling also as he leaned back on his hands. He supposed he could hang out with them for a while.

* * *

By half past eleven, three of the group were thoroughly sloshed. The bottle of vodka was almost empty, Ceris had vomited twice into the bushes, and Gethin had fallen off a nearby stone wall and twisted his ankle. Owen had managed to keep himself relatively sober by allowing the others to drink his share of the bottle. All talks of the ritual, the legend, and the devil had been forgotten by everyone apart from Owen, who eventually turned to Rhys.

'So…you ready to meet him?'

Rhys laughed and staggered slightly on his numb legs. 'R-Ready ta meet ooh?'

'The devil.'

More laughter. 'If you wanna meet 'im so bad, you do it.'

'Ah, come on, R-Rhys,' said Gethin, as he hiccupped. 'You gotta do it. Tis your idea.'

'Ch-Changed ma mind.'

'*Cachgu!*'

Rhys spat on the ground and wiped his mouth. 'I ain't a coward! I'll do it! I'll show ya *pen dicks* that I ain't scared.'

Gethin and Ceris roared with laughter as Rhys stormed up to the door of the chapel. Ceris fished her phone out of her bag and eagerly began filming. Owen's breath caught in his throat. He felt himself become alive with excitement and nerves as he watched Rhys who stopped at the door and raised his fist ready to knock.

Knock three times.

Run around the chapel three times counter-clockwise.

Knock three more times.

Rhys glanced over his shoulder at his friends, held his breath, and knocked three times on the solid door. The echo seemed to reverberate around the graveyard, knocking leaves out of the trees, but there was not a breath of wind.

Ceris gasped and clutched Owen's arm for moral support with her one free hand, but Owen didn't take his eyes from Rhys as he began to run around the chapel.

Once.

Twice.

Three times.

Silence followed.

Rhys came to a halt at the door again and raised his fist once more. Everyone held their breath, but he didn't knock. His fist was frozen, and he began shaking violently.

'Oh my God, what's wrong with him!' Gethin shouted while pointing with a shaking finger.

Rhys suddenly lurched to the side and vomited. Ceris and Gethin erupted into laughter once more as they dragged him away from the door, but Owen remained silent; the disappointment was clear on his face. He kept his gaze directed upon the door of the chapel.

It remained closed and dormant.

Of course it did.

Ceris and Gethin were still howling with laughter, barely able to contain themselves. It echoed around the graveyard, mocking the dead that were trying to sleep peacefully. Owen clenched his fists into balls and squeezed. The others had no respect, no moral code. He'd had enough.

'Stop it!' he shouted, but the laughter and jest continued. Rhys had finally stopped retching and was enjoying the banter, clearly forgetting the important task at hand. 'Stop it!' Owen shouted again.

Finally, the three of them all stopped and stared at him.

'Wassup with you?' Rhys spat onto a nearby gravestone.

Owen tightened his fists. 'You need ta finish it.'

'I don't need ta finish anything, mun.'

'You said you were gonna do the ritual. You said you wanted ta be the first person ta complete it all the way through.'

Rhys scoffed. 'If you want ta see it done so bad, you do it.'

'Yeah, go on, mun! You do it!' Gethin shouted as he thumped Rhys on the back. It appeared that he was on Rhys' side, as was expected.

Owen glanced at Ceris in the light of the moon. She had stopped laughing and had not made a sound since. She caught his eye and then immediately looked at the ground. It seemed Owen was outnumbered.

'Fine,' he said quietly. 'I'll do it. I ain't afraid.'

'Yeah, well, I ain't afraid neither!' Rhys spat again, but he began to take tentative steps away from the chapel, as did the other two. Ceris pulled out her phone once more and began filming.

Owen stepped forwards, keeping his eyes fixed on the door. His heart rate was steady, but loud. He could feel it pulsing throughout his body.

Thump. Thump. Thump.

He licked his lips and swallowed as he raised his fists.

Bang. Bang. Bang.

Without pausing, he took off running.

Once.

Twice.

Three times.

He stopped at the door, puffing slightly from the exertion, took a deep breath and...

Bang. Bang. Bang.

He heard an audible gasp from the group behind him and Ceris let out a little whimper, the hand holding her phone trembling. Owen held his breath as he stepped away from the door, as if he was expecting it to swing open towards him...but it remained closed.

Not even a rustle could be heard in the trees. A full two minutes passed before anyone said anything, and it was Rhys who eventually broke the deathly silence: 'Well, that was fucking anticlimactic!'

Ceris lowered her phone. 'I was expecting at least *something* to happen!'

Then they all began to laugh as they got back to finishing the bottle of vodka. Owen remained frozen in place, staring at the door, willing it to open.

Open...open...open.

The disappointment he felt ached throughout his entire body. He didn't want to move in case something happened, but the minutes ticked by, and he could hear the others settling down to tell some stories, but their words were muffled because he didn't want to listen. He wanted that damn door to unlock and open so he could meet the devil. He had never wanted anything so badly in his life, apart from seeing Luke again.

He began to think of Luke and how much he would have enjoyed this ritual. He'd had a fascination with all things devilish too, but he was gone now…dead…and it was all Owen's fault.

Finally, he dragged his eyes off the door and turned to the group. Ceris beckoned him over and he took a seat next to her. She linked her arm through his and snuggled up close, but he was careful not to return the gesture.

'You okay?' she asked.

'Yeah, I'm good.'

'You were very brave,' she added.

'Thanks.' He cracked a small smile for her, but then his face returned to the frown it was before as he listened to the boys tell the story of how they could see down the history teachers' blouse whenever she leaned over.

Owen felt the warmth of Ceris' body seeping into him as the air of the night turned cooler. In fact, a thin mist of fog was creeping its way over the ground, weaving in between the gravestones and over the grass. The moon was casting its light across the area, highlighting the white fog, but no one seemed to notice or care. Owen shuddered, which caused Ceris to raise her head off his chest and look at him.

The whites of her eyes were blood red; her pupils dilated to mere pinpricks. Her grey skin began to peel off in layers and he could see her blackened teeth as she grinned, her mouth getting wider and wider and…

Owen screamed as he scrambled to his feet, shoving her aside. Rhys and Gethin stared at him, but their faces were exactly the same. Their eyes were bleeding, their skin melting, their teeth bared…

Owen closed his eyes.

No no no no no no…

'What the fuck?' he heard Rhys ask.

Upon opening his eyes, Owen found all three of them glaring at him, looking perfectly normal, if slightly confused.

'I-I'm sorry,' he spluttered. 'I thought I saw…it's nothing. I've just had too much ta drink.'

Rhys and Gethin scoffed, but Ceris was still frowning at him. Owen felt himself blush and turned away from her. He looked out across the fog around the graveyard. The fog was expanding and now reached up into the trees and over the stone walls surrounding the area. The only part that wasn't covered with it was the place where the group were huddled. The fog was so thick that Owen couldn't see more than a few feet through it. He felt his chest tighten and a lump form in his throat.

'You sure you're okay?' asked Ceris. She'd appeared next to him.

'Y-Yes. Sorry…I just…does the fog always get this thick around here?'

'What are you talking about? What fog?'

Owen stared at her. She couldn't see it. None of them could. Ceris smiled up at him, completely oblivious to his growing dread as she turned and walked back to the other boys.

* * *

By one o'clock, everyone had started to get tired and began huddling under the blankets, settling down to sleep. Rhys and Ceris shared a blanket while Gethin and Owen had their own. One by one, they began to drop off, apart from Owen, who had set himself up so that he could stare at the chapel door all night long. The fog was still encircling the group, but it hadn't grown any thicker. In fact, it looked as if it was beginning to disperse a little because he could see further across the graveyard than he'd been able to an hour ago.

The chapel was illuminated by the moonlight, its stained-glass windows shining brightly, but the door remained closed. Owen was fighting the urge to sleep and finally, at just after two, his eyes closed, and he dreamed...

He was walking around the graveyard studying the headstones as he had done earlier in the evening. The fog had lifted, and it was a beautifully clear and peaceful night, but there wasn't a breath of wind or a single whisper from any nearby nocturnal wildlife. It was eerily quiet, not even his feet made a sound as he walked. It was as if he was floating inches off the ground. The only thing he could hear was his heartbeat, which was beating at a steady rhythm.

Owen stopped by a large headstone and bent down to inspect it. It was difficult to make out the inscription, but he could see it said something about a Welsh poet. Owen ran his fingers over the cold stone...

The ground began to tremble, so he stepped back, afraid that he had disturbed the grave. The very earth was moving. Something was coming up out of the soil...

Owen wanted to turn and run, but fear froze him in place as the ground parted and a skeletal hand clawed its way to the surface, making no sound whatsoever. He screamed a silent scream...

Owen opened his eyes. He was standing above the same grave. The earth was disturbed, as if something had climbed out of the ground.

233

He turned and glanced over at his friends, all of whom were still fast asleep, their blankets slightly askew. The fog was still there, but it was moving, as if it were alive somehow. Owen watched as the silky white mist swirled around the headstones. He held his breath as it then began to sink into the ground, slowly disappearing until there was nothing left.

Owen breathed a sigh of relief as he made his way back towards the group. As he got closer, he realised that something was wrong.

Gethin looked...different.

A person who was asleep usually still moved; their chest would fall and rise from breathing, maybe their eyelids would flutter while dreaming, but Gethin was still...completely still, his face a pale grey...as if he were...

'Gethin!' Owen rushed over and began to violently shake him. 'Wake up! Gethin, wake the fuck up!' Owen slapped him across the face.

Rhys and Ceris sat bolt upright.

'What the fuck, dude! What the...Gethin?' Rhys shoved his blanket aside and scrambled to his friends' side, joining Owen in his attempt to wake Gethin, but he remained grey and lifeless. Ceris screamed as she realised what had happened.

Owen and Rhys finally gave up and sat back on their heels, the body of their friend laying limp in their arms. Ceris wept as she sank to the ground.

'W-What h-happened?' she sobbed.

'I had a dream,' began Owen. 'I woke up over on the other side of the graveyard. I must have sleepwalked. I began to walk back and saw…'

'How the fuck could he have just died in his sleep?' demanded Rhys. He shoved the body aside, grabbed Owen by his t-shirt, and dragged him to his feet. 'You must've seen somethin'!'

'I didn't see nothing, I swear!' Owen held up his hands defensively.

Rhys finally released him. 'How much did he have ta drink?' he asked Ceris.

'No more t-than you or m-me,' she cried.

'Well, what the hell happened ta him then!'

Rhys and Ceris turned to Owen, who stood there shaking, unable to give them a straight answer. The truth was, he just didn't know, but he had a horrible suspicion that it had something to do with completing the ritual. They were being punished.

The trio left the body of their friend laying in an awkward position on the ground and huddled together in a group.

'Someone has to go and get help or call 999,' suggested Ceris. She was met with complete silence.

Owen eventually nodded slowly; he reluctantly glanced over her shoulder to where the body lay…but it was gone. Owen did a double take before pushing past Ceris. 'He's gone!'

'What?' demanded Rhys.

'He's gone. Gethin's gone.'

'How the fuck does a dead body just vanish?' Rhys stormed over to where Owen was frantically searching. 'Okay…I know what this is. This is some sick fucking joke. Gethin's having us on. He faked it! Come on out, Gethin! I'm gonna fucking kill ya, you motherfucker!'

Silence.

Not even a breath of wind.

'Gethin, this ain't funny no more,' pleaded Ceris. 'Please come out!'

Owen knew it wasn't a joke, but he didn't wish to panic the others. He looked towards the chapel; the door was still closed. Something was happening to them. Something was...

Rhys let out a blood-curdling scream as he collapsed to the ground and began violently shaking. White frothy bubbles erupted from his mouth as his body was overcome by a seizure. Ceris and Owen ran to his side to try and help him, but it was no use. Rhys became still seconds later...

'Call 999!' shouted Owen.

Ceris scrambled to her feet and began fumbling around on the ground for her phone. She found it and began to type the numbers, her hands trembling so badly she could barely keep hold of it. 'There's no signal!' she screamed.

Rhys laid perfectly still in Owen's arms, his eyes staring up in horror, as if he'd seen something ghastly before he had died. 'What have we done?' whispered Owen before slowly getting to his feet.

'We didn't do anything!' Ceris was nearing hysteria. 'It was just a legend, a horror story that's been passed down through generations. It's not real!'

'Seems pretty real to me,' spat Owen.

Ceris sobbed as she began walking backwards through the graveyard towards the exit. She was stepping on graves and flat tombstones, but she didn't care.

'Ceris! Stop!'

It was too late. An invisible force grabbed her ankles and she fell to the ground, her head smacking off a flat stone with a sickening crack. A high-pitched scream echoed around the area as she was violently dragged away, eventually disappearing into a grave.

Silence.

Owen closed his eyes as tight as they would go.

'This is just a dream. This is just a dream. Wake up, Owen.' He continued to repeat those words over and over, unwilling to open his eyes until he heard his friends' voices reassuring him that they were just messing with him or that he was sleepwalking again.

A loud crack emerged from the silence, followed by another, but Owen kept his eyes closed. It sounded like...a creaky old door opening...

He turned towards the noise. The creaking stopped and was replaced by eerie silence once more and then...

'Enter.'

The word came as a whisper in his ear, as if the person who'd spoken it were standing directly beside him.

Owen's body was flooded with goosebumps. He couldn't keep his eyes closed any longer. His body was forcing him to peel them open, and when he did, he was facing the chapel door, brightly illuminated by the moonlight.

The door was wide open.

'Who's there?' he stuttered.

Owen was trying his best to step backwards, but he couldn't move a muscle in any other direction other than forwards. It was as if he was being pulled; not by the invisible force that had taken Ceris away, but by his own morbid curiosity.

He'd wanted this.

He'd wanted to come here.

He'd been disappointed and angry that Rhys had given up.

He'd completed the ritual.

This was *his* doing, but he'd never felt such paralysing fear before; it rippled across every corner of his body. He wished he could take it back the same way he wished he could take back the fact that he'd made his best friend climb down into a cave with no safety rope. Luke had fallen to his death, and everyone had blamed Owen…and all because Owen had heard a rumour that the devil had lived in those caves.

Owen slowly stepped forwards as the fog began to reappear; it now encircled the chapel, closing in on him, getting thicker. Owen was at the door now, his feet on the large grey stone in front of it. He could see inside as the moonlight beamed through the stained-glass windows and cast rainbow patterns on the opposite wall.

The chapel was smaller than he'd imagined, home to only a dozen or so pews and a very small pulpit with a large wooden cross hanging above it. Owen's eyes grew wide as he took in his surroundings and stepped further inside the building. He turned around on the spot so that he could look back out of the door and into the graveyard where the fog had reached the door, trapping him inside.

'Welcome. You have finally found me, my child.'

The words were a mere whisper, but they echoed around the room and were followed by a loud bang as the door slammed shut, sealing Owen inside forever.

And thus, a new legend was born.

Chapter Six

Thursday

1. Mikhail Makes an Omelette

Mikhail bounded downstairs, his senses alive from the adrenaline rush of creativity and having so effortlessly bested his peers. He remembered the look on Pavel's face when he had told him of LaVey's invitation: kindness, yes, and that same naïve optimism, but also pity. He had gotten so angry at Pavel, not just because he hated being out of the loop, but because he despised all forms of charity.

We'll see who pities who now, Mikhail thought as he crossed the main foyer. Tucked away at the back, in the shadows, was another of LaVey's many intricately decorated doors. However, now that his story was completed, Mikhail had every intention of never giving any of LaVey's grandeur a second thought. Instead, he pushed open the door, stormed down a narrow corridor brightly lit by globe-like lamps, and barged into the kitchen. A far cry from his mother's humble kitchen at the old homestead, LaVey's kitchen was potentially bigger than Mikhail's whole apartment back in Voronezh and was the only room in the entire mansion that Mikhail had seen modern trappings married with the house's traditional, old-timey aesthetic.

The floor was made up of big stone slabs. A long rectangular oak table sat in the centre of the room and was home to various

240

chopping boards and jugs containing wooden spoons and other implements, and rows of wooden shelves ran underneath it which stored mixing bowls, cooking pots, and bags of flour. One side of the room was taken up by oak cupboards and drawers and a long kitchen counter; brass and silver pots, pans, mixing jugs, and knives were affixed to the wall overhead, allowing for easy access. A massive white ceramic sink sat at the end. Dish cloths and aprons were hung over a silver bar set into the front of it, and a large window was set into the wall above it. Small, rectangular windows lined the perimeter of the kitchen, no doubt allowing a great deal of natural light to enter.

The other side was far more modern and taken up by a gigantic, fifties-style refrigerator, two matching freezers, and a stainless steel work area on which was sat a number of cooking devices, including two microwaves, one at either end, flanked by two kettles (a more traditional teapot and crockery set sat on a shelf nearby), and other gadgets Mikhail didn't recognise, and beneath this were yet more kitchen gadgets.

Mikhail crossed the kitchen and opened the door at the far end, revealing a small, musty area that housed yet another freezer on the right (a smaller, chest-high model), a messy pantry on the left (in which were piled cans upon cans of food on rickety shelves, bags of potatoes, and crates of freshly-picked vegetables and fruits), and another matching door that led outside. *Probably to a vegetable patch of some sort*, Mikhail thought as he searched the pantry shelves.

After pushing aside tins of soup, creamed corn, fruit cocktail, and baked beans, and shifting through packs of buns, jars of cocoa powder, and a seemingly endless supply of tea bags and coffee granules, he finally found a stash of eggs and returned to the kitchen, leaving the door open behind him. Mikhail set the eggs down next to the massive, cast iron kitchen range. He grabbed a frying pan from a hook hanging above the hob and examined the cooker with momentary confusion. Although the kitchener had the capacity to be fuelled by coal, it was also gas-powered and, in moments, Mikhail had fired up the hob and set the pan upon the small ring of flames that had burst into life.

Mikhail searched through the nearby drawers, shifting through tea towels and cutlery (grabbing a knife and fork as he went) before finally finding a whisk. He whistled without even thinking about it. It was "Swan Lake," Lia's favourite of the classics, and he vaguely realised that he hadn't whistled or listened to Tchaikovsky in the years since she had passed, not until LaVey had played those first familiar notes the other day.

Lia had always made his omelettes using two eggs, which had left them thin and unsatisfying. Mikhail cracked three eggs into the jug, hesitated, then cracked a fourth. *Why the fuck not?* he thought as he whistled and whisked away. Once he was satisfied with the mixture, he rummaged through the potato sack until he found a couple of decent-sized potatoes; he cut them into small, unpeeled chunks and dropped them into the pan where they simmered away nicely.

Mikhail crossed over to LaVey's massive freezer, a blast of chilled air sweeping over him as he searched for a suitable meat. He pushed aside a packet of corned beef, left the pork luncheon tongue where it was, and had no desire to eat any more slimy chicken slices. He settled for a packet of cured ham. It wasn't буженина but it would have to do. Mikhail grabbed a block of cheese and two chunky tomatoes, kicked the fridge shut, and went back to the cooker. He shuffled the potatoes absently before slicing the other ingredients up, pouring his eggs over the potatoes, and sprinkling the ham and tomatoes over the bubbling mixture.

How he had loved the smell of Lia's omelettes, and how it had *infuriated* him that she couldn't replicate his mother's recipe with any kind of competency. '*Дурак!*' he would shout when she presented him with a plate of eggy mess. 'Can you do *nothing* right?'

She had never been much of a homemaker; she was always too busy daydreaming about the glitz and glamour of America. 'Is not like that мусор you watch,' he would say, but would she listen? Of course not.

Stubborn. Too stubborn for her own good sometimes, he thought as he gobbled up his perfectly-cooked omelette.

All he had wanted was a good, attentive wife. Even when his father had been at his very worst, his mother had been devoted and dutiful. Was it too much to ask for that kind of loyalty and commitment? He worked hard to provide for her and asked little in return; just a clean house, hearty meals, and children of his own, but she had shown very little interest in those reasonable demands. And no amount of reasoning or arguing would dissuade her. She had seemed dejected to find out that she was pregnant and had only grown more sullen after Luka was born: 'He is a *blessing*,' Mikhail had stressed when they had returned home with him.

Lia had remained unconvinced. She flinched whenever Luka cried, seemed disgusted at changing his nappy, and flat-out refused to breastfeed him. When the boy cried at night, Mikhail would have to attend to him; when he made his first teetering steps, Mikhail was there to catch him before he toppled over, and it was he who kept the boy occupied while Lia laid staring at the television.

Was it any wonder he had been stressed?

Who *wouldn't* have been stressed?

What man could say that they wouldn't have struck his wife after finding her holding a knife as their child lay wailing on the floor. 'I…I was…' Lia had stuttered, and then she had shrieked as Mikhail had shaken the knife from her hand and slapped her hard across the face.

'*Псих!*' he'd roared, seeing red, as Luka had bawled on the floor. '*What were you thinking!?*' and she'd sobbed, begging, as he had slapped her again, but he had lost himself to the rage. 'You get the fuck out!' he'd snarled, looming over her. 'Get the fuck out and *stay the fuck out!*'

'*Папа?*' Luka had asked later that night as Mikhail had sat in his favourite chair, moodily nestling a glass of vodka. 'When's Мама coming home?'

Mikhail had stroked his son's hair gently. 'We don't need her, малыш. We'll be just fine; you'll see.'

Thick smoke suddenly caused Mikhail to gag and tore him away from the memory. In his hunger and fatigue, he had forgotten to take the frying pan off the stove, and sizzling smoke was rising from the kitchener. Mikhail fumbled with the knobs and shut the cooker off, cursing his foolishness…not just with the kitchen, but at underestimating Lia's madness. He'd been just as stunned when he had found her ransacking their little house, frantically stuffing clothes and toys into a big suitcase at random, tears streaming down her blubbering cheeks.

'You're not taking him from me!' she'd babbled at him standing there, her eyes wide with fear. 'You'll *never* take him from me!'

She'd held that knife in her trembling hand.

Luka had been sat on the floor, two chubby fingers stuck in his mouth, his eyes so full of confusion and terror.

What   husband…what   *father*…wouldn't   have   reacted accordingly?

2. *Aster in the Hedge Maze*

This was the most productive I have been in some time. The solitude and lack of distractions (especially from social media because of the shitty internet) increased my focus on the project. Aside from going down to attend meals (mostly with Mr. LaVey and occasionally Mikhail), I was in my room, working hard on my piece for LaVey's anthology. When I was dedicated to something, everything else was forgotten until I was finished with the task at hand.

This short story—not to brag—was one of the best works I had done in a while. Everything was flowing nicely and, despite not writing out my usual rough outline, it was going well. 'I'll have to revisit this story and turn it into a novel down the road,' I said. 'I'll have to make a note of this.'

I should have tried to fit sleep somewhere in my schedule. It wasn't the first time I had gone over twenty-four hours without sleeping to work on a project. I knew it wasn't good for my health to get into this nasty habit, but I couldn't help myself and I was too stubborn for my own good. It had gotten so bad that I could swear I could hear voices.

'*Na–*'

It was definitely loud enough to be heard through the white noise coming from my headphones. Snapping my eyes from the laptop screen and removing my headphones, I glanced around the room and called out: 'Is anyone there? Mr. LaVey?'

I highly doubted LaVey would come into my room unannounced, but I couldn't be too sure. I hadn't actually seen much of him since the other day, and he could have been worried. The voice I heard, though, didn't sound like his at all. Another thing I noticed was how dark the room was.

I picked up my phone, it read 2:47 a.m. *Fuck. Been working for hours now. Honestly, I've lost count. A break wouldn't be a bad idea. Get up and stretch, give my eyes a break from the bright screen...*

Slowly getting up from the armchair, I twisted my body to the left and right to get my back to crack. Both sides released a satisfying popping sound and I could feel shivers run down my spine. Coming back from my second set of twists, I saw a flicker of white light from the window. I froze on the spot and watched it dance on the outer perimeters of the hedge maze. It was mesmerising as the light slowly made its way to the entrance of the maze. My feet moved on their own towards the window to see where it was headed next. While I could no longer see it, there was still a faint glow showing what direction the light was headed.

'*Come, Nao–*'

Slipping on my sweatshirt and boots, I quietly made my way out of my room, making sure to turn on my phone's flashlight before continuing down the hallway towards the two staircases, where I stopped in my tracks.

'What am I doing? Where am I going?' I mumbled to myself, looking around in the dark. 'Even I'm not that stupid. Going out, alone, in a foreign place is asking for trouble. If you're going to be an idiot, at least do it in the daylight with others awake to hear you scream.'

I took a deep breath before turning around and going back to my room. A slam of a door made me stop in my tracks again. I held my breath as I waited to hear any other noises. After a few moments of eerie silence, I exhaled cautiously and continued my way back to my room.

Sleep sounded like a fantastic idea. I changed out of my clothes and threw on my maroon tank top and fluffy blue pajama bottoms and crawled under the covers.

A bright light woke me from my slumber. *There was no way it could be morning already*, I thought. I rubbed my eyes sleepily and rolled over to the bedside table to grab my phone. There were four missed calls from Walter and three text messages, none of which I could make out due to my distorted vision.

'Shit,' I muttered. 'This isn't going to go well.' I had wanted to chuck my phone across the room after hearing Walter cuss me out, but it was probably best to get this out of the way now as opposed to putting it off until later. I hit the call button and waited. On the fourth ring, I heard an unfamiliar voice answer.

A woman's voice.

'Yuh-ello?'

My mind began to panic; a knot formed in my stomach, and I felt the familiar sensation of my eyes starting to sting before a crying fit started.

'Hello? Is someone there?'

My phone beeped in my ear, piercing my thoughts. I took it away from my head and stared at the screen: not only was it 1:58 p.m., but my phone was down to eight percent. I silenced the stranger's voice with a press of the screen and busied myself with fumbling through my bag. I dug out the charger, hooked it up to the adapter, and wandered over to the bedroom window in a daze.

I need to clear my head.

Looking out of the window down at the hedge maze, I decided that some fresh air would do me some good. It looked pleasant enough for me to stroll the grounds and explore the maze. There was plenty of daylight left as well, just in case I got stuck somewhere inside it. Though, I wasn't concerned; mazes and puzzles were something I excelled at. I changed into a blue knee-length dress. It was one of my favourites, and it could be worn for nearly any occasion. Slipping into my tennis shoes and grabbing my winter coat, I made my way outside. There was no doubt anyone who saw me would question my choice in wardrobe. Yes, I was unconventional, but I didn't care. What's the worst that would happen? My legs would get cold, and I'd have to throw on a pair of leggings.

As I made my way downstairs, I caught a glimpse of Mikhail making his way down the hall. I did my best to quietly descend the stairs and exit the front door before he noticed me. Getting into another verbal confrontation was the last thing I felt like dealing with. The cool air blasted me the moment I was out of the house, but it wasn't frigid like it would be back home. I followed the stone walls around to the back of the house where I had seen the maze. Opening the small gate, I continued to follow the path until I could see the maze in the distance. But that's when I noticed I wasn't alone; Rhiannon was sitting on the lone bench in the garden. She looked exhausted and was visibly shaking as she puffed away at her cigarette.

'Rhiannon!' I called to her. When she didn't look my way, I repeated her name.

Rhiannon jumped at her name, her eyes frantically searched the area until they landed on me. She gave a short wave. 'Hey, Aster...' she took a long drag and avoided looking at me.

'You all right? Haven't seen you for a few days.'

'Uh...yeah...just been writing, ya know? Once ya get started it's hard to stop...Just out here for a quick smoke. Want one?'

Rhiannon offered me one of her smokes, which I politely declined. The scent was bad enough, but the taste made me gag every single time. 'I'm just out here checking out the maze and getting some fresh air. Wanna join me?'

Rhiannon shook her head as she put out her cigarette. 'I should get back to writing, but we can talk later.'

Before I could reply, she was already through the back door and gone; the door made a loud slam that filled the otherwise silent garden grounds.

Huh, that was unusual. Hope I didn't offend her.

'Course you didn't. Stop thinking you're always in the wrong,' I answered myself. 'She said she needed to get back to writing...you can relate to that.'

Suddenly, the ball of light appeared at the entrance of the maze. Seeing it this close both surprised and terrified me. It showed itself... in broad daylight? I knew I wasn't seeing things now. The ball of light was real, and it felt like it was trying to tell me something. One thing I knew was that I wanted to sort this situation out once and for all.

As I approached it, the light darted further into the maze. This felt like a trap; another of those cliché setups that idiots in horror movies would fall for. However, I was too stubborn for my own good and that beat out my rational side.

I proceeded further into the maze. Everything became darker, but the light was always ahead of me, making sure I was aware of its presence.

The sound of children laughing filled the air. I stopped in my tracks. 'Hello?' I called out. I was met with silence. Children unnerved me, especially with their demented-sounding giggles. 'No kids here. It's just you. You're getting yourself worried for nothing...'

'*Aster...come play with us, Aster.*' It sounded like a chorus of little girls... and they sounded close.

A strangled chuckle fell from my lips. 'Stop scaring yourself...no one else is in here!'

The giggling stopped, and all was silent. This was one of several reasons I couldn't stand kids. Ever since I was a teenager, I never had the desire to procreate. Maybe that should have been my first sign to leave Walter. When he started talking about having a big family and was adamant I would change my mind, I stood firm on my beliefs, no matter how angry it made him. He always wanted to have sex whenever I was at my most fertile time (how he came to know this information I didn't know, but it was concerning) and I could always tell he was frustrated when I would get my monthly visitor. Maybe it was cruel of me not to tell him I was on the pill. That alone should have been a red flag in our relationship.

'But you thought you could change him,' I grumbled. However, I must have misplaced my current month's batch, which wasn't surprising for me. I had been under an enormous amount of stress trying to get *Masquerade* finished up for my ARC team and everything else in my life had taken a back seat. I hadn't been as good with taking them, and Walter had only wanted sex one time in the last few days. It wasn't in my fertile period, so I was in the clear. I made a mental note to get a new prescription ordered up once I got back to Iowa. The last thing I needed was to have a child.

Taking a deep breath, I continued forward before being forced to take a right. Rounding the corner, I saw a a line of incredible topiary animals. If I wasn't already on edge from the laughing phantom kids, I would have taken some time to admire them. A rumble of thunder above signalled it was going to rain soon. Maybe I should head back…

'*Hehehehe!*' A shrill titter rang out directly behind me. '*Why don't you want to play with us, Aster?*'

Whipping around, I expected to see a child staring at me. What I saw was worse: nothing. There wasn't anything or anyone behind me or nearby. The only noticeable difference was there was a white mist settling down in the corridors of the maze. *Where did this fog come from?* I thought. Maybe that storm was coming sooner than I assumed. It would be a good idea for me to make my way back. It was apparent that I was psyching myself out or—

The sound of a branch snapping stopped my thoughts. Okay, there definitely was someone else in here. My fear was replaced with anger.

'Okay, real funny! Mikhail! Brandis! You can come out now. I'm thoroughly terrified.' I began backing into one of the nearby walls of shrubbery. 'You succeeded in scaring me. Can you please come out now?'

Something cold gripped my arm. My body seized up for a moment before I dared to look down at what grabbed me. My eyes landed on a tiny hand wrapped around my forearm. Several others began to appear from the wall, reaching out to me, and trying to grab me and pull me through the shrubbery.

'*No!*' I screamed and yanked my arm from the child's grasp. I must have pulled back a little too hard as I lost my balance and stumbled to the ground. The sound of leaves and branches crackling filled the air, growing louder by the second. I stood up in a panic and locked eyes with one of the topiary lions. Its eyes blinked for a moment before staring directly at me, those two dark holes slowly glowing a bright red. Soon, the rest of the topiary animals were staring at me, eyes glowing ominously and making all kinds of strange growls tied in with the sound of children laughing.

My body went into fight-or-flight mode, and I chose flight. I could feel myself running faster than I ever had before in my life. Stumbling around a bit, I refused to look back. *Focus on what's in front of you. Looking back will only slow you down*, my mind cautioned. Something white flashed in my peripheral vision; I didn't need to look twice to see it was numerous chubby, small pairs of children's hands reaching out to try and grab me.

'*Fuck!*' I screamed, picking up my pace. The giggling children returned as I saw the exit of the maze. The rain was freezing against my skin and my legs were screaming in pain because of years of inactivity.

'Come on! You're almost there! There's the exit!' A face suddenly flashed in front of me and caused me to stumble to a halt. I immediately recognised it as Finley. What was he doing in here? His eyes were blacked out, yet he was staring directly at me.

'Aster. Are you ready for your future?' Finley's grin was unsettling as he flashed his blackened teeth at me. 'Are you ready?'

What the fuck was he talking about? I tried not to worry too much about the future unless it was called for. 'Finley, I don't understand. What's going on?'

His smile widened as his index finger pointed directly at my chest. 'You will be ready whether you want to be or not.'

I started to panic. This couldn't be the same sweet guy I had been chatting with a few days ago. No, this had to be another illusion, or whatever was going on in this maze. I sidestepped him, and he didn't try to stop me. Instead, Finley continued to watch me as I moved around him and gave him one last glance before running to the maze's exit.

Racing out of the maze, I didn't stop until I reached the back door of the house. Slamming it shut and locking it with the two deadbolts, I slid to the floor, trying to catch my breath. A loud sob escaped my throat, and I started convulsing.

What the ever-living fuck was that?! There was no way that could have been real. Inanimate objects couldn't come to life like that. It just wasn't possible!

'No, no, no, no, no,' was all I could mutter. I pressed a hand to my chest, trying to focus on my breathing. I needed to calm down; everything was all right now. Nothing from out there could get me in here. My eyes squeezed shut, tears threatening to spill out. I had never been so terrified in my life. Was I going crazy? Was that even real?

'Course it wasn't real! There was no one else out there! And hedge animals don't come to life. That's nonsense!

I slowly opened my eyes to see I was in the confines of LaVey's house.

No giggling children.

No red-eyed hedge animals.

This was a safe place.

There was nothing in here to harm me.

My breathing slowed and my thoughts settled down. I was still shaken up, but I was calming down. Using the door as a brace, I heaved myself to my feet and took a slow step forward.

'I need to get back to my room. It's safe there...nothing can hurt me there,' I whispered shakily. 'Come on, it's just out this room and up two flights of stairs.'

Taking notice of my surroundings, I realised that I was on something like a back porch. There was another door in front of me; I took a few trembling steps forward and turned the knob. It appeared I was in the kitchen, one room I had yet to explore properly.

'I'm in the kitchen...just need to find my way out of here...this shouldn't be too hard.'

It was dark in here, making navigation harder, but I was able to find my way to the archway leading me out to the main hallway. What I wasn't expecting was to be grabbed from behind and jerked back into the kitchen.

3. *Brandis Makes a Plan*

Having resigned myself to my self-imposed exile, I only ventured out of my room to load up a tray with food around lunch time and I was ashamed to say that I hadn't paced these meals out or picked anything even remotely healthy. 'Please, help yourselves,' LaVey had said the other day as he sat down to a bowl of porridge. 'The house is filled with everything you could want, or *ever* want for that matter, so indulge yourselves.'

My mother would've been mortified to see me take advantage of this. I loaded up plates of thick, soft bread, breaded ham, sumptuous cheese, and chocolate-stuffed flapjacks that I gobbled down as soon as I returned to my room. I yearned to sample the dinner selection, but I couldn't risk another conversation with Aster. So far, the entire event had been a spectacular debacle in terms of networking: Rhiannon was a drunk, Mikhail a complete dickhead, and Aster probably thought I was an asshole, so I highly doubted that I'd be acknowledged in her next book.

It was crazy how feeling ostracised and judged was somehow worse than the sheer dread I felt whenever I left my room. That decrepit, twisting monstrosity had been real, I'd no doubt about that, and it seemed to be tied to this house. If I left, it would stay rattling around in LaVey's attic and only torment me in nightmares, but my inability to establish relations would haunt me forever. I desperately wanted to apologise to Aster for my outburst, but what could I possibly say that wouldn't make me sound crazy, or just make things worse? It wasn't worth the risk.

I'd been a fool to think I'd be able to indulge my creative side here. No one in my ever-shrinking social circle was really that interested in learning about my writing. Whenever it came up, they generally dismissed it and never wanted to know the inspiration behind the words, the connection I felt to the characters, or the references I peppered throughout the text. They cared little that I'd written a short story with myself as an omniscient third-person narrator, a version of myself as the main character, and *another*, younger version of myself as the main character's hated rival, or that *Breath of Eden* was dedicated to my slaughtered friends.

To be fair, Dani had shown some interest. We often stepped away from the cafeteria (and our nosy colleagues) to a nearby park; a small island of overgrown grassland surrounded by large, leaning trees and a few battered, splintered benches that was often populated by guys in suits and ties and some of our more gossipy co-workers. We liked to wander around, chatting aimlessly, or sit and eat on the long grass on hot days.

'You wrote a *book!?*' she'd exclaimed when I'd casually mentioned that I'd been thinking about paying for some marketing.

'Uh…yeah…' I'd answered awkwardly. 'A while ago now.'

'Wow,' she'd marvelled, the twisted curls of her dark hair bobbing on the day's light breeze. 'I can hardly *read* a book!'

'*Hah!* Well, it's not for everyone,' I'd answered honestly. I'd once had a school friend who'd been so bored by reading that he hadn't read a single book for our English classes. Ironically, he'd also been aghast at his low grades, but all he ever cared about was his precious fuckin' football anyway. 'An' I wouldn't recommend writin' one, either.'

Her gleaming eyes had flashed at me (though I couldn't bring myself to look her in the eye): 'So's it, like, in shops? Can I go out an' buy it?'

I'd smirked without much humour. 'Well...turns out it's basically impossible t'do that, so it's online and such.'

She had whipped out her phone from her back pocket and started tapping at the screen. 'Tell me what it's called, I'm gonna buy it.'

I'd laughed this off, but she'd been insistent. As far as I knew, she'd gone through with it and started reading it, but I hadn't been able to work up the courage to ask what she thought of it. Work had picked up, then she'd had a week off, then I'd gotten LaVey's blasted invitation, and now I was sitting in bum-fuck-nowhere pissing everyone off.

I wish that I'd met Dani sooner, before my workplace had emotionally beaten me down and forced me to isolate myself from others, which made the hours drag and the days bleed into each other. Dani kept things interesting by sending me memes; she didn't judge me like everyone else; she laughed at my jokes, and seemed to enjoy my company.

At work, anyway.

I'd occasionally socialised with her outside of work, but only once where it had been just the two of us rather than a work event. I wanted to ask her out again, properly this time, but I'd been burned by haste before. Dani was certainly friendly and chatty with everyone, and I suspected that I'd misread the situation. Hell, for all I knew she already had a boyfriend (though she'd never mentioned one). To my dismay, she reminded me of Lucy: she'd been a bright-eyed, friendly, enthusiastic, and pretty girl who'd enjoyed being around me and always had a hug and a kind word to say. I'd wanted to ask her out, too, but had hesitated for many of the same reasons, and now I'd never get that chance.

Sat alone in my dark quarters, I was overwhelmed by the urge to contact Dani. Many were the times I'd been tempted to ask her out by the coffee machine, which seemed like the easiest thing in the world when driving to and from work or sitting at home with the cat. Maybe after this week was over, once these people were behind me, and LaVey's money was in my account...I sighed and swallowed my last Jaffa cake, comforted by my gorging, but as guilt-ridden by my dirty plates and bowls as I was about snapping at Aster.

Okay, fuck it. First, I'd take care of my cleaning, then I'd try to make amends with Aster, or at least offer an apology. *Then* I'd get back to work on my short story, which had stalled at around a thousand words. And maybe, after all that was done, I would ask Dani out and see what happened.

Though part of me was still unconvinced, I moved to take care of the first task and consoled myself with the comfort that there might be more snacks in LaVey's kitchen.

4. Mikhail's Darkest Hour

'What are you doing here, Lia?' Mikhail had asked, his eyes never leaving the glittering blade in his wife's hand. 'I told you to leave us alone.'

'He-he's mine!' she'd stammered, her slender body trembling all over, her face a mess of tears. 'My little angel…my everything.' She had whipped the blade before his eyes weakly, but dangerously enough. '*Stay back!*' she'd screamed frantically, and Mikhail had heard Luka scream in unison. 'He's cuh-coming with me!'

'You know I can't allow that,' Mikhail had reasoned, his hands held up to show he was harmless. 'You're sick, beloved. You need *help…*'

'*I DON'T NEED HELP FROM YOU!*' she'd screeched and swung the knife towards him. Mikhail had tried to grab at her wrists, but her skin had been sweaty, and he had lost his grip. She wasn't interested in tackling him head-on, however; she had merely wanted to ward him off so that she could clutch Luka tight against her hip.

No, no, no! I don't want to see this!

'My baby *needs* me!' Lia had hissed, groping at Luka's chest as he continued to suck on his fingers, his teary eyes never leaving Mikhail's. 'I can give him what you can't!'

Please! Please don't make me see this!

'You're bad for him, Lia,' Mikhail had said softly, not daring to step closer and unable to keep his eyes from the knife she held. 'Look at *yourself*, beloved. You know I'm right!'

A hideous sneer had crossed her face. 'Of course!' she'd spat. 'My husband, the great author, is always right! All-knowing, all-so-fucking caring!' she'd jabbed the knife towards him to emphasise each word, her eyes burning.

Not real! Not...Real! Just another nightmare! I can't see this again!

'*Папа!*' Luka had cried. 'Папа, I'm scared!'

'*Shhh*, my son. Don't be scared...Мама and Папа are just, just talking...'

'Oh, I'm *done* talking to *you!*' Lia had barked, tightening her grip on Luka.

'*Папа!* Please, don't let her...' Luka had bawled before Lia had slapped her hand around his mouth.

'Hush, baby boy,' she had soothed. 'There's no need to be afraid...'

Oh, God! Not again!

Please...

Please...Not again!

With Lia distracted by Luka, Mikhail had seized his chance and tackled her to the ground, easily overpowering her squirming form. '*Жопа!*' she'd spat. '*Fuck off and die!*' She was like a wild animal. She snapped her teeth at him, leaving bloody marks on his neck, and brought her knee into his groin, causing an explosion of hot pain to wash over him.

He had staggered aside, momentarily winded, as she had swept up her knife carelessly. The blade sliced down her face, spewing blood into Luka's beautiful hair. Incredibly, she had giggled and even lapped at the blood with her tongue, before dragging Luka into the lounge.

'*Help me, Пana! Please, help!*'

Get up! Get up, you idiot! Please…let it be different this time!

But Mikhail had been hurt; a great, hollow weight made it impossible for him to clamber to his feet. All he had been able to do was lie there, desperately reaching for his son, and watching as Lia struggled with the boy's thrashing, howling form. 'Hold…hold *still*, you brat! Mama's here now, she's here…hold…*still!*'

Oh, God…No…Not again!

The knife plunged into Luka's stomach with a wet sound similar to slicing a peach. The boy had uttered a strangled, gurgling croak that Mikhail had heard even over his anguished screams, and collapsed in a bloodied, quivering heap, his glassy eyes staring directly into those of his grief-stricken father. 'No…'

No…

'No!'

No!

'Not my boy!'

NOT MY BOY!

'See what you made me do?!' Lia had screamed as Mikhail had wrestled himself up. The pain in his gut was stamped down by his utter rage at the sight of the woman he had once loved standing over their son's lifeless body…the knife still stuck in the boy's stomach. '*Look what you made me do!*'

A red mist descended, sweeping away all thought and reason. In a blur of darkness and crimson, Mikhail pounced on his wife. He had barely felt her slapping, clawing struggles as he had forced his large hands around her neck and squeezed

Stop…

And squeezed.

Stop!

He had continued to throttle her long after life had left her body and she was little more than a flopping, useless thing in his hands.

* * *

'*Gah!*' Mikhail gagged suddenly. *Wherethefuck...?* He was still in LaVey's kitchen, thousands of miles and years away from that horrendous day, and drenched in sweat. 'Oh, dear God above...' he whispered as tears wormed their way down his quaking cheeks. Had he been dreaming...while awake? He tried to get himself under control, but his entire body shuddered involuntarily. In a fury, he swept at the plate that had held his omelette and it shattered on the stone floor, then he stumbled against the sink in the corner, cursing whatever gods were listening.

Bad dreams? LaVey's voice cut through his terror. *I used to have them when I grew up here...*

You're not taking him from me!

Houses have a way of...remembering things...

'*Stop!*' Mikhail bellowed, beating his fists against his sweat-drenched forehead. 'Stop, *stop, STOP!*'

'*I remember...everything...*'

Mikhail snapped his eyes open and clapped his hands to his mouth, his heart beating like a jackhammer as the kitchen's façade of normalcy literally bled away. The tiles, the paintwork, the very bricks themselves cracked and gushed with thick, oozing blood. It ran in geysers over everything; bulbs sputtered and shattered; the floor grew

263

tacky, and the room seemed to constrict around him. '*Another dream…Just another dream…*'

Mikhail gasped as a hand, bloody and gnarled, sprouted from the floor and seized him by the ankle. He shook his leg wildly, but to no avail. Bony fingers dug into his flesh as a bloodied corpse wrenched itself up from the viscera that was pooling around the kitchen. It was a grinning, toothy skull with dark, hollow eyes and yet, still, somehow recognisably Lia. Her jaw worked soundlessly, and yet still he could hear its words in his head: '*We're waiting…*'

Mikhail wrenched his foot away and the gibbering skeleton sank away as if dipping into quicksand. He slipped and clawed his way across the kitchen as the blood receded with a throaty chuckle, taking with it the once clean and well-kept furnishings, distorting them into a murky, dusty, splintered mess. Appliances sat in a mess of rust, dust, and cobwebs, the counters were filthy and littered with dead bugs and rodents, and the kitchen was as dark and repulsive as an age-old dungeon.

Mikhail gagged and suddenly spewed hot bile to the grimy floor as chunks of rotten mess spilled from his guts and every fibre of his body shivered uncontrollably. 'Держись подальше!' he snarled as he wiped away vomit with his shaking knuckles.

A shape loomed in the open doorway across the room. Bathed in shadows, and with his vision askew from terror, Mikhail saw the silhouette of a woman with long hair and a curvaceous form and leapt at the figure with a sudden burst of fury.

'*Fucking bitch!*' Mikhail shrieked as he wrenched at the hair of his long-dead wife. She screamed in surprise, and he yanked at her coat as he muscled her into the dank kitchen.

'What the hell is wrong with you?' Lia screamed. Losing her coat allowed her to nimbly escape his grasp and she glared at him with a ferocious intensity that was almost threatening.

Almost.

His mind a whirlwind of emotion, Mikhail glared at Aster's furious face. Her eyes were bloodshot, her pale skin covered in small scratches, her blue dress torn, and her hair a gnarled mess. He could *see* it was Aster and yet…he also saw Lia hovering before him, her face split and bloodied, her hand still holding that knife.

'I said, what the *hell* is…*ack!*' the Aster-Lia-*thing* gagged as Mikhail grabbed her throat.

She beat at his meaty arm pitifully as he easily manhandled her slender frame. 'Not this time!' he promised through gritted teeth. Lia's ethereal form lingered like smoke, sneering and taunting him. '*This time it will be different!*'

'Get…get *off* me!' Aster screamed. Her hair thrashed wildly, and her legs kicked into the air as Mikhail muscled her towards the door.

'*No!*' he barked, completely out of his mind. 'You will not have him this time!'

'*I will always have him…*' the phantasm cooed before fading away.

Burning rage flowed through Mikhail's veins; he saw the world only in a red haze as he dragged Aster away in a half-crazed lunacy. All logic and reason collapsed away. All he knew was that Lia must be stopped before she could hurt his son, and that he would do anything…*anything*…to keep him safe.

5. *Brandis Leaps In*

As soon as I went downstairs (like an idiot, I carried everything in one trip and almost sent LaVey's plates and cups toppling to the floor), I knew that I'd made a mistake even before I nudged open the door to the kitchen hallway.

I could hear raised voices echoing down the dark, narrow hallway, which was very bare compared to the others I'd visited so far. Everything was a very sparse, clinical grey that seemed to darken as the hallway ended at a set of plastic doors with two portholes set into them. Regardless, I'd come too far to turn back and, while it *was* tempting to simply set my load down and slink away, I decided to continue into the kitchen.

Before I could kick open the doors, the one closest to me suddenly swung towards me, and I half-expected that gruesome fiend to leap at me and take a bite out of my cheek with its rotted teeth. Instead, Aster came barging through the door, but my surprise was no less great; my tray was sent flying and its contents shattered against the wall as I stumbled backwards. I slapped against the wall to avoid tumbling onto my ass, and the red-haired American half-tripped into my arms.

'What the…' I started before Mikhail bashed open the other door.

'*Сука!*' he snarled, his face as white as a sheet and his dark eyes blazing with fury. Whatever had happened between the two had clearly riled the big Russian up; his jaw was clenched, and he grabbed a fistful of Aster's long, red hair with a meaty, blood-stained hand. 'Fucking *сука!*' he gnashed. 'You've been asking for this!'

Aster's slender form was torn from my arms before I could properly register what was happening. I was dumbfounded as Mikhail yanked her close and barked Russian slurs in her face as she struggled vainly in his grip. She was clearly in pain (I could see strands of her hair coming away in clumps between his fingers), but she ranted and beat at him with tightly balled fists. 'Fuckin' get *off* me!' she screamed.

I was suddenly overcome with rage. '*Oi!* What the hell...' Mikhail slapped a calloused palm to my face in a display of flippant dismissal and I was so taken aback that I slipped back and hit my head off the wall.

Mikhail stormed down the hallway. He switched his grip from Aster's hair and snatched her around the waist, though, even in the hallway's dim light, I could see that his beefy hand was clamped around her breast. She kicked and clawed at the air as he manhandled her, but to no avail. He obviously outweighed her and was carrying her away like a caveman. 'Let go of me you fuckin' psycho! Someone help! You fucking asshole...lemme go!' she hollered herself into a garbled mess, but the Russian seemed completely unfazed and oblivious.

I watched, dumbfounded, and was horrified that a part of me wanted to turn away and leave them to it. It was scary how tempting it was to simply step into the kitchen, wash my face and hands, and see if there was any chicken left in the fridge. After all, what was Aster to me? Nothing. A stranger at best, and just another person I'd pissed off at worst. I'd been so excited when she'd made her big entrance. I'd seen her Instagram posts, but it was different seeing her in the flesh, and it'd really hit home how insignificant I was compared to her. I couldn't hope to measure up to her success and everyone knew it. Although I'd published more books than each of them individually, I was the clear weak link in the group. I understood LaVey bringing Aster and Mikhail over to add to his anthology's international flavour, but where was the logic in drafting in a peon like me?

So, yes, I was ashamed that I was tempted to ignore it. Aster was a tough chick, and I was sure that someone would hear all the commotion Mikhail was causing. What could I possibly do to help her? I was massively outmatched. Mikhail was much taller than me and built like a brick shithouse, whereas I was a skinny runt in desperate need of a haircut and who'd ignored physical conflict his whole life.

No...it was better to let someone else handle it.

And yet...

Mikhail had wrenched her out of my shocked embrace with one hand; he'd spat all kinds of slurs into her horrified face, and he was dragging her away against her will...and I was really just going to watch that happen?

I watched him heave her away. In a couple of steps, he'd be in the main foyer.

I thought of that newspaper headline that'd broken something deep inside me: *Massacre on campus – Students found slaughtered in their rooms*.

In another world, I probably would've been counted amongst them. Instead, Lucy had died horribly and alone, another victim of a senseless killing spree. I'd often laid awake and wondered if I could've helped her, or Sam, if things'd been different; maybe we would've been at a pub quiz or chatting shit in the library, anything other than not even being there when it happened. Some cruel fate had spared me, and I'd squandered that gift on self-pity, jealous of the success of people I had no business comparing myself to.

I'd failed to honour them in my writing, but perhaps my fate was to honour them in deeds.

I stamped down my apathy and balled my trembling hands into fists so tight that my knuckles burned bone white. It was crazy…idiotic…the last thing I had any business doing, but I took after Mikhail in a flurry of footsteps and leapt at his broad back with a guttural howl. I didn't stay on Mikhail's back for long. He was burly and tall and my attack had faltered since I was so out of shape, but he'd been suitably staggered by the unexpectedness of my attack and finally released his grip on Aster, tumbling her to the hard floor.

I gave him a massive shove that was like pushing a brick wall; still, he was off-balance enough to stumble into the foyer. He stopped himself from cracking his head on the main staircase and glared at me, wiping drool from his bottom lip.

'*Ублюдок!*' he barked furiously. 'You want to test me?' he moved quicker than I expected and grabbed my collar, throwing me aside with a vicious swipe of his arm. '*Me!*' he roared as I skidded across LaVey's thin, bristly carpet. 'I shit bigger things than you, *карлик!*'

I scrambled away, barely avoiding the Russian's huge boot. My elbow caught the lowest step and I tried to pull myself up, but Mikhail beat me to it and wrenched me to my feet. He roared a torrent of Russian nonsense before delivering a hard slap with the back of his hand. I damn near crumbled from the blow but, incredibly, found myself laughing.

'What?' he sounded as confused as I felt. 'What is so funny, little man?'

I could barely form words, the giggles had struck me so completely. Tears streamed from my eyes as I coughed laughter louder and heartier as Mikhail shook me like a ragdoll in frustration. I patted his forearms with a condescension that only screwed his features up into a look of pure malice.

'B-big m-man...' I stuttered out. 'Beatin' o-on a girl 'cuz you're a f-few inches short down there.' I gave a little nod so he'd know exactly what I was referring to before spitting a huge wad of phlegm right into his furious eyes. 'Pathetic!'

That did it. If Mikhail hadn't been pissed off before, he definitely was now. He released his grip and I dropped to the floor, still grinning like an idiot even as he lashed out with a left hook. I heard a hard, meaty slap and everything spun into a swirling blackness. Bright fireworks exploded in my vision, and I heard a distant sound, so familiar and so deeply missed: Lucy's giggle.

The world swam back into focus. I was half-sprawled on the hard floor, my left leg and arm draped over the bottom step of the staircase, and one of LaVey's glistening chandeliers loomed overhead like the Sword of Damocles. The entire right side of my face throbbed with a grey pain that stung with each breath, but I couldn't help but smile at what my blurry eyes beheld: Aster was flailing a heavy, silver broadsword at Mikhail. I could just about see that one of LaVey's suits of armour was missing its weapon; clearly, Aster had grabbed it and was now threatening Mikhail with it. I couldn't see his face from my skewed position, but he held both hands up in a warding-off gesture.

'Back off!' Aster lunged with the sword. Although it was clearly taking a lot of effort for her to wield its weight, the tip looked sharp and dangerous enough, and she was clearly fired up. 'I dare you to take another step towards me or him,' she nodded at me. 'Try me. I will *not* hesitate to hurt you out of self-defence.'

She was furious. Her hair was a dishevelled mess of curls, but her face was flushed a deep red and her eyes blazed with all the furies of hell as she challenged Mikhail. She looked absolutely magnificent.

'You so much as look at me next time our paths cross, I'll make sure you leave here without your cock! Got it? Or do I need to repeat myself, you fucking bastard?'

Mikhail seemed convinced. He backed away and stepped on my right calf. I barked a yelp and kicked it out from under him. He glanced down at me; he seemed ashamed, enraged, and terrified all at once and I could see a small nick on his left cheek, possibly from the business end of Aster's broadsword. 'So real...' he muttered oddly, before glaring at Aster. 'You stay away from me, *пизда*.'

'Go on, git!' Aster tried to lift her weapon in a threatening manner, but finally succumbed to its weight, clanging the blade to the floor. 'Git outta 'ere, you sick fuck!'

Mikhail grumbled another unintelligible Russian insult before stomping up the stairs. A few seconds later, a door slammed and I dropped my head to the cold, hard, floor and felt the giggles overtake me again.

6. *Rhiannon Hears a Fight*

Over the next twenty-four hours, Rhiannon lived and breathed nothing but the short story, not even taking a break to recharge her batteries and sleep. She drank nothing but whiskey during this time and the bottle was now almost empty. The words flowed from her mind to her fingers and onto the page, one painstakingly slow letter at a time. She'd never used a typewriter before and she was pretty sure that, after this, she would never use one again as, if she made a mistake on the page, she had to type out the entire page again. She could feel the exhaustion and the alcohol taking over her body, but she fought it with everything she had. She began to feel that if she slept she would never wake up.

Maybe it was this house.

Maybe it was slowly eating away at her soul.

The incident in the library had shaken her to her very core. She wasn't herself at all. Normally, Rhiannon was fairly polite and approachable, but she could feel a kind of anger weaving its way through her bloodstream. Everything set her on edge; the wind howling outside, the strange noises that seemed to appear from nowhere, the loud voices…

'*Fucking…asking for this!*'

Who *was* that? Ah, of course…that vile Russian…

His voice seemed to reverberate up through the entire house, causing the crystal chandelier above Rhiannon's bed to shudder.

'Jesus,' she said aloud.

For the first time in twenty-four hours, her focus was drawn away from the typewriter and towards the sound of the commotion that was erupting downstairs.

'*Let go…Someone help!…lemme go!*'

That was Aster's voice!

Rhiannon jumped up from her chair (staggering slightly as her numb, alcohol-fuelled body fought to keep her upright) and pressed her ear against the thick door. All she could hear were dull sounds and muffled voices. They must have moved further away.

Overwhelmed with curiosity and concern, she unbolted the heavy door and yanked it open. Raised voices immediately wafted up from below, encircling the narrow corridors. Rhiannon cautiously crept along the hallway towards the irate sounds, using the walls as support. She heard more thuds, cracks, and shouts with the occasional Russian expletive making an appearance. She reached the top of the staircase, which overlooked the main hall, and surveyed the turmoil below with shock and awe.

Mikhail was beating the shit out of Brandis while Aster looked on, terrified, her eyes swimming with tears and her lip swollen and bloody. Brandis was lying on the hard floor of the main hall right at the bottom of the staircase while Mikhail loomed over him, red in the face and clearly enraged.

Rhiannon crouched low so as not to be seen. The last thing she wanted to do was get dragged into whatever the hell this was. Normally, she'd have done her best to defuse the situation, but after recent events she just didn't have the energy nor the inclination to get involved. All she wanted to do was be left alone.

She covered her mouth to stifle a gasp as she watched Aster grab a silver broadsword and swing it at Mikhail. A small smile crept over her face as she thought *you go girl!* The sword was clearly too heavy for her, but she wielded it as best she could. Rhiannon was mildly impressed.

When Aster screamed threats at Mikhail, Rhiannon raised her eyebrows at her tone, slightly shocked and bemused that such a tiny woman could sound so aggressive. All credit to her for saving Brandis, who looked like a shaking dog on the floor while Aster defended him. That did nothing to raise Rhiannon's impression of Brandis. The fact that he couldn't even defend himself was pathetic. She didn't know who or what had started the argument, but she suspected it had something to do with Brandis attempting to save Aster from Mikhail.

Typical man, thought Rhiannon. *Always trying to save the helpless woman...*

But it looked like Aster didn't need any help, not by the way she was brandishing that sword around.

Then a thought occurred to her. Maybe the reason she had a dislike for Brandis was because he reminded her a lot of her ex-husband. Not in his actions or the way he spoke, but they looked very similar. The same ungainly posture, unkempt hair—even the beard was familiar—and the way he seemed to silently judge everything and everyone around him with those cold, blue eyes. It obviously wasn't Brandis' fault that he looked like David, but she despised him all the same and held it against him. Maybe she hated all men now. She'd certainly been much happier these past ten years without a man constantly breathing down her neck, questioning everything she did and what she spent her money on. So what if she wanted to spend a few hundred pounds on a designer outfit or a lavish holiday for one? She had every right to enjoy her life and her money. She'd earned it, after all, and deserved every penny. She expected that she'd never find anyone else to settle down with now. At almost forty, she knew her most attractive years were behind her, but that didn't mean to say she didn't think of herself as attractive.

She was just…a little worn around the edges and set in her ways.

As Rhiannon watched the argument below her reach its climax, she allowed herself a coy smile, quietly enjoying the excessive swearing and swordplay. Finally, it appeared that Mikhail got the message and he stormed off, spluttering and still exceptionally scarlet in the face. She watched Aster and Brandis shake themselves off and survey the damage. She could have sworn that she saw them lock eyes for just slightly longer than was deemed appropriate for two people who were basically complete strangers.

Rhiannon decided that she'd seen enough and slowly headed back to her room, but she bumped into none other than Mr. LaVey as she rounded the corner. Despite her surprise, he showed no reaction to running into her at all. Had he been watching her while she watched the others?

'In a hurry are we, m'dear?'

'Sorry, Mr. LaVey! I didn't see you there!' she exclaimed as she clutched a hand to her heart in an attempt to steady it. He'd appeared out of nowhere, as if he'd materialised out of thin air.

'It's unwise to wander around the house so late, my child. These walls grow…restless when night falls.'

Somehow, the man looked even older than when she'd last set eyes on him, if that was at all possible. His skin was almost translucent under the glow of the lantern he was holding, which also cast great black shadows across the walls and ceiling. He clamped his eyes on her and she felt her breath escape her body. His eyes…they were glowing red…

'Goodness me, you're looking very pale, m'dear,' he said, raising his lantern up to Rhiannon's face; she squinted against the heat and the light. 'Are you still feeling unwell?'

Rhiannon shook her head and the glowing eyes vanished. She was losing the plot now, imagining that scary old men had glowing red eyes like a demon. Or maybe it was because the whiskey bottle was empty…

'Sorry…yes, I am feeling a bit…um…did you hear the argument just now downstairs?'

'I can't say that I did,' he answered as he finally lowered his lantern.

'The others were going at it in the hallway downstairs. Aster had a sword,' she said with a half laugh.

'I shouldn't worry about it, m'dear,' he said without much interest. 'These writer's circles can get very tense. It's all the egos and testosterone, I find. You young 'uns these days do love t'get your heckles up.'

'But…they seemed really angry about something.'

'Well, I can only hope that they are putting as much passion into their writing,' the old man stated.

Rhiannon sucked on her bottom lip to stop from arguing with him. Clearly, he wasn't concerned in the slightest. 'I best get back to my room,' she said as she attempted to sidestep around the frail Mr. LaVey, who followed her with his lantern held high.

'Of course, mustn't get complacent now. You take care, m'dear. Enjoy that whiskey...'tis one of my favourites.'

Rhiannon's heart thudded loudly in her chest as she felt her face grow red, but Mr. LaVey did not say anything further. She watched him glide away (was he gliding?) and then disappear around the corner (or did he sink into the wall?). She took a deep breath and scurried back to her room, slamming and locking the door behind her, puffing and panting.

'I'm going fooking crazy,' she muttered to herself. 'I need some fooking sleep.'

7. Aster Makes a Move

The sword clattered to the ground, the sound reverberating through the large, empty lobby. I fell to my knees, and a strangled sob escaped from deep within my chest. I really don't know what prompted me to grab that sword and face off against Mikhail like that. His crazed eyes…the way he'd gripped my hair, trying to rip it from my scalp…how he'd grabbed me and carried me off to do who knows what. I was so thankful that Brandis showed up—

Brandis! He… he saved me? But why? Our last interaction was less than desirable. What could have led him to do that? Was he being a good person and trying to help someone in need? Or maybe it was something else entirely?

The sound of someone giggling snapped me back to reality. I felt a cold chill up my back as I remembered the sounds of those laughing children from the maze. But this was different. This was coming from nearby, and it wasn't an unsettling sound. It sounded distressing. Scanning the room, I saw a figure lying on the ground. *Brandis. Oh God.*

'Brandis! Are you okay?'

Dropping to my knees, I gave him a quick glance over. It didn't appear that he had broken anything, but there was some swelling and redness near one eye. Probably from where Mikhail had hit him.

'Define "okay"?' he grunted as he wiped his bottom lip with the back of his hand; a small trickle of blood stained his skin. 'It ain't ev'ry day I get knocked on me ass by some Russian bastard'.

'Least let me help you up!'

'Nah', he groaned and waved a hand at me. I hesitated and kept my distance, watching with some confusion as he struggled to prop himself up on his elbows. He seemed to have a great deal of difficulty sitting up, but whether it was due to pain or the odd fit of giggles that continued to grip him, I didn't know. 'Actually...' he sighed, panting. 'Mebbe you *could* gimme a hand...'

I hoisted him up with my forearm; a brief look of gratitude flashed over his face, and then he dusted himself off once he was back on his feet. He looked around sheepishly, a little embarrassed, and mumbled some derogatory term about his own stupidity that I couldn't make out.

Suddenly, everything that had happened to me in the last few hours hit me. I became overwhelmed with emotion. My chest tightened, my throat closed up, and tears began spilling from my eyes. Millions of thoughts raced through my head with no sign of slowing. I could feel myself getting dizzy. Was the room spinning? *No, that was an illusion.* My breathing became erratic, no matter how much I tried to correct it. Another sob escaped me, and I couldn't stop crying. *Am I going crazy?* I thought. *What the fuck was that in the maze? Was it even real? What about Mikhail? He was so angry.*

'He could have...he could have...' I cried out, forgetting Brandis was there beside me. 'Oh my God!'

Brandis awkwardly looked down at me, saw the fat tears rolling down my flushed cheeks, and turned away. *He'll go*, I thought. *No one wants to see a hysterical woman crying!* Incredibly, though, he took a tentative step towards me and seemed to debate reaching a hand out to me. I wiped at my face, but the tears refused to stop, and I found my breath coming in panicked hitches. Through my blurry vision, I could

279

see his hand lingering in mid-air and wished very much for him to hold me in that moment, which caught me by surprise. After another second of deliberation, he dropped his hand, and I felt my heart drop with it.

'Are you all right?' he asked.

I flicked my eyes to his face and could see he knew as well as I did what a stupid question that was. He frowned and flexed his hands together distractedly, as if unsure of what he should do, or what was proper for him to do. 'Hey…Hey now, c'mon…' he tried to soothe me, but it would have been futile even if he had somehow found the right words to say. 'Um… c'mon, let's get you back to your room, yeah? I dunno 'bout you, but *I* could use a stiff drink.'

All I could do was nod at his suggestion and I allowed him to guide me up the stairs. He kept talking to me, and I felt rude for not paying better attention to what he was saying. 'You were badass with that sword back there. I actually thought f'r a second that you were gonna skewer him…'

I was still trying to absorb everything that had taken place and trying to calm myself down.

'…thought he was gonna stomp my friggin' head in there. Honestly, I dunno *wot* I was thinkin' when I…'

The next thing I remembered was a door creaking open, and I was in my room. Brandis followed behind; he kept his distance, but I could feel him watching me closely.

'Huh', he grunted. 'I guess all these rooms *are* th'same …'

I slowly made my way to the minibar and poured a shot of spiced rum. I downed it quickly, not even feeling the sweet burn. Before I poured my second one, I remembered Brandis was still in the room. *How rude of me*, I thought. *Didn't even offer him a drink, even after he saved your sorry ass.* Grabbing a second glass, I lifted it in the air, silently asking Brandis if he wanted something to drink.

He had been distracting himself with the large mirror affixed to the wall next to the door but spotted my gesture from the corner of his eye and stepped over. 'Yeah, g'wan then. You've twisted my arm.' I poured a quick shot into the glass, and he took a tentative sip, grimaced slightly, and then gave a slight nod of approval and took another sip.

I drained my second drink just as fast as the first one. I felt the burn this time, but it didn't compare to the fear still surging through my body. Reaching for the bottle, I was about to pour myself a third shot when Brandis grabbed the bottle from me.

'Mebbe that's enough?' he advised. 'LaVey's stuff is…pretty strong, and you don't wanna end up a borderline alcoholic like Rhiannon.'

I tried coming up with any kind of response but felt at a loss for words. Defeated, I took a small tumbler from the bar, placed three ice cubes in the glass, poured about a quarter of Coke and took the bottle from him so I could top the rest up with rum. As I placed the now empty bottle back down onto the bar and went to pick up the glass, it almost slipped from my hand and spilled all over the bar top.

'I mean…I don't wanna say "I told you so" but…'

'Zip it,' I snapped. Using all my focus, I lifted the glass again and took a slow sip.

Brandis shuffled over to the bar and rested against it with a wince. 'D'you feel better now?'

'I think so…I'm not sure.' Another sip. I always loved my rum and Coke. Walter didn't understand why I loved it so much.

'How could you drink that gasoline shit? You shouldn't drink at all. It does horrible things to your body and makes you fat.'

Walter's "advice" made me scoff in an irritated huff. I'd heard it more times than I could count, and other than it being bad for your body in large amounts, Walter was wrong about everything else. I would never tell him that though as I didn't want to get berated or backhanded for "mouthing-off." Besides, he was the biggest hypocrite. There were times he drank whiskey and scotch like it was water.

Brandis picked up the empty bottle of rum and studied the label. He smirked to himself and set it back down. 'I dunno where the old man gets this stuff from,' his eyes flicked to me and seemed to study my entire body and posture in a microsecond before turning down to the floor. 'You *look* better, at least…'

I raised my glass at him. 'Well, I should thank you for…is the term "saving me" the correct choice of words here?'

'Hah!' Brandis scoffed, the effort drawing another flinch of pain from him. His hand briefly dropped to his hip, which had most likely been bruised in his fall. 'I dunno if I'd call that "help," exactly.'

'Well, either way, I'm grateful.' I took a moment to study Brandis' appearance. His thick dark hair reminded me of my favourite guilty pleasure: dark chocolate. I had the sudden urge to run my fingers through it, but I was sure that wouldn't go over well at all. His steely eyes seemed to be desperately trying to hold back a deep pain that stemmed beyond the physical wounds he had suffered. Speaking of which, the swelling on his right eye was getting worse. I could see the discoloration getting darker. *Fuck that asshole, Mikhail.* My irritation soared at the very thought of that pretentious bastard; I could still feel where his beefy hands had grabbed me, causing a shudder to run through my body. It didn't matter to me why Brandis had been down there. If he hadn't shown up, I could have been raped, beaten…maybe even killed.

'Where'd you get this?' The question cut through my thoughts, and I blinked, momentarily disoriented, as Brandis shuffled over to my bedside table. I looked over my shoulder and saw him holding the paperback book I had placed there when I first arrived. 'This is…' he glanced at the cover in shock. 'This is my book?'

I took a sip from my glass, the spiced rum pleasant as it ran down my throat. 'I was going to ask you about it the other day, at breakfast,' I answered, and noticed a small cringe crease on his face at the memory of that morning. 'It took me a while to make the connection between you and the book but, yes, I've been reading it since the flight here.'

'But…how?' he seemed dumbfounded as he reviewed the back cover. 'How'd you even come across it?'

'I don't remember,' I answered honestly; the rum was making my head buzz a bit, and I welcomed the sensation. At least I wasn't a crying, emotional wreck anymore. 'It might've been a follow train or a recommendation, or something like that'. He frowned again. He didn't seem convinced. In fact, it was as if he had never seen a copy of his book before. 'In any case,' I continued, 'I saw the blurb and the cover and just had to get it.'

'Wouldn't it've been easier… cheaper… to get the digital version?'

I rubbed the back of my neck in embarrassment. 'I prefer the real thing,' I answered, my voice barely a whisper as I prepared to face his condemnation.

Instead, he placed the book back down and nodded. 'Same,' he replied. 'Don't get me wrong, digital *is* a lot cheaper an' it's wonders for buying uni books an' such but nothin' beats the real thing.'

I was shocked. More and more people these days were missing out on the joys of poking through the selection of novels in a book shop or settling down with a thick hardcover to browse through. It wasn't always a popular opinion to have, especially online, so I was reluctant to share it, but I couldn't contain my excitement at Brandis sharing the sentiment.

'I've really been enjoying it,' I said, motioning to *Breath of Eden.* 'It's very well written. I love the way you capture the essence of your characters in dialogue, even if I don't really understand it sometimes, being a dumb American.'

'C'mon, don't bullshit me,' he said curtly. I felt myself flushing slightly as he continued: 'D'you know what I'd give t'have the followers or even the engagement *you* have? That's the whole bloody reason I came all the way out here!'

I shook some loose hair from my face and regarded him closely. 'Haven't you written a bunch of books? I remember them listed inside the cover.'

He made that sharp scoffing cry again and wandered back over to the bar to pour himself a fresh drink. This time it was a slosh of whiskey in a glass with ice and a generous helping of Coke. 'I might as well've taken up jugglin' f'r'all they're worth.'

It took me a moment to decode his words; these Brits definitely had an odd and varied way of speaking. 'From what *I've* read, you're very talented.'

He smirked with little humour and tipped his glass to me in a mock salute. 'Well, thanks f'r that.'

'I *was* hoping to have finished it by now, but…' I trailed off, reluctant to say any more.

'After the way I acted th' other day, I'm surprised you ain't just chucked the stupid thing out,' he murmured, sipping his drink and turning his eyes from me.

I shrugged slightly and felt an awkwardness creep over me. I had been annoyed, insulted even, by the way he had gone off at me but, then again, he *had* just saved me, so I didn't want to make him feel bad. What else could I say but: 'It's all right…'

'No,' he immediately interrupted, 'it's not. You didn't deserve that. I was a dick and I'm…I'm sorry. It's just, everyone here's kinda treated me like shit.' He sipped his drink. 'Not that I blame them,' he mused.

I wasn't sure what to say to that. As much as I liked Rhiannon, I couldn't exactly deny that her treatment of Brandis had been frosty, and the less said about Mikhail the better. I tried to steer the conversation back towards more positive subjects: 'If they read your book…'

'Yeah,' he scoffed again. 'I doubt any of them even know, or cares, how hard I worked on that damned thing.'

I shifted my feet uncomfortably. 'It definitely shows in the book…I want to know, though: who are Sam and Lucy?' he stared at me blankly for a second, clearly blindsided. 'You…you dedicated it to them? I just wondered if they were friends, or siblings?'

'Friends of mine,' he answered bluntly. 'From a…a long time ago.'

'That's nice,' I answered, sensing a shift in the atmosphere. Clearly, I had hit a nerve without meaning to. This Brandis was full of surprises, it seemed. 'It didn't happen overnight, you know.' He finished his drink and looked at me, puzzled. 'My followers, I mean,' I clarified hastily. 'My first book was…' *Was what, exactly?* 'I had no idea what I was doing, let's just say that. I wanted to write. I always have, but I struggled so hard with getting my shit together for it, what with my studies and work and my…my fiancé. Well, we weren't engaged then, of course, but you know what I mean?'

'Sure,' he shrugged, grateful to have changed topics. 'I started that one when I was just a kid, then kept dipping in and out of it between life and work and shit.' He smiled dryly as he gazed over at the book. 'Maybe twenty percent of the first draft's even in the fuckin' thing.'

My eyes widened, and my heart skipped a beat. 'Oh my God, yes!' I exclaimed. 'I must have dumped about three chapters of *Only Come at Night*, and I completely changed the ending, *and* I ended up merging three characters into one! It was a nightmare!'

We ended up chatting for so long that I completely lost track of time. Brandis had moved over to where I sat on the bed, joining me, propping himself up against the headboard with one of the many cushions and pillows that came with the room. I found myself astounded by our similar writing experiences. From my perspective, Brandis had lived the dream I had longed for myself as he had actually studied writing at college.

'Over here, we call it "university". College means something completely different from what you're used to,' he had pointed out to me, chuckling softly at my embarrassment. Still, once he started talking

286

about his writing process, he really opened up. I found myself listening in awe as he described his inspirations and meticulous planning process.

'I'm such a pantser,' I laughed, crossing my legs on the soft mattress and giggling, feeling totally at ease. 'I get an idea and then I just write until it's out there, you know? But I'm such a perfectionist that I could spend days, weeks even, going over and over a single chapter or even one line of dialogue until I get it just right.'

It was refreshing to be so candid, and exactly what I had hoped for from the trip. The chance to connect with other writers, to share passions and ideas, and to feel that spark flare within me once again. Walter never wanted to talk to me about writing or any of the books I was reading. He would say things like it wasn't an interest of his or argue that the movies were better than the books, or that he had better things to do with his time than reading.

'I always wanted t'try and write a fantasy piece, y'know? But I could never wrap my head around how to describe things that weren't, like, real, if that makes sense?'

I nodded and murmured a reply, but I could not shake Walter from my mind. He really wasn't a great guy, and I questioned why I had endured his shit and abuse for all these years. *Because he's been gaslighting you for some time*, I thought. *First your parents and now Walter. Those three are perfect for each other.* It should be no shock; I have trust issues and depression. *Which you refuse to get help for.*

My mind started to see some things more clearly. I lifted my head and looked at Brandis for what felt like the first time. He had shifted topics to talk about a science-fiction book he'd read once and had become very animated. Even his swollen eye seemed to be alive with enthusiasm and a childlike grin was etched on his face as he rambled on. I felt a pang of guilt; it was unfair to say he was rambling. That had negative connotations that had no basis in reality. I found myself almost in awe of his passion and insight; his mind worked at a mile a minute and he seemed to conjure ideas on the spot without even realising it.

I could honestly listen to him talk for days and never get bored. It wasn't just the accent, either (though it *was* to die for…); it was the feeling of being valued, having my opinion and presence be appreciated rather than taken for granted. This stranger, Brandis, wasn't making demands of me, or putting me down, or making me feel worthless. He wasn't trying to leech off my talent or spend my money on alcohol or demand I hand over my phone so he could read through my messages and review my call list. I could sense that Brandis cared only for my talent and appreciated my company, and I felt a warm sense of belonging and…safety in his presence.

'I always say to people that it's the hardest gig in the world. It's like tryin' to apply for a job an' never gettin' to th' interview stage—or *havin'* the interview and never hearin' back. D'you know, one time, I sent a proposal to a lit'rary agent–'

I suddenly leaned towards him and cut his words off with a kiss. I don't know what came over me. It could have been a myriad of things, from the rum in my system to the giddiness of being appreciated by someone. My hands clutched the front of his shirt like he was going to fade away and though I felt him tense up, I didn't break the kiss. For the briefest moment, I wasn't thinking about Walter, or how this could impact any potential professional relationship I might have had with my unlikely saviour. I didn't even care how much his facial hair tickled at my face, which was something that usually annoyed me. The only thing

I cared about in that moment was how right it felt and how good it was to act on such a sudden and reckless impulse.

Brandis murmured only a brief, startled protest; I had obviously caught him completely off-guard. However, when I felt him lean into the kiss, a wave of reality hit me like a brick wall. *What am I doing?* I thought, horrified. *Kissing another man!*

I broke apart from Brandis at that moment, eyes wide and face burning red in shame. I found it impossible to even face him and turned away, apologies tumbling out of my mouth in an incoherent jumble. 'Oh God. I'm so sorry. Walter… God, what have I done?'

I could feel the shaking make its return. I hugged myself tightly and tried to compose myself, but all I could think of was how mad, how *furious*, Walter would be if he found out. *Oh, dear God, look at you, making excuses for that piece of shit again. Please take a moment to ask yourself how he would even find out?*

I couldn't decide what was more embarrassing: that I was already making excuses for that rat bastard, how I had reacted when Brandis kissed me back, or the kiss itself. I slid off the bed and wandered towards the bar, my arms still hugging my trembling body tightly. 'I've never done anything like that before. You must think I'm some sort of—'

I had a whole spiel to blurt out, but I found myself at a complete loss for words. Dropping to my knees, I stared at the bar in front of me and the empty bottle of rum. *Wish I hadn't finished it off. It would be nice to have something to take the edge off.*

'Why did I do that? Why?' I muttered. *He probably thinks you're insane or some kind of slut!* What the hell was wrong with me? I had never done something like that before, especially with a complete stranger! Maybe this house was causing me to go insane…or my depression could just be getting worse.

I was so caught up in my panicked thoughts I hadn't noticed that Brandis had risen from the bed until his hands were resting on my shoulders before slowly pulling me closer to his body in a gentle, but firm embrace. Truth be told, a small flinch shot through me as I felt his hands pulling me up, but I immediately relaxed when his grip didn't bite down into a pinching grasp. I closed my eyes and leaned my head back, resting against his shoulder. It felt so strange, yet sensual, to be held by arms that weren't burly and constricting. I couldn't help but make the comparisons between Brandis and Walter: where Walter was big, looming, and wide, Brandis was gentle and slight and ever so slightly awkward. A shiver ran down my spine as I felt his face brush against mine.

'You've nothin' t'be sorry for,' he breathed.

I allowed myself to enjoy the embrace for another minute before gently detaching myself from his arms. I turned my eyes down and prepared to offer further apologies for acting so hastily. Strangely, to my great despair, I could tell that he was about to do the same and I was alarmed. It made no sense, of course, and was massively hypocritical, but I didn't want him to spoil the moment, such as it was, with unnecessary apologies. I ran my hands over his face and held it as firmly as I dared.

'Shh,' I whispered. 'You don't have to say anythi—'

His lips found mine; a relief I hadn't expected rushed through me and my mind was a whirlwind of jumbled thoughts. He was passionate but tender; his hands plunged into my hair, causing me to gasp into his mouth. His eyes widened slightly, and he looked as though he was thinking about moving away, so I brought him closer. I gazed into his eyes, giving into the moment, and feeling a hot flush rush through me at the idea of being so…wanted.

Presently, he broke the kiss and rested his forehead against mine. He seemed to struggle with the same conflicting emotions as me…but wouldn't take his grey-blue eyes from my dark blue ones. I opened my mouth to say something. I had no idea what was going to come out of my mouth and surprised myself by blurting out: 'You want me.'

It wasn't a question. A flush came to his face, and he finally turned away. He stuttered a response, and I sighed heavily. 'Tell me,' I whispered.

'That obvious, huh?' he finally replied. He brought his hand to my cheek, gently stroking it with his thumb. He slowly made his way down and brushed it over my lips.

What was I doing? I couldn't stop…I didn't *want* to stop. I craned my head up and pecked his lips; the bristles of his beard tickled my chin, but I kissed him again, longer, and he lingered on my bottom lip for just a second.

He said the words I had been dreading to hear: 'We…we shouldn't…' It was clear he didn't mean them and was holding himself back out of chivalry. It was very sweet, and probably very true, but the last thing I wanted to hear at that moment. 'Y-you're engaged, after all, an' I'm just…'

He was right again, of course. Walter would probably kill me for even looking at another guy. *Why does it matter? He's back in Iowa; you're here…how would he even know?* He was far away, so very far away, and the more I thought about him, the further from my mind he seemed to get. I wasn't even sure I wanted to go back to him. Honestly, I felt like I had always intended to use this trip as an excuse to leave him but had been afraid, ashamed, to admit that to myself. It felt...wrong, dishonest, like I was betraying the sanctity of the sham that was our relationship. I sighed again, my thoughts still caught up in the moment's suddenness, and slipped my engagement ring off my finger without another word and simply looked Brandis dead in the eyes and said, with a voice that didn't quite sound like my own, 'You want me, don't you?'

Thankfully, this insightful, imaginative, enthusiastic man with the shaggy hair who had put himself in harm's way just to see that I was safe, gave a slow, shy nod, and I felt heat course through my body in a satisfying wave.

It all came upon me in such a blur. I threw myself at him and we kissed with such a passion that I found myself gasping for air against his beard but hungrily returned to his lips for more. My eyes were clamped shut, and I was lost in a blissful ecstasy as his hands ran all over my body, exploring it and clutching ever so tenderly in all the right places. I allowed myself to let go of my inhibitions, my caution, and my underlying fear. Something about this felt so right, and I was too busy getting lost in the moment to even question it.

Brandis scooped me up in a sudden movement and we toppled onto the bed, his lips still locked onto mine as I slowly brought my hands to the back of his neck. I lightly combed my fingers through his hair; a low growl escaped from deep in his throat.

'Tell me you've thought of this...' I breathed. Again, what was I even saying? This was so unlike me and yet...my hips clutched at his waist eagerly and I'd never wanted to hear his affirmation more.

He opened his eyes, the blue standing out prominently. I was captivated by them as his warm breath brushed against my face, and he lowered his lips to my earlobe and whispered, 'From the moment you came bargin' in, Aster.'

I felt that rush of heat flow through me again; a passionate urge gnawed at me. I held it at bay by running my hands across his shoulder blades and gazing into those honest eyes of his. It felt like, for the first time in forever, someone finally understood me.

'Naomi,' I whispered.

Brandis paused, his eyes full of confusion. 'What?' he asked. 'Who is that?'

A giggle escaped me. '*Me*. Aster Callahan is a pen name. My real name is Naomi Callahan.'

Brandis continued to look confused.

'It felt right to tell you who I really am. Very few know this information as I do an incredible job of keeping my writing persona and my personal life separate.'

'But…why tell me? I'm nobody.'

I shook my head. 'You're not a nobody. You did something millions of other people don't accomplish, you wrote an incredible book and got it published. That is something significant. Something to be proud of.'

He gazed at me longingly, stunned by my compliment. I could tell that it meant a lot to him, and he wasn't entirely sure how to process it. He was a sweet guy who looked so kind and vulnerable that I couldn't help but lean up to him and kiss him once more. He kissed me back intensely, all thoughts of chivalry and doubt forgotten. I could feel his hands tugging at my dress. Brandis opened his eyes, wordlessly asking me if it was all right. I responded by deepening the kiss, giving him confirmation. His hands found their way down my back, pulling the zipper down. Before too long, I was laying under him in nothing but my bra and panties.

I arched my back, my own fingers desperately clawing to get his shirt off. There was something about touching bare skin that made everything more sensual. Brandis wasted no time in heeding my wish; he tossed it aside and my lips travelled down his cheek and to his neck. He inhaled sharply at my nips to his flesh and plunged his hands into my hair. I could hear him muttering something, but I was too lost in the moment. I could feel his lips make their way down my cheeks and towards my earlobe where he caught it with his teeth and lightly nibbled.

I gasped, feeling that rush of heat and anticipation spark electricity throughout my body. It had been so long since I had felt so alive, such passion, and I moaned softly as he suckled gently on my neck. I needed more. I grabbed at his crotch, pushing his bottoms down, beaming a smile of pure ecstasy as his hands grasped the swell of my breasts before moving his hands down to the waistline of my panties, pulling them down in the process. His hands were smooth and tender, and his body was so lean and so unlike the bulging mass that heaved its way on top of me after a hockey game, or whenever he had a few too many whiskey and Cokes. I pushed those last lingering thoughts of Walter out, forcing them into a small box at the back of my mind as my lover met my passion head on and entered me with a gentle push that sent sparks flying before my eyes.

'Oh God! Brandis!' I moaned.

He silenced me with a kiss. 'Let's just stick to Freddy,' he whispered as he took me with a passionate vigour.

Interval Three

Aster at the Banquet on Saturday

I was in awe of Rhiannon's story and felt a twinge of sadness in my heart. Despite all those nasty things she had said about Freddy...about me...I still couldn't help but admire her and her work.

'Amazing,' I muttered as she sat down and, without looking at me, she gave a curt nod of acknowledgement. Hopefully, I could try to fix our professional relationship before departing tomorrow, but I wasn't counting on it. Still give it a shot, Naomi, *I thought. Looking down at my plate of food, I was embarrassed about eating so little. When Freddy and I came down, the various scents wafting through the air made my mouth water and my stomach grumble. However, I only took a few bites of my food before nerves began taking over. The lemon chicken was delightful and probably the one thing I ate the most of.*

I had tuned out most of Mikhail's story, something about a girl and monsters. I was glad Freddy reminded me about LaVey wanting our stories typed up on a typewriter. Unconventional, I had thought, but still a nice touch to the past. It didn't take me too long to type up what I had from my laptop onto the several sheets I ended up with from the typewriter. I gathered my papers in my hands and wondered if I was more nervous about reading it out or the storm that raged outside. Rain and hail hammered against the wall-to-ceiling windows behind us, but I was nice and warm thanks to the massive, roaring fireplace.

Something about it caught my eye; a curious decoration of rigid twigs that had been twisted into an odd symbol resembling a sideways triangle with a slash running through it. Mr. LaVey was just finishing a mouthful of peas when I asked him, quite unexpectedly, 'What is that, sir? Some kind of wreath?'

The old man swallowed and craned around his massive throne, before turning back to face me, one eye squinting beneath his monocle. 'It's Bile Dathi, m'dear. With the Blood Moon rising anon, it's only fitting that the house be prepared.'

'Is like Christmas, yes?' Mikhail frowned from across the table.

LaVey laughed heartily as he patted a silk napkin around his mouth. 'Nothing so commercial! This is a tradition of my family's that stretches back...oh, long before you were born.'

The table candles flickered on the slightest of breezes. The wreath was made of dark, brittle vines not unlike those that snaked around the outside of the house. 'You're a religious man?' I asked, still curious

LaVey laced his gnarled hands together; the reflection of the candle flames made his eyes glow fiercely. 'The old ways must be kept alive,' he mused. 'They teach us who we are, where we came from, and what is to come.'

Mikhail grimaced and shook his head, but I was suddenly reminded of those tumultuous family holidays. Thanksgiving, Christmas, birthdays...it seemed like my family delighted in ruining every single one of them with talk of politics, religion, money, and passive-aggressive comments. "When are you getting married?",

"When's the baby coming?", "Aren't you lucky to have a big, strong man beside you?", "Isn't it time you got a real job?", and hundreds more, seemingly designed to rile me up.

I could already feel myself getting antsy just thinking about it and found myself grateful to be shaken from these thoughts when I heard my name mentioned by Mr. LaVey. Freddy must have sensed my anxiety and gave my hand a gentle squeeze as I stood up, holding my typed pages in my hands. I took a shaky inhale and began reading my story.

Aster's Submission:

The Broadcast

'During the night of September 28, 2018,' KTCN head anchor Justine Kriener reported, 'our sister community of Castalia and its two hundred and seventy-three residents vanished. We do not know exactly what happened, only that a smoldering fissure remains where Castalia once sat.'

Justine's voice cracked after reading the intro segment, but she needed to persist until Officer Adams came on the line. When they had spoken earlier, he had specified not to bring any crew to the site and insisted on calling into the station to report what was going on. Odd, but if it was what was best, KTCN would heed his wishes.

'On the phone, we have Officer Henry Adams. Officer, can you shed some light on this tragic and horrific situation?'

There was a brief pause before Officer Adams responded. The reception wasn't great at the best of times. It must have been a nightmare, given the circumstances. 'Yes, I…you just…' The call was cutting out terribly, causing Justine's already uneasy state to grow.

'I'm so sorry. Can you repeat what you just said, officer? You're cutting out.'

Aside from the occasional static and a muffled word, the line was silent. 'Officer? Are you there? Can you hear me?'

A faint scream was heard, followed by piercing static and then the line dropped.

'Cut the feed!' someone commanded, causing Justine to jump. 'Cut it now!'

The cameras and audio were shut off, and the screens flashed up the 'technical difficulties' warning to any viewers watching. Justine tried to calm her shaking hands and get her breathing under control, but she couldn't stop the shiver that ran down her spine. The scream wasn't picked up on the live feed for viewers, but she heard it as plain as day. She couldn't have been the only one, right? The tech crew were trying to get Henry back on the line when a child's giggle sounded through the studio, causing everyone to stop amidst the chaos.

'Hello?' One of the tech guys called. Justine slowly started getting out of her chair, making as little sound as possible. No one uttered so much as a breath during those tense few seconds.

Twenty seconds…

Thirty seconds…

One minute.

No response.

The tension in the air settled for a moment. Justine exhaled the breath she had been holding in when all the lights in the studio went out.

* * *

September 15, 2018

'Breaking news for you early this morning. We have Charles Landt, Police Chief of the Ossian Police Department, with us regarding an

incident that happened in the community of Castalia last night,' Justine reported. 'For those of you who do not know, Castalia is in southern Winneshiek County and has a population of close to three hundred residents. Thank you, Chief Landt, for joining us'

The screen switched to Charles. He had been police chief for the last eight years, and those years hadn't been kind to him. He was in his early forties but was hardened by what he had endured in his job. It made him a fearless and reliable officer of the law, being one of the first on the scene and not letting high emotions or disruptions get the better of him.

'Thank you, Justine and KTCN. We had received a call around 9:45 p.m. from one of the town's residents reporting a strange rumbling sound coming from Jens Park. They said it reminded them of an earthquake.'

'That does sound strange indeed. Were there reports from other residents who experienced this?'

Charles took a deep breath, glancing behind him for a moment at his two other officers investigating the park. 'About fifty-eight residents had called into the station to report the incident. The last call was logged at 12:30 a.m.'

'Do you know if there was anything that might have been causing this disturbance? After all, we all know how kids can get, especially after the local high school wins a football game.' Justine couldn't help but cringe at her choice of words; she had been one of those very high school students during her senior year and certainly had upset her fair share of the older folks in Ossian.

'That was considered but has since been ruled out because the football game was still going on when the first call came in,' Chief

Landt quickly replied. 'There were a few residents who asked if there was after-hours construction still happening, as there had been some overdue repairs going on over the summer which had disturbed some residents.'

Justine kept her facial expression stoic but thought that was odd. When had construction projects ever gone past 6:00 p.m.? 'That is a fair point to consider but it doesn't sound like that was the case. Is there anything else you can report to us, Chief Landt? We know you probably need to get back to your investigation and don't want to keep you.'

'There's one more piece of information I can share…'

One of the officers came rushing up behind Charles, whispering something frantically. Justine watched Charles give him a nod before dismissing him off-camera. 'Apologies for that.'

A dark figure raced in the background behind Charles, causing Justine to yelp in surprise. 'Sir! What was that behind you?'

A puzzled look came across his features as he looked over his shoulder before coming back to face the camera. 'I don't see anything, Ms. Kriener. What did you see?'

'I thought I saw something move behind you, Chief Landt. I couldn't see any distinct features; it was moving too fast.'

'I had just adjusted the camera. Is it possible you could have seen a resident or one of the other officers?' her cameraman, Bryce, quietly commented. 'I didn't see anything unusual otherwise.'

Justine nodded her head. 'Yeah,' she said. 'That's what it probably was. But thank you so much to Police Chief Charles Landt of the Ossian Police Department for taking some time out of this *investigation to bring this situation to the attention of everyone in the surrounding area.'*

'Absolutely. If anyone has any information regarding this incident, please call into the non-emergency line at 563-545-8363,' Charles said before he stepped away.

* * *

Screams erupted throughout the studio and mingled with the sounds of people rushing about trying to find a switch to turn lights back on. Most began pulling out their phones to turn on their flashlights to navigate the dark space. Justine remained rooted to the spot. Despite not being able to see, she could *sense* something was there in the studio. A shiver coursed through her body. *Did it get colder in here?* Justine wrapped her arms around herself as she continued to listen to her co-workers rushing about in a panic.

You need to get out of here. Now. Justine nodded, agreeing with herself. Though she was terrified, she slowly began to move off the stage. Remembering her phone was in her pocket, she pulled it out and switched on the flashlight since she didn't want to navigate through the chaos in darkness.

Let's go to the break room. It'll be safe there. You can lock the door. You need to calm down. She pointed her phone down and made her way off the stage and onto the studio floor. Justine could barely hold her phone steady; her hands were shaking terribly as she continued to make her way across the floor. She was so focused on getting to her destination that she forced herself to drown out the sounds of everyone around her. *Focus on your breathing, Justine. Focus on your movement.*

Glancing up for a moment, she could see the exit door that would lead her to the back studio. She could see her destination within sight…and then she stopped. 'What the fuck?' she muttered. She tried to will her feet to take a step, but it was as though her feet were stuck to the floor. Justine tried to make any part of her body move, but it was useless. The panic rose; her breathing came in short hitches, a million thoughts raced through her head, and tears blurred her vision. She became hyper aware of her surroundings: the chaos and screaming of her co-workers had stopped, causing her to become more anxious. The only thing she could hear was her own interpretation of silence: a faint whistling of static white noise. Justine strained to hear something, anything, when a low chuckle pierced through the air, interrupting her concentration. Time itself seemed to stop as the laugh continued. Slowly, she realized she had heard it before. It had been a little over a week ago during the interview with Chief Landt…

* * *

September 18, 2018

'We are reporting live with Officer Jason Hovden. Officer Hovden, you had taken the first call regarding the incident of September 15. Is this the same situation?'

Officer Hovden straightened the microphone attached to his shirt. 'We're not currently sure, Justine. We received a call from a resident who not only heard the same rumbling sounds from the fifteenth, but when they went to check on the situation for themselves, they mentioned seeing a significant black opening in the sky.'

'A black opening in the sky?'

'That is what the initial report was before more calls came flooding in with similar sightings. Some say they even took photos of this black opening. However, every photo that we received came in looking blurry or distorted.'

Justine was confused. Surely people would not make up something so horrific; but the fact that every single photograph documented came out blurry or distorted was too coincidental. From what she remembered growing up, most people in Castalia were older and updated technology was something they avoided. Hell, most of them still had flip phones.

'That is strange indeed, Officer Hovden. Has an additional investigation been launched by your department?'

Before he could answer, Chief Landt walked into the camera's view. 'We have nothing additional to add, but we will keep you updated as we come to find out more. Thank you, Ms. Kriener.'

There was a brief, awkward silence that hung in the air as Justine tried to think of something to inform the viewers. A dark blur flashed across the screen, just like last time.

'Officers!' Justine shouted. 'There's something that ran over by that red house...just off to your left!' She watched as both officers drew their guns and made their way towards the house. As they approached, she saw a pair of red eyes looking right at her. A faint laugh came through her earpiece.

'Who...who's there?' Justine croaked. 'Wh-why are you laughing?'

Another chuckle. 'Careful. You don't want to ask questions when you're not prepared to hear the answer.'

* * *

Justine heard a soothing, deep voice in the darkness. 'We finally meet.'

'Wh-wh-who are you?'

'Not yet. You are not ready to see my true form yet.'

Terror seized Justine. The voice sounded close, and she was defenseless. 'W-w-w-who–'

'You have nothing to fear. I'm not here to harm you…unless you choose to act out. Then I can't say for sure you'll be safe.'

How did you…what in the hell? How did you know what I was going to say or what I was thinking?

'I have not limited your speaking abilities, you know. You're perfectly capable of talking normally.' A flash of light caught her attention and, when she fixed her gaze in its direction, her heart stopped: it was the same pair of red eyes she had seen ten days ago. 'You are remembering when you first saw me. You know I could hear you…it wasn't nice of you to inform them about me. That was rude of you, Justine.'

Her blood turned to ice upon hearing her name. 'Who are you?' she whispered.

Another giggle. 'Who I am doesn't matter. I have a mission to fulfill. That stupid police chief couldn't help me. He really fought hard until the end, you know…'

Justine could feel tears running down her face. She didn't understand what was happening. Also, why was no one helping her? Couldn't they see what was going on? She tried to focus on her surroundings, listening for anything that wasn't her own breathing. When she realized it was silent, a fresh wave of dread consumed her.

'No, they cannot hear you or see you,' the voice continued. 'We are still in the studio, but in our own separate reality. I needed to get you alone, Justine. You are the key to making my reawakening a reality.'

'Why me?' Justine squeaked.

* * *

September 24, 2018

'We have another concerning update to provide to you coming from Castalia. We have our cameraman Bryce Schissel on the scene with Police Chief Charles Landt of the Ossian Police Department.'

The camera feed switched over to Chief Landt; his eyes had large, dark bags under them. His facial expression was that of resignation, but he still stood in front of the camera with a commanding presence. 'Thank you, Ms. Kriener. The last update that came in was regarding the black openings in the sky was from September 18th.'

Justine nodded her head. 'Yes, that is correct, sir. Were you able to get to the bottom of that?' She saw him shake his head.

'Unfortunately, we did not. We even had to call on fellow officers over from the Decorah Police Department to help us look into the matter.'

'So this is becoming a county-wide investigation? What can you tell us, Chief Landt?'

As he was about to speak, he stopped; his mouth still open and his eyes preoccupied with something off to his right. This lasted a few moments before he brought his attention back to the camera. 'Apologies for that. Thought I heard one of my guys say he found something. Just a false alarm.'

Justine noticed he seemed tense as he continued talking. 'After collecting statements from nearby neighbors outside of Castalia, we discovered something unusual. We learned anyone who lived outside of the city limits of Castalia did not see any black opening in the sky.'

Justine narrowed her eyes upon hearing this. 'I'm not sure I understand,' she tapped her fingers on the desk nervously. 'No one else saw this strange opening in the sky...except for people who lived in the city limits? Am I understanding this correctly?'

Chief Landt nodded. 'I know. I didn't believe it myself. Every resident we could talk to in the Castalia limits reported the opening; anyone and everyone outside saw nothing. I didn't see anything until I entered city limits.'

'It's getting bigger!' someone screamed in the background, causing Chief Landt and Justine to jump. 'The hole! It's getting bigger!'

Justine didn't know what to do. She was frozen in terror. Her fear grew when she saw the daylight disappear, plunging the town into darkness. 'Chief Landt! What's going on?!' She screamed.

She could tell he was trying to keep a calm demeanor but whatever was going on had spooked him. 'I honestly don't know, Justine.' More screams erupted, causing Justine to rip out her earpiece. What the fuck was going on?

'Charles! We need your help!' Justine watched as Officer Adams made his way over to the chief, fear apparent in his eyes. 'People are going missing! I can't find Officer Hovden anywhere!'

Chaos ensued. Justine could faintly hear Bryce asking her if he should stop filming. She fumbled with her earbuds and pushed them back in. 'No, I want you to get as much of this as you are able to safely. If it becomes too dangerous, get out.'

Bryce repositioned the camera as the two officers made their way to a crowd of panicked people who were pointing upwards. It panned up to show the black hole in the sky. An explosion in the distance caused Bryce to move the camera to a cornfield...it was on fire! 'When did that happen? What is going on?!' Justine wasn't even hiding the terror in her voice at this point.

'Oh my God...what happened to him?' She heard Bryce ask someone off-camera; however, she was concerned with the fire as she saw some residents make their way to it...and walk right in. She couldn't believe what she was seeing. Were those people really walking into the fire? Justine muffled a scream; tears began running down her face as she saw people burn like paper.

'Justine...' She heard a dark voice say over her earpiece. 'Justine...'

She ripped her earpiece out again and threw it as far as she could. Who the hell was that? That was not *Bryce. It made her unsettled. Looking back to the fire, she watched more people walk into it; but something else caught her attention. Her eyes locked with the pair she could see coming from inside the fire. How could it be coming from inside?! This was the second time she'd seen those eyes. They were real...weren't they?*

'Justine, get your earpiece back in,' one of the tech guys handed it to her. 'Bryce needs to talk to you. There is a situation...' Putting it back in her ear, she heard Bryce's voice immediately.

'Justine! Justine!'

'Y-y-yes, Bryce?'

'I was trying to tell you to turn away from what you were seeing. Did your mic cut out or something?'

'What did I just see, Bryce? Who would do such an insane thing like that?!'

She heard Bryce take a shaky breath before responding, 'That was Officer Hovden who just walked into the fire. He's dead.'

* * *

'I will explain why in due time.'

Justine swallowed, trying to calm herself. 'Do you have a name?'

It chuckled. 'I go by many titles; none of which is even my true name. You can almost say that, depending on your belief, I can go by this name or that one. It doesn't matter. Monikers are meaningless.'

Taking a deep breath, she focused on her heartbeat. Even though she was scared beyond belief, she needed to calm down. 'Can I at least see what you look like?'

Without saying a word, it stepped away from its spot and came into her light's path. This thing reminded her of someone wearing an all-black bodysuit; however, she was pretty sure normal people didn't float in the air and have a smoky-like quality to their form. She blinked rapidly, trying to process what she was looking at. Had she finally lost her mind? Was this some kind of fucked up nightmare? Through her panicked confusion and dread, one thing stood out in her mind.

'It was you! You're the one who I've been seeing in the background of the reports! You're the one who I saw in the fire! You lured Officer Hovden to his death!'

A chuckle. 'You really are an observant one.'

'And all those people who went missing? Over a hundred people...? Was that–'

'Yes,' it replied darkly, 'that was quite the glorious moment. Hearing those screams and those burning bodies was a pleasure to witness.'

Justine's fear was slowly being replaced with anger. 'You bastard! What did they do to you?! Why would you harm innocent people like that?!'

'Now is the time!' The figure said suddenly; she could have sworn she saw a grin appear on its featureless face.

'Time for what?'

A tearing sensation started at her feet and coursed through her body. She let out a scream, as it felt like she was being ripped into two.

* * *

September 25, 2018

'Breaking news out of Castalia. Reporting live with KTCN is Officer Henry Adams of the Ossian Police Department.'

'Thank you for having me,' Henry's hoarse voice responded.

'So, I'm trying to understand what you said when we spoke earlier. All the residents who went missing yesterday were...found?' Justine asked, her voice full of hope. However, that hope faded when

311

she saw Officer Adams' eyes staring into the camera. They were filled with dread.

'Those one-hundred-and-five residents,' he sharply inhaled, 'were found.'

She didn't like the tone his voice had taken. 'Are they...all right?'

He stared at her through the camera's lens. '...we found their burnt bodies.'

Justine didn't even try to hide the startled yelp that left her lips. She had hoped he would give her a different outcome. The picture flickered for a moment, catching her attention. There was something very wrong with this situation, but she needed to keep her composure for the viewers.

'Oh my God!' a deep voice shouted in the background. 'Adams...I need your help now!'

Justine watched as Officer Adams and Bryce made a mad dash towards the voice. Though muffled, Justine picked up that it was Chief Landt. When the camera focused on him, there was blood splattered across his uniform.

'I think it would be wise to–'

'Bryce, I swear if you cut away now, you will not have a job in the morning!' Justine couldn't believe she had snapped like that.

'Ms. Kriener, I think it would be best to–'

Without taking her eyes off the screen, she repeated her threat before adding that this was critical for people to know and to keep them informed about the situation.

'Oh my God! Justine, cut the feed!'

The camera jerked without warning, showing Charles screaming out in agony. Blood poured from his wounds in spurts; his body violently jerking about almost inhumanly before going still.

Five seconds.

Ten seconds.

No one dared to move or speak.

Thirty seconds.

'*Should we call an ambulance–*'

A deafening roar escaped from Chief Landt. His body lurched forwards viciously as he made his way to his feet. Blood continued to pour down his body.

'*Sir? Are you okay? We need to get you to a hospital! You've lost a lot of blood,*' *Officer Adams said.*

A chuckle escaped from Landt's lips. '*I'm perfectly fine, Henry. It looks worse than what it actually is.*'

Justine felt troubled. There was something really wrong. I think Officer Adams and Bryce can sense it too, *she thought.* 'Bryce...I think *now would be the time to come back to the studio. Make up a reason,*' *she whispered into her earpiece. Seeing the camera jerk once as a response, Justine heard Bryce mumble something to Officer Adams before he started walking away.*

'*I will get him to a–hey, help! Stop him!*' *Justine heard Officer Adams faintly through Bryce's earpiece.* '*Catch him!*'

* * *

313

Justine fought as hard as she could, but it was no use; this…*thing* had taken over her body. She screamed and cried out for help, begging for someone in the studio to hear her desperate pleas.

'Don't you understand, Justine? There is no one here to help you. We killed everyone here. Loads of dead bodies for my companions to consume when they finally arrive.'

The lights flickered back on, and Justine suppressed a scream; there was blood all over the walls and floor of the studio. There weren't any bodies to speak of; all she could see were their remains scattered everywhere. Justine heard herself chuckle at the sight of the carnage. Picking up a severed arm, she lapped the blood before taking a healthy bite from it. *I can't believe this is happening*, she thought. *This isn't happening. I'm just having another nightmare. Wake up, Justine!*

Those red eyes gleamed back at her in the darkness. She shut her eyes, but it was no use, she couldn't block them out. 'This is all very real. All your co-workers are dead and I killed that wretched police chief before making my way to visit you. Don't worry…this will all be over soon.'

'I don't understand. *What do you mean*?' She could almost feel her heart stop for a moment. 'Are you going to kill me, too?'

He snorted. 'Oh no…no, I have much bigger plans for you. I can't go around in my current form, and I'm still very weak after being resurrected. Originally, it was my plan to take over that miserable police chief…'

'It was you that killed Officer Adams?!' Justine screamed.

'No…it was Charles Landt's last act before his body gave out completely. He was weaker than I thought. He had a different monster destroying him from the inside. There was nothing left for me to consume, so I needed to find a new body.'

Justine couldn't find words. She had a feeling she knew what was going to happen to her, and she was powerless to stop it.

'I needed a young, strong, and supple body to consume. One that will last me quite some time. You were the perfect candidate. So, I thank you for your sacrifice. Your body will not be used in vain.'

Justine could feel tears stinging her eyes. Yes, she was terrified, never in her life did she expect to go out like this, but she needed to remain brave until the end. She needed to figure out a way to get this thing out of her body.

'Why did you do this? Those people did nothing to you!'

Another dark chuckle. 'I do this for fun, you see. There are so many like us out in this world. You humans are so ignorant and easy to fool, it's almost no fun. Don't worry, dear Justine. In a few short moments, I will take full control of you. You won't feel a thing.'

Justine could feel herself fading, her mind blanking. 'Just give in. It will make everything so much easier. Besides, we also have a breaking news story to report to your viewers. More vessels to draw in.'

Gritting her teeth, Justine fought back. She willed herself to take back her consciousness before her body made it to her desk. The camera lights flicked on, the standby light illuminating the back wall. As she was about to ascend the steps, Justine made her body stop, preventing from going forward. 'I will not let you win!'

* * *

'This is KTCN's Justine Kriener reporting. We finally have an update to provide to you about the Castalia situation. Our breaking coverage on it three nights ago was interrupted, technical difficulties.'

Justine tried to take her mind to a happy place before continuing. 'Unfortunately, we have a report regarding Officer Henry Adams. He has been shot and had to be rushed to Gunderson Medical Center in nearby Decorah.'

Someone started speaking into her earpiece. Justine closed her eyes for the briefest of moments. 'I'm just getting word now that Officer Adams has passed. We send our condolences and prayers to his family. The search for Chief Landt is still ongoing and Chief Harper of the Decorah Police Department says they won't stop looking until he is found.'

Another message came through her earpiece. She went still but continued to stare into the camera. 'Another update. Chief Harper has informed me of the status of Castalia.'

A pause.

'Castalia and all of its residents have vanished. All that remains is a scorched black hole.'

Justine stared into the camera, unblinking and unmoving. Slowly, a smile spread across her delicate features; the sounds of screams could be heard through her earpiece. 'What a tragedy indeed.'

Chapter Seven

Friday

1. *Brandis Dreams Again*

I was filled with suffocating dread.

Pure, primal, dread.

Walls of impossibly high black stone surrounded me; they stretched to the squalor in the sky and ahead into a broiling darkness as thick as fog that swirled around me.

Everywhere I looked, I saw either a dark void or a very faint, grey light winking at me out of the blackness.

I felt trapped, lost, but definitely not alone. Sounds were as meaningless as time and air, and yet I could still hear something lurking, stalking, leering far

(*ahead?*)

behind me. I could feel it watching me, its breath on my neck, and so I ran. My legs were like lead weights; the ground was sloppy mud, and although the walls rushed past me it felt like I was standing completely still.

The walls were the crumbling, age-old bricks of LaVey House; they even had those same knotted, twisted vines growing out of them. I reached towards them, and they whipped at me viciously. A cackle, like the wrinkling of decayed leaves, rose around me and the walls fell away and suddenly I was falling, falling fast…or was I being propelled? Grey fireworks burst in my vision and smoke billowed in a brief storm and I watched, frozen, as it stretched towards me like grasping hands.

Dreaming, I thought. *I'm dreaming. Nothing more than a dream.*

I felt no comfort from this realisation; in fact, my dread grew, even though I knew those smoke hands couldn't harm me. I defiantly passed through them, shuddering at the sensation, and sensed something black and huge fluttering overhead. I couldn't see it, but I could hear its flapping wings and imagined a great crow passing and cawing above, and, as if in response, black feathers rained all around in a cascade. I realised all too late that that it was a distraction to keep me from noticing the shadows that were closing in, constricting, and taking physical form

(*behind?*)

all around me. It rushed at me like a prism of living, clutching darkness and wrapped around me so tightly that I could scarcely breathe. I felt pinned (although I also had the sensation of standing up) as a part of me was effortlessly and spitefully drained from my body.

I tried to tell myself it was just a dream…

A trick of the mind and nothing more.

My head flailed as cold icicles caressed the back of my neck and the impossible darkness of that *thing's* eyes glared at me with sheer malice and sin. Its face was that grotesque melting mask of flesh, tendons, and gore. What was left of its lips leered gruesomely and it licked a thick, grey tongue over its drooling features as it barked one word before reality came swimming back into my brain: "*Black!*"

I awoke not with a scream or covered in sweat, but with the gentle and grateful realisation that I'd been dreaming. The part of me that was still a child afraid of the dark had been somewhat convinced that I was trapped up in that attic again or lost deep within LaVey's house. After all, it wouldn't be the first time I'd woken up in a strange place with no idea how I had gotten there. I'd once upset Lucy and Sam by randomly leaving a nightclub and stumbled back to campus without a key and had passed out on the lawn in front of the tower block.

This was different, though; I knew where I was, but my surroundings were definitely not what I'd grown accustomed to lately. I sat up slightly and wiped a hand over my face to shake off the lingering nightmare and felt my heart racing for two very distinct and equally excitable reasons. The first was that, for the first time in over a year, I'd actually had, and remembered, a nightmare. My heart dropped that I couldn't jot it down in my notebook, but it had been so vivid that my nerves were alive with energy and creativity. My nightmares had always bothered me, but ever since I'd stopped having them, I'd felt so empty. Now suddenly, I felt more like myself than I had in a long time, and I wondered if she, the other reason for my excitement, was the reason why.

Aster (*No*, I corrected myself. *Naomi. She'd said her name was Naomi*) was lying on the other side of the bed. The duvet was crumpled between our bodies, but I could easily stroke my hand down her bare shoulder blades if I wanted. It was tempting, but she was fast asleep, and I didn't want to disturb her or risk waking her and have her realise that she'd just made a massive mistake. I propped myself against the bed's uncomfortable headboard and watched her sleep. The mess of her thick, long mane was curled all over her pillow and she was lying on her stomach, her face turned away from me and partially buried in that same pillow. The duvet covered most of her slender, naked body and I could hear her soft, whispery breaths as she slept. She was so still that, were it not for that gentle breathing, I would've thought her dead.

Last night had been a blur of intensity and passion. I don't know what had come over me; I haven't been that bold with a girl for ages and had almost forgotten what it felt like to have that first kiss and that raw feeling of lust overtake me. Even now, I struggled. She'd clearly had a traumatic experience and had hit LaVey's rum pretty hard and, even though I wanted her badly, I also didn't want to take advantage of her.

If anything, I smirked, she *took advantage of* you. That was a humbling thought that made me feel strangely good. It'd been like my deepest fantasy come to life. This gorgeous woman, a successful and striking author who I'd followed and fantasised about for the longest time, had suddenly been in my arms and pulling at my clothes. The feeling of her body, her breasts, had been indescribable; she'd felt so soft, so smooth, so unbelievably divine, and I'd completely abandoned any inhibitions.

I'd felt alive in a way that I hadn't since starting university, when all we'd done was throw caution to the wind, stealing kisses on the dancefloor, having shots, and singing bad karaoke, or heading home with a willing girl in your arms or a greasy cheeseburger as a consolation prize. The sensation of being young and alive and free had been so real…and so fleeting. If I'd known that it wouldn't last, I would've done more, *said* more, and taken more chances.

But then again, the brightest flames burn the shortest, or whatever that fuckin' saying was.

Naomi stirred abruptly and jolted awake with a little cry that surprised me. She rolled onto her back. Her hair fell about her face comically and she placed a hand to her forehead wearily. 'Mmm...'sit?' she groaned.

I couldn't help but laugh. Obviously, she was not a morning person. I cleared my throat and hoped to God that she remembered what had happened last night or else I was liable to get another black eye. 'Mornin',' I greeted, a dumb smile on my face as her dark eyes rolled up towards me. 'How're you feelin'?'

'Like shit,' she coughed with a pleasant smile. She rolled over, making no attempt to cover her modesty, and I forced my gaze on her eyes rather than the delicious temptation of her cleavage. 'So sorry, but could I trouble you for a glass of water?' her cheeks flushed a bit, and she turned her eyes away. I wondered if she was always so formal after sleeping with someone.

'Sure, yeah,' I chuckled before slipping out of bed with a grimace. I'd landed awkwardly on my hip after Mikhail's punch and could feel a painful bruise forming there.

I crossed Naomi's bedroom and filled a tumbler with tap water; she took it gratefully as I retrieved my clothes. I didn't normally sleep naked, and I felt very awkward just standing there with everything on show, so I turned away and pulled on my clothes as she finished her water.

'Thank you,' came her timid voice.

I turned back to her and nodded. 'No worries. I usually spend the entire next day drinkin' water after bein' on the lash.'

There was a noticeable pause and I flinched slightly as her hand suddenly touched my back. 'I meant for last night.'

A rush of heat flushed my cheeks as I slipped my t-shirt over my thin frame. I turned and looked down at her. She'd shifted over onto my side of the bed and basically took up the entire mattress with her body at a slight angle. Again, I couldn't help but smile; she wasn't the first girl I'd known to hog the bed.

'I don't want things to be awkward, but...'

'Yeah, no,' I answered much too quickly. 'It's one of them...things.' What even were words at this point? I could talk about purple monkeys and dishwashers and it'd have the same fuckin' meaning.

'I mean...' *Here it comes*, I thought dismally. *Here comes the standard, "You're a nice guy but..." speech.* I dunno why I was surprised, to be honest; she was engaged, after all. 'I guess I didn't realise how much I needed that...'

My mind reeled in surprise. 'Same,' I answered in more of a croaked whisper. She wearily stretched a hand up to my beard and I took it eagerly, kissing her soft skin lightly. All I wanted was to lose myself in her once more, to feel her need and desire around me again, but I could also sense that the moment wasn't quite right. I settled on simply saying: 'Thank *you*.'

She smiled and rolled back onto her back, wrapping herself up snugly in the duvet. 'I could stay like this forever,' she mused sleepily. 'Far away, in the middle of nowhere. Just me, my books, and a big, comfy bed.'

'And your rum,' I quipped.

She giggled. 'And my rum.'

Her eyes closed as she drifted off, so I rose and searched for my trainers; one was near the bar and the other was against the wall. I pulled them on and tied them up. When I looked over at her she seemed fast asleep, but she surprised me by mumbling: 'I'd love to see you later…'

'Yeah,' I answered, trying to contain my delight. 'Of course.'

As I stepped to the door, I felt something under my foot. I stooped down and picked up a glittering silver ring. Her engagement ring. I rolled it between my thumb and my forefinger as I watched her dozing and quietly placed it upon her dresser as I stepped into the hallway.

2. *Rhiannon's Breakfast Confrontation*

Having eventually succumbed to exhaustion late into the night, Rhiannon woke the next morning absolutely famished and decided that, unless she wanted to starve to death, she needed to venture out again to eat. Her stomach grumbled loudly as she opened the door. It was early so she prayed she wouldn't see anyone else. Also, she hoped she'd be able to find another bottle of something on her travels. The dull buzz was wearing off and had been replaced by an almighty headache.

As she made her way down the various corridors, she spied the helmet room in front of her. She vaguely remembered that Aster had been staying in that room…but why the hell was Brandis coming out of it? His hair was ruffled, his clothes were slightly askew, and he wore a slight, smug smile on his face. The truth hit Rhiannon like a thud to the chest as she ducked behind the nearest suit of armour.

How dare that pathetic excuse of a man use Aster for his own sordid gratification! Rhiannon clenched her jaw and desperately fought back the urge to jump out from her hiding place and confront him. She watched, seething, as he strolled past, completely oblivious to the fact that he was in danger of being shoved off the nearest balcony to the hallway below. His stupid face made her want to punch him until his smirk disappeared forever.

When Brandis walked out of sight, she immediately felt her anger and tension begin to decrease. What was happening to her? Why was she full of…hatred…for a man she barely knew…and why was she feeling so protective of Aster? Was it because she reminded her so much of her own daughter? Possibly. Or maybe she just didn't like it when men took advantage of women.

Rhiannon peered out from behind the armour, checking in both directions before descending the stairs and heading for the dining hall. She could smell the warm aromas of freshly baked breads and pastries. Surely, Mr. LaVey didn't bake all this himself? Where the hell was all the food coming from? It was mind-boggling to think that he was doing all this solo…unless he'd ordered the food in, but that seemed just as unlikely, as she had never seen any vehicles arriving or seen any signs of a delivery.

As soon as she saw the wide array of food on offer, she forgot about how it had appeared there and began to pile up her plate. A humungous cafetière of hot coffee sat steaming on the table, so she filled up a mug and added a splash of cream. Maybe coffee was a more appropriate beverage for this time of morning.

A creaking sound from behind startled her and a few drops of cream spilled onto the clean, white tablecloth. Rhiannon glanced behind her apprehensively and saw the mountain of a man that was Mikhail standing with his gigantic arms crossed over his chest. He was glaring at her as if she had no right to be in his presence.

'Good morning,' she squeaked, realising that her throat was dry and sore.

'What's so good about it? Why are you here?' Mikhail spat, his voice low and gravelly.

'Erm…I was just…you know what? I don't have to explain myself to you. I'm getting breakfast, what the fook does it look like I'm doing?'

'You better watch your tongue, or you end up with it cut out.'

Rhiannon chose to ignore the threat. 'Heard a little girl kicked your ass with a sword yesterday.' A statement, not a question.

'There was no ass kicking. They ganged up on me.'

'What started the fight anyway?'

'None of your fucking business, woman.'

'All right then, don't tell me. You know, it wouldn't hurt to be a bit more pleasant to people...you're a bit of a fooking asshole.'

Rhiannon had no idea where her sudden bravery (or maybe it was stupidity?) had come from. She knew that Mikhail could respond in one of two ways: either he would ignore her, or he'd beat her to death. She watched as his eyes narrowed and he puffed out his chest, but she held her ground. She didn't want to appear weak and, if needed, she thought she could remember a bit of self-defence from her few short lessons. If not, then smashing the cafetière over his head would certainly make him think twice.

Luckily, the behemoth merely grunted at her and began to serve himself from the table. Rhiannon took that as her cue to leave and took her food and coffee back to her room, deciding that she would leave the hunt for more alcohol until later that night.

3. Aster Gets Judged

The bright sun peeking through the thick curtain roused me from my slumber. It was the best night's sleep I'd had in some time. *Pretty sure the sex you had with Freddy had something to do with that*, my inner voice mocked. *How was that, by the way? Was he worth cheating on your fiancé with?*

A fleeting feeling of remorse ran through me, but I had already decided. 'Yes, yes, it was worth it.' This wasn't any kind of sick payback for all those times Walter had cheated on me, but I'd be lying to myself if I didn't feel smug about having someone desire me like that. It really boosted my self-confidence as I honestly didn't think of myself as anything special: I was short, had a little extra pudge around my tummy, and had a tendency to appear bitchy or rude with my facial expressions, so why would Freddy be attracted to someone like me? He had mentioned that he'd wanted me since I'd arrived, as well as being in awe regarding my success and Instagram following, so he must have been following me there. A wave of guilt hit me, thinking about how I could have gotten to know him sooner.

I picked up my phone and scrolled through one of my accounts. Even my mobile data was on the slower side today, as it took longer than usual to load. Once Instagram was up, I started typing any name that made sense, and I quickly found him under '*author.f.brandis.*' To my surprise, I realised I was already following him but had never given him a second glance. He had under a thousand followers and posted very little, let alone anything personal beyond a simple profile picture. *No wonder*, I thought. *I usually pay attention to accounts that have daily content or ones that actively engage with my posts.* Maybe he was too shy to comment on anything, or he could be a newer user. Either way, I made a mental note to take the time to keep in touch after this collaboration was over. I made a second mental note to boost several smaller accounts that deserved proper recognition. It brought me immense joy helping others, and this experience with Freddy had opened my eyes to that oversight.

I checked the time; it was 10:36 a.m., so probably not a good time to call Walter. He would be finishing up his shift and immediately crashing once he'd arrived home. Not that I really wanted to speak to him as we hadn't been in communication since he'd snapped at me while out drunk with his friends.

My stomach grumbled loudly, alerting me that eating wouldn't be a terrible idea. I would think more about the Walter situation after I had some food. Getting up from the warm, comfortable bed was difficult, but I just about managed it. I threw on an old college t-shirt and my pyjama bottoms and made my way downstairs and into the dining area where the usual breakfast foods were laid out. Most of it had already been picked over, but that didn't bother me; I only wanted to grab a bagel and some juice before going back up to my room. There wasn't anyone else around, so I grabbed my food and hurried back upstairs. Once I got to the second floor, someone called out to me.

'So…saw Brandis leaving your room this morning. What was that all about?' Rhiannon's voice caught me off-guard. I opened my mouth to answer but she quickly shut me down by raising her hand into the air. 'Never mind, I have a pretty good idea what that was about. How could you stoop so low?'

I blinked a few times, confused by her comments. 'What do you mean "how could I stoop so low"? Admittedly, I made a different kind of mistake before–'

'Just sayin', I think you can do better than that loser.'

'Actually, Freddy is an incredibly talented writer. He wrote—'

'I don't give a fook what that imposter has written. I'm sure it was trash, just like him.' She got right up in my face, her eyes narrowed. 'But you're worse than he is!'

Taking a step back from her, my eyes widened with tears threatening to spill. 'Okay, I don't understand the full story of why you don't like him, and I suppose I never will understand. That's fine, you have your reasons, but don't you dare, for one second, stoop so low as to call me trashy! You don't even know what really happened!'

Rhiannon dryly chuckled. 'I don't have to know what happened. It's written all over your face, *bach*.'

'What does it matter to you?'

She shook her head at me. 'I thought you were better than that. After all, you are engaged,' Rhiannon pointed to my ring finger and stopped for a moment, her lips pursed tightly. 'Funny. Why aren't you wearing it now?'

'Because I'm going to be ending things with my fiancé!' I screamed, frustrated by the turn of events. I thought Rhiannon had a higher opinion of me. I didn't understand why sleeping with Freddy would make her change so quickly.

'Such a shame...' Without finishing her sentence, she brushed past me and made her way towards her room; the sound of the door slamming reverberated through the empty hallway.

I stood there, my mouth still hanging open. I wasn't going to kid myself; it hurt to hear her snide comments. Personally, I thought she had more respect for me than that. To be fair, she wasn't entirely wrong to call me out on sleeping with someone while I was engaged to someone else, but what business was that of hers? Walter and I could have been in an open relationship as far as anyone knew! If she was going to make such a rash judgment call like that, maybe it was for the best that we didn't connect on a personal level. Professionally, I still respected her. That couldn't be denied; her work was exceptional, and I would continue to strive to be just like her. However, I would not try to pursue a friendship with someone who was *that* arrogant and full of herself.

If she just got to know Freddy, maybe she would see what I saw: an extremely talented, albeit shy, author who deserved more recognition than what he got. On the other hand, she still seemed set in her ways and would continue to look down on him, even if he became a bestselling author. Shaking my head, I continued to make my way back to my room. I had a piece to finish…and a fiancé to break up with.

4. *Rhiannon Prepares to Finish*

A few hours passed and Rhiannon felt the overwhelming urge for another smoke break. Her fingers were sore from using the typewriter and her neck was beginning to stiffen. She breathed in the smoke as deeply as she could, feeling the burning sensation fill her lungs. She hadn't been for a run since...*it* had happened, so maybe after this she'd put on her trainers and go for a short jog. The thought made her shudder. Running brought her pleasure and the idea of having fun after such a harrowing incident was unthinkable. She needed to recover and made a mental note to check in with her therapist when she returned home.

While Rhiannon was walking along the second-floor corridor back towards her room, she spied Aster carrying a bagel and a glass of freshly squeezed orange juice. Rhiannon decided to confront her about Brandis leaving her room earlier that morning. The woman was engaged after all, and she'd thought she had more respect for herself than that.

Unfortunately, the confrontation ended with a few hate-filled words and left a sick feeling in her stomach, but Rhiannon didn't care about attempting to be polite to Aster anymore. She'd had enough of this house and these people, none of whom were worth being friends with. Aster was just like the rest of them: selfish.

Rhiannon slammed the door to her room harder than she anticipated, which caused the chandelier above her head to judder. She stared at the typewriter. It was mocking her. Tomorrow was the banquet where all the stories were to be revealed and she was determined that her story was going to be the best of them all.

'Let's do this,' she muttered as she took her seat.

5. *Brandis Finds His Motivation*

I'd barely been able to contain myself when I'd gotten back to my room; I'd pushed LaVey's typewriter aside, opened my laptop to give it time to warm up, and showered quickly. I'd never been a big fan of showers; I'd been wary of them ever since we'd been forced to share a cramped, stained bathroom at university and much preferred a long, hot soak in a bath, but I needed to freshen up. I could still smell Naomi's intoxicating scent on me and, while it wasn't unpleasant and I'd much prefer to experience more of it, I needed to eliminate the distraction it caused.

I dried off and caught sight of myself in the small mirror above the sink; I looked a bit dishevelled, but that was nothing new, but the unmistakable glint in my eyes gave me pause. I couldn't believe how invigorated I felt, but I had no intention of questioning it. After all, who knew how long the feeling would last! I tugged on an old pair of joggers and a hoodie. The morning was a bit chilly and I wanted to be as comfortable as possible if I was going to let my writing take me over as completely as I suspected it would. I could feel the words pawing at my mind like a curious kitten as my documents struggled to load up.

On the journey down to Arklington, I'd tried exploring some ideas for LaVey's book but had drawn nothing but duds, and I'd looked at a few underdeveloped ideas I had saved but nothing had jumped out at me. There was maybe enough content for a side story or an interlude, but nothing I felt confident to hit LaVey's minimum word count. Five thousand words wasn't much to work with; just enough to tantalise the reader, and I didn't want to waste my time on a concept that could barely clear one thousand words.

The sad fact was that a lot of these underdeveloped ideas were just incoherent nightmares from my youth, and they rarely evolved into anything other than passing mentions in other, unrelated books. In *Breath of Eden*, for example, my main character was often plagued by horrible nightmares, which allowed me to give those scribbles a chance to take life, but the rest ended up completely abandoned.

It didn't help that LaVey's instructions had been frustratingly vague. The old man seemed pleasant and accommodating enough but he seemed to be holding his cards very close to his chest regarding the specifics of *Even Death May Die*. 'I like to publish an anthology or two each year, yes,' he'd mused the other day when I'd cornered him. 'It helps to offer some variety, y'see? Cast a wider net, so to speak.'

The old man had been busying himself in a drawing room, half-heartedly waving a feather duster about and dressed in a three-piece striped suit, a gold pocket watch slipped into the pocket of his glistening waistcoat and a cravat of pure Egyptian cotton wrapped loosely around his neck. He looked a bit like he was late for an important dinner date, and yet continued to chat as if he had all the time in the world. Oddly, I also noticed that he'd taken to wearing a monocle over his left eye, which seemed noticeably squinted that day, something I hadn't noticed before.

I had ignored this and tried to push him for more specifics: 'But, like, what're you actually lookin' for? Ghosts? Gore? Summink more, I dunno, metaphorical?'

'Hm?' he had continued dusting, lost in his own thoughts. It was like trying to talk to my increasingly senile father. 'I should think you, as an artist, would appreciate having some freedom to indulge your creativity.'

Shit, I'd thought. *Had I offended him?* It was impossible to tell; the old man's features were locked in a look of permanent, grandfatherly benevolence. 'It's not that I ain't *grateful*,' I had stressed.

The old man chuckled. 'Of course not, m'boy.' Normally, I hated being referred to as "boy," but it seemed to be an old habit of LaVey's, and I decided to let it slide. LaVey had then finally stopped dusting and turned towards me, his hands clasped behind his slightly stooped back. '*Carte blanche*,' he said with a smile.

I'd blinked, momentarily stupefied, feeling like a schoolboy under the watchful eye of a kind, but stern, head teacher. 'I don't…'

LaVey plucked the monocle from his eye and breathed on it, misting the lens, before cleaning it on his waistcoat. 'In many ways, the subject doesn't matter,' he explained as he blinked the monocle back into position; I was somewhat amused to notice that his silk waistcoat had only further stained the lens. 'My desire is to bring you fine writers together, to house you here and foster your creativity, and to reap the rewards of what comes from your time here. When you walk my halls, do you feel a sense of being watched? Do you see the Devil's eyes blinking at you in the dark corners of my abode? Perhaps the chill that whistles through the windows is my dear old aunt Delilah searching for her long-lost son. It's not for me to say.'

I'd chosen not to reply; LaVey tended to talk in cryptic, almost nonsensical riddles. If I'd told him that his mansion probably *was* haunted, then he'd most likely have thought me mad. He surprised me then by saying: 'You attended that institute with those gruesome murders a while back, yes?'

'I...was there, yeah,' I'd replied uncomfortably. 'Not when it happened but...yeah.'

The old man tutted sympathetically and shook his head. 'Nasty business; it was in the papers even down here, y'know. Nasty, nasty business, and just another sign of how far we have fallen. Men, I mean.' He'd given a chuckle that seemed a bit inappropriate but, again, I didn't question it; sometimes, it was better to just stay quiet. 'We've been falling for some time though, wouldn't you say? Scripture tells us that we couldn't even get it right on day one! Imagine that.'

'I...guess?'

The old man's features had cracked into a warm smile. 'The point is, m'boy, we stumbled in the Lord's garden and we stumbled in Judea. We stumbled at Golgotha, when the spear pierced His side, and we've been trying to pick up the pieces ever since.'

Realisation had dawned on me and was quickly chased by curiosity. 'I didn't know you were a religious man, sir.'

LaVey had chuckled again and rocked slightly on his heels. 'I am a purveyor of *many* teachings, m'boy. Visit my library sometime; you'd be fascinated by some of the tomes I have locked away there. Religion, science, philosophy, even...*heh*...even some astrological meditations, yes. I find one can never have too much knowledge; with knowledge, maybe we could have saved ourselves from stumbling in the past, yes?'

I'd pondered this briefly before spying a flaw in his logic. 'But...Adam didn't know any better. How was he to know an *apple* would cause such a problem?'

LaVey's eyes had sparkled. '*Exactly!*' he cried. 'Exactly! He didn't know any better; I couldn't have put it better myself! *He* didn't know any better, Jerod didn't know any better; how many men throughout our history, real *and* fictional, simply acted without full knowledge of what their actions would bring? And *that's* the key, m'boy. Knowledge. Foresight. The ability to *think*, to *learn* from the past, no matter how gruesome it may be. You'd be surprised—*heh*, yes—surprised to know what you can learn from even the most forgotten, ancient texts.'

The conversation with LaVey hadn't really helped illuminate me much. I'd returned to my room and failed to produce anything but a series of disconnected, anti-religious sentiments that I wasn't prepared to indulge any further, but his words had stuck with me. My interpretation now was that the old man had basically been saying "forewarned is forearmed," and to learn from past mistakes. Why he couldn't just *say* those things was beyond me, but I suspected that LaVey was trying to make me realise something for myself rather than simply telling me the answer. My unproduced ideas weren't the answer; none of them sparked my creativity and I'd wasted enough of the week trying to force something to come out of it. I only had two days left and I needed to take advantage of my newfound enthusiasm.

I had no doubt that the key was in the past; Lucy, Sam, and all the colourful characters I'd known at university. Better, simpler days when our concerns were small, and our spirits were high.

'Y'know what I'd *love* t'do?' Lucy had slurred to me once while drunk. 'Jus'…jus' go climb a *mountain*, y'know? Fuck off down t'Snowdon or…or just, y'know, *travel*. Do sumfin' *wild!* Like skydivin'! Or helicopter lessons!'

I'd laughed her off, of course. She'd always been desperate to travel and wanted to try everything, but she didn't drive (which had hampered matters somewhat) and was deathly afraid of heights. Yet, she'd been determined to overcome those issues and come back with some interesting stories, and my heart ached that she'd been robbed of that chance. I wished that I could say that I did it in her stead, but it wasn't like I could just pack up off to Australia and leave my life behind.

Excuses, Lucy's voice scoffed.

Maybe she was right, maybe not, but it had been her dream to do something absolutely mental.

Sam had always been the big joker, always been the first to get the drinks in and then slip a tenner behind the bar to convince the waitress to cook up some ungodly concoction that one of us (usually him) would have to gulp down while the others hooted '*See it away! See it away!*' A night out with Sam could start as innocently as having a quick pint at the local pub and end with us changing into a shirt, tie, and shoes and blowing hundreds of pounds in the strip club at the end of town.

I'd always just gone along with it. Sam's carefree attitude had been infectious and livened up even the dullest of night's out, and Lucy's warmth and ability to be both rational and feisty had always meant that we both worked hard and played hard. Everything since then had been a mere shadow. Nightclubs weren't as alluring, lectures had seemed lifeless, and I don't think anyone had really felt comfortable revelling or even in some cases still walking around campus when so many had been so brutally and senselessly taken away. Many, myself included, actively avoided certain areas of campus out of both irrational fears of disturbing the dead and the real concerns of seeing a single bloodstain missed by the cleaners.

I'd been grateful to get out of there. The whole campus carried an ominous dread not unlike that found in LaVey's House, but there had been something more unsettling about being in a wide open, familiar, and previously safe environment full of nothing more scary than horny students and dull grey buildings and feeling as though some maniac could come charging through the gates and finish the job.

If I couldn't honour Lucy and Sam by living the dreams that had been stolen from them, it was the least I could do to try and let them live on in my writing. I usually avoided using the names of people I knew and places I'd lived; I found a freedom in crafting completely original locations that were a mish-mash of different places I'd lived in over the years, and the last thing I needed was someone I'd known getting all pissed off because I'd used their name for a psychopathic killer, but this was different. *Even Death May Die* was guaranteed to be published, to be read and seen by countless readers potentially the world over, and I wanted those readers to see Sam and Lucy's names in my story so that they would finally be able to live on.

6. *Mikhail on the Edge*

Mikhail sat on the floor of his bedroom shrouded in darkness, an empty glass nestled between his trembling, bruised knuckles.

After the…incident in the main hall, he had stormed back to his room in a fit of rage and humiliation and ransacked LaVey's fine furnishings, wrenching the wardrobe door from its hinges and launching the bedside table lamp at the huge lattice window doors, leaving a web-like crack spreading up the glass. Then, he'd raided the liquor cabinet, swigging everything straight from the bottle and casting each aside when they were done, saving the Beluga until last.

The results had been catastrophic, to say the least. He'd drifted in and out of consciousness, raged at shadows and left splintered holes in the bedroom walls, and thrown up sickening bile, the alcohol successfully numbing any concerns he might have had about the piercing pain in his lower back and the tint of red in his urine and vomit. Finally, he had collapsed into a heap on the floor.

With the greatest of pained efforts, he had propped himself against the bed, wearily dropped ice cubes that were littered across the lush, thick, vomit-stained carpet into a glass, and got to work on the Beluga. Each hit dulled the shame he felt at being so easily bested by the Америкос whore and increased the seemingly never-ending tirade of memories and taunting jeers the fading ghosts of the past hurled at him.

Жалкий! came his father's voice. *Pathetic runt!* How desperately he had wanted to keep his father from hurting his mother and sisters, and how badly he had paid the price for his insolence.

It is not new...the people need new, came Pavel, that sincere look glistening in his eyes. Kind-hearted Pavel, who had only his best interests at heart, but Mikhail could tell that even his oldest friend had lost patience with him.

Hurt мой ангел, Lia's father had warned him on their wedding day, *and, so help me God, I will break you*. A judgemental, overbearing old fool, he always thought he knew what was best, always interfered, and was forever undermining him.

My husband, Lia mocked. *All knowing, all-so-fucking caring!* How had this once sweet, innocent woman turned into such a pitiful creature?

The glass tumbled from Mikhail's hands and rolled lazily; the bottle of Beluga toppled over, spilling the last few drops onto the carpet. *A waste of good vodka!* Rodion cried, dismayed.

'Shut up,' Mikhail croaked as he angrily wiped tears from his eyes. 'Please…just shut up!'

A darkness, heavy and black, wrapped its cold claws around his heart, which beat much too fast within his panting chest. His head ached as much as his bladder and his back. His knuckles screamed from the ugly bruises he had received from hitting Brandis, and blood seeped from a dozen puncture wounds caused from small splinters.

'Never should have come here…' he muttered, staring vacantly past the cracked glass of his window doors and to the endless void of the night sky. The stars had been snuffed out by a vast, wispy grey cloud that lazily drifted across the blanket of infinity. Rain splattered relentlessly like the pattering of feet, yet his thoughts drifted to the foggy memories of long ago, when he had sat behind the wheel of his car and barrelled across the city with two bloodied, dismembered corpses that had once been his whole world wrapped up in black bags and duct tape on the back seat.

With Lia and Luka dead on the floor, Mikhail's first instinct had been to bolt into the kitchen and slather his bloodstained hands with soap until his flesh wrinkled and burned a bright pink. He'd been staring vacantly out of a window then, too, at their small, overgrown garden. *When are you going to tidy that shit up?* Lia had fussed at the back of his mind, and he had whipped around, fully expecting her to be standing in the doorway moaning about his lack of garden maintenance.

Realisation had hit him then and Mikhail had gagged on vomit as he lumbered towards the front door, his keys dropping to the floor as his shaking hands desperately tried to hold them steady so he could jump in the car and race far away from those bodies. Halfway to the door, he caught sight of his loved ones lying in thick pools of blood. *That stain'll* never *wash out,* he had thought incoherently, and suddenly found himself tempted to burn the whole place down.

With him in it.

The thought had hit him like a wall. Suddenly, it had seemed like the most logical idea in the world: set the house ablaze, purge all evidence of his heinous act, and spare himself the judgement of his friends, peers, and society. His life could have limped along if just one of them had perished...but *both* of them, one of them by his own hands no less, meant he may as well have gone with them.

Some primal instinct had taken over then. It wasn't like earlier, in the hall, when a black fog of madness and rage had overwhelmed him and driven him to attack Aster. He had allowed this instinct to guide him to grab fistfuls of black bags and a huge roll of duct tape, but all he remembered past that was that he had whistled as he wrapped up the still-warm bodies of his wife and son. 'Swan Lake,' he whispered into the darkness as he relived these memories.

Then, he was barrelling towards the Don River as dusk settled overhead; the streets were quieting as he pulled up a dirt track and trundled towards those calm, dark waters. Mikhail had sat there for some time and contemplated simply driving onwards and losing himself to the cold, murky depths. '*Join us*,' Lia had seemed to whisper from the backseat but, when Mikhail had whipped his head around, he had seen only those still, wrapped up bodies lying there.

Shrouded in darkness, Mikhail had carried out his dark deed. He had pulled Lia's body out first, carrying her near weightlessness in his burly arms and still whistling between his strangled sobs. Lia's lifeless, blood-streaked arm had tumbled from the wrappings and brushed against his leg; Mikhail had let out a strained cry and dropped her body to the frosty dirt. With great trepidation, he had dragged her the rest of the way to the water's edge, drenching his jeans as he waded into the Don with his unholy offering. As he repeated the same section of "Swan Lake" over and over, Mikhail had stroked Lia's blood-soaked hair from her face, which had frozen in a wide-eyed stare of terror. 'Sleep, любимый,' he'd whispered as he planted a small kiss to her forehead and gave her a gentle push. He had stood in the freezing water and watched her float away and be swallowed by the thin layer of mist that covered the area.

With a heavy sigh, Mikhail had sloshed back to the car and carried Luka's tiny, limp body to the same fate. Tears had streamed from Mikhail's eyes as he had told Luka all the things he had planned for them to do tomorrow, and the next day, and in the future. He had chattered endlessly, regaling his dead son with tales of adventure and excitement, love and heartbreak, and silently vowed: 'I shall dedicate my next book to you, мой сын. Won't that be nice? You'll be the son of the famous Mikhail Orlov!'

Luka's doe-like eyes had simply stared right through Mikhail's, his little mouth hanging open lifelessly, and Mikhail had sent his boy on his way with a gut-wrenching sob. He had returned to the car and sat there, staring out at the Don, and wondered if his loved ones would wash ashore, all covered in slime and dirt and hungry for human flesh.

Now he knew better.

Now he knew the real truth.

The dead didn't stay dead. They moved on, but not to a better place or some nirvana.

They came here, to LaVey House.

Some force drew them here like magnets. Restless spirits, vengeful ghouls, lost souls who had wandered too far…the house was like a beacon calling out to them and trapping them there, where they waited, hungry and spiteful, to torment the living. Mikhail felt a seething fury bubble within him at the idea that this decrepit, faraway place should be where his loved ones should find themselves trapped.

How he had longed to join them in the depths of those waters. The following weeks and months had been a nightmare as people had bombarded him with questions, but he had played the part of a shell-shocked, grieving man to perfection. Lia's father suspected, of course, but had no evidence. Pavel and Rodion had been stunned at the idea that Lia had gone so terribly off the deep end that she had abducted, or possibly killed, Luka while Mikhail had been out at work and Mikhail had been mildly amused to see his book sales get a brief spike due to the short-lived media attention. As soon as he could, he had packed up and moved to a small apartment across the city and had spent the remainder of his days desperately trying to drown out the memories with alcohol.

This house, though...

It had stirred those memories, overwhelmed him, and now he just felt...drained.

Lifeless.

Suddenly, he needed fresh air, not the musty, suffocating stench of LaVey's mansion. Summoning what remained of his strength, Mikhail hauled himself up. His legs buckled and the world swam in grey waves but he somehow managed to stumble towards the windows, which lined the far wall and ran about eight feet from the floor to an elaborate cornice around the ceiling. He opened the window out onto the small, stone balcony and was immediately pelted by rain. The balcony was just a few feet across and was littered with dried, curled leaves and decomposing vines of ivy.

Overcome with grief, Mikhail collapsed against the four-foot high, crumbling stone wall. 'Lia...' he whispered. 'Luka...' The sound of the knife piercing Luka's soft flesh and Lia's gurgling choking had haunted his dreams, and he had done everything possible to bury his feelings of utter helplessness and grief right along with them, but now it was back...and it was *hungry*. It was a foe that no amount of bravado or alcohol could chase away. 'It should've b-been *me*...' Mikhail muttered. 'I...I should've done *more*...'

It's not as if the world would notice. Who was he, in the grand scheme of things? Here, on the other side of the world, life rolled on regardless of whether he had strangled his wife to death or not. The very next day after that heinous deed, Pavel had probably woken and prepared for his day as normal despite the fact that Luka's life had been so horribly snuffed out.

What did it matter?

What did *anything* matter?

Mikhail smirked at the irony. Had he not accused Brandis of being less than dirt? The truth was that he, all of them, *everyone* was little more than stardust amidst the great wheel of fate…and life. They were simply killing time, counting down the days, desperately trying to fill every waking moment with some kind of accomplishment, some rationalisation to justify a bleak, pointless existence. He had never realised it before because he'd had Luka, something tangible to leave behind. Seeing it so violently and easily ripped away from him had broken Mikhail in a way that he had never thought possible, and he remembered that the first time he had reached for a bottle of Beluga had been when he had returned home after sending his wife and child into the Don.

That fear, that conviction, had terrified him more than anything, and he had thrown himself completely into forcing it into a deep, dark hole. LaVey House had shown him that this was a fool's errand; the fear had *always* been there, haunting him as surely as LaVey's phantoms, driving him here to this dilapidated house full of condescending foreigners and restless spirits wandering where they didn't belong.

'Дурак,' Mikhail smacked his fist against the low stone wall that separated him from a nearly fifty-foot drop to the rugged, overgrown flower beds below. 'Дурак!' he repeated over and over, slamming his fist down again and again until his words were a mere roar of despair and blood oozed from his shredded flesh.

Mikhail clutched at the fragile stone, grasping brittle ivy and fragments of brick in his torn-up hands, and gasped for breath. He had been denied the murky depths of the Don, but perhaps LaVey House held the answer. It wouldn't take much; a simple hop over the edge and he would plummet to the ground below, surely breaking his neck and ending his travesty swiftly and mercilessly.

Good riddance, they'd all say.

Shit, that could be carved onto his tombstone!

So great was Mikhail's desire to be rid of his torment, to never again be bothered by his memories or his guilt or his nightmares, that he actually found himself clambering onto the cold stone wall. He swung his legs so they dangled precariously over the edge; just a slight shift and that would be it. A short fall followed by a sudden, sharp stop and the welcome embrace of eternal darkness…and maybe even the forgiving arms of his wife and child.

Or…would he also find his way back here? Would he follow a pulsating, ethereal light and long for it to be Heaven only to find himself in LaVey House and stalking the living as some unholy spirit? Would he, Lia, and Luka be forever bound by whatever force lurked there?

The vodka had fried Mikhail's mind, the night air numbed his body, and so no answers could be gained while he still drew breath. Only by taking that plunge would he know for sure what lay beyond, and what had happened to his family.

Папочка?

Startled, Mikhail turned back towards the darkness of his bedroom. After a moment, the murky shadows bled away, banished by a brilliant flare of white and warm orange. Everything it touched was transformed, reinvigorated, until the strange room in this strange house was replaced by Luka's old bedroom. The bed, the sheets, even the bright blue wallpaper were the same; everything, right down to the chipped, over-stuffed toy box and the frayed carpet he had always meant to replace.

At the centre of the light was a small, distorted shape. The light was too bright (and Mikhail's brain too frazzled) for him to make it out, but the familiarity was so overpowering that Mikhail burst into tears with a whimpering gulp. 'Luka…' he dropped to the balcony and took one step closer before his resolve faltered. The warmth, the intensity, of the light was overpowering and he felt…unworthy, like he might taint its purity, somehow.

Не ехать еще, Папочка, Luka's voice whispered from the light, which was already beginning to recede, returning the darkness to the bedroom. *Это не время.*

'Stay with me!' Mikhail cried, falling to his knees and reaching his bloodied hands towards the retreating light. 'Please, *please* stay with me. D-don't…don't leave me here…' The light pulsated briefly, then, in the blink of an eye, all that was left was Mikhail's weeping form kneeling on the cold, chipped stone, and the empty bedroom before him.

Mikhail struggled to his feet, suddenly feeling very faint, and staggered into the bedroom, sweeping the window shut behind him. His boot came crunching down on his discarded tumbler, but he barely noticed. Instead, his eyes were drawn to a single, very faint light at the far side of the room, opposite the bed. Though smaller than the flare he had just witnessed, it was also familiar, but for entirely different and far less supernatural reasons. It was the gentle, red-orange glow of a bulb struggling to flicker to life.

'Luka?' he said, hopefully.

No, it was merely his desk lamp struggling to light up. Mikhail flicked the switch, and that familiar electric glow illuminated the desk. There, bathed in that gentle glow, was his manuscript; just a handful of heavily plagiarised words, but the key to Mikhail ensuring that his son lived on as he had promised him in those cold, dark waters.

Mikhail gathered up the papers; the story still lacked a new title. *Mara's Secret* wouldn't do; it had died the moment he had erased Sophia Novaskaya's name and replaced it with his own. With only a tinge of irony, considering everything he had experienced since arriving at LaVey House and the utter anguish he had suffered in the last few hours, Mikhail snatched up a pen and scribbled a new title onto the first page:

Это все в вашей голове.

It was all he had left now.

Tomorrow, he would present it before those who would think themselves his peers and then his name…and the name of his son…would be immortalised across the world.

Maybe that would banish those dark thoughts and allow him to rest, once and for all.

7. *Aster Completes the Assignment*

I was very pleased with this piece. It could definitely be extended into a full-fledged novel, or I could submit it to an anthology; the possibilities were endless. Inadvertently, there were parallels between the life of the police chief in the story and my own. Despite the uncertainties and warnings of going to that forsaken town, he had a duty to find answers about what happened to those people. He was brave and faced a scary situation head-on—just as I was about to do the same with my soon-to-be ex-fiancé.

First, I cancelled my plane ticket for Sunday. I would have to see if Eloise would let me stay with her until I could get myself established somewhere as she had offered to have me stay with her multiple times whenever I got around to visiting the United Kingdom.

I sent Walter a text message saying that he needed to call me as soon as he could because there was something important I needed to tell him. It might have been cowardly to send a text but I was trying to be courteous because I knew Walter would still be sleeping. A wave of nausea hit me and I barely made it to the bathroom before I emptied my stomach of the contents of my light breakfast. As I stood up to clean myself up and rid my mouth of the horrid taste, I stopped dead in my tracks. A horrible thought hit me: was I...? No, that wasn't possible.

Think about it, Naomi, my inner voice mocked. *Yesterday morning, you were vomiting the previous night's dinner. The day before that, it was breakfast...and before that—*

'Yeah, yeah. I see what you're trying to get at. Stop it,' I muttered. I was chalking it up to stress. It wasn't the first time I had missed my monthly visitor because of being too anxious.

But what about your breasts being tender and your increased trips to the bathroom to pee?

I rolled my eyes. I was getting myself worked up over nothing! Walter and I had been careful; however, accidents happened. Once this meet up was concluded, I would have Eloise take me to a doctor to put my thoughts at ease. Then I recalled the encounter in the maze…when I'd heard those giggling children, it was almost as though I felt something physically stir inside me, as though something tangible within me was reacting to those giggles.

'Knock it off! You're panicking for no reason! First, you need to think about what you're going to do once this event is over! You need a plan!' Not having a plan was abnormal for me; being impulsive and reckless terrified me and I had avoided it as much as I could. Things must have been worse than I thought if I'd taken such drastic measures and not only cancelled my flight back home, but was also preparing to end things with the man I was supposed to marry in three months! I was embarrassed that I hadn't realised his abhorrent behaviour sooner. I was smarter than that and had seen too many friends go through similar situations, and always advised that they leave that shitty person because what they were doing wasn't healthy. I could feel the hypocrisy flood through me at not heeding my own advice. *Suppose it's better to realise it now as opposed to down the road*, I thought. *No, stop lying to yourself. You were afraid to leave him because you craved companionship. Since your parents died, despite their many flaws, you* hated *being alone.*

'I need a break. I should go see what Freddy is up to. He'll make me feel better. But first I need a shower.'

Shedding out of my clothes, I made my way to the large bathroom and started the shower. The hot water felt phenomenal on my aching body as I took my time getting cleaned up. Once I was finished, I wrapped a fluffy white towel around me and made my way back to the bedroom and opened the wardrobe. It didn't take long for me to decide what to wear: a black dress with a delicate lacy pattern that would allow the rose tattoo on my sternum to peek out. I purposely chose that dress as Freddy had expressed an admiration for the design. I took the time to brush my bushy hair into a sleek style with soft curls. Applying some light make-up and putting on my trademark fashion glasses, I grabbed my phone and was about to exit the room when I caught a glint from the dresser in the corner of my eye. My engagement ring. Picking it up and rolling it between my fingers, I didn't give it a second thought and set it back down where I had found it.

'Hopefully I can get some money for it.'

8. *Brandis Gets a Surprise Visit*

Time slipped away from me by the time I switched over to the heavy typewriter. It was quite an adjustment after all these years of using modern keyboards, so I'd made sure to save it until I had typed up a few rough drafts on my laptop.

I'd spent about an hour fleshing out a run-down of my characters. Characters have always been important to me and my works, which was just another reason why it was so frustrating and disappointing that people couldn't be more like Naomi and actually read my stuff. I don't really like having too many characters; I find the more voices you have, the more muddled and confusing things become, and it's far easier to focus on a handful of core characters and infuse them with distinct traits.

Traditionally, I liked to write in the third-person; I had been forced to use first-person a few times at uni and I wasn't much of a fan. That was Lucy's ballpark. She crafted intricate narratives told entirely through one character's eyes and could even skip between two or three characters and always kept it clear who was talking and how they were unique. I'd been incredibly envious of this but was comfortable with my third-person prose; however, I tended to be a little too wordy (if you can believe that!) and I didn't want to submit something unnecessarily bloated so, to challenge myself and try to keep things focused, I stepped out of my comfort zone and wrote in the first-person through the eyes of a fictionalised version of Sam.

I'd known Sam pretty well. His carefree nature made him extremely approachable but he also hid a surprising intellect. While

Lucy poured herself into research and rolled her eyes at Sam's shenanigans, even she would admit that he knew his stuff when push came to shove. While he hadn't been much of a negotiator and mediator, I like to think he could've been, so the fictional Sam became someone up for an adventure but also the more level-headed and informed of the group, something I imagined the real Sam would've found amusing.

After my deliberation, I decided that the fictional Lucy would be elusive, but still a significant presence as a point of contention to show just how influential and important she'd been in my life. The other three characters, as always, would be extensions of myself. Marshall would be the joker of the group whose recklessness would lead them into danger, Peter would be the antagonistic and abrasive sceptic, and Bart would be the poor sap caught in the middle who just wanted everyone to get along. My aim was to capture some of the banter I'd experienced in our ever-changing social circle. Sometimes tensions and relationships between friends would be frayed, even hostile, over the smallest things, disagreements, or even instances of adultery, which created a melting pot of conflicting emotions.

I couldn't help but smile to myself as I wrote their dialogue, something I always enjoyed writing and tried to make as natural and realistic as possible. I regretted that I hadn't used my phone to record conversations in real time because it was difficult thinking up witty remarks and speech patterns on the spot. The little village I'd grown up in, Haverhill, had a very distinctive and lazy dialectic; t's were frequently dropped, a's became o's, and *ph* and *th* were often replaced with *f*. Considering how well-spoken a lot of the older inhabitants were, it was amazing how we'd grown up with such a sloth-like drawl.

Northward was only around thirty miles north of Haverhill, but their dialect was entirely different: *barf-tub* became *baff-tub*, *karpet* became *carr-pett*, and *wa'r* became *war-tar*.

My interactions with Naomi had inspired me to really ramp this up. She seemed fascinated by my accent, and the different accents amongst our writers circle, and I adored the way she watched, awestruck, at how different our words and inflections were. I'd never seen someone so interested in hearing me speak, but the feeling was more than mutual. There was something about hearing the drawling twang of an American accent in person that was different from hearing it in movies.

I also wanted my characters to be fractured by Lucy's absence, and struggling to repair their friendship and rediscover that spark of adventure. I think Lucy would've enjoyed that. She'd never been one for the limelight and had been extremely humble, and I'm sure she would have giggled at the idea of being so deeply integral and influential to someone.

Since researching the focus of their adventure was a chore thanks to LaVey's crappy internet, I decided that I'd much rather craft my own fictional location. Fictional environments were very freeing to me; they allowed me to dictate the geometry, weather, and scenery without any restrictions, and it meant I could include a mish-mash of aesthetics and create a lore that was influenced by multiple sources and time periods without being handcuffed by reality.

Just as the characters had arrived at their destination, I took a well-deserved break. I winced at the pain in my hip and the ache in my lower back (LaVey's antique furniture was far from comfortable) as I brewed myself a mug of tea, grabbed myself four chunky cookies, and stared at the awful wallpaper plastered to the bedroom walls and pondered what threat would spell the ultimate doom of my characters.

Of course, there was only one real solution: the ghoul from LaVey's attic.

While that twisted wretch had been an explicit, explosive horror, though, I felt something more intangible, almost beautiful, would be more fitting. My previous horror stories had favoured sudden, bloody deaths since I had a fondness for eighties splatter horror and slasher movies, but I wanted to use this newfound motivation to try something more subtle, something more alluring and chilling. I switched back to my laptop and allowed Lucy's influence to help me craft this being. She had adored Japanese mythology and had longed to travel to Japan and throw herself into the culture. Personally, I couldn't stand the thought of trying to adapt to their cuisine. Still, she had been captivated by their colourful lore, which was made up of spirits of all kinds that walked their graveyards, watched over their shrines, and lingered in homes, and I felt like taking a quiet, restless spectre and infusing it with the qualities of a siren, banshee, and succubus could give it a splendour that was directly at odds with the ghastly wretch I'd encountered.

Once I was happy with the rough electronic draft, I returned to the typewriter and typed as though possessed. I wasn't too concerned by minor errors or smudges from the ink as LaVey hadn't specified that we had to worry about that—and, honestly, if he *was* concerned then he shouldn't have had us type our work up on a typewriter. The rush of creativity was palpable, and I barely even noticed that I'd forgotten my tea, which sat cold and neglected on my desk. I was almost tempted to return to the attic and challenge the phantom to reappear to relive the terror it'd instilled in me (and, also, to validate if it'd actually been real), but I pushed this impulse aside and focused on the task at hand.

As the sun set, fatigue set in, and I began to wind down. I flicked through my typed pages, ignoring the erratic letters and smudges. There were a few errors here and there but, for the most part, it matched with what I'd written on my laptop. I'd left the narrator and his abrasive friend in a precarious situation, but my wrists were aching almost as much as my back, and my stomach was growling. I'd worked through the entire afternoon but had gained over three thousand five hundred words. A wave of emotion welled up inside of me as I realised that there was only one section of about two-thousand words left to wrap things up.

I'd forgotten how gratifying it was to produce something I was actually proud of. I wouldn't go as far as to say it was my best work, or something I could really turn into a full-blown novella, but it was something I was happy with, at least. I didn't even care if Mikhail or Rhiannon turned their noses up at it; I'd finally written something that would be published. I could only hope that Lucy and Sam and all the others would be happy to see themselves immortalised in my own small way.

My stomach growled again, and I suddenly found myself hankering for a bacon, cheese, sausage, and egg bap; it was an oddly specific yearning but quickly became all I could think about. I pushed myself away from my desk and prepared to head downstairs—not really caring if I bumped into one of those assholes—when a small knock came at my door. I was so euphoric that I didn't even consider that it could've been Mikhail coming to finish the job, or even that gruesome fiend looking to rip its jagged claws into my throat and bathe in my arterial spray.

Instead, much to my surprise and pleasure, I opened the door to find Naomi standing there with a beaming smile on her face, a bottle of wine in one hand, and a bag full of snacks in the other.

9. Aster's Definitive Decision

I didn't think Freddy would mind if I came by to tell him the good news about finishing my story, or my impulse to not go back to Walter. Still, I was nervous. I must have wandered across the hall four or five times as I struggled to work up the courage to knock on his door. I was just about to rap on his door when I considered the time and thought back to the other day, at breakfast. To buy myself a little more time to compose myself, I dashed downstairs and into the small dining room. I grabbed a few snacks and some food from the buffet table without really thinking too much, as well as a glistening bottle of red. *Fuck it*, I thought. *I'm happy and I want to celebrate!* I carried my load back upstairs, stopped to check my reflection in a large full-length mirror in the hallway, and took a deep breath before finally knocking on Freddy's door, my hands shook while I waited for him to answer. I really hoped that I wasn't bothering him from his work or distracting him from something else that was much more important.

'Naomi?' I jumped a little. I'd been so lost in my thoughts that I hadn't even noticed that he had opened the door. His face wore an amusing mixture of surprise, embarrassment, and intrigue.

'H-hey Freddy,' I said softly, my face starting to blush.

'Y'alright?' he asked in that adorable accent of his. I wished we had connected sooner. 'What's up?'

'I finished my piece for LaVey, and I was excited to tell someone about it. Hope I'm not distracting you any.'

'No,' he answered immediately. 'No, of course not. I was just takin' a break myself.' He lingered in the doorway for a minute and then sheepishly realised that he hadn't yet invited me in. 'You wanna come in an' tell me about it?'

Following him into his room, his comment last night made more sense: the room looked almost identical to mine, aside from minor differences. I could see a neat stack of papers next to his typewriter, which had a half-typed sheet of paper stuck in it, confirming that he had at least been working on something. Freddy gestured for me to sit in the armchair that was located across from his workspace.

'So, you've finished, yeah?' he asked, gesturing to the bar.

I sat down, brought out my bottle of wine, and gave it a little shake. 'Yeah,' I replied as he took the bottle from me and struggled with the cork. 'Finally! I was having some struggles with the middle sections and connecting them to the main plot.'

'That's...' he gave a grunt and the cork finally popped loose. 'That's fantastic. If it's anythin' like *Shattered Faces*, I'm sure it'll be great. I loved how you captured tension in that one.'

He handed me a wine glass that was a little overfilled for me, but I took it gratefully and sipped the sweet liquid. A flush came over me, and it wasn't because of the alcohol; I was flattered by his insight into my works. 'Well, it's a little different from that. It goes back and forth between the present with a news anchor reporting on strange events happening in a neighbouring small town, and the past where the reader gets to see snippets of said events.'

Freddy's eyes widened a bit. 'Sounds interesting. Can't wait t'hear the rest of it.'

'I'm excited! It's out of my usual element. The only common factor is the build of tension until the climax of the piece.'

'I bet,' Freddy said. He seemed troubled as he settled down into the chair opposite his desk. 'I only wish I'd brought your books with me so you could sign them.'

'Speaking of...' I reached into the bag I had brought with me. A packet of chips and cookies tumbled out, and I muttered a curse before pulling out my copy of *Breath of Eden*. 'I was wondering if you could...'

Freddy seemed taken aback. He took the book from me and looked around wildly for a pen; it was very amusing to see his facial expressions jump between confusion, frustration, and embarrassment. He found a pen and opened the book but paused a few pages in and looked at me sheepishly. 'I've, ah...I've never actually signed a copy before...'

A giggle escaped me; he was so adorable. 'Just write whatever.'

As he clicked the pen and wrote with a flourish, I shifted in my seat as I watched him. I adored the way his dark, shaggy hair hung over his eyes, and the sheer concentration that radiated from his posture. Presently, he handed the book back to me and I opened it up to read:

For Naomi,
Thank you for buying my book and actually giving me the time of day.
You've been the best part of this entire experience!
All the best,
F. Brandis x

'I know,' he said with a shrug. 'It's not the best.'

'No, no! It's lovely. Thank you.' I closed the book and put it carefully back in my bag before offering him some of the food I had brought up. It was as heart-warming to see his eyes light up in excitement as it was to read his cute dedication once more and he eagerly took some slices of ham and stuffed them into the tiger rolls to construct a make-shift sandwich. 'So…How is your own story coming along?" I asked. "Hope things are going well.'

'Good. Great, actually,' he answered, covering his mouth with the back of his hand as he ate. He seemed to be absolutely famished; I wondered if he had eaten at all today. 'I dunno wot it is about this place, but I finally felt mo'ivated t'actually write somethin' and just ran with it.'

'That's fantastic! Can't wait to hear it tomorrow night at the banquet.'

Freddy nodded thoughtfully and swallowed down the last of the ham roll before enthusiastically accepting a packet of cookies and a shining green apple. 'I love apples; I usually have t'eat at least one a day.'

'Really?' I asked, curious. 'What happens if you don't eat an apple every day?'

Freddy stopped mid-bite and stared at me for a second. He gulped down the apple chunk and coughed a little. 'I dunno,' he answered with a shrug. 'I pr'bly just have a pear or somethin'?'

'Oh!' I exclaimed. 'I thought it was for a medical reason!'

He chuckled; it was a lovely sound to hear and immediately put my foolishness at ease and brought a red tint to my cheeks.

'No! It's just the closest I get to eatin' healthy, is all. I do love me some fruit.'

Taking another sip of my wine, I plucked a small cake out of a plastic packet. 'What *is* this?' I asked, hoping it wasn't another stupid question, but I was amused by the small, glistening cherry on top of the treat's white frosting.

'It's a Bakewell tart,' Freddy answered, enthusiastically taking one for himself. 'It's like a little cake with jam in the middle.'

He picked the glacé cherry from the frosting and popped it into his mouth. I mimicked the action and felt a rush of sweetness flow over my tongue; it was like eating a squishy ball of pure cherry jam. Biting into the soft little treat was equally exhilarating. 'Oh, my lawd,' I mumbled through a mouthful of tart. 'Everything tastes so much better over here!'

'I'll say…' Freddy murmured, his eyes turned away.

Was that…was that an innuendo?

I watched him closely as I finished my wine. A brief silence fell between us, and I broke it by asking: 'How do you think the meal will go tomorrow night?'

Freddy settled back in his chair, clasping his hands together thoughtfully. 'Honestly, I ain't really thought 'bout it. I was more worried 'bout actually havin' somethin' to submit. Somethin' worthwhile, anyway. Public speakin' ain't really my thing, though.'

'That surprises me,' I replied. 'I find you eloquent…and I adore your accent.' I felt my fingers tangling into my hair playfully and I dropped them back down to my lap, fearing that I looked like some giddy teenage schoolgirl.

'Hah, well, thanks f'r that,' he replied with that trademark smirk. 'But it's nothing compared t'yah fancy American twang.'

That hot flush came over me again. Talking with Freddy was so unlike talking to anyone else in my life. I had been dismayed by just how many distasteful and disgusting men there were when I had first set

363

up my Instagram account. At first, I had named and shamed these individuals who thought it was appropriate to proposition women online and send them pictures of their dicks, but soon I had settled for simply blocking and reporting them at every opportunity. Men always seemed to have their mind on one thing and one thing alone and, while I could now attest that Freddy was more than capable in that regard, his primary focus was always on being complimentary and humble. Even before we had slept together, I felt as though I could trust what he was saying. He had some cheesy lines and was a little awkward, but he clearly wasn't trying to trick me into bed at every opportunity and seemed genuinely pleased to sit and talk with me.

'Can I read some of what you've written?' I asked, unaware that I was even going to speak.

Freddy's eyes widened in shock, narrowed in suspicion, and then finally settled on curiosity. 'I guess so. It's not finished, and there's prob'ly some typos, and I still need to…'

'That's fine,' I interrupted his rambling and stepped over to his desk.

Freddy sat in his seat and watched me as I leaned over to the typewriter and began reading. I knew he was watching me, that he seemed incapable of taking his eyes off me, but I was too busy being captivated by his words. He had a genuine talent for the craft, that much was undeniable. And while I didn't agree with some of his punctuation choices, he painted such a picture with his writing that it was almost as if he were an artist rather than a writer. I glanced at another page and then forced myself away, not wanting to spoil the story for myself, and turned towards him, brushing my hair back over my ear. He looked nervous as I did my best to articulate my admiration for his writing. 'I can't wait to see how it turns out,' I concluded, honestly.

Freddy grinned and appeared to be happy, but he still seemed tense. It was interesting trying to get a read on him. He seemed to be constantly debating within himself while projecting...

'Mph!' I cried in surprise; Freddy had left his chair and pulled me into his arms. His lips were pressed to mine. I reciprocated the gesture instinctively; my hands plunged into his hair, running my fingers through his thick strands. Sighing in his mouth, my body relaxed at his touch. How did this person, someone whom I had only met a few days ago, have this much effect on me? I considered myself to be rational, trying to keep my feelings and emotions in check, but Freddy was someone who came and messed it up.

'It's gonna suck when we have t'leave,' he said against my lips, those unbelievable eyes staring into mine.

He made me feel something I hadn't felt in a long time; it both terrified and enthralled me. 'I'm not going back,' I blurted out.

I felt him stiffen, and he broke our kiss. Confusion was written on his face. 'What d'you mean you ain't goin' back? What about your life, friends, family? Not t'mention your fiancé!'

Pulling away from his arms, I took a few steps back. 'I decided not to go back to him. Walter is not who I thought he was.' I shrugged with indifference. 'I don't need someone like that in my life. Someone who doesn't value me or even consider my dreams, my aspirations. I'm ending our engagement.'

'Jesus,' he breathed. 'That's pretty heavy. I dunno if I could make a decision that big.'

'I'm absolutely terrified! All my life, I've always had a plan. I was never reckless or impulsive!' Making my way to the window and staring out into nothing, I remained silent, contemplating what more I wanted to say. It was snowing lightly, and it reminded me of home. It snowed a lot around this time of year back in Iowa; the temperatures were bitter, and icy conditions weren't uncommon. Memories of my soon-to-be former home flooded my mind for a moment, but I felt nothing. I had mostly terrible memories associated with that place, and it made me realise my decision not to go back was one that had been coming for a long time. I was glad I had finally done it.

'Why him? What made you choose 'im?' Freddy asked sincerely. 'You seem too smart to be with sumone so dreadful.'

I couldn't look at Freddy. I was ashamed to admit the truth, but the words just came tumbling out. 'There are a lot of reasons. I suppose the biggest one is that I was too scared to be alone. I crave companionship. My biggest fear is being alone in this world. That probably sounds silly, but it's true. I don't get to see most of my friends anymore mostly because of him or because they're busy with their own lives.' I wiped a lone tear from my eye. 'He wasn't all bad at first. We had met through a mutual friend, and everything seemed to be wonderful, but things gradually got worse…'

'You don't have to say any more, Naomi,' Freddy cut me off. 'I ain't judgin' you. We all have our reasons.'

'No, it's okay.' I squeezed my eyes shut, tears flowing down. 'He was never physically abusive, but the verbal abuse…is awful. I should have seen it because my own parents were just like him! But it's better late than never. It was too early in the morning back home when I came to this decision, so I sent him a message saying we need to talk when he got up. I'm not changing my mind. I'm done with him.'

Warm arms wrapped around my waist as Freddy sidled up behind me. 'I'm proud of you,' he whispered, kissing my cheek lightly. I covered my hands over his and squeezed them, grateful for his embrace. 'Where you gonna go? What's the plan?'

'I really don't know,' I answered, still staring out of the window. 'I have some money, and a friend I could stay with, but I'm just going to take it one day at a time.'

There was another pause. Snowflakes melted against the window and time seemed to slow. It was a nice, cosy moment to find myself in.

'Y-you could always come back with me...' Freddy said, his voice barely above a whisper. I turned around in his arms to look at him. He was staring out the window, lost in thought. 'I-if you wanted, I mean. Just for a bit, like. I only have a small place, and I'm not sure I can really *have* anyone staying there... and you'd have to compete with the cat, but if you needed somewhere, I'd be more than happy to—'

I placed a finger to his lips, silencing him. 'You're sweet,' I said. 'I couldn't impose, though. I have a friend in Ire-chezter who can put me up.'

'Wait...D'you mean *Irchester*?'

'Is *that* how you say it? I've only ever seen it written but, yes, *Urr*-chesster.'

He chuckled again at my odd pronunciation and looked at me solemnly as he tucked a loose strand of hair behind my ear. 'Irchester's pretty close to where I live, like twenny-five miles or somethin' like that.'

'No way!' I was shocked; but then again, the United Kingdom was tiny compared to even my home state.

'So, like, I could at least come visit you, mebbe?'

I gazed up into his sweet face. 'I'd like that very much.'

He smiled back and swallowed. 'And you're sure you wanna go through with this?'

'Yes. I'm sure it's the right thing for me to do.'

He placed a hand on my cheek, softly stroking it as his face drew closer. My breath hitched in my throat; his lips mere inches from mine. Suddenly, my phone started playing the Imperial March from the *Star Wars* films.

I froze.

That was Walter's ringtone.

I was terrified to answer.

As though he could sense my panic, Freddy bit his bottom lip in frustration, pulled away from me, and stepped over to my phone. He snatched it up and glanced at the screen and, for one horrible moment, I thought he was going to answer it. Instead, he held the button on the side and the ringing abruptly died along with the screen light.

Freddy set my phone back down and returned to me in a few steps; the look in his eyes said everything.

'That takes care of that interruption,' he said before cupping my face with his warm hands and kissing me with such fervency that I nearly melted on the spot.

I felt myself being backed towards his bed and didn't even try to fight it; I simply gave in and let the moment overtake me.

Interval Four

Brandis at the Banquet on Saturday

This was it.

We'd eaten well and the others had all had their turns, and now all that remained was for me to share my story.

"Nervous" didn't cover the breadth of the anxiety I felt welling within me. All of them, even Mikhail, had produced some first-rate material and LaVey, sitting at the head of the table and bathing in the glow of candlelight, seemed deeply satisfied. Behind him burned a great roaring fire that danced flickering embers and living shadows across the old man's features and made him resemble the great puppet master and deceiver, Mephistopheles.

The grandfather clock ticked away ominously across the room, persistently counting down the minutes and hours of the evening and making itself known even over the discourse raised from our gathering. The mood was dark and gloomy, and I felt the atmosphere had shifted noticeably compared to when I had first arrived and even when I first sat down at LaVey's grand dining table and tucked into the gloriously roasted meats and potatoes laid out for our feast. I'd taken slices of beef, turkey, and honey-glazed gammon, piled both mashed and roasted potatoes on my plate, slipped a couple of puffy Yorkshire puddings on there for good measure, and drowned it all with a thick and luscious helping of gravy and gorged myself as the others had shared their tales of terror.

All eyes were on me now, watching expectantly. Even Mikhail had laced his hands together and prepared himself to hear my story, and were it not for Naomi gripping my hand tightly under the table and flashing me a look of support, I don't know if I would've found the strength to rise from my chair and read the words I'd agonised over since receiving LaVey's invitation.

This was it.

This was my story ...

Brandis's Submission:

The Peak

Of course, it'd been Marshall's idea to avoid Mount Fuji.

'Mate,' he'd said, that goofy grin shining beneath his bristly orange-red beard. 'It's a total tourist trap! You wanna go hikin' up somethin' *real* then *this* is the only place t'go!'

He'd been proudly waving a crumpled map in the small log cabin we'd rented for the week. He laid it out on the coffee table and the four of us—Marshall, Peter, Bart, and I—crowded around, grateful for the extra body heat. 'We're in peak sheeple season for Mount Fuji, m'dudes,' he'd said, tapping the mountain range for emphasis. 'I'm talkin' families, crowds up the nines, and queues, mates. Queues!'

'I'm familiar with queues,' Bart muttered. 'Get t'dah bloody point!'

'You're finkin' Mount Goemon, ain'tcha?' Peter was staring daggers at Marshall.

Marshall's face had fallen. 'Way t'piss on my barbecue, dude,' he sighed and swept his hand over the Mount Goemon range some one hundred kilometres from the more popular Mount Fuji. 'Yeah, I'm thinkin' Mount Goemon.'

'Mental,' Peter spat, shaking his head.

'Why?'

'Don't gimme that shit!' Peter snapped. He and Marshall hadn't been the same since all that crap with Lucy. I'd hoped that coming out here like in the old days would have helped smooth things over, but, apparently, there was still a lot of bad blood. 'One,' he continued, 'we're under-equipped. Also, it's about two thousand feet taller than Mount Fuji. Three…Um…*Three!* It's got summa th' worst climbin' conditions you could ask for! Hell, in th' last fifteen years there's gotta've been what? Twenny people who've died jus' tryin' t'get halfway up there!'

I actually knew something about this so I figured that this would be a good time to chime in. 'Twelve deaths, six cases of severe frostbite—two that required amputation—and at least three people unaccounted for in seventeen years.' The others frowned at me. 'What? I read,' I shrugged.

'I don't care,' Marshall snapped. '*This…*' he paused for dramatic emphasis, 'is where we're goin'.'

'*You* go,' Peter huffed. 'I'm stayin' here.'

'Oh' c'mon, man!' Bart whined. 'Don't be like that. Look, we got all the gear we'd need for Fuji; it ain't our first barn dance!'

He was certainly right about that. To say the four of us were adrenaline junkies was putting it mildly. Hell, we'd all met in hospital nursing broken bones and a couple of pretty severe concussions (Peter still complained of crippling headaches every now and then and I'm pretty sure that he swallowed an assortment of multicoloured pills just to get to sleep at night), but that hadn't stopped us. Nothing was off limits; rallying, skydiving, you name it. Marshall was two tours into a career as a paratrooper for fuck's sake. Bart had trained for six months to get in the octagon and fight professionally and ended up being

372

knocked out within fifteen seconds. I, on the other hand, preferred conquering the elements at ground level. I was a rambler, a skier, a hiker, and there was nothing I enjoyed more than a bit of free climbing or taking on nature's greatest mountains and harsh environments both up *and* down.

I'd once been trapped in a network of uncharted caves off the north coast of Scotland for over three days. With limited light and resources, I'd spent hours wandering the dark, rationing my water supply, and following a faint breeze until clawing my way to freedom, heavily dehydrated and having lost about four stone. That had probably been the most harrowing experience of my life; worse than the broken leg I'd suffered on our trip up Snowdon (we went back one year to the day later so I could finish the job), or that time my main 'chute had failed less than six thousand feet from the ground.

Still, life's too short, and sometimes you just can't fight the adrenaline rush.

I looked at my friends. Marshall was still arguing with Peter while Bart tried desperately to be the voice of reason. We never should've let Lucy come between us. And to think, it was less than a year ago that she and Peter had been all set to get married.

We needed this.

'Marshall's right,' I announced.

'*What?!*' Peter cried.

I met his glare. 'He's right. Mount Fuji's overplayed and overrated. It's tapped out. There's nuffin' t'gain by climbin' it 'cept some fancy magnets from th' gift shop.'

'Sam...' Peter tried to interrupt, but I raised my hand to cut him off.

'No,' I said simply. 'We're doin' this. It ain't impossible. Bart's right: we came prepared t'climb a mountain, and now we get t'beat *Goemon!*'

'Exactly!' Marshall cried enthusiastically. He turned to Peter. 'I ain't just pulled this outta my ass, y'know. I got it all worked out.'

'Yeah,' Peter scoffed. 'I'll jus' *bet* you 'ave.'

'Well, we gotta climb *sumfin'*,' Bart insisted. 'We flew all t'way out here, after all!'

I looked at each of them in turn. While I couldn't be completely certain that Marshall had properly researched Mount Goemon, the statistics *I* was aware of made my stomach churn. It was dangerous, stupid even, but you better fuckin' believe I felt that spark of life flaring up beneath my skin!

'We're going,' I said finally.

* * *

The rickety little bus was absolutely packed and wobbled uncertainly as it trundled along a rugged path that had been trampled through the wilderness over time. We'd been forced to sit (or stand, in Bart's case) away from each other. I had two extremely enthusiastic Japanese teenagers chattering on my left and poor old Bart was being crushed between tourists decked out in fluorescent gear and reflective sunglasses.

As we bounced along, Mount Fuji loomed ominously to the west. Despite what myself and Marshall had said, it was truly a magnificent sight. I remembered when we'd seen the pyramids for the first time. Their grandeur was just as affecting but somewhat stagnated by the fact that civilisation had overtaken the area. Here, the mountains and wilds of nature stood untainted—at least from this distance. I was convinced that the closer we got we'd see a museum, a gift shop, and a way station where visitors could go through safety briefings and whatnot.

The bus bombed past the great mountain. Part of me was disappointed to not be conquering it but I could literally taste the anticipation of tackling Mount Goemon. The bus wouldn't drop us at the foot of the mountain, of course; the weather and terrain were far too bad for that. No, we'd have to get off and hike about thirty kilometres or so and even though our equipment was heavy, and the weather was bitter, it all added to the excitement.

When the bus skidded to an abrupt halt, confused chatter filled the tight quarters and I heard Marshall politely apologising as he pushed his way past the gaggle of passengers. When I awkwardly stood to leave, the Japanese couple sat next to me spoke words I could never hope to understand. I could hardly speak English let alone one of the most complex languages in the modern world, so I simply flashed an apologetic smile and tried to push past. They stayed right where they were and barked more gibberish at me.

'Sorry, can I just...?' I didn't want to barge past them. Considering how bulky I was with all my gear, I was liable to knock them flying if they didn't move.

The slim little man muttered something as he finally stood. I have no idea what he said; he could've been calling me an asshole for all I knew. It sounded like *oon-meh* but I honestly had no idea.

'Thanks. Sorry,' I said as I finally got past.

Once we were off, the bus immediately sputtered to life and drove away. The day was deceptively bright, as I found it often seemed in other parts of the world, where it appeared like the glaring eye of a titanic deity was looking down on a colony of ants. I slipped my shades on and was grateful for the filter, but the bitter chill of the day penetrated my many layers of clothing.

Marshall was consulting his map and that same damn chipped compass he always had attached to his belt. It'd been a gift from his dad, right before he died. 'Looks like we're headin' north,' he called over a howl of wind.

Bart smacked him playfully on his shoulder. 'Ya think?' he jerked a thumb at the intimidating shadow of Mount Goemon dominating the horizon.

I adjusted my bag and set off, unsurprised to see that Peter and Marshall were never near each other. The mountain loomed like a Titan. While Mount Fuji had been this pristine, natural peak into the heavens, Mount Goemon was a jagged, distorted fist that punched defiantly at the sky. The peak was partially obscured by clouds of fog, and snow stretched down the rugged landscape in angry slashes. The mountain slanted as though it were on the verge of collapsing, and the only sounds were our inane banter and the banshee-like wind.

The ground quickly grew muddy and wild; our boots squelched and tripped, and walking slowed considerably. Hail suddenly drenched us, the tiny shards nipping at the few exposed parts of our flesh, and Peter's mood soon soured. The deluge had caught him off guard and he dropped his hat and gloves to the ground and planted a boot onto them, leaving them muddy and drenched in his haste to cover up. The hail passed as swiftly as it had come by the time we reached the foot of the mountain, and Bart was in the process of scoping out a decent campsite when he stopped and laughed.

'What is it?' I asked, my voice muffled by my face coverings.

'We're already *on* the damn fing!'

We looked around to confirm. The slope up onto Mount Goemon had been so gradual that, between the elements and the swamp-like ground, we hadn't even noticed that we were already about twenty feet up it.

'*Ya-hoo!*' Marshall cried, pumping his fists into the air. 'That's progress, at least!'

* * *

The hail picked as soon as we made camp. By the time we were all set up, it had whipped up into a violent snowstorm and we'd been forced to venture a little further up to fresh ground into a small alcove for better shelter. This low down the mountain, the ground was incredibly uncomfortable, but it was at least free from the ice and snow that awaited us further up. The twists of foliage that sprung from the soil were like the roots of some age-old tree, and flowers the likes of which I'd never seen bloomed everywhere; brilliant white and yellow petals bloomed on tall, sturdy stalks and remained steadfast despite the frigid and tumultuous weather.

'Chrysanthemums,' Bart said as he walked past me.

'Since when did *you* become a flower expert?' I shot back.

'My mum's a florist,' he answered as he began setting up our new camp site. 'You can believe that if y'want.'

Soon, the storm had died down to a bitter wind and we were huddled around a flickering fire and roasting sausages. I was glad to have a flask of piping hot tomato and carrot soup to warm me as well. Marshall had gone for tea, Bart had a canteen of his "special brew," and Peter was slipping a hot water bottle down the front of his coat.

'Y'know why it's called Mount Goemon, don'tcha?' Marshall asked.

The others shook their heads; Peter barely glanced up. I remained impassive and was interested to see what bullshit story Marshall would concoct. It wouldn't be the first time we'd sat around a fire and told ghost stories.

'Well…' he shifted into a more comfortable position. 'There was this outlaw, kinda like a highwayman, named Goemon, back in t'shogun days.'

I grinned at this but said nothing.

'He was kinda like the Japanese Robin Hood, stealin' from the rich an' all that. He was also basic'ly the first ninja!'

'Ain't ninjas Chinese?' Bart pulled a sausage from the fire; it was a little crispy, but he seemed happy to take a bite out of it.

'Chinese, Japanese, s'all the same thing,' Marshall said without skipping a beat. I could see Peter biting back a retort to *that* statement. 'Anyway,' Marshall continued, 'one time, he's asked by the empr'r t'kill this clan leader, right? Sorta t'pardon all his crimes or whatnot. So, Goemon sneaks into the clan's temple, right? All shrouded in the shadows an' he pulls out this pipe…' Incredibly, Marshall pulled a thin, slender object from one of his many coat pouches and held it out. It was wooden and had *kanji* inscribed into it. 'He puts it to his lips and *ptoo!*

Shoots a poison dart right at the head honcho, who collapses an' chokes t'death.'

'*Ack-kk-gh!*' Bart mimed, drawing a chuckle from us (except for Peter, who sat with his hands tucked under his arm pits).

'But when he goes back t'the empr'r, Goemon's sentenced to death! They's gonna boil him alive in oil, or broth, or whatever. Goemon, though, he's too cunnin' f'r that an' he takes the empr'r's daughter hostage. "I ain't bein' boiled alive t'day, y'hear?" he shouts!'

I giggled. 'Is that an exact quote?'

Marshall grinned back. 'I might be paraphrasin'. Anyway, he flees with the empr'r's daughter to this mountain, with the empr'r's guards in hot pursuit. The princess's a prim an' proper, sheltered lass so she slows him down, right? But he can't just let her go; he needs the leverage.'

'Sure, sure,' Bart mused, finishing his sausage and slipping another onto his skewer.

'So, they get 'bout halfway up...right up to that part there...' Marshall pointed above us to a slight indent in the mountain that was given an ominous glow by the fire's flicking embers. 'An' *that's* where one of the guards shoots 'im with an arrow. *Urk!* Right through th' heart!'

'Aw, and so close, as well,' Peter murmured; he frowned when he saw that his sausage was a chargrilled husk.

'They never found 'is body, or the princess neither. They searched all over for days an' just got themselves frozen t'death. Apparently, their restless spirits lure people to their deaths. *That's* why no one's ever reached the top. That point up there? They call it *Goemonbūro*, "Goemon's Tomb".'

I burst out laughing.

'What?' Marshall looked hurt. 'It's *true!*'

I couldn't even formulate words. Tears rolled down my cheeks as Bart looked at me confused and Peter raised a single bushy eyebrow. I slowly got myself under control and my laughter tapered off. 'Oh, man,' I managed. 'You are somethin' else.'

'Did I miss the joke?' Bart asked, puzzled.

'Did you not see that shop in town th' other day? That sold hot tubs an' shit?' Bart shook his head slowly, still not getting it. I locked eyes with Marshall and smirked. '*Goemonbūro* is a bathtub! Kinda like a hot tub!'

'No!' Bart cried. He walloped Marshall with his elbow. 'You *fucker!*'

Marshall rocked from the blow and covered his mouth so that we wouldn't see the big stupid grin that was so obviously plastered to his face. 'Nah, nah,' he insisted. 'Th-they just use that to, y'know, tie into the story!'

'Such a bullshitter,' Peter muttered. 'I'm goin' t'bed.'

'Aw, c'mon, don't be like that!' Marshall moaned.

Peter glared back at him. 'I'm *not* bein' like *anythin'* but It's late, I'm tired o' your shit, and I wanna rest up before we climb this thing.'

With that, he disappeared into his tent and zipped it shut.

I broke the uncomfortable silence by saying to Marshall, 'For what it's worth, you were almost right.'

* * *

When we awoke, Bart was gone.

'He was right *here!*' Marshall exclaimed, motioning towards Bart's empty and snow-swept tent.

'I *know* where he fuckin' *was!*' Peter roared back. 'But where's 'e now?!'

'How t'fuck should *I* know?'

Their incessant arguing was hurting my head, which was oddly frazzled and heavy from a troubled night's sleep. Bart's tent sat in a small drift of snow; his sleeping bag was a crumpled mess inside.

I ran a gloved hand down my face and looked around. The fire had long since died out and the glaring daylight showed footprints leading away from the tent. 'He's must've gone that way...' I murmured, following the tracks cautiously.

'*Hey!*' Marshall called, panicked. 'Sam! Wait!'

I turned back. 'Just grab the stuff and c'mon!' The tracks were faint, and the night's snowfall was already obscuring them, but they wound up towards the alcove Marshall had pointed to when telling his story.

Soon, Marshall and Peter caught up with me. I slung on my haphazardly packed bag and Marshall looked at me sceptically. 'I don't think we should head up there.'

'Why?' Peter snapped back. 'The tracks clearly go this way.'

Marshall flicked a troubled glance at the rugged, uninviting mountainside but said nothing; he simply stared at the snow-covered ground and trudged on.

The ground soon took on a loose, rocky surface made all the more slippery by a crust of ice. Thankfully, we were wearing the right boots for the job and were able to haul ourselves up, but it was hard work. Normally, we'd better prepare for such a hike but there was no time for that now. For a while, the climb became so steep and unstable that we were forced to half-crawl, half-drag ourselves up across dirty snow and mud.

Once the ground levelled out, Peter glanced back at the route we'd taken; our campsite laid down a steep, rocky incline and he looked at me doubtfully. 'You really think he clawed his way all the way out here?'

All I could do was shrug. The tracks were gone. If Bart *had* come up this way, it seemed the only logical place he could've gone was a sharp recess etched into the landscape. As I stepped towards it, Marshall frantically grabbed at my arm and pointed at the chrysanthemums that snaked their way to the alcove. 'Mate, I'm tellin' you this's a bad idea!'

I snatched my arm away and hissed at him: 'What t'hell's the *matter* with you?' and strode away, annoyed. I was beginning to think this was one of their stupid pranks.

Soon, I reached the stony recess. It was as though some eldritch beast had taken a chunk out of the mountain and left this jagged semi-cave. The inside was covered in a fine, decaying moss-like foliage and ribbons of cloth that were nailed into the rock and fluttered in the breeze. The alcove wasn't very deep, and the ribbons were arranged around a curious stone sculpture that'd been carved out of the mountain rock, covered in the same dry moss and weathered by the elements and the ravages of time. The carving depicted a figure, possibly a mother, hugging a weeping child.

The ground was littered with those white and yellow flowers. They sprouted around mounds of snow around five-foot high and around each of those were half a dozen strange piles of smooth, oval stones that seemed to have been freshly laid.

'*Goemonbūro...*' Marshall whispered.

'Would you *stop* with that bullshit?' Peter barked. He swept a gloved hand over the nearest mound of snow and yelped, snatching his hand away quickly.

'What?' I looked around, startled. I'd been looking at the *kanji* on the ribbons, baffled by what they could be communicating. Peter had fallen to one knee and was grasping his wrist; his eyes bulged and, when I saw why, I felt hot bile bubble up my gullet and my ears were pained by the roar of Marshall's ghastly scream as we beheld what laid beneath the snow mound.

It was Bart. He was hunched into a gnarled, agonised figure of ice. Peter scrambled to his feet and frantically wiped away more of the snow which flew into the breeze in a flurry, and it took all the strength I had to restrain him as he degenerated into a blubbering mess as we saw our friend's mangled corpse. He was still wearing his parka and one arm was raised over his face as if to ward off an attack. His frozen mouth was an open in an empty scream, and his eyes were mercifully clamped shut. Ice clung to his skin, tinting it a horrifying blue, and cracks crept along the surface of his icy corpse from the sudden change in temperature.

A whistling breeze suddenly flared up, as though a scream were cutting through the air, and we were pelted by an unexpected flurry of snow and ice that toppled Marshall to the ground and drove me and Peter further into the alcove. Thanks to the pure white sky, the fresh snow on the ground, and the glare of the day, I was practically blinded, but could just barely see Marshall struggling to his feet in the blizzard.

Rather than join us, though, he seemed unduly distracted by something beyond the alcove.

'*Marshall!*' I called, my shouts completely lost in the howling storm. 'Get your ass in here right now!'

The wind was a shrieking squall that whipped around my hood and assaulted my ears, but I could just barely hear Marshall scream back: '*I can see her!*'

Any response I had would've been lost to the uproar, but Marshall stomped away without even waiting for a reply. He slipped slightly but fought his way through the sudden whiteout with a dogged determination. 'Where t'fuck's he goin'?' Peter roared.

I stumbled out from the alcove and was blasted by a sideswipe of wind and snow. Although I tripped over my heavy boots and twisted my ankle, I was happy to avoid colliding with Bart's frozen corpse. Those strange oval stones went flying as I slipped to the ground with a cry and the wind seemed to squeal in anger. Suddenly, I felt Peter hauling me to my feet; he was frantically pointing up the length of the mountain and yelling something that I couldn't hope to make out as the storm raged around us.

Though momentarily snow-blinded, I could just about make out the bright red of Marshall's heavy snow coat. He'd clambered up the incline just past the makeshift cave and seemed to be half-crawling, half-climbing up a sheet of glistening ice, snow, and dirt. I cupped my gloved hands around my mouth and screamed his name and was surprised to find that I could actually hear my voice echoing back to me.

Peter and I looked around, completely dumbfounded as the storm whipped into an abrupt frenzy, assaulting us with flurries of snow and jagged shards of hail, as it blasted up the mountain. '*Marshall!*' I screamed again as the gale blasted him to his knees. He clawed at the slick ground to keep himself from tumbling and probably breaking his leg…or neck.

The storm swiftly relented. The clouds silently drifted by, and I prepared to intercept my fallen friend when all of the breath in my body died on my lips.

'What's wro—' Peter stopped abruptly as he saw the same inexplicable thing that'd caused my eyes to widen in my skull and all the salvia in my mouth to dry up.

The remnants of the storm swirled like a small, localised twister. I'd seen such a phenomenon before when we'd been passing through Fort Dodge a few years ago. The storms had been so unlike anything we'd seen before and Lucy had been terrified, and seeking refuge in a storm shelter hadn't done much for her nerves either, nor had the mild flooding and power outage that'd left us all trapped for six hours before the storms had safely passed by. Even Bart had been left in a stunned melancholy as we'd passed by the sheer destruction wrought by those unforgiving and seemingly malevolent storms that day.

This was, of course, nothing like that…and yet the same feeling of impassive malice was undeniable. The snowy twister intensified, kicking up dirt ice from the mountainside and spewing it into the air before dissipating in an ice-cold blast. I could see Marshall shielding himself and then dropping his arms slowly as he beheld the same figure that had driven the air from my body.

It was a woman. Tall and slender, she seemed to float on the breeze, her white kimono fluttering behind her as her impossibly long, coal-black hair billowed around her head. Her arms were spread out and her face was entirely obscured by her tangled locks, but I was sure I could see the jagged outcrop of the mountain through her body. A gentle, enticing whisper tingled at my ears as the phantom glided through the remnants of the blizzard with an aching, agonising slowness.

Marshall climbed to his feet on trembling legs as the apparition hovered before him. Her hair whipped in thick tendrils, and I found myself captivated, convinced that this spectre was a vision of unspeakable beauty and magnificence and that to behold her visage was to feel all woes and troubles melt away. I felt envy and anger unlike anything I'd ever experienced, at Marshall's fortune to be so close to that enchanting vision, and would have happily trampled over him to see the sparkle in her eyes (which were surely the cool, pure blue of the clear sky).

'Yō-si-lu...' it spoke with a soothing, beguiling grace. Although I had no idea what it was saying, I was reminded of Lucy's reassuring voice. 'Yō-si-lu...Gi-seei.'

'Marshall, don't!' Peter suddenly screamed, breaking the illusion, but it was too late.

Marshall took barely one step towards the phantasm and was enveloped first by its thrashing locks and then by its arms, which clamped around his body like pincers. The blizzard burst into life once more as though the ground beneath them had exploded from a landmine, and the blast of frigid air was enough to knock both of us down. As the wind howled, there was a brief, bone-chilling scream of terror that was drowned out by a banshee-like shriek so piercing and intense that I slapped my hands to my ears, shut my eyes, and screamed until it finally, mercifully, passed and all that was left was another mound of snow where my friend had once stood.

* * *

Stunned, we trudged our way towards Marshall's flash-frozen corpse as the biting cold burned at our exposed flesh. Peter couldn't bring himself to approach Marshall's mangled form. He stood, staring vacantly at the foreboding mountain peak, as I stumbled through snow that now came to my shins.

Like Bart, Marshall was buried beneath a thick layer of snow; his face a contorted grimace of pain and terror, one arm partially, uselessly, trying to shield himself from harm. Whatever that thing had been, whatever it had done, it had turned him into little more than another ice sculpture. His father's compass lay in the snow near his feet. Sombrely, I picked it up and glanced at it; the little needle was spinning crazily. I snapped it shut and briefly thought about placing a tender hand on my friend's icy corpse, but my arm dropped powerless to my side.

'G'bye, bro,' I whispered, my voice cracking slightly.

'Now what?' Peter asked.

I squinted back down the mountain pass; our campsite was gone, enveloped by the raging, sporadic snowstorms. The gale was already kicking up again. Without shelter, we'd be hard pressed to carry on, and I felt fatigue and despair teasing my heart.

'This way,' I grumbled. There was another jagged alcove of rock a few feet up the mountain where the path seemed less treacherous. 'Maybe we can get down easier over this side.'

Peter followed without much protest and remained uncharacteristically silent as we fought through the snow. Perhaps he was thinking about how he and Marshall would never be able to work things out. Maybe he was thinking about the half-drunken brawl they'd had when he'd found out about Marshall and Lucy. That had been an ugly sight. In their wild thrashing, they'd broken Bart's nose and earned themselves a stay in the cells.

We stomped through the thick snow at a slight angle for about a half hour or so before the ground levelled out. Those fabulous flowers bloomed regardless of the frigid temperatures and I was so busy keeping my eyes locked on that large alcove of rock that I barely even heard Peter wail from behind me.

I spun around, grabbing at one of my climbing axes, only to find Peter had tripped over something half-buried in the snow. I stepped over to him and almost slipped over myself as he scrambled to his feet and looked around aghast. 'Jesus...' he choked.

A dozen twisted, mangled animal corpses were buried all around us. The snowfall was lighter on this path, and we could see the contorted bodies of birds, foxes, and squirrels half-rotting in the glaring daylight. Peter had tripped over the hind leg of a massive, half-obscured bear. The gigantic animal lay on its side, rigid and glistening.

I urged Peter on. Though I tried to be mindful of my steps, I could hear the dry crunching of bones as I tramped towards our refuge, which was surrounded by a wash of dirt and vegetation. The alcove itself was a large, jutting tooth of grey rock; sharp icicles hung from the ceiling and a curious blossoming vine snaked around it. Peter let out a low moan as three—no, five—of those snowy mounds were peppered around the landscape. Each was surrounded by those same oval stones. Peter snatched one up and seemed transfixed by it.

I motioned him into the dark recess of the cave and, finally sheltered from the howling winds, cobbled together a makeshift fire. There wasn't much available for kindling, but I felt I had to at least try. Peter, however, ducked into the cave and shone his torch over the curious symbols carved into the rock and ice on the back wall.

'They *worship* that thing...' he whispered.

'Fire's started,' I replied, ignoring him. I didn't want to hear any more ghost stories; I just wanted to get the hell out of there.

I dropped to the hard ground with a sigh and huddled closer to the pathetic flame I'd coaxed out of some dry grass and twigs. It was a dismal effort; Lucy wouldn't have been impressed.

Peter came and sat by me. He dropped a bundle of vines onto the fire and the flame lapped at them hungrily, flushing us with a blast of warmth. He pulled out the small oval stone he'd picked up.

'I think those piles are *càirns*,' he mused, turning the stone over in his hand. 'They mark gravesites and ward off devil spirits.'

'Doin' a bang-up job 'round 'ere,' I muttered, desperately willing the fire to burn a little brighter and a little longer.

'Did you *see* that thing?'

I shot Peter a scowl. 'Of *course* I fuckin' saw it!'

'It was...beautiful...'

'Not the word *I'd* use.'

'He *went* to it....' I turned towards Peter, who seemed hypnotised by the swirling snow falling outside. 'He *wanted* it to take him.'

'You didn't see his face,' I grumbled.

A piercing shrill came on a gust of sudden wind; the fire struggled weakly before being snuffed out. I muttered a curse and was fumbling for my lighter when I saw that Peter was up on his feet. He was working that smooth stone between his fingertips, his gloves cast aside and forgotten on the cave floor.

'Hey!' I called. 'What're you doin'?'

'Can't you hear her callin' me?'

I pulled him back roughly. 'It's the *wind*, you idiot!'

Peter shrugged me off with surprising force. 'It's *her*. She's callin' me...'

He stepped out of the cave despite my desperate pleading. I followed but couldn't bring myself to leave the sanctuary. The blizzard was raging, but Peter walked into it willingly, bereft of his coat. Through the tumultuous snowstorm, I could just barely see the flicker of that ghoul's jet-black hair. Peter walked towards it, his arms outstretched, deaf to my frantic screams. The phantom glared at me through the snowstorm, angered at my defiance, and I retreated back into the dark safety of the cave before I could witness its horrific embrace of my last friend.

Distraught, I fought the urge to make a run for it. The cave held no hope of salvation. Its rocky walls were covered in *kanji* and archaic symbols that offered no insight. Part of the wall had been gouged out to form a crude depiction of the spectre that haunted this godforsaken mountain. She had her arms and hair wrapped tightly, securely, around a young child.

Marshall had screwed up the timeline when telling his story about the mountain, and Goemon. He'd made it seem like it had all taken place in a few days but, in actuality, Goemon and the emperor's daughter had disappeared for years. Crucially, he'd neglected to say that the two had birthed a child and lived peacefully on the mountain before the emperor had tracked them down and brutally enacted his vengeance.

'*Yō-si-lu...*' the wind shrieked in a primeval bawl that wracked my body with a trembling shudder.

I whirled around to find the cave mouth enveloped in darkness; a freezing blast of wind pelted me with rock-hard hail and drove me to my knees. I shielded myself from the attack, gritted my teeth, and snatched up my climbing axe, ready to fight to the death if need be.

The spectre drifted into the cave like a wraith; its black hair a tangled, writhing mess that seemed to merge with the shadows. Its eyes were the dark and piercing cosmic ballet that danced through the sky at only the furthest reaches of the world. Its arms were outstretched, welcoming, as it whispered: '*Yō-si-lu...Gi-seei.*'

I raised my little jagged pickaxe as it drew nearer. Its movements were both graceful and haunting as it floated above the cave floor, its feet obscured by its long, snow-white kimono.

'*Yō-si-lu...,*' it slowly beckoned at me, and I tried to turn away, but something caught my eye through the phantasm's translucent form.

It was Marshall.

And Peter.

And Bart

And dozens, maybe hundreds, of others.

They stared vacantly, their eyes white and blank, their faces as stoic and expressionless as stone. The storm raged around them, *through* them, and their mouths moved each time the spectre spoke, creating a chanting dirge that bore into my very soul.

At the head of this gathering of lost souls was a grim-faced man with long hair that spilled down over grand ceremonial armour. One hand was gripped to the hilt of a sword strapped to his waist; a small child clutched at the other side of his body.

'*Gi-seei*,' they all chanted.

The ghoul bore down on me. A putrid stench of rotting flowers and decay wafted over me as it stroked at my cheeks, filling me with a dread beyond anything I had known. The lady in white regarded me with a morbid curiosity and cocked her head back on her shoulder. She called to the boy with a word I couldn't begin to comprehend, and he came willingly, shyly, his arms outstretched towards me.

The spectre pulled back, one hand teasing, tingling, at the back of my head. '*Yō-si-lu*,' she murmured as the boy approached. I glanced pleadingly at the spirits of my friends, but they simply stared back at me, their eyes watching expectantly, chanting those haunting words over and over as the boy readied himself to embrace me and end my life as so many had been taken before.

At the last second, I positioned my axe between myself and the boy, surprised to find it held him back. His hands clutched at nothing but thin air and his mother lingered over me like a vast, ice-cold shadow. '*Ná-lu*,' she sighed and, with the boy's hands safely away from me, I clamped my eyes shut and wrapped my trembling arms around him in a tight embrace.

I was expecting cold.

Dark, freezing, terrifying death.

Instead, there was a soothing warmth that flowed through me like liquid. A gust of wind followed, but not from outside, where the blizzard was raging. This came from beneath me, where the timid spirit stood.

When I opened my eyes, I was on my knees on the rocky cave floor, my skin tingling from the lingering heat. I looked up and all around wildly, but I was alone. The spirits were gone. Where the boy had been was another of those curious stone piles.

'*Càirns*,' I mumbled, barely aware that I had spoken.

The snowstorm had subsided. I stumbled out, leaning against the cave wall, and marvelled at the beauty of the landscape around me. The thick, white clouds had parted, those horrifying snow mounds were gone, replaced by more *càirns*, and I could quite plainly see a safe path back down the mountain.

I pulled out Marshall's beloved compass. The needle quivered slightly at due west. I snapped it shut and put it back in my pocket and, without glancing back, took my first step out onto my long road home.

Chapter Eight

Saturday – Witching Hour

1. *LaVey at the End*

The blazing fire crackled and spat as Brandis finished his story. The four guests and their host sat around the long, centuries-old dining table, their bellies full and their eyes wide. Words seemed to have escaped each of them and they wore the same solemn, haunted looks of the ragged and the damned.

To LaVey, his guests appeared to be little more than expressionless mannequins. Had it not been for the subtle rise and fall of their chests, he would have been hard pressed to tell that that were actually alive and not corpses strung up in some macabre mockery of high society.

Everything was exactly as expected.

LaVey sat back in his chair, a grand oak construct that seemed to swallow him with its sheer size. It was fitting that the master of the house should have a throne at the head of the table where he entertained his guests, fostering their creativity and stoking the flames of their imaginations. The evening—and the entire week for that matter—couldn't have gone any better. From the moment his guests had arrived, discord had been rife and tensions had flared, awakening things long dormant from the darkest corners of the house, and the old man had been positively giddy at feeling the old place live once again.

LaVey watched in a stoic, observant silence after raising a goblet of his finest wine and saying a few words. It amused him a little to see them stumble at the gesture and reach for their brass cups in their haste, and to see them consciously sit according to the social groups they had established over the last few days. The four had eaten heartily and one thing was for certain: they enjoyed taking advantage of his gracious hospitality.

The part of him that had once been a father and grandfather many moons ago felt a swell of delight at entertaining them, housing them, and sharing the luxuries of his wealth and abode to their individual needs. Another part, the darker side that knew what needed to be done, pitied them for their ignorance. Which side won out in the end was a debate that would never be revealed, for LaVey lapsed into a morose silence. None of them, not even the most inquisitive amongst them, really noticed that their host had hardly touched a bite or said a word; the old man simply watched with placid fascination as they each told their stories, sipping from his goblet and relishing the taste of the pure virgin's blood contained within.

Having finished his story, Brandis sat back down, and the mood settled. LaVey saw his guests turn towards him, but his cold eyes were turned towards the ancient grandfather clock on the west wall of the room. As the redheaded Aster offered praise to Brandis (who was clearly her new lover), the heavy, rusted brass hands clicked over and the clock chimed midnight. The brute, Mikhail, who had spoken to him so disrespectfully throughout the week, sat pouting and picking at the remnants of his lemon meringue pie with a cake fork, while the alcoholic, Rhiannon, polished off the goblet of viscera that she thought was wine. They seemed to be waiting for his feedback, perhaps some words of praise, or talk of logistics. He had spoken to each of them on more than one occasion regarding the publication, the financial compensation, and the specifics of the book they believed would be published from their works, and they had bought his act as a doddering old man hook, line, and sinker.

As the last chime from the grandfather clock echoed throughout the dining room, a chill of anticipation ran up LaVey's spine. *Witching hour*, he thought before rising from his grand chair and spreading his arms in joy.

'Many thanks, my friends!' he cried, clasping his hands together before his chest. 'You've all performed admirably. I couldn't have asked for more potent words. At this hour, the evocation is completed...finally.'

Rhiannon, clearly intoxicated, struggled to focus on her host through the glare of the roaring fire. 'Are you happy with our work, Mr. LaVey?'

'Happy?' LaVey cried, clapping his palms to the table. 'M'dear, I'm positively ecstatic!'

Mikhail wore an ignorant scowl on his face. 'Then what is this word you speak?'

'Evocation,' LaVey repeated as if talking to a child. 'A summoning, my brutish friend.'

LaVey was not surprised to see a confused, hushed silence fall upon them. Brandis broke it with the most natural, obvious, and predictable of questions: 'A summoning of what?'

'Choices are made not being free,' LaVey growled, glaring at him pointedly. 'Another pull and give as if to need...The ones that speak of what is me.' He snatched up his steak knife and clasped his left hand around the blade, ripping his palm across it in a violent jerk that caused a yelp to jump out of Aster's throat. LaVey held his shredded, bloody palm up to his guests so they could behold his bright, streaming blood and the gorge torn into his paper-thin flesh. With an elated smile, the old man lapped his tongue over the wound and then slapped his bloody palm to his face, smearing it with a red streak. 'The *Great Duke* comes! Through dark words and life's blood, I evoke *His* name!'

The table rocked suddenly, spilling goblets and tipping over bottles of wine. Brandis grabbed the table's edge on instinct and jerked his hands away with a hiss as dozens of splinters punctured his palms.

'A shadow's life of make believe,' the old man cackled. 'Lost in time we live...and breathe!' The fireplace billowed behind LaVey, who brayed a guttural laugh, the flames lapping hungrily and pumping a thick, noxious smoke into the room. '*Astaroth!*'

In an instant, all lights were extinguished. The fire withdrew, as if subjected to a sudden vacuum, and small orange flames struggled to life around the charred logs. LaVey's eyes glistened despite the suffocating shadows that now enveloped the room, and he stood hunched before them, glaring, saliva dripping from his crooked, leering lips.

'*He* walks among us once more...'

'What is...' Mikhail started before suddenly uttering a series of choking, coughing gasps.

'*Silence!*' came a rasping, inhuman voice that was little more than bile and spite making a mockery of language.

'If this is your idea of a joke...' Rhiannon mumbled and then hitched a breath as something cold, dark, and hideous stroked its way across the bare skin of her collar bone and silenced her.

'Into the light, I command thee...' LaVey whispered, and with those words the candles on the table burst to life once more. The lamps lining the dining room walls flickered into existence or shattered entirely, and the fire roused itself back to life to cast an eerie orange glow throughout the room that banished the shadows to the darkest corners.

'Naomi...!' Brandis gasped; he made a half-hearted effort to stand and then dropped back to his seat.

The redhead had stood during the blackout, as LaVey knew she would, and had come towards him the moment he had evoked that lost and ancient name. Her head was turned to the side, one cheek resting against her shoulder, and her eyes were turned all the way back so that only the gleaming whites showed. She hung in the air like a puppet, as was only fitting, her toes pointing downwards as she hovered within arm's reach of LaVey.

'There is no "Naomi",' LaVey spat as he snatched up the knife once more. He placed his bloody palm to Aster's face and plunged the knife deep in her belly before the others could even think of reacting.

'*No!*' cried Brandis, though he remained pinned in his chair by an unseen force of great heat and power.

'Aster!' Rhiannon screamed, her hands clutching at the armrest of her chair, her eyes widening with dread.

'*There is no Aster!*' LaVey roared, his voice gravelly and full of wicked intent. Then he cupped both hands to Aster's cheeks and a single tear leaked from the corner of her eye. 'There is only Astaroth.'

Aster's body jerked in sudden spasms and a wailing, shrieking moan escaped her gnashing, frothing lips. Brandis forced himself to his feet, thinking to help her, and was violently thrust backwards, a stinging red mark instantly appearing on his face. The others simply sat, transfixed and horrified, as Aster's body shuddered and convulsed and rose two feet into the air. Her hair was little more than a flailing red cloud of strands that billowed around her head, and her skin darkened as invisible hands grabbed and clutched at her flesh. She threw her head back and let out a choking death rattle that shattered every window in the room and the ornate mirror placed above the fireplace, and then dropped to the floor in a heap of limbs.

'Naomi…' Brandis whispered, one hand clutching his face. He glared at LaVey. 'Whu-what did you—'

'Words could never convey the actions we have all taken this day,' LaVey interrupted without looking at him. His dark eyes were focused squarely on Aster's crumbled form, his breath coming in excited pants. 'Aeons *He* has slept, trapped in the darkest nether. Can you imagine?' he looked at each of them in turn, a spiteful shadow of disgust etched into his face. 'You can't even begin to imagine how long the Great Duke has toiled in those depths, longing to walk amongst us once more. Thanks to this place, thanks to *you*, *He* is among us at long last.'

'The old man is mad,' Mikhail growled, but his eyes told a different story; he was terrified beyond belief, and utterly powerless to act.

'Mad?' LaVey glared at him. '*Mad*, am I? All my life has led to this moment, every step meticulously planned and prepared for, every tome and ancient incantation memorised, and every element needed assembled here, along with all of you.' He bent down and hauled up Aster's lifeless form; she teetered slightly on her heels. 'And you say I am mad? Then so be it, if madness beholds this beauty.'

His guests stared in horror at Aster's slumped form. Before their eyes, she stood without aid, a dark red clot forming around the knife protruding from her belly. LaVey took her by one limp wrist and patted her hand as a father would a crying child. 'Awaken, m'dear. Too long have you slept.'

'*Ye-ee-esss…*' came that same dark, chilling voice. It was like nails on a chalkboard, the mocking growl of some unspeakable living darkness that lurked in the corner of every room. It was as though malevolence had been given a voice as icy as the deep cold of the endless void between worlds.

LaVey smiled, tears of joy leaking from his eyes. He launched into a jubilant soliloquy, peppering the entity that now wore Aster's skin with promises of riches and conquest. Aster, her body merely the shell to house the demon, watched him with a festering loathing through unblinking, cat-like eyes.

'It can all be yours; everything, everything you could want…everything you could *ever* want!' the old man vowed, clasping both hands around Aster's deathly pale and cold ones. 'I did it all, everything, for you, my dearest Lord of Lords!'

The creature stirred with a curious jerk of its head. Aster's once shining red hair was tattered and dishevelled and fell in twisted clumps down the ghoul's hunched back, and its eyes were so impossibly black that the others found their minds unravelling as they stared into them. LaVey, however, never broke eye contact with the entity he had unleashed upon the world.

'*Annnnd you shall be...rewarded...*'

A grateful, loving smile washed over LaVey's wrinkled features that, for a second, made him resemble a giddy schoolboy, before being replaced with a look of utter disbelief.

'*Ughnk...*' he gagged, blood spitting from his trembling lips. With the greatest of efforts, he looked down and saw the same blade he had stuck Aster with now stuck into his breast, right where his frail, black heart beat within his chest.

Astaroth gave the old man the lightest of pushes and he slumped to his throne, his quivering hands reaching pathetically for the knife. Yet, as he turned his tired and glassy eyes towards the creature, LaVey wore an expression of acceptance and reverence in his final moments.

'Long live...the King...' he wheezed before falling silent for eternity.

2. *Brandis Bears Witness*

'Naomi…' I struggled to speak, or even move. I couldn't see the force holding me back, but I could damn sure feel it. My cheek stung as though burned, my hands dripped with blood from the splinters stuck in them, and no matter how hard I tried to force my way up, I remained pinned to my chair. '*Naomi!*' I called, desperately. 'Please, stop this!'

Naomi simply screeched with laughter. It was her…and yet it was decidedly *not* her. Her entire body rippled and jerked with every movement as spasms racked her limbs; her face was twisted and glaring, and her eyes were black pits. She curled talon-like fingers around the knife handle and wrenched it from LaVey's chest, running her tongue along the blade before swiping it at the exposed flesh of her forearms over and over. Words, or curses of some kind, that defied my understanding barked and snarled from her split and frothing lips as she slashed deep cuts into her tattooed skin. Bloody chunks of meat and arterial spray spat from the wounds, yet still she continued with her assault, cackling with glee as cuts criss-crossed her flesh and blood stained her clothing.

'Oh, Jesus Christ…' I murmured, my strength draining away in a flood.

The creature that had been Naomi roared in disgust and outrage. It slapped its hands to its face and clawed its fingernails down its screaming cheeks. '*Do not speak that name to us!*'

This was crazy; *everything* was crazy! I couldn't even begin to process what was happening as this thing, this…Astaroth…flailed at the head of the table, grabbing at the meats and foods and the sickeningly sweet wine LaVey had served and gorging itself in a frenzy. It gnashed and gnawed, ripping huge meaty chunks from the remains of the turkey, splashing wine all over its face and running it through Naomi's once-luscious hair. It tossed aside plates and cutlery and goblets as it fed with a voracious hunger that was more animal than human, and I felt a terror overcome me the likes of which I had never known. The room, the entire house, seemed to have closed in on us; the heat from the fireplace was almost unbearable, and the creature's ravenous squeals and grunts of delight drowned out all sound, all conscious thought, save for a curious and mind-numbing buzzing in my ears, as though thousands of locusts were nestled there.

After I'd finished my story, my nerves had been shot and my stomach had been churning, but I'd been happy with how it turned out—and with my delivery, for I liked to think that I had a flair for the theatrical that others in our group, especially Mikhail, were sorely lacking—and had been grateful to feel Naomi's warm hand clutch at mine afterwards. She had favoured me with the sweetest smile and a look of such pride and wonder that words had completely escaped me. I had simply looked back shyly, a goofy smile on my face, breathed a sigh of relief, and was absolutely captivated by her warmth, her beauty, and her belief.

She had been holding my hand the entire time but, when the lights had suddenly been snuffed out and that rancid darkness had swept over me, she had been snatched away from my grip like a leaf in the wind. I'd just about gone out of my mind when LaVey had stabbed her, but seeing her corpse explode to life as this animalistic dervish caused an icy tightness to clamp itself around my heart. I strained my eyes and saw only my same terror reflected on the faces of the others. And while

Rhiannon appeared to have given in to her fear completely, Mikhail was struggling against his with all his might.

The burly Russian writhed in his chair, tendons and veins bulging as he desperately tried to overpower the strange, powerful force holding him back. A string of unintelligible insults tumbled from his mouth, and I was appalled to see that, in his mania, he had chewed meaty lumps out of his bottom lip.

'You are an abomination!' he raved, his eyes wild with fury and horror. 'You do not belong! Демон, I renounce you!'

Astaroth glowered at Mikhail, burning holes through him with its eyes. With a shriek that pierced my ears like a drill, it swiped a bloodied arm at LaVey's chair and cast it aside as if it (and the body sat in it) were little more than a child's toy, and the sheer ferocity of the fireplace caused tears to stream from my eyes. With a gangly grace that was both clumsy and unsettling, it clambered onto the table and stalked over to Mikhail like a ghastly arachnid.

'*Insignificant fool,*' it croaked, caressing Mikhail's face with one gnarled hand. At Astaroth's lightest touch, Mikhail rose from his chair, his hands balled into fists so tight that I could see thin trails of blood from where his nails were digging into his skin. When the wretch spoke again, it was with the distinct, dulcet tones of a female. Though I didn't recognise the voice, Mikhail certainly did. Upon hearing its soft whispers, his body slumped as if drained of all its strength. 'Join me, beloved,' the voice cooed. 'I wait for you in Hell. Come, join me.'

Mikhail stared the creature right in its eyes, seemingly unable to break from its gaze, and then slowly turned away, a tear rolling from his eye. He took a single lumbering step away from the table, and then another; his movements jerked as if he were a marionette. '*Mikhail!*' I screeched, my throat as dry as desert sand. '*Stop, for fuck's sake!*'

Suddenly, something hard and metallic struck me across the forehead, just above my right eye, and knocked me loopy. The world swam in waves of grey and black dots exploded before my eyes. Astaroth sat cross-legged on the table, rocking back and forth and cackling maniacally as she watched Mikhail step closer and closer towards the fireplace. I shook my head, trying to clear the cobwebs, and saw the flames billow invitingly as the brawny Russian came within an arm's reach of the great, Yorkstone decoration. As powerless as he was to resist the force propelling him along, so too was I unable to turn my face away. A strong, deathly cold grip forced me to witness first-hand Mikhail's gruesome end.

At first, the flames lapped and engulfed him like harmless smoke. As they pulled back, though, I could see that his clothing was enflamed at the arms and knees. He uttered a strained, warbling cry like some nightmarish banshee as the fire spread...and still he continued walking, until he was right inside the flames; he even stooped lower and kicked aside the charred logs in order to fit better, even as the blazing heat liquefied his flesh. His eyeballs burst from the intense fires and bubbled down his cheeks like yolk. His burning hands flew to his screaming face and succeeded only in peeling back his melting skin, exposing bloodied tendons and his shrieking skull for the briefest of bone-chilling moments. Finally, the fireplace consumed him whole, like a rapacious beast. The flames crashed together like great waves, and billowed fiercely before dying down, as though satisfied, to get to work on immolating Mikhail's charred remains.

'This…this can't be happening. This can't be happening!' Rhiannon screeched. She flailed and struggled and screamed until she was horse, her face a disturbing shade of red and purple, and her breath coming in dry, strained gasps. Her chest heaved and her lips trembled uncontrollably; it was as though she was having a full-on panic attack, like the one Naomi had been on the verge of the other night, and it only got worse as Astaroth rose up.

Rhiannon blubbered and struggled for breath as Astaroth padded across the tabletop towards her. The creature seemed unfazed by the food and cutlery strewn across the table, and even crossed each footstep over the other in a taunting gesture as she inched ever closer. 'Come, my dear; don't cry now. There'sss no need to fear…'

Astaroth squatted down before Rhiannon, who desperately tried to turn away from the creature's glaring eyes. Rhiannon snapped her head from side to side and clamped her eyes shut, but gagged on her own panicked, wheezing breaths. Astaroth lowered itself with an inhuman, almost insectile grace, Naomi's striking hair dropping down over its hunched back and covering its ghastly visage. It reached out and stroked Rhiannon's hair and made soothing, calming sounds. It was like watching a mother comfort a crying child, except with every touch of Astaroth's hand it snaked its fingers around Rhiannon's hair and tugged it out first in strands and then in tangled clumps.

'I-I…I cuh-can't…' Rhiannon whimpered and then grimaced, a muffled cry escaping her throat as Astaroth placed one bony finger to Rhiannon's lips, and the unmistakable smell and sound of sizzling meat filled the room.

'Hush, child. Hush,' it cooed. 'Your whining bores me.'

Astaroth leaned in close to Rhiannon and, for a second, I thought it was going to plant a kiss right on her lips, but then the creature reared back and gagged. It turned towards the ceiling as it choked with a broiled, throttling series of coughs not unlike how Bert struggled with hairballs. I grimaced with disgust at the thought of this inhuman thing spitting up something like that, and then felt bile burst from my lips in a sudden froth as Astaroth vomited dark, viscous fluid from its gullet all over Rhiannon's face and torso.

Rhiannon wailed in revulsion as the foul viscera drenched her. It sloshed into her screaming mouth and matted the remains of her hair, staining her clothes and leaving ungodly bile and chunks of entrails splattered all over her. Rhiannon's scream soon turned into a shriek of utter, unimaginable suffering, however, as Astaroth's fetid puke began to sizzle and eat away at her skin like acid. Astaroth dropped back to the tabletop and watched as Rhiannon writhed and screamed in indescribable anguish as her flesh split and slapped to the floor in gloopy tendrils and then a spew of dark, chattering beetles burrowed their way out from the bloody remains of her skin. A great, slimy centipede skittered out through what little remained of Rhiannon's lips and her one remaining eye, wide and alive with horror and agony, stared at me with a desperate, silent plea that I was unable to answer.

Rhiannon's convulsions ceased within seconds and all that was left of her was a stinking, rotten mess of sizzling meat and glistening bones. Strands of muscle and great droplets of fat leaked from her corpse into a sickening puddle and the discoloured remains of her largely skeletal face leered at me across the table. The heat and stench in the room was unbearably nauseating and I swallowed back another rush of vomit with a revolted grimace. My body felt numb and cold and distant; my head swam, and I felt myself drifting away. I welcomed the sensation, desperate to spare myself from further horrors, but the creature was on me before I was even aware.

I fell to the floor in a helpless sprawl, my head thumping off the thick rug and my chair clattering along with me. I felt myself being rolled over; a claw-like hand grasped the front of my shirt and hauled me up so that I had no choice but to stare into those cold, dead eyes and see up close the wretched thing that Naomi had become.

'Poor, sweet boy,' Astaroth mocked through jagged teeth. 'Don't you find me desirable anymore?'

Its cackling jeers sent a shiver down my spine, and I was completely helpless against the malice of this entity. 'Naomi...' I whispered. 'Please...'

'*Don't!*' the creature roared, slapping my face with a blow that damn near dislocated my jaw. '*Do* not *tell her to fight!*' It shook me violently, as though I were a weightless ragdoll. 'There is *no* "Naomi", *no* "Aster." She's *dead! Gone!* The nether welcomed her with open arms!' The creature ranted and raved, rancid spittle flying from its lips and scorching my skin. 'This vessel is *mine*, as was fated to be! Pathetic, mewling quim of a mortal! I claimed her long before your hands ever touched her!'

Astaroth straddled me. The weight was almost unbearable and easily three times what Naomi had weighed when she'd been in a similar position. Its skeletal talons caressed my face and shirt, ripping it open and scrawling crude symbols into my flesh in thin, bloody trails. 'Four brought to one,' it mused with a sigh. 'But where there is one, there is life within, and from their loss shall call forth *He* who has been entrapped for dark aeons.' Cold, peeling, corpse-like hands caressed my face. 'And the world shall die alone.'

I blinked, swallowing back tears. My thoughts turned to Dani; to Lucy and Sam; to my mother, my daft old father, Bert, and old friends long since passed. I thought of Naomi; how she had come to me the other night and the connection I felt to her. The glimmer of hope that maybe there could have been something more between us had filled me with an ecstasy I'd never experienced before, and it had felt so good to be needed, respected, and appreciated for a change. I could see us together, after some awkwardness, cementing those bonds and fostering our imaginations and creativity in so many ways, and just the idea of living out such a fantasy had made the entire trip down here worthwhile.

Now, Naomi was gone, and where once there was a faint hope there was now a bitter, gut-wrenching dread. Astaroth, perhaps sensing my despair, favoured me with a look that was a twisted mockery of Naomi's usual warm, radiant gaze. Those muddy, glowering eyes dissipated for the smallest of seconds, flooding them with life and the captivating allure of Naomi's gaze, and I could have sworn I heard her voice escape from those sneering lips: 'I would've gone with you...'

I stared into Naomi's eyes one last time, feeling nothing but bewilderment and helplessness. The creature that wore her skin appeared to weep, its hands clutched to its face, but those sounds quickly turned to low, gurgling chuckles. Sheer blackness swam in its eyes and fangs dripping with saliva burst from its gums as its jaw exploded in a flood of gore. More fangs, long and slender as the spines of a porcupine, pushed through the thing's slashed and bloodied flesh.

Its serrated fingernails cracked and fell away as the skin on its hands split up the middle, revealing insectile appendages slick with viscera.

The moment I saw a similar gash creep up the middle of the remains of Naomi's gruesome visage, and the entity that now inhabited her skin rearing back and preparing to pounce, I clamped my eyes shut and surrendered myself to the Black…

3. Astaroth Walks the Earth

Freedom.

At long last…

After untold aeons…

Freedom.

I stood amidst the flames and bathed in their magnificence. The heat was tangible, exhilarating, and the purity of the fire destroying the wretched earthly construct brought a smile to my face.

As the flames billowed around me, turning the old man's beloved shrine to my name to little more than charred wood and piles of ash, I gazed up at the infinite void above and marvelled at the stars. I had longed to be beneath the constellations once more, to feel the awesome power they exerted upon the cosmos, and felt myself finally whole after countless epochs lost in the swirling darkness.

If those Old Ones could see what their hubris had wrought unto this world once more…but they slept, powerless and lost to the void, their influence long gone and long forgotten.

The fire parted before my path with but the merest squint of my eyes, allowing me safe passage from the blazing abode. A trail stretched out before me, seeped in darkness and smoke, that led to the huge iron gate and the quiet town at the foot of the incline.

And beyond that…the world.

I took a breath I didn't need and flexed hands my host would barely have recognised. Although the woman's flesh was decaying as my true form imposed itself, her body was strong, her imagination potent and alive. It would not be long before I had fully asserted myself and quieted the distant screams that still echoed at the back of my mind.

I turned back to bask in the splendour of the burning building. The smoke was thick, black, and noxious and swirled into the night sky in a tribute as fitting to my coming as the blood-red moon that sat amidst those twinkling stars. I drank in the flames, allowing their scorching heat to invigorate my flesh, and gave my thanks to those who had been drawn here to ensure my return.

They would not be the last to fall in my name.

The straggly remains of the woman's hair fell about my face as I turned away from my earthly prison. Never again would I allow myself to be contained, to be dependent on antiquated incantations, or to be returned to the dreadful black of the deepest nether.

This world was rich and alive, and ripe for my return. With each step I took, the grass withered before bursting into flames; with each breath (a reflex I would soon stamp out), the air grew cold. The light of life and colour was snuffed out as I made my way down the path, the woman's feet dangling uselessly above the ground as I effortlessly drifted through the night air.

The gate was nothing, easily swept aside with the slightest of movements. My strength grew with every passing moment, fuelled as much by my elation at finally being free as it was by my dark designs for this world. The woman's voice begged and cried as I passed the threshold of the old man's land, but it was trivial compared to the entire world that awaited me beyond those grounds.

The old man's house burned behind me, taking with it those who had been summoned and all the illusions contained within, replacing them only with the coldness of the Black. It enveloped me, enclosing around me and feeding my strength as the final façade of the woman's form slipped from my bones and I passed beyond the gates and took my first steps into a world that I would see suffer in fire and decay.

About the Authors

Dr. Stuart Knott is a PhD graduate of De Montfort University, Leicester, who lives in Bedfordshire. He has been writing from an early age and published a number of books in addition to his academic accomplishments. Influenced by science fiction, horror, and action movies of the eighties and nineties, as well as comic books and videogames, he posts regular articles and reviews on his website, *Dr. K's Waiting Room*. It also took him six attempts to pass his driving test.

Stuart wrote the character of Frederick Brandis, the short story *The Peak*, and contributed heavily to the character of Mikhail Orlov.

Harriet Everend grew up in small-town Iowa, USA, and always had bigger dreams than staying in her hometown—so she ended up moving to the big city of Cedar Rapids. She had dreams of being a writer since she was twelve and obtained her B.A. in Marketing from Upper Iowa University in 2011. *Cursed Legacy*, her debut novel, was released in June 2021. Some of her hobbies include kayaking, scrapbooking, genealogy, drinking wine, and living life to the fullest potential.

Harriet wrote the character of Aster Callahan, the short story *The Broadcast*, and contributed heavily to the character of Mikhail Orlov, with language assistance from Daria Lavrenteva.

Jessica Huntley wrote her first book at age six and wrote ten full-length fiction novels between the ages of ten and eighteen as a hobby. At age eighteen, she left her hobby behind and spent the next four and a half years as an Intelligence Analyst in the British Army. After leaving the army, Jessica became a mature student at Southampton Solent University and studied Fitness and Personal Training, and she still enjoys keeping fit and exercising daily. She is now a wife and a stay-at-home mum to a crazy toddler and lives in Edinburgh.

During the first national lockdown of 2020, she signed up to a novel writing course on a whim, recently completed a Level 3 Diploma in Editing and Proofreading, and is currently working on the final novel in her "*My...Self*" series.

Jessica wrote the character of Rhiannon Hughes and the short story *The Devil's Graveyard*.

Alice Stone wrote the Prologue chapter of *The Summoning*. She is a queer MA student studying Creative Writing. She grew up in the Lake District and developed her talent for writing at Edgehill University. Her aim as an author is to challenge her readers with something new and to add her own spin on the horror genre whilst giving representation to lesser known voices. Alice is currently writing her debut novel, and her short story *The Muscus* can be found on The Black Petals Magazine website.

Shantel Brunton is the Canadian author of *Tortured Innocence* who wrote the short story *It's All In Your Head*. She holds a bachelor's degree in psychology, and her love of psychology inspires her writing. When she's not writing and doesn't have her nose buried in a book, she's either working out, drawing, painting, or wandering into the shadows. She has three snake babies who keep her sane enough.

Acknowledgements

Dr. Stuart Knott

To Siân, who begrudgingly allows me to skip housework to write, to my fellow authors who joined this project, to indie authors everywhere (especially Amanda Jaeger, Gillian Church, Jayne Clarkson, and Nic Winter), and to the darkest time of my life and all of those who made it happen…and helped me through it.

THE SUMMONING *began life as a bold idea to take my undeveloped short stories, expand them, and weave them all together with a framing narrative not unlike the horror anthology shows I grew up with. Thanks to encouragement from Harriet Everend, it grew to include other indie authors and expanded into easily my most ambitious project to date.*

Thankfully, I was working with some extremely talented, enthusiastic, and imaginative writers and the process gelled so much better than I could have ever expected.

Harriet Everend

To my husband, Jeremy, for tolerating my many late nights and absences while working on this book. I also want to thank my fellow co-

authors on this project, Stuart and Jessica. You are both an inspiration to me and it's been a pleasure to work with you on this.

Jessica Huntley

First and foremost, I must thank Stuart and Harriet for giving me the opportunity to work with them. I've not worked with other authors before and I've thoroughly enjoyed the process. Thank you also to Alice and Shantel for being part of the project.

Thanks to all my close friends and family for their support throughout my writing career so far. I've only just started, but I don't plan on stopping, so your support is very much appreciated. Final thanks to my best friend Katie Hughes for helping me with THE DEVIL'S GRAVEYARD *and refreshing my memory about the legend in our local village growing up, and also for helping me with the Welsh words!*

THE DEVIL'S GRAVEYARD *is loosely set in a real village in Wales called Pontrhydfendigaid. It lies on the western flank of the Cambrian Mountains between Devil's Bridge and Tregaron. I grew up only a few miles from the village and my best friend actually lived there. The abbey spoken about in the story is based on the Strata Florida abbey in the village, and the graveyard is situated next to it. The chapel described is based on St Mary's Church located within the graveyard in the abbey. The legend is actually loosely based on a random rumour that the local children spoke about. I don't know when or how it started or why, but often me, my sister and our friends would visit the graveyard and attempt to do the ritual (knock three times, run around the chapel three times, and knock three times again), but we were always too scared to complete it!*

Alice Stone

I'd like to thank Dr. Stuart Knott for inviting me to the project, and the rest of the team for being so great to work with, and my amazing friends, without whom I wouldn't be where I am today.

Also, a special thank you to my partner for sticking with me through my penniless writer phase, and of course to our readers for taking time to enjoy this novel, on which we've all worked so hard.

Shantel Brunton

I'd like to thank Harriet for inviting me to join the project and contribute my short story. I also owe a huge thank you to Annasbooknook, one of my best Instagram friends, for doing edits for me. Last, a huge thank you to my amazing partner Allen for always supporting me.

Further Reading

Also by Dr. Stuart Knott:

Nightshade: The Inception – Here There Be – Campus

The Teamos Connection
Loose Ends – Parasite – The Late Shift –
Outbreak – The Morning After – Consequences

Also by Harriet Everend:

Cursed Legacy

Also by Jessica Huntley:

The Darkness Within Ourselves

The *My…Self* Trilogy
Book One: My Dark Self
Book Two: My True Self
Book Three: My Real Self

Also by Shantel Brunton:

Tortured Innocence

Coming Soon from Alice Stone:

For Esmae

Printed in Great Britain
by Amazon

81643835R00244